The Humanisphere

IN THE SAME SERIES

The Humanisphere
and Other Utopian Fantasies

translated, annotated and introduced by
Brian Stableford

A Black Coat Press Book

ISBN 978-1-61227-511-6. First Printing. May 2016. Published by Black Coat Press, an imprint of Hollywood Comics.com, LLC, P.O. Box 17270, Encino, CA 91416. All rights reserved. Except for review purposes, no part of this book may be reproduced or transmitted in any form or by any means, electronic or mechanical, including photocopying, recording, or by any information storage and retrieval system, without permission in writing from the publisher. The stories and characters depicted in this novel are entirely fictional. Printed in the United States of America.

TABLE OF CONTENTS

Introduction

This collection of four "utopian fantasies" first requires some explanation of the evolution of that term and the manner in which it had been further elaborated since its initial adaptation from the title of Thomas More's *Utopia* (1516). More intended the coinage as a derivative of the Greek *outopos* [no place], and his depiction of an imaginary society is primarily satirical, but the image of Utopian society was widely misconstrued as a design for a hypothetical ideal society, comparable to Plato's *Republic* (although the latter also contains more sarcasm than is sometimes credited to it). The derivative adjective was thus used by many of those who adopted it as if it were derived from *eutopos* [better place], and could be used from the very outset either as a label for any non-existent location imagined for literary purposes, or, more specifically, for attempts to design ideal societies. The situation was further complicated in France because the French adaptation *utopie* permitted the term to be applied to fanciful ideas in general.

The frequent use of "utopia" to mean, tacitly, "eutopia," eventually encouraged the invention of an opposite term to refer to worse places: "dystopia." That word appears to have been first used in English by John Stuart Mill in 1868, but it was not adopted into the critical jargon of historians of imaginative fiction as a necessary distinction until the 1960s. The equivalent French term, *dystopie*, took even longer to catch on, slightly handicapped by competition from a pre-existent medical term defining a particular defect of eyesight. Long before then, however, French writers had begun to produce satirical images of hypothetical societies worse than our own—utopias in the broad sense, but definitely not eutopias—often in order to mock or contradict eutopian ideas, the most striking ground-breaking work of that kind being *Le Monde tel qu'il sera* (1846) by Émile Souvestre.

By the time "dystopia" became commonplace in critical parlance, however, other distinctions had become useful, and perhaps necessary. In his exemplary anthology *Utopias and Utopian Thought* (1966), Frank Manuel argued that the history of utopian thought had undergone two crucial transitions, the first in the late eighteenth century—primarily and crucially in France—when "eutopian" imagery and thinking had begun to be gradually and largely displaced by "euchronian" imagery and thinking, in which hypothetical ideal societies were located in a hypothetical historical future rather than in an imaginary geographical space. The second shift, he argued, had begun in the twentieth century, when the emphasis of much imagery and thinking in that vein had gradually shifted into a "eupsychian" mode, which sought an existential ideal in a better state of mind instead of a better formula of government and social organization.

The four works in this collection illustrate not only the ambiguities in the term "utopia" but also the evolution of ideas and methods that encouraged the coinage of the variant terms "dystopia," "euchronia" and "eupsychia." The first of them is a utopia in the broad sense, in which the hypothetical society described is only related to existing society in satirical terms, and very subtly. The second and third are both set in future Paris, one being an archetypal euchronia imagining the supposedly ideal society that might result from the thoroughgoing application of the politics of Anarchism, and the other an archetypal dystopia arguing, on the contrary, that a thoroughgoing application of the political principles of Socialism would produce a disastrously vile society. The fourth reverts to the utopian plan, but presents a society that, although founded by eutopians with a firm euchronian agenda, has produced a strangely compromised result, in which eutopian and dystopian elements are fused, thus raising the question of whether any program of eutopian political reform could possibly produce the intended results, given the limited malleability of human nature, and wondering exactly what kinds of psychological adaptation, if any, might really qualify as a recipe for general happiness.

Each of the four works has virtues of its own—all four were ground-breaking in their day—and also faults of its own, some generated by dubious logic and others by the innate awkwardness of adapting their narrative strategies to their utopian subject-matter, but they become even more fascinating in juxtaposition, illustrating aspects of a spectrum rather than isolated endeavors. One virtue that they all share is that of being relatively short—although I have, admittedly, shorn all four of them of supplementary non-fictional material that increased both the ponderousness and prolixity of their original versions, allowing their narrative components to speak for themselves, as none of the authors quite dared to do, in an era when utopian fiction as still relatively unfamiliar to general readers, and not a genre able to assume any advance sympathy on the part of potential readers. That querulousness was probably unnecessary, as the texts are all, in fact, quite lively in parts as well as thought-provoking, and perfectly readable.

Publication complète des nouvelles découvertes de sir John Herschel dans le ciel austral et dans la lune by Victor Considerant, here translated as "The Complete News from the Moon" was originally published in Paris by Masson and Dupré in 1836. The story takes the form of a sequel to the text of the New York *Sun*'s famous "Moon Hoax," which first appeared in that newspaper as a series of six articles, beginning on 25 August 1835, ostensibly reporting discoveries made by a group of astronomers headed by Sir John Herschel employing a new telescope built at the Cape of God Hope. The story was credited to a fictitious associate of Herschel's, Andrew Grant, but its actual author was probably the *Sun* reporter Richard Adams Locke. From modest beginnings, the hoax articles moved on to pile improbability upon improbability in its descriptions of the fauna of the Moon, culminating in descriptions of its winged humanoid inhabitants, beginning with a seemingly-flightless species with bat-like wings, re-

9

ported on the fourth day and provisionally dubbed *Vespertilio-homo*, and then a related but taller and seemingly more advanced species of whom a brief glimpse was reported on the sixth and final day.

The hoax articles caused a sensation, and were rapidly reprinted in other newspapers; the sensation was repeated when translated appeared in various European nations, but had a particular impact in Paris, where it stimulated several responses in kind, including four satirical pieces by Joseph Méry subsequently reprinted as "Les Lunariens" (tr. as "The Lunarians"). Considerant's sequel was, however, by far the longest and most substantial.

Although the consensus among astronomers in 1835 was that the Moon had no atmosphere, and was therefore lifeless, there was a stubborn minority view claiming that the satellite did have an atmosphere, and various items of evidence were still occasionally cited in support of that view. A number of astronomers also continued to construe features observed on the lunar surface as evidence of intelligent construction, and thus that the Moon had been inhabited in the past, even if it was not now. The German astronomer Franz Gruithuisen had published an account of observations he considered to be those of relics of a supposed lunar civilization in 1824. The idea also received continuing support from the minority of theologians who clung to the "principle of plenitude"—the argument that God would not have filled the universe with worlds only to leave them barren, and must therefore have populated all of them with beings made, at least approximately, in his image.

The Masson and Dupré book takes some trouble to establish its "credentials," including an effusive dedication by Herschel and two prefaces by "the editors" and "the translator," which I have considered to be superfluous and have omitted, only reproducing the account of the supposed further observations of the lunar civilization of the angelically-winged "Séléniens" and their interactions with the bat-winged "Vespertilios," many of whom have been domesticated and now provide the Séléniens with one of its servant classes, although the "savage" Vespertilios living on the part of the Moon's surface invisible from the Earth still mount occasional nocturnal raids on the Séléniens, having long since obliged the Séléniens to place their heavily fortified homes on mountaintops and to maintain a constant vigilance. (At the time it was so widely believed as almost to be taken for granted that the Moon's many craters were volcanic, and hence qualified as mountains.)

In Considerant's version of Herschel's discoveries, which are not entirely consistent with the allegations of the original hoax, the domesticated Vespertilios only fill the median position in the lunar social hierarchy, the heaviest and dirtiest manual labor being carried out by the wingless Castors [Beavers], thus completing a parallel of sorts to the Earthly social hierarchy of the aristocracy, the bourgeoisie and the proletariat, but the resultant element of social satire is only one element of the story's satirical purpose, and not the more important one. The early sections of the text show the astronomers scrupulously recording and collating their observations, gradually building up an image of the hypothetical "anthropology" of the three alien races, including the effects on their culture of the long cycle of their days and nights. Up to that point, the work is interesting not only as the most elaborate description yet provided of a fictitious alien culture, in terms of its adaptation to its environment, but also as the most elaborate fictional account yet provided of scientific observations made and reported in careful and disciplined fashion. It is, however, a parody, ultimately intended not to praise its hypothetical observers but to demolish them—or, at least, one aspect of their attitude.

The later sections of Considerant's text, which deal with the astronomers' attempt to study the lunar religion and to draw inferences from their observations, take the rhetoric in a different direction, mounting a subtle but devastating attack on a tendency among some contemporary scientists to what was known in England as "natural theology": the idea that by studying nature one could obtain an insight into the mind and methods of the Creator that would support and confirm religious faith rather than threatening it. While continuing hypocritically to assert their objectivity, Considerant's astronomers describe a religious ceremony from which the reader might well draw inferences quite different from theirs, and the text concludes with an addendum in which a minor character suggests further inferences that might be drawn from the contemplation of lunar life—a passage that might well owe something to the author's reflections on Bernardin de Saint-Pierre's posthumously-published and lyrical account of *Harmonies de la nature* (1815). I shall leave it to the reader to decide what attitude the real author is inviting the reader to take to that conclusion.

Victor Considerant (1808-1893) was one of the staunchest disciples of the great French utopian writer Charles Fourier, working with Fourier on the propagandizing periodicals *La Phalanstère* and *La Phalange*. After Fourier's death in 1837 he became the effective leader of the movement, and he wrote a good deal of campaigning non-fiction in the cause of democratic socialism, championing a right to work and devising the proportional representation system of democratic election, but he wrote no further fiction. He eventually followed the example of another famous French utopian, Étienne Cabet, in attempting to found a utopian community in Texas, in 1852, but it did not survive the Civil War and he returned to France in time to support the Paris Commune of 1871, although he did not suffer execution or deportation in consequence, perhaps because he still held an American passport.

The edition of *L'Humanisphère, utopia anarchique* [The Humanisphere: An Anarchic Utopia] by Joseph Déjacque held by the Bibliothèque Nationale has a title page indicating publication by the Bibliothèque des "Temps Nouveaux" in Brussels, which the library dates 1899, not necessarily correctly, but the edition in question is advertised internally as a reprint, and it is probable that an earlier edition of the text was printed clandestinely in Paris. What is certain, however, is that the material therein had initially been published in serial form in the U.S.A. in Déjacque's periodical *Le Libertaire* [Libertarianism], which published twenty-seven issues between June 1858 to February 1861. The section entitled "Le Monde futur," here translated as "The Future World (of the Humanisphere)" is the penultimate chapter of the book, presenting a vision of the implementation of the anarchist political scheme that Déjacque attempted to develop in the theoretical articles he published in the pages of the periodical.

Joseph Déjacque (1821-1864) was the most extreme of all the French political radicals of the nineteenth century—a title for which there was certainly no shortage of competition. Like Victor Considerant, he was an enthusiastic supporter of the 1848 Revolution, but he was imprisoned for socialist agitation before the *coup d'état* of 1851. He seems to have escaped from prison during that upheaval, and then followed Considerant's example by fleeing the country, initially making his way to England. As with most agitators, imprisonment had only made him more determined to continue the struggle; and while he was resident in Jersey—also Victor Hugo's place of exile—he published an article that is nowadays regarded as one of the foundation-stones of the French political philosophy of Anarchism, although Déjacque used the term *anarchie* interchangeably with *libertaire.*

In the pages of *Le Libertaire* Déjacque published a substantial series of related texts, of which *L'Humanisphère* is a drastically-abridged summary, giving pride of place to his vision of the ideal society that the complete application of the anarchist philosophy ought to produce. Whereas most later writers attempting to design an "anarchist" eutopia compromise to some extent with the principle of total liberty, Déjacque does not; although clearly aware that skeptics might consider his account of the probable consequences of a complete absence of any regulation or restriction in education, labor and matters of amour a trifle over-optimistic, he defends his position robustly. From a literary viewpoint, the narrative of the futuristic vision is relatively uninteresting, containing

13

no characters, no dialogue and little concrete description of the anarchist way of life, but it does contain some plangent rhetoric, and a concise summary of the anarchist ideal that is particularly interesting in comparison to other accounts of the role of science and technology in hypothetical eutopian societies.

Déjacque's ideal anarchist society, organized around huge edifices of a kind that would subsequently be dubbed "urban monads" in the late twentieth century, is only feasible because of dramatic improvements in technology, intrinsic to which are abundant power supplied in the form of electricity, elaborate agricultural and industrial machinery, and sophisticated means of transport, including aerial transport. It is a highly mechanized and largely automated world, which inevitably places Science at the very heart of its educational system and central to its atheistic reverence. In Déjacque's vision, Anarchism and advanced technology are intimately interlinked, and his thesis is, in a sense, the ultimate extrapolation of the eighteenth-century philosophy that saw technological and social progress as different aspects of the same process.

Other political philosophies, of course, could equally well envisage the future development of science and technology, and would have been foolish not to do so in the years of the Second Empire, but to say the least, Déjacque's vision of a high-tech society, more elaborately advanced than the vast majority of such visions produced thus far, and his forging of a firm link between the image of an electrically-powered, mechanically elaborate society and the philosophy of anarchism, were not likely to incline diehard opponents of anarchism in favor of such imagery. Nor could the ban on his ideas discriminate between his politics and his technological anticipations, and anyone who contrived to become acquainted with his work in spite of the censors was bound to associate the thrill of the forbidden with all the aspects of the text.

By virtue of those circumstances, Déjacque's account of "Le Monde futur" is not only interesting for its reflection of and contribution to the development of political philosophy, but also, and perhaps more so, for its reflection of and contribution to the hopes and expectations of the social transformations that technological progress might facilitate and might perhaps encourage. It is, at any rate, a fascinating experiment in ideas, in spite of its shortcomings as an engaging narrative.

La Cité nouvelle was originally published anonymously in Paris by Amyot in 1868. It author, Fernand Giraudeau (1835-1904) was located at the opposite end of the spectrum of Second Empire politics from Déjacque, being Napoléon III's most outspoken apologist; *La Cité nouvelle* is, in part, an angry reply to the emperor's critics, and includes a long account by a historian supposedly speaking at the end of the twentieth century, who assesses Napoléon III's reign as the greatest in the history of European society.

The nature of the exercise compels that account to extend beyond the date of the book's publication, which we can now see, with the aid of hindsight, to have been a trifle unfortunate, being only two years ahead of the Franco-Prussian War that brought the reign in question to a catastrophic end. In the "future history" mapped out by Giraudeau—which the passage of time rapidly turned into a an "alternative history"—that does not happen, of course; in a brief military campaign that hardly qualifies as a war, the emperor puts the Prussians in their place and secures Alsace and Lorraine for France permanently, and then goes from strength to strength until he is succeeded by his son, who is compelled to engage in the first genuinely worldwide conflict, when France, England and Germany are allied against Russia and the U.S.A., and from which that alliance emerges triumphant.

The imaginary history is then obliged to progress, however, to account for the bizarre society described in the opening chapters, which, although it contains numerous comical episodes, is by far the angriest and most detailed account of a comprehensively wrecked society produced in the nineteenth century, and a much closer analogue of the many twentieth-century anti-socialist dystopia than Souvestre's *Le Monde tel qu'il sera*.

Giraudeau did not embark upon any further ventures in speculative fiction after *La Cité nouvelle*, perhaps working on the principle of once burned, twice shy, but the rapid falsification of his hypothetical future history did not cause him to modify his opinions; he spend the rest of his literary career—having, of course, lost the plum government job that the emperor had given him after the publication of his propaganda piece—writing eulogistic accounts of Napoléon III and deeply regretting the fact that the great man had been unjustly robbed of the opportunity to complete the program laid out in his own imaginary history, and that the entire human world was worse off in consequence.

Lettres de Malaisie by Paul Adam, here translated as "Letters from Malaisie" was originally published in Paris by Éditions de la Revue Blanche in 1898. Although Malaisie could, and perhaps should, be translated as "Malaysia," I have left the French spelling in place in the present translation because it preserves a deliberate reflection of the word *malaise*, which would be lost by substituting the English spelling. The "Malaise" from which the letters come is not so much the geographical Malaysia as the Land of Unease.

Paul Adam (1862-1920) was a prolific novelist explicitly affiliated to both the Naturalist and Symbolist schools, which were often considered to be opposed rivals in the French *fin-de-siècle*. Several of his Naturalistic novels contain digressions into utopian speculation, and he had written a brief futuristic fantasy constituting propaganda for pacifism *Le Conte futur* (1893) before embarking on the far more complicated and sophisticated examination of the central ideas of the French eutopian tradition in *Lettres de Malaisie*, which adopts the hypothesis that a disciple of Étienne Cabet, disillusioned by the fate of Cabet's Icarian colonies in the U.S.A., had set out to carry out a similar experiment in the isles of the Indian Ocean, under the collective influence of the Comte de Saint-Simon, Fourier and Cabet. The preface is, however, careful to emphasize in advance, that the society depicted by the letters is *not* an ideal, and puts that statement in capital letters to make sure that the reader gets the message. In fact no other work more clearly justifies the utility of differentiating between utopias and eutopias.

The preface to the letters refers to all the utopian writers of the early nineteenth century, in whose ideas the narrative is rooted, and also likens the exercise explicitly to More's pioneering exemplar, but the main text also has an extensive series of footnotes consisting of long quotes from François Fénelon's *Aventures de Télémaque* (1699), drawing comparisons between the advice offered therein by Telemachus' tutor Mentor on how to construct a wisely-governed society and the society described by the letters, although the contrasts are much more striking than the similarities. I have considered those footnotes to be superfluous to the present translation, and have omitted them.

The conspicuously prim Fénelon, a devout Catholic clergyman, would certainly not have approved of the reprinting of his words in a book that he would undoubtedly have considered to be obscene, and which must have seemed pornographic even to many of the readers of the *fin-de-siècle*, who had grown accustomed to a much greater degree of license in fiction than would have been permitted two centuries earlier. Fénelon would probably have been appalled, too, by the horrific aspects of the text's lubricity. Evidently bearing in mind what actually happened to the communities that Cabet, Victor Considerant and others of their ilk tried to establish in various parts of the world, Adam describes a society that has been forced by circumstance to become extremely authoritarian in order to maintain an ostentatious philosophy of liberty that really does not extend much beyond the orgiastic application of complete amorous license.

Joseph Déjacque would also have been horrified by Adam's account of the likely consequences of amorous anarchy, which make a striking contrast with his own estimation of what the results of such a liberation would be. Déjacque would, however, have found much that was similar to his own

17

ideas in the advanced electrification and mechanization of the cities of the new society. Although the complete community of property and the corollary absence of money are strongly reinforced by law in Adam's hypothetical society rather than purely voluntary, as in Déjacque's, they are supported and sustained in much the same way, and just as necessarily, by technological sophistication and the resultant abundance of food and physical comforts.

Unlike Déjacque's "humanispheres," the cities of Adam's new society are carefully specialized, each symbolized by the name of a Roman deity, although the founder of the colony has rejected Déjacquian atheism is favor of a functionally and philosophically redesigned Catholicism, complete with a the new catechism, of which even Fénelon—a flexible and tolerant theologian, unlike many of his contemporaries— might have approved in part. Perhaps the most remarkable aspect of that specialization is the different character of the orgies that take place in the various cities. Even the one described by Théa as having taken place in Diane, and the one in Minerve in which the narrator is a participant horrify and sicken him, but as he witnesses others in Mars and, perhaps surprisingly, in Mercure, the city of science, the pitch of his nausea is markedly increased as the screw of perversity is relentlessly turned—although the sequence eventually acquires a strange twist in the final erotic scene set in the industrial city of Vulcan; once again, I shall leave it to the reader to decide exactly what attitude the author is inviting the reader to take to Pythie's final declaration, and what attitude ought to be adopted, rationally considered.

Lettres de Malaisie is perhaps the most interesting of all nineteenth-century utopian satires, in the way it gathers so many threads of eutopian thought together, in order to expose their supposed paradoxicality and potential perversion, while simultaneously allowing the voices of the imagined society to argue, forcefully and cogently, that the societies of Europe are far worse and far more absurd than theirs. It is certainly the most sophisticated and ingenious of the century's ambivalent dystopias, and it really does provide a significant series of dispatches from the psychological realm of Unease. No other work is as conscientiously nightmarish in amalgamating eutopian ideals with their nightmarish underside.

Adam scrupulously includes in his survey all the imagery of technological advancement that *roman scientifique* had enabled to become conventional by the end of the nineteenth century, combining the relevant wonders, hopes and anxieties in a more insidious but no less effective fashion than Albert Robida's classic skeptical account of *La Vie électrique* (1892; tr. as *Electric Life*). He illustrates, more graphically than anyone had previously done, the clash of Déjacquian optimism with an insidious disenchantment that was to make further progress in the early years twentieth century, even before the Great War and its aftermath seemingly abolished the optimism of such thought permanently. His work therefore makes a fitting conclusion to the collection, in terms of the comparisons and contrasts it offers with the other three works.

The translations of *Publication complete des nouvelles découvertes de sir John Herschel dans le ciel austral et dans la lune* and *La Cité nouvelle* were made from the versions reproduced on Google Books. The other two translations were made from the copies of the relevant texts reproduced on the Bibliothèque Nationale *gallica* website.

Brian Stableford

Victor Considerant: *The Complete News from the Moon*
(1836)

First Fragment: ASTRONOMICAL NOTIONS

An attentive observation of the Moon does not take long to conclude that it is animated by a proper movement in the celestial sphere. If, at a certain moment, it is found in the sky near a star, one sees it draw away therefrom increasingly, and, in one night, travel a very obvious arc through the vault of the heavens. Thus, the Moon independently of the movement of rotation that it appears to have in common with all the stars in the firmament, possesses a particular movement in the sky. We know that the common movement is only apparent, and that it is the Earth that, rotating on its axis, permits an observer placed on its surface successively to embrace the whole of the infinity of luminous globes dispersed in space.

Our satellite traces an elliptical curve around us that hardly differs from a circle. The Earth occupies one of the focal points of that ellipse. It takes the Moon about twenty-eight days to complete its orbit—which is to say, to return to coincidence with the same star in the sky. During that revolution, the Moon sometimes presents itself to us in the form of a crescent with horns, sometimes in the form of a semicircle and subsequently in a complete circle; then it re-passes through all its phases of grandeur, gradually diminishing to the extent of disappearing completely. It is the passage through those different periods that constitutes the "phases" of the Moon.

When the Moon, in its motion, places itself between the Earth and the Sun, the half that faces the Sun is illuminated and the half the faces the Earth is in darkness; the Moon is new and we do not see it. On the other hand, when, after half a

21

revolution, the Moon is placed behind the Earth, the half that faces us is illuminated; the Moon is then full. When the new Moon, the dark disk that is facing us, receives light reflected by the Earth, it is sufficiently illuminated by that reverberation to be easily visible to the naked eye if the sky is cloudless. The kind of light that the Moon has when it is between three and five days old is known as "ashen light."

Our satellite, as is proven by observation of certain ever-apparent and well-defined points of its disk, constantly presents the same hemisphere to the Earth, and, in consequence, rotates on its axis in the same time as it travels its entire orbit. In that the Moon is like a person who departs from one point of a round table and goes all around the perimeter with his face turned to the center; it is evident that when the person reaches his point of departure he has made a complete rotation of his body.

The result of that fixity of position in relation to our globe is that only half on the Moon cam be studied by us, and that it is not given to humans to know the other hemisphere by direct observation. However, although we cannot see the second half of the Moon, the phenomenon known as libration permits perception of the polar regions and the parts close to the edges of the hemisphere turned toward us. The librations are, in fact, merely an effect of slight vacillations of the heavenly body in the directions of its axis and equator. One can easily visualize these small derangements by comparing them those a person makes with his head to affirm or deny, indicating yes or no.

The librations are due, firstly, to the fact that the Moon's axis is not perpendicular to the plane of its orbit and, secondly, to the fact that the velocity of our satellite in the orbit it travels is not uniform. The first of these causes will be easily understood if one applied to the Moon what happens on Earth. We know that the line around which our planet turns is not perpendicular to the plane of its orbit; otherwise there would be no seasons on our globe; the days would be equal to the nights for all its points, throughout the year. As the axis of the Earth

22

remains constantly parallel to itself as it moves through its orbit, the Sun sometimes illuminates one pole and sometimes the other; hence the six-month-long day and nights that are the prerogative of the circumpolar regions. In the same way that an observer of the Sun would see the Earth's axis going up and down, we see the Moon's axis sometimes inclined toward us and sometimes tilted away; that kind of movement is called latitudinal libration.

In order to visualize the second kind of oscillation, known as longitudinal libration, it is necessary to imagine a straight line drawn from the center of the Earth to the center of the Moon. That line encounters the surface of the sphere at a point that would obviously remain invariable if our satellite, while rotating uniformly on its axis, also circled around us at a uniform velocity. Because that is not the case, it is obvious that the point of that encounter on the Moon's surface is mobile: that it travels in one direction when our satellites accelerates, and in the reverse direction with its velocity diminishes. The Moon therefore oscillates indefinitely around a median position, and allows the sight of several degrees of extent either to the east or the west of the visible hemisphere.

Intelligence of the preceding information is sufficient to comprehend the greater part of my observations. Before giving a description of them, however, I shall cast a glance at the ensemble of those that have been made before, with regard to the physical constitution of the Moon, and I shall say a few words about the consequences that have been drawn therefrom, as well as the different theories that scholars, both ancient and modern, have established to proved that our satellite is either provided with or deprived of living beings.

It has been observed that the Moon sometimes disappears from a clear and serene sky, in such a fashion that it cannot even be seen with instruments endowed with the strongest magnification. Kepler witnessed the phenomenon twice in 1581 and 1583. It was observed by Helvetius in 1620, by Riccioli, other Jesuits of Bologne and many other people in Holland on 14 April 1642. On 23 December 1703, another total disappearance of the Moon occurred. The heavenly body, which appeared to be yellow-brown at Arles, was red and transparent, as if the sun were shining through it, in Avignon; at Marseille, one of its sides seemed red and the other very obscure; in the end, it disappeared completely, although the weather was perfectly serene. The astronomer of the last century claimed that these strange phenomena could only be produced by a substance enveloping the Moon and disposed to give passage to rays of a particular color.[1]

Helvetius reports that he has often found, when the atmosphere is perfectly clear, that the Moon and its patches are not always equally clear and visible; that they are brighter, purer and more distinct at times than at others. Thus, that astronomer, along with Lalande, d'Alembert and many others, affirm that it is necessary not to seek the reason for the phenomenon in question either in the air that surrounds us or in the substance of the moon, but in something else that surrounds the body of our satellite.

Cassini has observed that Saturn, Jupiter and the fixed stars, when they are hidden behind the Moon, appear to take on close to its rim, whether light or dark, an elongated shape, but in other observations he has not found any alteration. The same phenomena are sometimes presented on the Earth for the Sun and the Moon; they are due to the refraction of luminous rays in atmospheric layers of different densities, Cassini his therefore concluded from the similarity of the two phenomena that he Moon is sometimes surrounded by a dense matter, which is sometimes only found in a state of excessive rarefaction.

During a solar eclipse, one sees the Moon surrounded by a luminous ring parallel to its circumference. That is what was observed in London in 1715; in Leipzig, by Wolff, in 1706; in Antwerp, by Kepler, in 1695; and finally, long ago, at Geffa,

---

[1] The usual explanation of these "disappearances" is, of course that they were lunar eclipses during which the Moon was covered by the Earth's shadow.

six or seven miles from Cairo, in 978 by the astronomers of King Abu-Haly-Almanzor, ruler of Egypt. The observations of the later astronomers are recorded in a very curious manuscript of Ibn Yunus. Wolff, in his *Acta Eruditorum*,[2] observes that the brightest part is that closest to the Moon; he hastens to conclude that the atmospheric layers are weaker in density as their distance from the lunar surface increases.

I shall also cite the total solar eclipse of 16 June 1806. It was observed by Ferrer, a skillful Spanish astronomer, who went for that purpose from New York to Kinderhook. Ferrer reports that the lunar disk appeared to be illuminated seven minutes before the conclusion of the obscurity; that seems, he says, to be the effect of a small lunar atmosphere. He also observed a concentric luminous ring around the Sun about 45 or 50 degrees in diameter; the edge of the Moon was indistinctly terminated; small columns of very thin vapor were departing from it, which dissipated in the luminous ring. I shall explain these phenomena, as curious as they are bizarre, in due course.

I ought also to say that in the last century, the duration of the occultation of a star having been calculated by reference to its mean velocity before and after its passage behind the Moon, it was found that the time was exactly equal to the observation made directly, from which it was concluded that the Moon had no atmosphere, for if the luminous rays had traversed a gaseous milieu they would have been refracted; in consequence the duration of the occultation furnished by observation would be less than the duration given by calculation. I shall return later to that conclusion, which I have enunciated in my elementary work on astronomy.

As it is the nearest heavenly body to the Earth, the Moon has been submitted to observation more than any other planet in our vortex. With the aid of powerful astronomical binoculars or good telescopes, certain principal points have been rec-

---

[2] *Acta Eruditorum* [Reports of the Scholars] was a pioneering scientific journal published in Leipzig between 1682 and 1782. Christian Wolff was one of its many contributors.

ognized that are brighter than all the others, and others more obscure, and finally, large dull gray patches. These points being sufficiently distinct to be completely definable, it has been possible to project them on to a plan surface; hence maps of the Moon, and therefore selenography.

If one directs the axis of an astronomical instrument at the disk of the Moon when it is entirely illuminated by the Sun, the eye, struck by the glare of the light, has difficulty at first in distinguishing the objects that are in the field of view. After a few seconds, however, pronounced undulations are easy to recognize; the observer can follow long veins much brighter than the surrounding areas, and perceive immense plains dimly lit and variable in brightness. In addition to these differences in the intensity of the light, he can also, through a very favorable atmosphere, remark specifically different colors, notably green, sometimes ruddy and yellow-brown; the later hues are, however, less pronounced. The most considerable of the greenish surfaces form the interior of the *Mare Serenitatis*.

If the observations are made when the Moon is in its first quarter, directing the axis of the instrument at the illuminated part, the crests of the mountains reflect the solar light that strikes them obliquely, and one can measure the immense shadows that they project into the valleys. Here and there, in the obscure part, one finds bright spots that are evidently the highest points of the mountain summits.

Among the men who have occupied themselves most with selenography, it is necessary to cite Helvetius, who adopted the geographical principle for the nomenclature of the Lunar features, and Riccioli, who chose the names of illustrious men to designate the features. All the selenographers of modern times have followed Riccioli's denominations, and have added to them the names of scientists, dead or still alive, especially for craters and plans closed by circumvolutions. They have similarly conserved for the seas or gray surfaces the bizarre named of the Sea of Sleep, the Lake of Death, The Sea of Putridity, Rainbow Gulf, by allusion to lunar influences then universally admitted. I shall not change any of the denominations accepted thus far, and as for those I shall introduce to designate new points on the lunar surface, I shall try to give them a significative value.

Such is the ensemble of the knowledge resulting from observations made of the Moon previous to the employment of my telescope. I shall not pause on the consequences that have been drawn from them. Some are true, others false; the description of the planet I shall give in accordance with our work will permit people versed in these matters to distinguish the judicious appreciations from the erroneous opinions.

It was not until 10 January 1835—which is to say, after three months of work, that we were finally able to commence our observations. We needed that time to establish the immense telescope whose description is given in a special chapter in the full report.

I owe the local inhabitants thanks for the kind assistance that they procured me, and it is with the greatest pleasure that I inscribe the names of my honorable collaborators, Messrs. Grant (Andrew), Drummond, ship's lieutenant, Major Muller and Herbert Holms, the expedition's artist.

It is, in fact, impossible that their memory will be effaced from human memory so long as the scientific notions endure that we are transmitting regarding the material organization of the globe neighboring our own, the developments of the animate beings that move on its surface, and finally the magnificent creature that Providence has placed there to be its master and rector.

The Sun had disappeared, the Moon was rising over the horizon, gradually disengaging itself from the vapors that were obscuring its light. The sky still conserved a hint of cerise red in the occident. The direction and inclination of the instrument had been calculated in such a manner that its axis would encounter the circle traced in space by the center of our satellite. An unforeseen accident overtaking the frames of our two lenses endowed with the greatest refractive power prevented us from obtaining the greatest magnification in the observations of the first few days. The lens mounted would permit us a magnification of 5,000.

Everything was ready, and we were waiting for the moment when the heavenly body would enter the field of the instrument; each of us, during that moment of expectation, projected his thoughts toward the globe that we were finally about to know and travel in every direction, as if a powerful charm were drawing us into its atmosphere less than a mile from its surface. Our imaginations revealed precipices and prairies, volcanoes, rocks, scoria, crevasse and glaciers. Several of us experienced nervous tremors that could not be mastered. All of us had hearts and minds constricted in a condition impossible to describe.

Finally, a general cry put an end to that anxiety.

That first night and the following ones were employed in scanning the lunar globe. Conserving the same magnification, it was possible for us to make out the points already known and to identify a large number of others that were to serve as reference points when out most powerful lenses were mounted and the field of vision reduced. That investigation permitted us to revise the lunar maps already known, and to assess the degree of their precision. Those of Messrs. Guillaume Beer and Jean-Henri Muller, of which only two quarters have appeared, are undoubtedly the most accurate.

Second Fragment: SELENOGRAPHY

The mountainous countries of the Moon present a constant and invariable configuration. Everywhere, the crests of the mountains embrace curves, either circular or elliptical, almost all of whose points are situated in the same plane. Those crests are redoubled and form several stages, the heights of which decrease as one approaches the center. Those various stages are separated by immense crevasses, whose depth it is impossible to determine. No trace of vegetation can be perceived on those mountains, and the immense banks of rock that compose them have the appearance of volcanic lava congealed by a sudden cooling. From the steep crests of the final stage gigantic rock faces fall almost vertically, and one sees enormous masses of rocks forming steps of a sort at the bases of those walls, which are several miles high. The floors of those immense wells are slightly inclined toward the center, with the result that all the waters on the valley flow to the lowest point of the basin, where they form a great lake, the banks of which must extend or shrink in accordance with the fraction of the water that streams and rivulets bring them they distribute into the atmosphere by evaporation.

From the center of the lake, in the form of an exceedingly steep cone, one or several almost-crystalline masses rises, affecting various bright colors. The number of these peaks varies between one and five. They are always unequal in height, the tallest only a mile and a quarter. They are very often terminated by conoid surfaces so regular that we were obliged to recognize them immediately as the product of intelligence and to refuse nature the ability to have created them.

Independently of the mountain systems we have just described, the Moon presents immense plains of great fertility; the number of vegetables that we have discovered there merits such special mention that we shall devote several chapters to it.

The first aspect that struck our gaze was a green rock like certain frequently-irrigated lichens; its hue was not due to a cause of that kind, to judge by its elevated position and its rather rapid slope, which doubtless furnished superabundant dew with an easy, even prompt flow. From the fact that lichens do not participate in that mineral coloration, it ought not to be concluded that another plant of the family of mosses sought its existence there. No, it is certain that the bright color in question was that of stone, and frequent encounters with analogous substances have provide that to us with conclusive evidence.

Soon, that rock was succeeded by a myriad of small brown, sharp pebbles, a kind of natural mosaic, a sharply-outlined pavement with which we had nothing to compare.

Cavities and crests were almost equal in number there, and the former might have served as molds for the latter.

The rocks were composed of poorly developed, idiosyncratic crystals, with calcareous monads intermingled with micaceous scales. Those lavas had the most incoherent positions.

In the middle of that sterile, rocky country, among the high rocks deprived of all vegetation, which corresponded to the country that Riccioli, following a rather unfortunate inspiration, called Lacus Somnorium, in a place where it seemed impossible for it to exist, we chanced to recognize a creature among blocks of a granitic appearance, a monster endowed with locomotive faculties. To explain its presence and its *modus vivendi* would be impossible. Let us limit ourselves to its form.

The head, a kind of fleshy triangle covered with sky gray leather, bore at its anterior extremity a horn divided into three branches for half its length, estimable at a foot and a half. From that point on it sticks up sharply. The beast had no visible ears, and its eyes, placed on top of its head and protected by a visor of skin that could be withdrawn at will, could see into the rocks and the sky, doubtless to protect it from some voracious bird. Its body, about the girth of that of a wolf, was much more elongated, which gave the head, very disproportionate, and which swung from right to left, a frightful aspect.

The animal was bipedal, its legs short and its feet very broad. The skin resembled that of a rhinoceros, and from the rump projected a flat tail articulated by rings, terminated by a bony spatula framed with long spikes, which it used to anchor itself and raise itself upright in the midst of those rugged rocks. We have described that monster because we never saw it again, and it seemed to be born for the nature that surrounded it.

Soon, the face of the landscape became more varied, and violet flowers were a prelude to the spectacle of the most cheerful nature...

Third Fragment: INTELLIGENT RACES;
PHYSIOLOGY; WARS

The intelligent creature is what we sought most avidly on that globe, open for the first time to the eye of science. As soon as we had encountered it, nothing could detach us from that contemplation. How many times Mr. Hamilton, my noble friend and I, congratulated ourselves on having found for the result of our discoveries not merely the rectification of lunar maps, an advantage already precious, or the acquisition of very interesting astronomical details, which would have been more than sufficient to recompense us for our efforts, but also to have responded to the most noble tendency of our epoch, in aiding by the patent development of science the occult work of the moral amelioration of humans!

We have recognized, therefore, among the beings whose existence was successively revealed to us, three creatures worthy of being set apart by virtue of their forms and habits, although they do not occupy an equal rank in the scale of creations, and the same functions are not identically assigned to them, as will be observed in due course; but they rise, as much by virtue of their respective functions as by the nature of their physiological constitution, so far above all the others that they appeared to us to be the true representatives of intelligence on the planet, and, in spite of the line of demarcation traced between them by nature, they undoubtedly constitute the "lunar human race."

The first of those beings was manifest for the first time to our gaze on the edge of a forest of trees that were reminiscent of both *Cupressus* and *Pinus maritima*.[3] We had too little time to characterize it; it disappeared so promptly that we mistook it for a large bird.

Soon, our field of vision embraced a mountain surmounted by a large building—we were in the south of

---

[3] The pine tree initially classified as *Pinus maritima* is nowadays known as *Pinus pinaster*.

31

Longrenus. We were undecided at first as to whether to attribute the construction to nature or art, but the reappearance of a legion of beings similar to the one that had caused our surprise settled the question in favor of art.

Those animals—that is how they are designated in our journal the first time there is mention of them—were agglomerated on a small clear sloping plain. Scarcely had we turned out eyes in their direction than they all disappeared in the same direction, cleaving the air with great beats of the wings that veiled their bodies. They came back thereafter with other beings of the same genre, but not the same species, which we had already perceived a month before, but too vaguely to be able to form any conjectures. We saw them again frequently, always in the same company, and it was as easily as it was flattering for us to identify them as two races of "androselenians." Only the more perfect of the two conserves that name in our reports.

Selenians are scarcely more than two feet eight inches in average height. Their body is supple and elongated; their articulations have the appearance of vigor; their shoulders are endowed with vast wings, longer in the female, reminiscent by the nature of the plumage and the joints of the wings of an ostrich. The analogy stops there, for the pinions are longer, and stiff and slender near the edges, like those of a gull, but much longer. Thus, Selenians enjoy a very bold flight; they soar like birds of prey, and maintain themselves above the water over which they pass with celerity.

That aggregation of faculties in a single being confirmed the opinions we had already formed in advance; it is impossible, in fact, not to suppose that the lunarian humans must accomplish all, or at least the greater part, of their functions in the atmosphere. What are those functions? Apart from the difficulty of extending our inductions as far as phenomena so different from those accomplished for us on Earth, the field of observations is too extensive for us to permit us to indulge in metaphysical conjectures, less interesting because they are less positive, and because they would contribute in a less direct manner to astronomical progress.

Later, however, we shall develop considerations on that subject that can only be born from experience.

It is important, in order to distinguish the beings that occupy us presently from the one that will shortly be the object of our analysis, to remember that, similar to the wings of the ostrich, those of the Selenians are covered with plumes, and that those plumes, attached uniquely to the wings, contrast with the absolute nudity of the rest of the body, on which hair cannot be detected. It is to that absence of a pilous system in Selenians that we must attribute the perfect knowledge we have acquired, satisfying to the highest degree, of the whiteness of their skin. By an admirable contrast, their eyes are dark, and the hair on the head black. That hair, in falling backwards, frames with its bushy mass the two wings, when they are deployed, and nothing equals the beauty that results from the accord in question.

We have said that alongside the beings that appeared to us to occupy the first rank on the satellite, our objective manifested a second, similar to the other in certain respects, and distant from it in many others.

That new race has wings like the first, but deprived of feathers; and in that regard, if the Androselenians offered us an analogy with the ostrich, the species that we shall designate by the name of *Vespertilio* presented us one with bats.

Vespertilios are about four feet tall, and rise up by means of their wings into the high atmosphere, but it seems to us that they are less at home there than the Selenians, for they do not have the faculty, as the latter do, of traversing very considerable distances without exhausting themselves. It seems that their aerial faculties are less important; they have only received from the Creator half the power attributed to the Selenians. They rest frequently, doubtless by necessity, and we have often remarked that, with the objective of renewing the vigor of their membranous wings by means of an astringent immersion after a relatively brief flight, they alight on a river or a lake and steep themselves therein.

Only that hygienic motive has explained the frequency of those baths to us.

Vespertilios are brownish gray. Can one not believe that the Creator, with regard to that feature, wanted to establish the most exaggerated contrast between them and the androselenians? The field of philosophy has always been vast, and has become even more so since study has delivered the secrets of our satellite to us. I bequeath the conjectures to those who will follow me; my mission is limited at present to divulging my astronomical observations, and that is already important enough.

The constitution of the Vespertilios does not differ from that of humans with regret to the other organs, but they bear all the external signs of their intellectual authority. Their facial angle is less developed than that of the Selenians; the head is flat, the neck slender and elongated; and if we cast a glance over the physiognomic appearance in general, we find that it is far from presenting the signs of domination that are the pre-rogative of the Selenian race, properly speaking.

The female Vespertilio is difficult to distinguish from the male when one only considers them from the viewpoint of form. She differs in that from the female Selenian, who, as much by the length of her wings as by the color of her plum-age, is essentially separate from the individual of the other sex.

The female Selenian has, moreover, the greater delicacy of the limbs, with which she combines the vigor that results from the harmony of her proportions. The female Vespertilio, on the contrary, is heavy and well-muscled. We attribute that physical development to a thousand causes, but principally to the industrial exercises and base functions that are shared without distinction between the two sexes of that race.

On exploring more attentively than we had yet done the characteristics appropriate to each sex, we obtained for a result the most curious of singularities. If we have deferred making it known until now, it is because, far from constituting a general law, it is subject to numerous exceptions. The female Vespertilio is not veritably gray, but a gray that approaches black in its dark hue. We were deceived momentarily by that bizarrerie, and were on the point of believing in a new race of humans when irrefutable and scrupulous observations brought us back to the truth.

It is time to say that before those two races we had discovered a third, of which I have put off until now furnishing a description because it only occupies the third rank on the satellite—that, at least, results not only from the attentive examination of its physical being but also the analysis of the functions to which is habitually devotes itself.

The Beaver—we are all agreed in giving it that name—appeared to us for the first time on the edge of a lake or broad stream surrounded by small gray eminences of which we were unable at first to determine the nature; but a thick smoke escaping from them did not leave us in doubt for long, especially when we saw a large number of Beavers leaving the edge of the lake to go to those monticules and, at the moment when we had the greatest desire to follow them, suddenly vanish. We therefore concluded that the eminences could only be their huts, and that they entered or exited therefrom on the side opposite to the direction of our instrument. The smoke enabled us to presume, moreover, that the Beavers were intelligent, and you shall soon see that that presumption was not long in being converted into a certainty.

Beavers are bipedal; that, as is evident, is the character common to the three andro-selenian species. Like the Vespertilios, they are almost always four feet in height, rarely less and never more. Furthermore, apart from their intelligence, manifested by a facial angle of greater opening, they offer the greatest analogy with terrestrial beavers; they could even be confused with the latter if they were not upright on their feet, if they had a smaller stature and if their arms had not been designed by the Creator to accomplish the part they play in lunarian industry.

Such are the three very distinct races that inhabit the globe of the Moon. Nevertheless, numerous and clear-cut as those natural distinctions are, they are feeble by comparison with social distinctions. In fact, although the Vespertilios live in the same places as the Selenians, it is not in the same capacity; if, like them, they mingle in various kinds of labor, they are not of the same quality; and above all, the occupations of either are completely different from those of the Beavers.

Strictly speaking, houses do not exist on the Moon, but rather manors, often octagonal in form or conical, susceptible by their extent of containing two or three hundred individuals. Those manors are sometimes separated from one another by large spaces populated with trees, which cannot be called gardens because they do not include anything analogous to leguminous or fructigenic plantations. The trees in question seem entirely designed for ornamentation or salubrity.

We have noticed troops of Selenians still young and small frolicking in these plantations. Each group was under the surveillance or the safeguard of a Vespertilio. As only individuals of the Selenian race are found among those children, that first observation put us on the track of discovering a multitude of other customs that would otherwise have escaped us. The Vespertilios thus seemed to us to be fulfilling functions analogous to those of the pedagogues of Rome, who were all slaves. Once that analogy was found, we extended it, and eventually discovered that the Vespertilios were the slaves of the Selenians.

We have seen Vespertilios working on the land, and never Selenians. The latter were exercising a sort of surveillance over them, not individually but grouped into ambulant committees. We concluded therefrom that property in the land in question might well be common. Other arguments came to fortify our opinion, and give us reason to think that the community in question even extends to different orders of relationship. Is that a bad thing or a good thing? Does it offer evidence of a social estate more or less advanced than ours?

I know that in recent times philosophy has agitated those questions a great deal; but, preoccupied by my scientific endeavors, I was unable to listen to the debates, and besides which, I cannot, informed as I now am of the mores of our satellite, adopt an opinion in that regard without giving the lunar race the advantage over us or taking it away from it, and I do not want to reduce myself to that extremity.

Alongside Vespertilios and with them we have seen Beavers working the land. Their number was always more considerable than that of the Vespertilios. We concluded from that observation that the latter never took part, in all the orders of industrial functions, in any but the less tedious and less coarse work, that they were like the foremen of the Beavers, who were themselves unable to escape all that manual labor presents of the rudest and most fatiguing.

Fishing and hunting are the favorite occupations of the Selenians, of which they have the exclusive privilege. Fishing in rivers is the only kind we have observed. In the lunar planet, bristling with mountains and fissures, we have encountered few rivers in the sense that we give to that word; we have accorded that denomination to streams and ravines whose course in sometimes interrupted by the steepness of the slope and sometimes transformed into a deep pool.

Fish are scarce there but crustaceans pullulate. Those animals, whose incoherent and multiple forms are difficult to describe, appear to us to be almost all armed with pincers or jaws, and powerful means of defense, and in spite of the dexterity of the Selenians, as they only ever make use of their fingers in fishing, we have perceived that they are bitten quite frequently.

In spite of our humanity, we experienced satisfaction one day when that accident happened to a fisher who had been the object of all our attention for some time, and whose image stood out very clearly in the objective. We owed it to that accident, in fact, to remark for the first time that the blood of lunarian humans is not red like ours but a milky blue; the extent of the wound caused a quantity to flow sufficiently considerable to remove all doubt in that regard.

Although the ravines are not very profound, they end in basins whose bed is very deep. One night I perceived a Selenian diving into one of these basins and, curious to see the result, I waited for his return to the surface. He took his time; I even thought momentarily that he had drowned; but after twenty minutes he reappeared, holding in his hand two fish, round in form and passably stout, which seemed to us to have a considerable analogy with marine turtles. I renewed my observations in that regard and have been able to convince myself that Selenians are amphibious.

We have collected few documents on hunting; that which is done in the mountains has remained unknown to us, so difficult is it to penetrate by gaze, at such an enormous distance, the masses of trees and rocks of which those mountains are composed.

On 7 February, at eleven o'clock in the evening, regions thought to be uninhabitable having entered our field of view, we discovered on the rocks that we were disposed to examine a multitude of winged beings who were mingling and colliding without our being able to determine whether they were Selenians or Vespertilios, so abrupt and rapid were their movements.

After half an hour, the crowd being less dense, we recognized that they were, in fact, Vespertilios, who were fighting against another species of winged beings. The latter offered the most astonishing similarity to the Verspertilios. Their organic constitution was the same, and a more attentive examination soon forced us to agree that they were identical, of the same race.

We perceived, in fact, in the midst of Selenians, Vespertilios of the species already known, and the result of the comparison was as I have just said. These, however, were naked, unlike the latter, which, without being dressed like the Selenians, are covered by a kind of loincloth and a vest that

38

extends from their waist to their chin. These garments had prevented us until then from knowing for certain whether the Vespertilios were hairy, even though we could conclude it from the presence of an enormous beard extended over the whole face, just as we had concluded, with regard to Selenians, from the absolute privation of facial hair, an absence of hair over the rest of the body. Furthermore, the nudity that had initially astonished us in the Vespertilios of the new species, ceased to surprise us when we saw that it was in harmony with the dirty and repulsive exterior of those beings, whose hair is matted with ordure, and whose physiognomy is simultaneously bloodthirsty and stupid.

From that mass of observations we concluded on the same day that there is between the two sorts of Vespertilios the same difference as there is between civilized humans and savages. It seemed, in addition, that the former were the enemies of the latter, since, as we have already said, they fought in the same ranks as the Selenians. But what was the cause of the battle? What role did the Vespertilio savage play in the lunar world? That was what we could only hope to discover after long observation.

We recognized subsequently that those battles were frequent, but not always as terrible. The first time, the confusion was so great that we were unable to distinguish anything, whereas in subsequent observations, there were little more than skirmishes, in which the savage Vespertilios usually succumbed under the blows of an ever-alert enemy difficult to take by surprise. However, if it happened that a Selenian was killed, the Vespertilios immediately took possession of the body, after having divided it into pieces in order to reduce the weight, which caused us to presume that they were androseleniphages.

The savage hordes appeared to have another goal as well as that of war. They were often seen rising from the ground and carrying away various roots, like marauders. A few Selenians pursued them, but they, however numerous, did not even think of putting up a futile defense and were content to

39

flee. They always headed in the same direction—which is to say, as far as our field of view permitted us to follow them, toward the part of the Moon that is invisible for us, and in which we suppose that little exists except for volcanoes, precipices and marshes.

That is perhaps where the savage Vespertilios live, and it is necessary to agree that the abode is worthy of them. It is doubtless to shelter them from pillage that the Selenians have established in that direction forts of a kind, in which civilized Vespertilios are placed as sentinels. The latter, even more relentlessly opposed to the savages than the Selenians, give the signal.

We have not, in the course of our observations, seen savage prisoners taken, from which it can be concluded that the distinction has existed for a long time between the two Vespertilio races that makes one the enemies of the Selenians and the other their most devoted servants. The existence of that barbaric race is perhaps the sole obstacle to the development of Selenian civilization.

That is only offered as a humble supposition.

It was necessary to wait for sixteen days before being able to study the curious phenomena that occur on the surface of the Moon during the night—which is to say, when it is only illuminated by the Earth. Ashen light has permitted us to make observations of the obscure disk for nine days in each lunation, so the state of our knowledge of what happens among our neighbors during their long fourteen-day nights leaves nothing to be desired, although it required nocturnal observations for no less than three entire lunations to coordinate the facts, classify them entirely and obtain a theory sufficiently complete for the explanation of the various phenomena that I proposed during the second lunation to seem convincing to my collaborators.

When the Sun has ceased to illuminate a mountain and its valley on the lunar surface for two days, objects begin to become obscure; a kind of excessively white fleecy matter forms, which we mistook at first for snow covering the lunar ground. Its movement, sometimes slow and sometimes rapid, did not take long to accuse our hypothesis of falsity. The matter in question, which seems to descend from the mountaintops, is evidently held in suspension in the atmosphere; the central peak is gradually effaced, and the mists thicken so much that one can no longer perceive anything but the mountain crests, which then form a series of unified crowns designed in black against a mat white background.

On 17 March a very large number of black dots was distinguished on the horizon; some seemed to be moving with great rapidity, and it did not take us long to observe several that were circulating with rapidity above the valley on which all our attention as fixed. Suddenly, those black dots disappeared as if they had plunged into the ocean of mist. The chronometer marked 2:11. At 2:34 they reemerged from the valley, but Dr. Grant, who had counted 79 of them, found 116 in the second enumeration.

After that simple observation the phenomenon began to be less embarrassing, for it was obvious that the black dots we had seen initially were individuals of the savage Vespertilio race; they had doubtless come to carry out some atrocious actions, and the Selenians were pursuing them. In fact, the black dots were coming together continually in the air and appeared to be colliding violently; numerous combatants, doubtless wounded, disappeared into the thick vapors covering the valley. Finally, the Selenians appeared to be put to flight, and the Vespertilios came to settle on the crests of the mountains, for they ceased to be perceptible as soon as their shadows were projected on the dark crowns that dominated the valley.

We had been reflecting for a few minutes on the nocturnal combat in order to determine its cause when the tympanum of the Observatory was struck by a violet-tinted red light comparable to that given by the flame of strontium salts. Our doubts were removed at that moment and several of our suppositions were, unfortunately, only too well confirmed. A number of Vespertilios were lying on banks of volcanic rock; one of them was dividing up the limbs of a child and distributing them to his hideous companions.

Three other children were a few paces away from that cannibal feast; they were agitating their wings and appeared to be crying out; their feet were trapped beneath an enormous stone, and a cord passed around their wings bound their arms behind the head. By the whiteness of their skin and the bright colors of their wings, we could not doubt that the children belonged to the Selenian race.

The luminous meteor that traversed the atmosphere of the Moon was a stroke of luck for me because, while all attention was fixed on the revolting scene that I have just described, I was surprised to see the fuliginous masses that were covering the valley emerge from a kind of crevasse situated about four hundred feet from the crest and extending around the entire perimeter of the mountain. I advanced the opinion—to the great surprise of my companions, who had not observed the same phenomenon—that all those mountains were as many volcanoes, no longer launching ardent lava, ash or smoke, but vapor at a high temperature. That opinion was admitted by everyone when a sufficient number of observations and a more attentive study of the mountains when they were directly illuminated by the Sun had enabled us to see that those craters existed everywhere.

Fourth Fragment: SELENOLOGICAL OBSERVATIONS

A few nights went by between the last proofs and those which remain for us to consign.

Vapors enwrapped the Moon with considerable persistence—an extraordinarily rare accident—and that veil was only lifted on 5 March at 10:34. I had been careful to mount lens Zz, designed for minute observations; and at the time indicated above, the very considerably crystals with which Cleomenes is bristling were displaying their colors and accumulated crests in the field of view.

That lunar region, situated thirty degrees south of Endymion, which corresponds to N2 on Blunt's map, presents the aspect of sterility commonplace in regions neighboring the sea. The reefs with which it abounds have a darker tint, and constantly affect the form of little mounds rounded at the top.

The crystals are irregular; they are often encased in dull matrices, with which they form a body, and which present to the eye a considerable analogy with mercury and lead sulfides.

A few rocks have shown us the specific characteristics of metallic oxides analogous to those of iron, without, however, our being able to affirm on that subject anything except our visual impressions, for no appearance of iron is clearly designed, in a compound analogous to our knowledge of that metal.

It is probable that the element in question, which plays such an important role in the terrestrial world, is not identified in the lunar clime, and our fortunate discovery regarding the blood of the Selenians comes to the aid of that hypothesis. That constant observation obliges the search for another origin for the ferruginous masses known as aeroliths, which scientists have attributed thus far to the fall into the sphere of terrestrial attraction of matter ejected by lunar volcanoes.

Another natural product of that soil appears to us to be worthy of attention. It consists of crystalline blocks of a beautiful translucency and a magnificent crimson color, the examination of which has led us to suppose that copper protoxide, so resistant to human efforts to incorporate it into glass, is mingled by the Creator with those diaphanous masses, which effect the form of polyhedra derived from hexagonal prisms.

We are, of course, only placing that classification in the category of probabilities. In fact, it would be imprudent to assign positive values to the various figures of everything lunar, and to make them enter into account with admitted reasoning. We have encountered dry strands, silky to the eye, which made us think of asbestos. Some rocks have appeared to us to be calcareous, others flint-like; those characteristics only serve as instruments of comparison, nothing more.

At the extremity of the aforementioned reefs, the earth—we cannot find any other word—becomes humid and descends for a long time in a gentle slope. The strand in question is gray, and there, as throughout the satellite, the tint of ocher is only found once. Beyond that ground a sea begins whose extent our objective cannot encompass.

That liquid plain offers us a singular sight: the totality of the waves turned in the direction of our world affect a conical form like the mountains; the waters present a mass raised in the middle as if drawn into the air by an invisible force, which is terrestrial attraction, much more powerful on the Moon than that of the latter on our planet.

No traces of navigation on the part of the winged inhabitants are evident on that sea. As for the aquatic population, our ignorance on that subject is understandable. We have, however, seen gliding over the surface of the water, without plunging into it, reptiles of large dimension. Those creatures of an extraordinary length might be more advantageously compared to Vibrions—such as hydrated acetic acid contains—considered under a solar microscope, albeit with infinitely multiplied proportions.[4] Their head is armed with two pincers similar in shape to a cow's horns, but smaller and incisive, which they doubtless bring together in order to lacerate or seize. A shiny envelope like that of scales covers their back, separated by membranous ventral fins bristling with a kind of mossy fur like that of a sea-spider.

No marine plants carpet the shores—those, at least, that we have examined.

Among the animals of those regions we ought not to forget an amphibian reminiscent of a seal but much more voluminous. Further inland we have encountered many mastodons; there are some that are similar to elephants, with the difference

---

[4] The term vibrion was once used to refer generally to micro-organisms only perfectible under a microscope; the ones that the writer has in mind are probably rotifers.

that they sometimes have white patches on the rump, and always have larger ears than those of the world we inhabit.

Birds are very rare in that region of the Moon; most of the time their wings are only short feathered stumps that they use for rowing in the air, which imparts an incomparable rapidity to their running.

In spite of the interest of these observations of the lunar soil, after having examined its general surface, our minds, accustomed to a scrupulous search for the truth, became weary of struggling against the impossibility of scientific proofs. In fact, for all of the geological fraction, chemistry would have been constantly necessary.

That is why we were impatient to find organized beings again, lunarians susceptible of indicating the nature of inert substances by the employment they assigned to them, and capable of being analyzed with certainty, given that life retraces its instincts and characteristics in its movements. We have therefore, undertaken in more detail that analysis accessible to the eyes, driven by our system of sacrifices to the search for the truth.

However, that branch of our discoveries, the most fecund in certainties and irrevocable arguments, is, it seems to us, the most surprising; but that astonishment disappears under the sagacity of a reflection made by my savant collaborator, Mr. Drummond. I ask permission to expose it before going any further.

"Sir," I said to him, almost doubting my reason, "this is more fanciful than the islands of Thomas More; will London dare to believe it?"

"Doctor," he replied, "the scientists who have spoken about the Moon have imagined glaciers there and have refused it an atmosphere; now, glaciers cannot exist in a void, but they have been believed without hesitation. If we had seen an entire vegetable kingdom without a single animal, the vulgar would have accepted it, and yet a similar organism, if it could exist, would be the most improbable absurdity. We have observed singular things, but which do not contradict the laws of providential harmony; the eye of science will not be deceived thereby. Outside of that, what does it matter to us if his weakness transforms the man in the street into a skeptic?"

We shared his generous warmth, which, however, I calmed with a word from the great Bacon, a word too commonly employed for there to be any need for it to be cited;[5] and it was then that we resolved to show the Selenians as they are, in all their aspects.

One trait that I have not yet had occasion to mention with regard to Selenians, which I shall consign immediately, is their notion of musical harmony. That observation is of great interest and it is consoling to think that the glories of the author of worlds are suing everywhere.

We have reason to believe that their melody is very primitive and little different from that of negroes. The beauty of the latter is measured in accordance with the violence of the noise. The effort of the lungs that the attitude and the faces of the Selenians rendered sensible enabled us to presume that. As for the measure, it is not appreciable, to judge by the irregular bounds of dancers excited by the orchestra which is composed, in addition to voices, by two instruments, each formed of eleven tubes terminating in a drum or reservoir open at the summit. Eleven instrumentalists applied to the mouths of the tubes appeared to us to be blowing into them vehemently.

Fifth Fragment: NUPTIAL CEREMONIES

The rocky surface of Cleomenes offers little of interest; we have let it go by and have attained Longrenus, which almost touches the longitudinal libration. An expanse of water had entered our field of view, when the landscape was suddenly tarnished by a gray shadow, the cause of which has remained unknown. Soon, vision recovered its clarity. The water

---

[5] The notional author's reference is not as obvious as he pretends to think, but he might mean: "There is in human nature generally more of the fool than the wise."

previously uncovered had become a thread intersecting the field of view at right angles, and beyond that long narrow lake, whose waves appeared black, a wooded country, cultivated and facile, gave us reason to hope for a further encounter with animate beings.

Our expectation was not disappointed; an extraordinary movement was manifest at the issue from a somber forest, and we distinctly saw emerging from the wood an entire boscage, which traveled through the atmosphere, glided over the lake, went over a hill and came to rest on a high conical mountain truncated at the summit. Only then was I able to comprehend that displacement and to divine the motors of that vegetable caravan.

Those branches, taken from the nearby forest, hid the gray wings of an army of Vespertilio domestics, who were transporting shade to the hill with an objective that we had been a long time in suspecting. They planted their branches in a circle around the superior platform with a facility that surprised us all the more because the ground appeared to be formed by a monolithic siliceous crust. The height of the bushes inspired us with a high idea of the strength of the wings of those anthropornithians, in spite of their subservience to the Selenians.

That work concluded, the valets of the superior inhabitants of the planet extended their flight in the direction of another mountain terminated by a white cylindrical mass, around which were arranged four brown cones. The Vespertilios lined up at the base of these habitations, while one of them began flying to the summit of that kind of *castrum*, and, suddenly furling his wings, allowed himself to fall vertically on to the summit of an open roof and disappeared. That simple and unornamented construction was, however, beautifully proportioned; its symmetry was perfect. The Vespertilio stayed there for some time, during which Mr. Drummond pointed out to me at two-thirds of the height of the cylinder, or tower, an elliptical frame, in the middle of which we saw the contours of a symbolic design somewhat analogous to certain Indian figures. We had seen the sign before on two huts, and worn by the chief of the Verpertilios. We finally dared to articulate, in a timid voice, the word "coat-of-arms."

The invention of that usage in the lunar world astonished us less than one might think, if one did not know that such signs are encountered in all terrestrial peoples, in very different epochs, and that everywhere that the vanity of mortals has separated castes, it has created ornaments to announce conventional grandeur to all eyes. Egypt has known armories; the peoples of India have possessed special characters of the same genre, and the companions of Captain A. del Rio have seen neatly-carved escutcheons under the debris of Mitla.[6]

I was, therefore, unsurprising to see that institution in vogue among the Selenians, not for distinguishing the Vespertilios—nature has posed sufficiently sharp distinctions between them—but to mark divisions between beings of the same species corresponding to the hierarchies whose existence we had observed.

We have said that the organization of those singular peoples seemed to us to be a patriarchy degenerated into feudalism—which is to say that individual pride was beginning to break up the family; it is therefore no longer necessary to be surprised that that sentiment had created a form, that of sentiment itself, and to recognize the universality of the divine word. Did not King Solomon exclaim: *All is vanity under the sun*?—and it is the Sun that illuminates the Lunarians.[7]

However, all this rests on a series of observations whose sum is not equivalent to a geometrical proof; I offer them for what they are; in due course, other facts will provide them with further support.

The first sentiment that ought to ensue from this discovery is that of humility: perhaps everything has not been creat-

---

[6] Andrés del Rio (1764-1849) is famous for his discoveries in chemist, but did visit the ruins of Mitla in Mexico, which later became an archeological site of great importance.

[7] The Biblical quotation actually comes from *Ecclesiastes*.

ed for humankind. The second is a hymn of admiration in honor of the creator of several worlds so varied. God is great in is works, and the heavens, seen at close range, give us a very imposing lesson.

Let us return to our observations, too long interrupted.

One of the Vespertilios had penetrated into the habitation while the others were perhaps awaiting new orders. He emerged again after a quarter of an hour, holding something of which it would be as difficult to describe the utility as the form, and of which only a drawing could reproduce the contours. He put that unknown object to his mouth, and the air was suddenly populated by a multitude of Lunarians coming toward him from all directions.

The winged domestics lined up to either side of the troop, and the ensemble went to alight on the mountain artificially shaded by the Vespertilios, who arranged themselves in a circle at the base of the cone. They remained at rest momentarily, after which several Selenian males descended over the lake in single file, at rather long intervals.

In that blue-black streak an isolated rocky islet rose up, as transparent as crystal and somewhat pointed. At the summit of the reef a Selenian female was posed, easy to recognize by the length of her wings, their colors, and by her costume. She was motionless, her wings folded against her body like two bucklers—except that she turned her mat white head from time to time.

The Selenian male who arrived above her began circling, drawing closer, thus tracing in his flight a cylindrical helix from top to bottom, as far as the level of the rock. Having arrived there, his plumes described the basal circle three times in the air, while his head was directed toward the female, who remained still, and he drew away, swimming.

After him came another Selenian male, and then a third; then forty male Selenians succeeded one another, so rapidly that their combination seemed to form a living tower around the female Selenian's head. That crowd thinned out; the fluttering relented, and we were able to observe that the beings who formed it, after throwing themselves into the water, did not turn to look back at the motionless female, and did not come back. Other Selenians were still fluttering around the latter; there was one of them who stayed in the air longer than the others, and suddenly descended in front of the rock. The Selenian female extended her wings and flapped them several times.

Immediately, the whole troop disappeared.

Left alone, those two individual flew back to the mountain. We thought that the Selenian female had just chosen a spouse.

That solemn election proved to us the liberty of the Selenian female; a liberty in which she shares all the advantages of the male, as we have observed in fishing, in hunting and elsewhere. In the battle against the Vespertilios, the Lunarian females shared the hazards of war.

We have found, I believe, the reason for the casual attitude of the Lunarians with regard to their females, in observing that the latter are as strong as them. It appears, in addition, that the mentality of the males is not yet sufficiently developed to lead them to repudiate the assistance and labor of the females and reduce them to inaction.

As for the solemnity deployed in the choice of a lover, the Selenian women surprised us, for we knew already, after numerous inspections, that fidelity is not a virtue of the Lunarian females, that they do not enchain themselves eternally, and search for mates rather than husbands.

We have concluded from that the custom in question that nature has more authority than morality in their legislation, which is a poor argument in favor of their civilization.

However, with regard to that reprehensible independence, I have seen so much decency, a mixture of simplicity and mystery so praiseworthy—if one remembers that they do not link themselves together for life—that I have found it difficult to reach a conclusion.

Our Selenian couple had found the mountain deserted. Alighted on the summit, facing the sky and us, they were about to consummate the act of reproduction.

"Oh!" exclaimed my collaborator, Andrew Grant, "those are individuals who have sought solitude, and who do not suspect that from one world to the other..."

That reflection inspired us with a kind of shame for partaking of such a sight; but the duty of a scientist cannot be intimidated by such thoughts. At least we agreed, for the sake of decency, that I would be the only witness, and that observations of that sort would only be made by one person at a time.

The union of lunar beings only offered me two curious observations, which are only of interest to physiologists, to which we shall transmit them.

1. Nec istis sicut feminis vulva supposita; sed altius et propter umbilicum. Stant in copulando Lunarii; brevis conjunctio et duplex; namque ab ore simul et genetricibus membris amplectuntur, ut duobus modis aligerum et terrestrium donati, duobus ideo fruantur in copulate.

2. Lunariam inter et Vespertilionem horrescit natura coitum; huic namque repugnans intemperantia virgae.

After a few moments, our lovers leaned over the edge of the hill. Immediately, all the branches with which the Vespertilios had dressed it were taken up and heaped at the summit on the nuptial bed of the two spouses. Vespertilios penetrated into the circle and set fire to the branches, which burned with promptitude. When the smoke appeared we saw Selenians arriving in a host from all around the mountain and lining up there.

As soon as everything was burned, the crowd precipitated into the theater of that singular marriage; they fluttered for a long time at ground level over the warm ashes, as if to respire some amorous trace that had escaped the flame. After which Selenians of each sex sought one another, selected one another and formed couples that took flight in all directions, lavishing caresses more tender than chaste in mid-air.

Long before their return, however, the two lovers who were the objects of the ceremony—we conjectured that such details only took place in connection with the marriage of Selenian virgins—had quit the "hymeneal mountain," as we agreed unanimously to call it, and directed their swift and precipitate flight above uninhabited crests, beyond which they left our field of view, the narrow perimeter of which rendered them the mystery that they seemed to be pursuing with so much anxiety.

Sixth Fragment: HABITATIONS

The majority of the summits were crowned by constructions, conical in form, which seemed at first glance to be part of the mountain itself, to the extent that, on seeing the Selenians introduce themselves into the interior of those masses through rather narrow openings, we assumed at first that the interior cavities into which we saw them penetrate and remain in large numbers must have been hollowed out in the mountains, like the subterranean galleries that one encounters in the mountains of Upper Egypt and in those of the countries of India. In brief, we were persuaded that the Selenians were completely ignorant of the art of building and had thus been reduced to enlarging natural grottos, or carving out artificial ones, for their habitations.

We did not take long to be completely undeceived on that subject, however, and we remained penetrated by admiration for the art of the Selenians and the resources of their intelligence, when we had had the opportunity to observe the immense and magnificent constructions that they had built in certain regions of the globe they inhabit. But let us not anticipate the progress of our discoveries.

The Vespertilios, we had noticed, also came to alight on the immense conical towers inhabited by the Selenians, although they penetrated into them by different opening, usually

52

placed in the lower part of the edifice. It required several weeks, though, before we had sufficiently complete observations on the relationship between the two races for it to be possible for us to form a precise opinion on the relative importance that we ought to assign to each of the thousand details of their social life. However, as we have established previously, it was easy for us to observe that the Vespertilios lived in a kind of servitude, in an incontestable dependency of the Selenians, for they lived in the interior part of the communal edifice, and every time they made a journey or undertook an action of any importance, they seemed to be obeying a signal from a Selenian, whom their leader sometimes approached in an attitude of submission, as if to receive his orders.

If you have followed our description of the mountains of the Moon attentively you will recall that they are ordinarily terminated by a mound emerging in the middle of a crater whose rim has conserved very recognizable traces of their volcanic origin; on that crest, separated by a fairly deep natural ditch from the central hillock that dominates it, four lodgments are built, similar to cages, or sentry-boxes, to put it better, constructed with materials that appeared to us to be remarkably solid. Each of them is regularly pierced in its upper part by narrow circular openings. The opening at the summit is always vertical, while those that come after it incline successively toward all the parts of the sky; all are defended by long metallic spikes of a sort, very sharp and very close to one another, which, from our viewpoint, gave each of the sentry-boxes the appearance of a rolled-up porcupine.

A sentry-box of the same form, but much smaller and much more solid in appearance, was placed at the top of almost all the edifices that we had seen thus far. The lower sentry-boxes were placed precisely in accordance with the four cardinal points—which led us to observe that, in spite of their usually circular form, the edifices of the Moon are all perfectly orientated by the openings contrived for entry into them as well as their exterior decoration. Those four sentry-boxes are occupied by four Vespertilios who come out from time to time—capriciously, it appeared to us-in order to walk or fly around the surrounding area. Several times a day, at regular intervals, which we recognized to be two hours and forty-five minutes, on the signal of a Selenian, they are relieved by their comrades.

On substituting lens Zz for lens Dz, of which we had made use to make the preceding observations, we saw distinctly that the individuals placed in the sentry-boxes had their eyes directed at the sky, which caused us to suppose that they were occupied in astronomical work. The perfect orientation of their monuments proved to us, moreover, that they were not complete strangers to the ancient science of the Chaldeans, which is today the object of our most interesting studies.

We were further encouraged to admit that interpretation because the sentry-box remarked at the summit of the edifice was always inhabited by a Selenian, who, looking alternately toward the sky and the Vespertilios in the inferior sentry-boxes, seemed to be communicating with them by means of signs; thus, the latter, whose intellectual inferiority we had already recognized, must have been employed in simultaneously observing the facts on their own part, and keeping, each on his side, an exact note of them under the direction of the Selenian, while the later, then speculating on the combination of the five simultaneous observations would be able at leisure to coordinate scientifically the facts so methodically observed. But it was not possible for us, that night, to form an exact idea of the nature of their observations, and we redirected all our attention to the edifice we had before our eyes.

It was a regular cone having its base on the entire breadth of the mound that occupies the center of the crater long observed with ancient instruments, at the summit of the highest mountains of the Moon. The edifice tapers until it no longer presents a diameter of approximately three feet. It is terminated by the sentry-box described above. The walls of that strange construction presented to us a shiny and polished surface, divided with a great deal of artistry by ornate marble compartments of the brightest colors, which form exceedingly

54

complicated regular designs after the fashion of Arab mosaics, to which I was all the more willing to compare them because we likewise never encountered in them the slightest intention of representing any depiction of plants, animals or humans. The design of those compartments is very complicated; in fact, two identical figures could not be found over the entire surface of the edifice, and we have been obliged to copy the ensemble every time we wanted to give a complete account of the decoration.

The walls of the edifice are pierced by eight openings or unsealed skylights. So far as we have been able to judge, those openings fulfill the function of doors rather than windows, for the mosaic presents at intervals crystal compartments of the greatest beauty and perfectly transparent, through which a very pure light must penetrate the interior of the habitations. They were not a great resource for us, however, to see what was happening inside because of the great obliquity of the plane from which they presented themselves to our gaze.

The openings just mentioned are disposed four by four in two planes rather distant from one another; those down below pierced about a third of the way up the edifice are noticeably larger than those higher up, but they did not appear to us to be much more elongated. All of them are decorated by two colonnettes, surmounted, for the lower ones, by a single flat stone built into the wall, and for the higher ones, by two stones similarly embedded, supported one on top of another, which form a kind of fronton.

The colonnettes repose on the exterior edge of the wall and rise up perpendicularly, departing sufficiently from the body of the edifice for the crown they sustain to offer a free space of a certain breadth, an area surmounted by a truncated cone that reproduces exactly the form of volcanic mountains; for one can observe a little crater at their summit, in the middle of which rises a very long projection. On either side of that steeple of sorts, at the corner left free, directly above the colonnettes, two very small steeples are placed, but with a form almost exactly similar to the one just described. Before each of the doors is a small platform similar to one of our balconies deprived of its balustrade. Those platforms can be raised at will and thus close nearly half the opening.

Numerous Selenians and Vespertilios, coming and going, landed on the platform and went in, or, if they were coming out, took flight from there; but the field of our vision had been so restricted by the powerful lenses that we were employing to study the details of the edifice, while Herbert Holms drew them, that we lost sight of those who drew away by a few feet.

Meanwhile, the Moon had declined so far toward the horizon that everything was soon blurred by the interposition of the moist vapor that the proximity of the sea almost always maintains in the atmosphere at a certain elevation. Finally, we lost sight completely of the objects that interested us so powerfully.

Then we began to communicate to one another the thoughts that had been suggested to us by such an unexpected observation. We raised the question of why beings endowed with the faculty of flight did not equip their habitations with entrances sufficiently spacious to go into them with wings extended, without being obliged to alight and fold them up.

Dr. Grant suggested that it was to protect them from the extreme heat that must reign in summer in that zone, and cited to support his opinion the low and narrow doors adopted on our globe in almost all hot countries; and perhaps that it was also to protect them from noxious insects, as in certain countries of southern Africa. But I made the observation that whatever the temperature might be in the depths of the valleys, it was scarcely possible to admit that the heat could ever be unbearable at the summit of such high mountains, and so isolated their they were exposed to all the air currents. As for insects of the mosquito family, supposing that a few species of them existed to the Moon, they would live in the depths of valleys where the heat and humidity ought to be entirely suitable to their multiplication in certain seasons of the year, rather than the summits of mountains, on which they would not find any of the conditions necessary to their existence. That, at least, was what it was necessary to conclude on the basis of what happens on our globe, where one is only inconvenienced by mosquitoes, gnats and midges in low-lying and humid regions, on the edges of marshes and pools, while one never encounters them above a certain elevation in the mountains. But all that did not explain the lack of width of the reserved openings of the Selenian castles, and we only discovered the true reason a long time afterwards.

Several weeks passed without our observing anything new regarding those matters, but finally, on 24 March, at about 10:45 at night. Ptolemy having entered our field of vision, we were studying the castle that crowned its summit. We were somewhat surprised to find that edifice crowned by a platform, in contrast to those we had remarked in three or four analogous monuments that had been previously submitted to our observations, and it was a new opportunity for us to be humiliated before the sovereign arbiter of things, to recognize how infirm and presumptuous our nature is, how subject we are to error and prompt to content ourselves with the first somewhat plausible solution that we are in haste to cause to prevail, in our vanity, because it is our own, whereas a more persistent and attentive examination would soon enable us to recognize our error.

The error into which we had just slipped was one reason more to mistrust ourselves and redouble our attention in our studies. In fact, it was quite frequent for us to find that we had taken for a general rule what was only an extremely rare particularity. This is how we succeeded in assuring ourselves of that.

We replaced the powerful lenses that we had been using in the preceding observations, and substituted the excellent lenses fabricated by S. J. Davy, and enlarged the field of vision as much as possible while conserving a sufficient dimension for objects not to confuse them; then, adding out reflectors in such a manner as to give the greatest possible clarity to the smallest objects that were about to pass before our eyes, I asked Dr. Grant to regulate the movement of the telescope so that we could observe successively all the parts of the Moon visible that day. By that means we recognized quickly the parts that ought to be the preferential objects of our detailed observation.

Thus, we recognized in the most formal fashion the existence of an immense city at 15 degrees 40 minutes of longitude and 57 degrees 53 minutes of north latitude, and we had soon observed all the systems of habitation adopted by the three intelligent races that inhabit the Moon. (We count degrees of longitude from the peak Arago, which we have recognized as having a slope much steeper that those of all the other mountains of the Moon; it has no crater and is terminated by an indefinitely prolonged spike. We have been glad to give that mark of deference to our honorable colleague and friend, the Director of the Paris Observatoire. In addition, the singular form of the peak that bears his name, and the place that it occupies, makes a very recognizable reference point for a terrestrial observer.)

The habitations of the Beavers are very badly constructed, uncomfortable and poorly sheltered from seasonal bad weather; they generally only have one opening giving entry to a single chamber, in which individuals of all ages and both sexes seem to us to live pell-mell, in scant accord with the prescriptions of hygiene and morality. The agglomeration of those dirty huts forms a disagreeable ensemble of an aspect similar enough to that of the majority of our European villages.

The form of the huts is conical, like those of all isolated edifices that we have observed on the Moon; they are constructed with tree-branches planted in the earth and linked together by a kind of mortar that, on drying, acquires a great hardness; several observations gave us the certainty of that. In the upper part a fairly broad opening is contrived, the only one by which daylight can penetrate and smoke can escape. The hearth is always placed directly below that chimney of sorts, and we have had several opportunities to observe the inhabitants of the hut roasting some of the crustaceans we have previously described over an ardent fire.

In the vicinity of a Beaver village and in a more elevated place, to the extent that nature permits, we have always observed a vast granary, a kind of well-aerated drying-room into which crops are packed; they undergo several preparations there, and the portion reserved for the nourishment of the Selenians and Vespertilios is transported by the latter into vast storehouses designed to receive them.

Here, we are passing over a host of details curious in more than one regard, but of minor scientific importance, in order to arrive at descriptions of surveillance castles; the country houses of the Selenians in the upper part and, in the lower section, the habitual dwellings of the majority of the civilized Vespertilios, who, like farmers of a sort, remain masters of the house in the absence of the owner.

These isolated manors, built on the summits of all the summits of all the volcanic mountains, differ essentially from fortress-castles. First of all, they are devoid of the observation-boxes; secondly, they have the form of a truncated cone, like the mountains on which they are built, and not that of a regular cone; now, that latter form not being encountered in any natural objects observed on the Moon, cannot be the result of the imitative instinct recognized in the Lunarians, and can only have been shown to them by the revelatory necessity of great things.

These, so far as we have been able to understand them, are the circumstances that might have give rise to that necessity. The Selenians must have established a very long time ago, in the regions that they inhabit and which they have subjected to cultivation, lines of observation in order to watch for the invasions of the savage Vespertilios and oppose their ravages. In the beginning, probably, the places of observation did not differ in any respect from the houses of pleasure that dress all the lunar summits. Then the savage Vespertilios, noticing that the signal to attack had always come from the same place, must have turned all their efforts toward those places, and, in order to destroy them, they will have employed means in accordance with their primitive intelligence. They will have raised enormous stones up to a great height and, letting them fall in great number, crushing the castle and burying the boldest of its defenders under the ruins, thus destroying a large number of those observatories. They would then have been able to exercise their ravages and devastations at their ease over the civilized lands.

I offer that hypothesis for what it is worth; it is one of the probabilities that are present to my mind. I ought to add that we have twice been witness to attacks of the kind that we have just described; they were stubborn enough, but neither succeeded, and it was precisely the form of the edifice against which they were directed that we have been obliged to attribute their lack of success. In fact, the stones launched by the Vespertilios either broke on the metallic points of the superior sentry-box or, falling on the body of the edifice, following a very acute angle, slid away without producing any notable damage. Soon, Selenians and civilized Vespertilios arrived *en masse* to assist the attacked fortress, and the savages were forced to renounce their reckless enterprise.

These attacks seem to be rare, however, and no longer seem to be on the part of those undertaking them to be anything but a reminiscence of successes obtained in the past, conserved among them by tradition. Thus, most of the time, they are content to attempt surprise attacks and to ravage in all haste regions on which they fall unexpectedly, as the Northern hordes do; then, like them, they flee with their booty without waiting for anyone to set out in pursuit of them.

These attacks take place against rural areas in the epoch when the fruits have attained their maturity, and sometimes against the granaries placed at the head of villages when the crops have been stored therein, but never against the pleasure-house castles, probably because the savages, caring little about the objects of luxury that they contain, do not hope to find sufficient booty there to compensate them for the danger they would be running.

However, we have perceived them sometimes prowling around during the night; half-hidden in the vapors then condensed in the depths of all the valleys, they lie in wait in case some Selenian might imprudently venture outside the common dwelling; then they throw themselves in large numbers on the isolated individual, drag him away and disappear suddenly with their prey into the mist. Doubtless attracted by the cries of the victim, Vespertilios and Selenians emerge in force, launching themselves in a certain direction; and then, as if the cries had suddenly ceased, they abruptly renounce a pursuit that could only compromise them pointlessly.

The isolated edifices around which these surprises sometimes take place are composed of two divisions that do not appear to us to have any direct communications between them. As in the fortress, the domestic or civilized Vespertilios live in the inferior part, into which they penetrate via four openings orientated and disposed in the same fashion; but the upper part of the fortified castle differs in that it is terminated by a broad platform at the center of which a circular aperture has been excavated, closed by a strong metallic grille that is lowered inside in order to open it. That trap-door of sorts is the most important external issue that we have recognized in the edifice.

In front of that tower of sorts, and on the most elevated plateau of the mountain that serves as its base, there is sometimes an octagonal enclosure closed by walls of medium height. At each of the corners is constructed, depending on the location, an edifice of varying shape and size. The area enclosed by the octagon is usually planted with trees. I definitely recall, however, having seen several in which nothing was cultivated by a plant that rose to a height of two feet above the soil at the most.

We have also observed, in several places, an edifice quite similar to that one at first glance, but which nevertheless differs from it essentially. As it is not exactly a habitation, but more like a kind of religious monument, we shall describe it completely in the appropriate place.

In the pleasure-castles, the decoration of the principal edifice is quite similar to that of a fortress. One can assure oneself of that by comparing the different drawings that Herbert Holms has traced in the course of our observations. The platform that crowns them is ordinary formed by a monolith of extraordinary thickness; its surface, sometimes smooth and polished, is sometimes ornamented by capricious and bizarre mosaics, of which we give several examples in our atlas.

Our studies of the monuments of the Moon have been long and persevering. Interrupted several times by various accidents, they have always been resumed with a new ardor. We are proud to have brought to our European civilization these incontestable proofs of Selenian civilization. Several very keen debates have been engaged between us on the matter on matters of the most serious gravity, but we have succeeded in agreeing among ourselves on the most important things; discussion has reciprocally clarified us on many matters, and if some differences of opinion remain among us, they only relate now to objects of such secondary importance that we can regard ourselves as being in complete accord. That divergence of opinions and the discussions that have been its consequence have sometimes led us to important discoveries.

One singular remark by Lieutenant Drummond, which led us to results of that nature, was that while the castles built on the mountains of the central part of the hemisphere that we had before our eyes all have the axis of the conoid that envelops them converging on the center of the face of the Moon, it is not the same for those that are distant from that central region. On the contrary, the more distant they are from it, and draw closer to one of the poles or to regions subject to librations, the axis of the conical surface appears to converge less and less toward the center off the face of our satellite. We have also recognized that the difference in question increases in a perfectly regular proportion, and that it becomes very pronounced in the lands neighboring the libration and the polar regions.

The first time that the constructions of a great city of the circumpolar regions were submitted to our observation, the unexpected inclination of its tallest monuments astonished us so much that we were convinced by the sight of those numerable towers, spires, steeples and turrets, all equally inclined, that the architects who had built them had wanted to achieve a *tour de force* analogous to that of the leaning towers seen in Pisa and one or two other cities in Italy. But after having observed that the inclination is everywhere the same on each circumference described around the central point of the hemisphere facing us, and that it diminishes or increases as that circle shrinks or expands, it was evident that it could not be caused by the variable caprice of architects. It is impossible to account for the strangeness of those constructions unless one admits, as we do, that the center of gravity of the Moon does not coincide with the center of its apparent face, but that it is much closer to our planet than the latter.

In fact, the Moon having originally been liquid, as will doubtless be proven by the specific details that we shall subsequently devote to selenology, its form is necessarily modified by the attraction of the terrestrial spheroid. In the same way that our seas, obedient to the attraction of our satellite, rises and forms tides, the fluid elements that constituted the lunar mass during its liquefaction were accumulated toward the point closest to us. The face of the Moon is elongated, and as all the molecules, once arrived at their point of equilibrium have no longer been stirred by the same cause, in cooling that have conserved the position that they had attained, and their total mass has formed a solid somewhat elongated toward the Earth. Their general center of gravity is thus displaced in our direction.

The quantity by which it is displaced is easily calculable; it is between eighty-three and eighty-four miles. By virtue of that the inclination of the axis of a habitation twenty-five degrees from the pole ought to be eleven degrees. Now, observations made with the greatest care have always given us seventeen degrees for that inclination. How can that strange difficulty be explained?

Lieutenant Drummond, I might say, is the only one among us who has proposed a solution: I am in haste to make it known, believing it to be very appropriate to demonstrate how powerful the entirely experimental method followed since Newton by the astronomical school is. I shall leave my young friend to express himself in this circumstance, and it is his notes that I am transcribing here:

"We have constantly observed," he said, "that that in the excursions that have always taken place when the sun is no longer illuminating the lunar hemisphere turned toward us, the savage Vespertilios seemed to launch themselves into the remotest regions, and they were seen to disappear at the horizon as if they were taking refuge in the hemisphere opposed to the Earth. It was impossible for us to conserve any doubt in that regard after the observation we made on 17 September 1835.

"From that fact, it results necessarily that the hemisphere that we can perceive differs essentially from the one that it is given to us to observe. In fact, nowhere, except in the great fissures that the craters of extinct craters present, does one encounter beings belonging to that savage and bloodthirsty race. Everywhere that the Selenians have been able to establish their dwellings, they have destroyed, or at least expelled, that enemy race.

"In consequence, since the unknown hemisphere of the Moon serves as a refuge for those savages, we are forced to conclude that it is entirely dissimilar to the known hemisphere. It doubtless presents immense fissures, enormous craters, infinite precipices, such that one can see all the way to the center of the planet. In sum, the Moon presents something akin to a concavity in its invisible hemisphere. From that mathematical consequence it results quite naturally, by the sole fact of the lunar from, that he center of gravity is more than eighty-three miles closer to the Earth than the sphere that would have for its circumference the apparent disk of the Moon. The inclination of the polar edifices thus no longer has anything surprising about it."

That conclusion is certainly worthy of the present state of science, and I adopt it with great satisfaction. I ought, however to add that before Lieutenant Drummond, Helvetius had announced the principle that serves as a base for that ingenious theory of the figure of the Moon, in order that justice can be rendered to everyone; for in the sciences, an invention belongs to the first to stake a claim by delivering an idea to publicity. Now, Helvetius wrote in 1647:

Quod si in Luna dentur res creatae viventes, illae quae habitant in hemisphaerio Lunae patente et aperto Terrae, ratione luminis sunt melioris conditionis quam illae quae colunt hemisphaerium Lunae nobis absconditum ac latens.

That posited, we can proceed boldly with the description of the capital of the Moon—or, to put it better, the only agglomeration of edifices that we have found sufficiently large to merit bearing the name of city.

Selenopolis, the name we have given to it by common accord, is situated, as we have said above, at 0 degrees 48 minutes of longitude and 0 degrees 53 minutes of north latitude. It is built in an uneven, broken, fissured ground where bottomless abysses are found at every instant at the foot of a gigantic peak; there are a few scattered plateaux of medium extent, and a few pleasant valleys planted with trees that seem to be public gardens, but more frequently steep mountains in the form of bizarrely truncated conoids and varying distances from one another. That is the ground on which the Seleniabns have built their capital.

We have been unable to reach complete agreement on the reasons that might have determined the choice of that rugged and broken region in preference to more cheerful and more fortunate regions. The only reasonable hypothesis that has been presented to our minds is that they wanted to supervise at the closest possible range the factories that we have distinguished in the depths of the abovementioned fissures. They wanted by their number and by their continuous presence to protect their subjects against the disasters that the spirit of sedition and revolt would not fail to bring down on their heads if they could ever formulate the idea of an enterprise crowned with some success. They must have preferred to intimidate them and impose a salutary terror upon them, rather than find themselves constrained to make terrible examples to repress their disorders.

Whether it was politics or the instinct of self-preservation, however, whether hazard or unknown causes led the Selenians to build their city in that place, the fact remains, and it is with the facts before anything else that we have to occupy ourselves.

The plan of Selenopolis presents something approximating to a regular octagon. At each angle there is an observation castle, the utility of which might have been very great in the past but which is presently much less, because, for the eleven months that our observations lasted, we did not see a single savage Vespertilio approach, even remotely, the regions neighboring the city. The memory of numerous defeats had doubtless made them avoid the area.

The entire southern part of the city is very populous; it is there that the most numerous habitations are found. The buildings are generally circular; the two walls that enclose them describe two concentric circles. The space, sometimes very extensive, left empty inside is planted with trees whose distribution is so carefully organized by species, in accordance with the seasons, that we did not observe them a single time without finding some in flower, some in fruit and others in full maturity, always one after another successively, which necessarily supposes a great variety of endeavors and occupations, and, in consequence, a long series of observations of culture and climatic variations.

The habitations of the Selenian city are not isolated from one another as blocks of houses are separated by streets in all terrestrial cities; on the contrary, they communicate by means of open galleries carried by bridges every time they pass over the abysses described above. We shall remark here that the openings made in the walls to perform the functions of doors as well as windows are triangular in all the edifices of Selenopolis, contrary to what we observed in the castles and isolated monuments. In cities, where one can neglect precautions of defense, one is only occupied with the conveniences of purpose, so the windows have the form of isosceles triangles whose base is placed horizontally at the upper part of the opening; the corresponding angle is 96 degrees, which gives 42 degrees for each of the two superior angles. The singular form of those tapering windows caused us the greatest astonishment, but it soon disappeared on seeing the admirable facility with which the Selenians and civilized Vespertilios enter and exit from them flying. Then we understood that the form in question had been decided with a view to the purpose of the opening that it was designed to frame.

The aspect of those openings has the most beautiful effect on the immense facades, which are decorated with marbles and metallic ornaments in all the monuments of a certain importance.

The richest and vastest of these edifices are located in the northern part of the city. We have not been able to discover a plausible reason for that disposition, so we shall not seek to explain it. There, we have observed two vast elliptical monuments whose greatest diameter is no less than half a mile in length, and which are separated by the entire width of the city. An octagonal expanse of water five hundred feet in diameter, which appeared to us to be very deep, is located at the center of one of the uncovered areas left empty between the walls of these monuments; the corresponding area is occupied in the other by an observation castle similar in every respect to those we have described. Around that expanse of water, eight long needles in the form of triangular obelisks are distributed, which, with another placed at the center and much longer, form a set of nine.

The walls that enclose those vast enclosures are pierced at intervals by openings disposed in such a fashion that the Selenians need the greatest skill to pass through them without suspending the rapidity of their flight. Those windows, triangular, like all those we have observed in the city, are distributed regularly in nine rows at different heights throughout the circumference of the edifice. Contrary to the usage observed among us, however, the windows of the various rows are not arranged directly above one another, but distributed in such a fashion that the one in the upper row is directly above the middle of the space separating those below; thus, the Selenians have established in principle the theory of fillings above voids, of which a few trials are found in Gothic edifices.

These monuments appear to us to be designed for the exercises of young Selenians. It is where they come to train, by means of simulated conflict with civilized Vespertilios, for combat with savage Vespertilios. In those exercises, one of the troops is always composed of mingled Selenians and Vespertilios, while the other is made up only of Vespertilios. We have observed them in these exercises several times; they launch themselves with incredible rapidity, rising, descending, passing through the thousand openings in that arena of sorts; then, depending on the location, they plunge into the expanse of water or gather in number around the fortress, continually brushing in their multiple evolutions the sharp spikes of the observation-boxes.

Several times, I ought to say, those interesting spectacles attracted our attention to the point of rendering us passionate spectators and making us lose sight of our role as scientific observers , and it was difficult not to abandon oneself to that involvement; in fact, I do not know whether any spectacle exists more interesting than that of intelligent beings deploying all their resources of cunning, skill and physical and mental power in a goal of practical utility and without great danger to their person—for their skill is such that in those dangerous exercises, accidents appeared to us to be extremely rare.

The space contained between these two monuments and a third, different fort placed in the center of the city and forming an equilateral triangle with them is evidently the richest and most animated part of the city.

There, as elsewhere, bridges of several tiers are extended over the abysses between two rocks, sometimes only between two sharp peaks; some are formed of a single stone, others of two enormous masses of rock between which a third is fitted like the keystone of an arch. There, as elsewhere, all the peaks, all the summits and all the houses are decorated variously with metallic spikes, or clusters of triangular obelisks, plantations of various sorts; but, more than anywhere else, the monuments are rich, numerous and very extensive.

Nothing equals the splendor, ostentation and originality of a construction of strange taste extended between the highest two peaks in the central part of the city. It is like an immense wall built with the most precious materials, pierced at entirely irregular intervals by large triangular openings, with the form, unlike those we have observed almost everywhere else, of equilateral triangles. The upper part is bizarrely terminated by crenellations separated at intervals by triangular gaps disposed three by three at unequal heights. Over each of the crenellations, in a space expressly contrived, rises a triangular obelisk of a bright blue material, mixed with yellow threads like gold.

We were so dazzled by the richness and glamour of all those monuments of the most diverse forms that it took us several days to remark what was happening in the depths of the vast abysses that we had identified at the very beginning. It was something hideous and repulsive. As the depth increased, the walls of rock became viscous and smoky, and at the very bottom, we saw something turbulent and filthy stirring in places, to which we were not able to put a name.

After having vanquished our repugnance, however, we discovered, on looking more closely, immense machines that were visibly operating with great regularity. Here, we distinguished immense pendulums, there large wheels rotated manually by beings who race it was impossible for us to recognize, so uncertain and unsteady as the little light that penetrated to those depths.

Sometimes the depths of those immense fissures suddenly became an ardent red, like the fire of a blast furnace, but an instant later such a thick smoke rose up that it hid everything from our gaze before we could recover from the dazzle caused by the sudden brightness, and it was not possible for us to observe anything. On seeing a few civilized Vespertilios plunge into those deep fissures occasionally, and come back as quickly as possible, we thought that they had gone to give orders for the work that was doubtless being done in those horrible abodes, and that the workers might be Beavers, doubtless condemned to that harsh labor.

And we wondered whether it really was from those somber factories that the rich fabrics emerged in which the Selenians were clad, and all the apparatus of luxury that surrounded them, all the ornaments with which they decorated their edifices, their metals and their marbles, so admirable sculpted.

It was, in consequence, there that the materials had been prepared of the admirable temple placed in the center of the city in front of the pierced wall that we have described, forming an equilateral triangle with the two arenas. It seemed to us then quite different from the way we had seen it at first; its richness produced a very different impression on us, now that we knew all the dolors that it had cost.

The plan of that edifice presents a precise equilateral triangle, each angle of which is blunted and rounded. It is supported by thirty-six columns devoid of bases or capitals, distributed in sequence around the edifice, nine on each side and three on each curved section. Those columns are surmounted by a platform supported on the other side by a wall, from which they are nine feet distant, a separation three times that which separates them from one another. They support a wall of an elevation double their length, and on which a monolith is set that covers the whole edifice, which is a single massive block of a milky gray substance, which we presume might be unpolished crystal.

That opaque body appears to us to let some light penetrate the interior of the edifice, but it prevented us from seeing anything that might be happening there. Mr. Drummond thought that if the crystal was unpolished, it was doubtless a precaution to shelter the mysteries from the indiscretion of civilized Vespertilios, who were, in any case, not admitted to the interior of the unitary temple, toward which the faces of all the inhabitants of the Moon are directed at times of prayer.

At the three angles of the edifice are three elongated triangular pyramids, which appeared to us, like the columns sustaining them, to be carved in the blues of a mineral product, which, by the brightness of its blue color and the seams of gold that we saw mixed in with it, appears to us to have a considerable analogy with the precious stone known as lapis lazuli, from which we derive the color commonly known as ultramarine.

The windows of the temple, bordered by a strip of that beautiful marble, are also fitted with unpolished crystal, and we have presumed that the interval between the wall supported on the columns and the interior wall rising to the top might well have been contrived with the aim of preventing Vespertilios from seeing anything of the interior of the sanctuary when the Selenians admitted thereto open the windows to introduce themselves.

Seventh Fragment: CONJECTURES ON WORSHIP AND RELIGION

Thus far, in the report of so many astonishing discoveries, and in order to communicate the elements of our conviction to the scientific world, it is evident that we have consistently proceeded to philosophical deductions solely by the examination of the facts and the relationships between them. To embark on the exploration of facts of a major order, however, perhaps requires, *a priori*, to suppose them and to proceed to their encounter by way of the conjectural method. The history of science shows clearly enough that more than one discovery has resulted from hypothesis, and that the experimental method alone, by paralyzing the temerities of the human mind, would have imprisoned it and condemned it to crawl in the narrow main of known facts.

My colleagues and I, therefore, did not refrain from proposing hypotheses, sometimes frivolous, which helped us rest from our labors during the stormy nights that the equinoxes commonly bring to the extreme regions of southern Africa.

During one of those nights, one of the boldest and most important conjectures was submitted to us by the honorable Sir William Cobett, a member of the Biblical Society who had arrived at the Cape shortly before, momentarily deflected from the voyage he was making to India by the desire to meet up with his young and savant friend Lieutenant Drummond.

The hypothesis that he introduced into our conversations was significant and serious; it concerned primarily the dogma of revelation; Sir William Cobett only produced it tremulously himself. It was a matter of deciding, in accordance with the errant and fragmentary observations that we had collected scrupulously up to that point, still awaiting a decisive incident that would rally them under a single point of view, whether the Selenians, and the species of an inferior nature that are immediately subordinate to them, recognize a supreme God and, in consequence, honor him.

That proposition encloses a second, and one of superior interest, which had not at first been formulated by any of us, although the Selenians might certainly have been pagans or idolaters, without having the slightest acquaintance with the eternal verities propagated by the Gospel. Newton had moist eyes every time he pronounced the name of the Eternal! Without the revelation, our world would still be languishing in darkness. In any case, as one can imagine, it was not for Christian Englishmen, enlightened by the luminaries philosophy and the progress of civilization, to pose a question unfortunately defended by the skeptic Bayle as to whether an atheistic civilization could exist.[8]

---

[8] Pierre Bayle (1647-1706) addressed that question in his *Dictionnaire historique et critique* (1695-1697). As a French

Our terrestrial globe—which of us is unaware of it?—has presented here and there in the course of the centuries a few attempts at realization so deadly as to attest to the human mind one obvious fact: that the propagation of the poisonous maxims of atheism have consistently ended in bloodshed, after having covered the planet with scandals and ravages and causing retrogression to a state of barbarity. It is by laws, natural or revealed, that societies are organized and subsist. The superhuman notions of devotion, morality and resignation, by establishing order and progress in the privileged races of the universe, moderate the egotism and destructive spirit of the personality, while the negation of God leads to the negation of all social order. The harmonies of the Selenian world immediately reject the merest admissibility of those deplorable attempts.

It therefore remained to put a finger on the emblems of worship and to extract, from the special character of those emblems, indications as to the nature of the benevolent manifestations of the divine power in favor of the inhabitants of our satellite.

Each of us was keenly preoccupied by that.

This time, there were only serious words between us, worthy in every way of the infinite research to which our hopes rose up in concert. Is there any need here to explain under what influence we were necessarily obliged to bring up and assemble the notions already collected on that capital point? In trying to lift one of the corners of the veil of that vast sanctuary where created beings drew closer to the source from which all intelligence emanates, and which, from planet to planet, and doubtless even beyond our vortex, observes the universal alliance of superior races in the bosom of contemplation and prayer, with God their sovereign legislator, how could

---

Protestant, Bayle was naturally in favour of tolerance and opposed to Catholic dogmatism—an opposition that led him to a more thoroughgoing skepticism.

73

we have avoided the accusation of mingling a little enthusiasm with the austerity of scientific language?

A remark by Dr. Grant, after having initially received from all my friends—and, I must admit, from me—an ironic welcome, in that it seemed to us to belong to exclusively to terrestrial bias, as well as to the superstition of numbers and the Cabala, penetrated us gradually with a religious emotion as soon as Mr. Drummond had insisted, by developing forcefully a certain quantity of analogous remarks.

According to the young lieutenant, the ternary number was reproduced with a singular constancy in a host of occasions, and apparently deliberately multiplied in taking on several forms alternately, incessantly, like a element of action or order, and with regard to a series of facts linked together by relations until then neglected or noted very indifferently in the course of our general observations. The lieutenant hastened to clarify what was obscure and apparently hazardous is that assertion, by reminding us of instances that seemed immediately to be revealed everywhere; and that first remark was on enveloped by a mass of dazzling proofs, and, so to speak, a body of doctrine.

In fact, in the depths of thousands of extinct craters that were perceptible from the summits of the plateaux of the mountains that furrowed the visible portion of the lunar disk in all directions, the prodigious cordon of fortresses and observatories that we have already identified, offered lacunae at intervals Those fortresses and observatories gave way to arenas, whose circular walls were bizarrely pierced by triangular niches hollowed in the rock, in the manner of inverted cones, as we had previously noted for the windows of the edifices of the Selenian capital, and placed in three vertical stages, like the stalls of an infinite circus. In the center of the arena rose four blocks or pyramids, similarly triangular, and one of those four pyramids dominated the others, in such a fashion that their equilibrium offered the mass of a powerful triangle.

It did not take us long to conjecture that those habitually deserted arenas, which, on the basis of an excessively superficial examination, had appeared to us to be rudimentary constructions or ruins—for we had only considered them in relation to the general system of the Selenians' defense against the hostilities of the savage Vespertilios—might well be religious stations for the usage of countless bands we had seen, at various times and in various circumstances, heading processionally through our telescopic field of vision to disappear at its edge.

The result of our observation of the pace and organization of these processional bands took the supposition a step further. A constant regularity in the progress of the flying squadrons; the order that the Selenians observed in their groups, advancing three abreast and three deep; the whole series of the groups, which general ensemble formed a triangle, since their flanks, after a rapid development, were suddenly cut off in the vicinity of the rear-guard by a straight line; such an affectation reproduced point for point in the number, form and movement, as if decisively, had to be the expression of a thought, the translation of a ritual or the accomplishment of a law.

The field enlarged before the hypothesis. After the examination of all our particular remarks, their concordance proved to us in an irrefutable manner that, during the 350 hours that form, very nearly, the duration of the Selenian day, those phenomena of great processions had been revealed to us exactly three times, while the sun's rays were in contact with the central point of the hemisphere of which the satellite offers us the eternal aspect. That particularity was therefore offered, if one can make use in this circumstance of sublunar terminology, first in the morning, then at midday and finally in the evening—which is to say, as soon as solar light reached, illuminated in full or deserted the central point of the Moon. Subject to verification by subsequent observation, that accord in our annotations, that simultaneity on a point that had initially seemed to us to have to little value, appeared to us at that moment to be singularly remarkable.

The same number triumphed everywhere. It remained for us to consult, laboriously, the other analogies of that genre, and, as it were, to catch the religion of the Selenians in the act, *in flagrante delicto*, before risking a conclusion that each of us feared to launch recklessly.

Sir William Cobett resolved to stay with us until the opportunity was offered to us to carry the spirit of investigation and analysis into the profound examination of that interesting problem. There was, from that moment on, something unusual in the solemn form in which we proceeded with our astronomical operations. Science was rising up this time to the heights of religion; no more beautiful enigma had ever disturbed the human mind.

It was 23 December, at eleven o'clock in the evening, the hour calculated on the basis of previous observations for devoting ourselves to that examination, that the axis of the telescope was directed toward the fringe of the lunar fortresses, maneuvering the instrument in such a way as to scan the entire chain of mountains and to choose very scrupulously the point at which our investigations ought to commence. The sun's light was rendering the heavenly body full. The lunar day was at its mid-point. The movement of the telescope, initially a rapid and simple scan, was soon slowed down and determined by the double calculation of the velocity of our globe and its satellite, in order not to lose any of the details of the singular spectacle that realized our conjectures.

We saw an immense arena populated by Selenians, all with wings extended, standing in the niches of the rock faces that formed the walls of the crater. Just as we had remarked during the details previously given on the occasion of the nuptial election of the nobles of the Lunarian race, prodigious vegetal transplantations must have taken place on the perimeter of the ring around that point of rendezvous. The animated colors of that transplantation formed a striking contrast with the dead and somber hues of the vast arena, where, visibly, those masses of verdure could not have grown. The undulation of the branches was feeble; it attested to the calm of the air during the hours when the Sun fully illuminates the apparent disk of the Moon; and, unless the verdure of those unusual arbors was spreading some freshness in the surroundings —a supposition that nothing justifies—it was initially impossible for us to agree among ourselves as to the goal and the positive utility of that luxury of verdure.

The evaluation of the number of Selenians could not be fixed at less than ten thousand. The bottom of the vast basin that they were overlooking from the height of their niches, reminding us of the symmetry of the statues of saints that garnish the perimeter of the naves in Catholic cathedrals, presented a dense and compact mass of Vespertilios lying face down and motionless, whom one might have thought struck by death but for the extreme regularity of their disposition. That disposition, in order to be so correct, had to be voluntary and simultaneous. In fact, the heads of the Vespertilios were uniformly turned in the direction of the pyramids; their feet were touching the heads of other slaves, and so on, over a distance of more than three hundred toises. The ground seemed literally paved with them, like an infinite mosaic; their number appeared to us to be four times as considerable as that of the Selenians; one manifestation more in favor of the celestial justice that submits strength and number to intelligence, in the same way that it opens the rich sanctuary of infinity, populated by the vortices of the universe, to the humble gazes of the imperceptible scientists of our world.

The immobility of the two races, the free race and the domestic race, appeared to us to be general in spite of the variation of attitudes. There was no individual of the beaver race there, which seemed never to emerge from the depths of its valleys or the vicinity of lakes. Perhaps beavers would perish on the mountain plateaux; perhaps, too, they would be unable to climb the steep slopes.

We were beginning to believe that the worship of the first two races might well offer, save for nuances between them, some analogy with the ecstatic contemplations of Indian dervishes. That induction came to mind above all because of one Selenian who was standing alone, like a stylite, perched on the extreme tip of the central pyramid; when suddenly, the latter seemed suddenly to attain more developed proportions—doubtless by rising up in definite flight and hovering in space, and all the Vespertilios leapt to their feet. We presumed that it must have been in accordance with a resounding signal, for the movement was nervous and simultaneous among the forty thousand Vespertilios; their wings quivered and folded up again. They were arranged in circles, disposed in concentric rings. The narrowest of those rings was at a distance of four feet from the pyramid, and the last against the walls of the arena to which the Selenians were as if attached.

That movement was followed by another. The Vespertilios separated themselves into groups of three; abruptly, the left side turned toward the center of the triangle; for nearly twenty minutes, with a kind of furious competition, they flagellated one another reciprocally and relentlessly, the first striking the second, the second striking the third and the third striking the first, while the Selenians quit their niches and flew above the host of slaves, making a processional tour of the arena. That soon formed the most extraordinary variegation of movements and colors, like the radiation of the spokes of a dazzlingly white wheel against a black background. One might have thought it the bars of a cage rotating on a pivot. That spontaneous mortification of slaves who were striking one another under the gaze of their masters, and whom the masters were not imitating, appeared to us to be the symbolic expression of a religious faith in the hierarchy of the ranks and the destinies of each of the races, on the Selenian globe as for any other world.

Throughout the time that the circulation lasted, we suspended any further conjecture. Finally, and probably in response to the repetition of the same signal that must regulate everything, the Selenians resumed their places, the Vespertilio triangles were reformulated into lines and those lines into circles; the solitary of the pyramid appeared to be getting sensibly closer to his shadow, which was vacillating to our eyes all around him on the walls of his pedestal. Abruptly, he refolded his wings, and the civilized Vespertilios fell face down in the arena again.

A thought seized us then, in combining the simultaneity of the various movements, which was that the civilized Vespertilios were worshiping their masters like beings of an infinitely superior nature, and that religion, among the Selenians, was restricted to the calculation of political subjection, in which the dominators, denuded of beliefs, positioned themselves as gods above the rabble.

That thought, which afflicted us, did not endure; for, supposing that the individuals of the domestic race revered the Selenians for their real superiority, that veneration must only be, at the most, the well-understood admission of a relative preeminence, and could not go as far as idolatry for perishable beings that the Vespertilios of the barbaric countries of the Moon dared to attack even in their fortresses, put to death and probably devour.

The analogy of terrestrial events sufficed to refute our first suspicion. The Americans ceased to tremble religiously at the sight of Cortes and Pizarro as soon as they perceived that the Spaniards did not form an indivisible whole with their horses, and that the frightful monsters who disposed of thunderbolts were mortal like them. We returned to the idea of a certain unity in the religion, but with political modifications between the races.

It was then that Sir William Cobett, whose indefatigable attention did not neglect any of the details of the vast ensemble represented in our field of vision, pointed out to us groups of Selenian females in the thickets of verdure on the rim of the crater, in isolated groups of three, around a kind of dais or palanquin of foliage in which a bird was perched. That bird might be an object of sacrifice. It became interesting to determine its species. By virtue of its almost white color and one very curious particularity—the bird only supported itself on one leg—we thought we recognized in it the Founingo, or green wood-pigeon of Madagascar, a variety of pigeon singularly stronger than the one to which ornithologists apply that nomenclature in Europe, and even at the Cape of Good Hope.

The unipedal pigeon was not attached; it was fluttering hither and yon freely, which set aside any idea of sacrifice. Sir William Cobett also pointed out to us that the Selenian on the pyramid was also carrying one of those pigeons in his arms, against his breast.

At that moment, the Selenian, turning round, appeared to offer that bird to general adoration. The festivals of Venus and Adonis on the island of Cyprus, the Egyptians' worship of animals and the Judaic oblations in the Temple of Solomon came to mind, with a host of increasingly bold, perhaps audacious, suppositions, which the frequent repetition of the ternary number seemed to constrain us to deduce as a sequence of rigorous consequences; but we hesitated, and the conclusion remained suspended on our lips.

Finally, the Vespertilios of the great circle broke away rapidly from all points of the arena, like enemy cavaliers charging one another in a battle, or swarms of insects colliding; they were followed almost immediately in that surge by the Vespertilios of the second circle, and the other circles followed, exchanging blow for blow, until the last. In the blink of an eye, with the prodigious strength that is decidedly the prerogative of that inferior race, they had stripped the margin of the crater of the vegetation covering it, which we had reason to believe to be foreign to that elevated region.

As soon as the position of the branches ceased to be aligned with the telescopic axis, we were able to appreciate their form and grandeur; their length could not have been less than twenty feet; their very compact foliage was composed of densely packed leaves, like those of the laurel, but much larger and of a pearly gray whose reflection sparkled in the sunlight like polished steel. Then a cortege was organized; the Vespertilios hastened to form a double line and incline their branches toward one another in the form of a vault.

That movement was executed with a regularity that appeared to us to be marvelous, for the last to arrive of the slave race rapidly ran to the head of the column to extend the avenue infinitely, and the line of shadow into which the Selenians of both sexes precipitated themselves. It was necessary to calculate the movement of the telescope to follow that procession in its journey over the plains, lakes and mountains, which rolled before our eyes like the movement of a cylinder, in a direction contrary to the course of the caravan.

The Selenians always seemed to be on the point of overflowing the avenue in which they were enclosed, and yet, by virtue of an infinite relay, as soon as a void was established at the rear extremity of the avenue, the Vespertilios posted momentarily at the tail of the column transported themselves to the head of the cortege with a hasty acceleration.

Some of the unfortunates, exhausted by that violent exercise, or chastised by their chiefs by means of a kind of lasso whose usage we had noticed during combat and hunting, plunged through the air and were broken against the rocks, without the accident interrupting the pace of the general progress. For us that was a specimen of the severity that reigns in discipline with regard to the slaves, and the disdain that those slaves had between themselves for members of their own race, since the Vespertilios' chiefs were Vespertilios themselves.

That will not astonish people who are acquainted, even superficially, with the regime of our colonies, and who have seen negroes laboring under the discipline of men of the same color.

But let us return to the cortege, of which, after all, the Vespertilios only formed the border. Harnessed, in a sense, to the dais of foliage that bore the bird, the young Selenian females came first, two in front and the third behind the dais. We counted three thousand of them. The Selenian of the pyramid came after them; he raised the pigeon above his head, and he crowd of Selenians followed him in parallel lines.

That was no longer in conformity with our previous observations of the triangular formation of all the formalities of the ceremony, and for the moment, we were obliged to tell ourselves—which was subsequently confirmed—that the re-

81

turn journey after religious solemnities was not subject to the same rules of order and movement as the departure. Nevertheless, in the partial organization of groups, and in the ensemble of the cortege, it was still easy to observe a hierarchy of ranks and functions among the Selenians, and in all things, the supremacy of the priestly hierarchy over the purely civil hierarchies—manifest testimony of a legislation that drew its principal authority from the promulgation of a spiritual and religious code.

But whence came that promulgation? Did it come from the Selenians or the Eternal?

That was not for us to answer. Perhaps we have assembled enough striking indications and irrefutable evidence to enable Christian minds to share the conviction that took possession of us; but that conviction, solemn as it is for the first witnesses of so many marvels, for us, who now owe ourselves the felicitation of thinking that revelation has not limited the benefit of its mercy to our planet alone; for us, in sum, who do not pronounce without a respectful tremor the names of the three persons of the Holy Trinity, who in the series of revelations, have seen each of those three persons announced in turn or seconded by the other two, by the law dictated in Sinai, by the sacrifice of Calvary and the tongues of fire of Pentecost, that conviction surpasses the narrow bounds of Science. It will remain in the sanctuary of our intimate persuasion; it will brave the fanatical insults of incredulity. Those flagellations, those numbers and those symbols speak clearly enough for us.

The winged caravan continued on its way for nearly forty-five minutes, and we saw arriving, as if to meet it, the conical roofs and crystal platforms of the Selenian metropolis. The rapid evolution of the telescope was moderated with the movement of the general halt, and it was revealed to us that the powerful mass to which we have made allusion in our considerations of the architecture of lunar races was their temple. It was not permitted to us, any more than to the Vespertilios to penetrate the mysteries of that religious enclosure.

The young Selenian females harnessed to the doves disappeared thereinto; then the leader of the ceremony; and then the principal group leaders. The other Selenians flew off in all directions; and yet it was necessary to believe that the ritual was not entirely complete, for throughout the time when we were able to follow the Moon above the horizon, groups of the premier race brought offerings of crustaceans, fruits of conical form bright with a thousand colors and foodstuffs whose form we could not determine, on crystal trays, which were accept by the elect at the balustrade of the temple. None of those whose offerings were accepted, however, went inside, either because they were unworthy, although their offerings were not, or because they were not initiates, or because the interior of the temple was only accessible to superior officers and priests.

As for the Vespertilios, they remained torpid and grounded in the surroundings, perhaps to rest from the unusual fatigues of the religious ceremony; neither their fatigue nor their relative weakness had been spared.

The Moon, almost at that moment, was lost in the vapors of our horizon.

Let us stop here; other revelations have clarified other mysteries for us, and in due course we shall present our remarks on the race of Beavers and our conjectures on their religion, which seems to us to present some similarities to that of the Sabeans.

Eighth Fragment: LUNAR HARMONIES

Given these numerous observations, several times renewed by the honorable and eminent men I have named, we are already able to describe here, at least in part, the moral condition of the Selenians; for, in the same way that the material details of that world have been revealed to us through the lenses of our telescope, through those material details, if I might put it thus, the secrets of the moral world have been revealed to philosophical eyes. But it seems to us that perhaps the moment has not yet come to proceed in a complete manner with that interpretation.

For one thing, the people of our own world will already have enough difficulty recovering from the amazement caused by these important discoveries, and we are hesitant for the moment to mingle with those irrefutable material details other details that will not have in the eyes of everyone the same degree of certainty as in ours; and when I think of it, I thank God from the bottom of my heart for permitting, in the interests of science, that these observations could be made at the Cape of Good Hope, to which all the scientists in Europe might soon flood; for if I had written what I am writing today in the depths of some distant country, my voice and those of my fellow observers would have been stifled by the incredulous clamors of ignorance, and no one would have wanted to take the trouble to verify the veracity of our story. Eternal thanks be rendered, therefore, to divine Providence, which has doubtless played a large part in all of this.

We shall therefore only deliver to the public the whole of our moral inductions when people are already familiar with that new material world, and we have completed our observations. Then, recovered from the initial stupefaction, quite natural in a world that encounters a differently ordered one, the people of Earth, with a better appreciation of what might appear to them at first to be problematic or bizarre in the constitution and customs of the Selenians, will follow us more easily and will even assist us in our laborious investigations.

Then again, it must also be said, in matters of a moral order, it has always been more difficult for humans to arrive at the same unity of views as in the establishment of facts or material phenomena; and that difficulty we have encountered ourselves in approaching the Selenian moral world. As we advanced further in the exploration of that world, three of us strove by way of interpretation to arrive at an understanding of the moral world: the honorable Dr. Bruce, Captain Muller and Herbert Holms had established from the earliest days three imposing theories, essentially different from one another, it is true, but which all three founded on arguments difficult to combat, and on considerations as elevated as they are ingenious. That will not astonish intelligent men habituated to seeking the reason of things; they know that it is only after difficult groping, after many bold hypotheses, that one finally arrives at the discovery of the truth.

As the initially isolated and confused details were slowly classified in a harmonious assembly, however, the various theories of our colleagues also gradually came together and arrived at a state bordering on unity.

The moment has not yet come, as I have just said, to deliver that vast and conscientious labor to the public; you will understand with what powerful emotion, what continual palpitation must have presided over that extraordinary task of the edification of a new moral world in accordance with a new material world; you will understand, in such an unusual—I might even say unprecedented—situation, a few preoccupations could even have afflicted grave and cool-headed men, and that pages written at a moment when the calculation is only made with a vague feverish excitement, need to be reviewed with calm and collection.

While waiting, therefore, until we can deliver that work to the meditations of the thinkers and philosophers of our globe, in order that they can comment on and discuss them, we shall, by way of introduction, extract from the journal of the honorable Herbert Holms a few pages inscribed at the highest point of a noble religious sentiment. They are, in any case, a victorious response to the prejudice so fatally spread by the philosophy of the eighteenth century against men devoted to the exact sciences, who are always assumed to be drawn at an equal pace into the profundities of science and the darkness of atheism.

"Doubtless this planet has not, like ours, merited wrath, or at least celestial disfavor, for God appears to have lavished upon it means of harmony and peace. After so many scrupulous observations of the majority of the Lunarians of three races, on their customs and their mores, it is evident that the race that dominates, and enjoys all the advantages, has only obtained that domination by intelligence. On our planet too, it is doubtless intelligence that dominates, but that domination is only maintained by a difficult struggle, which singularly diminishes the pleasures and advantages of domination, for God, in giving all of us the same physical organization, has wanted to create hereby for our planet a fecund means of expiation, an incessant case of lacerations and sufferings, that apparent equality naturally leading humans to the deadly belief that everyone on Earth ought to have an equal share of wellbeing and happiness. In the Selenian world, however, in order to avoid any attempt at usurpation, God has been able to separate the three classes and indicate to each one its immutable destiny.

"To one, he refuses the wings that he grants to the other two, in order to make it understand the abasement to which it is condemned. To another, he grants wings, but does not permit it to rise as high as the class of predilection. At the same time, he grants its members double the strength accorded to the Selenians, in order that they should comprehend that they ought not to work and take trouble for themselves alone.[9]

"It is truly a great and ingenious idea to have established the power and superiority of races on the greater or lesser faulty of flight. To begin with, one wonders why God, after having inspired the inhabitants of the Earth with such a powerful attraction to that enterprise, has not facilitated their means of following it, but after the first cry of plaint and desire that

---

[9] Note in the original text, presumably attributable to the execrable Herbert Holms: "How have the negroes been able to misunderstand, as they have done, the evident intention of the creator? To arrive at that, the perversity of the human mind had to be pushed to an extreme in the last century; how was God able to permit that assault on the order he had established? That can only be explained by admitting a modification of his original will."

escapes before reason and philosophy have spoken, one comprehends the motives of divine wisdom. If God had given wings to us, who, in expiating great faults, must inhabit this vale of tears, our life would doubtless have been a perpetual attempt to escape this accursed planet, to which we have been so justly deported. To be sure, we would not have been able to cross the atmospheric barriers, but our life would have gone by, no longer on the ground but in the ambient air, which might not have entered into the designs of divine Providence. Thus, O my Lord, everything that you have done on Earth as on the Moon, as on all the other worlds that we do not know yet, you have done well.

"In the first place, the race of savage Vespertilios, who often come to attach the Selenians' dwellings, appear to contradict that benevolent intention of Providence, but that contradiction disappears, if one considers that the race in question was never very dangerous to the Selenians, who have expelled it from all the places they want to occupy, and are always certain of repelling it advantageously when they have taken the precaution of organizing a defense, the principal care of which they confide to the Vespertilios. Those wars—or, rather, skirmishes—cost the Selenians no more blood than jousting and passes of arms once cost knights, and one can affirm that the struggle with the savage Vespertilios is only regarded by the Selenians as a perilous distraction, as hunting bears and wild boar is for our great lords, with the difference that in order to flush out one of those animals and force it to engage in battle, our hunters sometimes have to tire themselves out for days on end, while the savage Vespertilio always comes to offer himself to the Selenian hunt.

"The providential mission of the savage Vespertilio appears to us, in addition, to have been, by forcing the Selenians always to remain on the defensive, to hasten the development of architectural art and all the industrial arts attached thereto, thus fecundating the genius of civilization. It is also necessary to add that in stealing the Selenians' children, they maintain among them a certain equilibrium of population.

"Then again, what perfect harmony the various lunar creations have with the places they are destined to occupy! Thus, when we observe the savage Vespertilios in their horrible retreats, where the ground is covered with rocks and lava debris, rent by the craters of extinct volcanoes, we always experience a profound impression resulting from those somber but harmonious accords; whereas the Selenians, with their great silky wings, tend incessantly to get closer to the heavens, whose almost always light hues mingle and melt marvelously with the gray-blue of their wings.

"One cannot admire too much the infinite foresight of God in the astonishing phenomenon of the formation and condensation of vapor; in fact, here is a globe submissive to excessive alternations of heat and cold; sometimes the Sun darts its burning rays vertically upon this ground, sometimes the most intense chill extends over its surface, for fourteen days a heat greater than the equator, for fourteen days a cold more extraordinary than that of the polar regions; in brief, everything seems contrary to the existence of animate beings.

"Well, Providence harmonizes everything: it makes immense mountains surge forth, to which it gives circular form; it hollows out profound valleys, placing high mounds at their center in order that the Selenians can establish themselves there during the planet's long nights, the warm vapors escaping from the flanks of the mountain warm the atmosphere and fall as dew as radiation causes them to lose the gaseous form. The plain is flooded, the waters rise, the land is invaded, the inferior habitations are attained, everything disappears; but the beings that have to live in the depths of the valleys are amphibious, their cabins are heavy and have nothing to fear from the effects of currents; they can sleep tranquil while their fields are fertilized; the water keeps rising, always rising, but the Selenians on top of their rocks can contemplate tranquilly the sea that surrounds them, swelling continuously, for they know that God has assigned them a height that it can never attain.

"The Sun appears, and everything is reborn with its light. The mists dissipate, the vapors remain condensed by heat in the depths of their craters, the sky becomes pure and serene; the atmosphere arms up, the waters in the valley evaporate and refresh it; the earth is laid bare, the inhabitants of the valley depths emerge from their long sleep and spread out into their fields to harvest the plants that grow under the benevolent influence of the Sun, and the civilized Vespertilios come to receive from their hands the fruits of the earth and everything that is destined for the nourishment of the Selenians. Fatigue comes with the end of the day, and when the Sun sinks gradually over the horizon, and they only receive the light reflected by the Earth—which, for them, is fixed in the sky—sleep doubtless comes to take possession of them, and it in the mildness of repose that they await the fine season.

"Everywhere, in sum, what a constant imitation of nature! Their habitations always affect a conical form, in imitation of their mountains; in imitation of birds, they clave the air with their wings, and sojourn for a long time beneath the waters in imitation of fish—if, that is, fish exist in their waters, which Major Muller formally denies for reasons too long to deduce here, but which he intends to develop in a paper addressed to the Royal Society.

"Finally, to all the natural and social advantages that God had accorded to the Selenians, he has added the greatest favor of all, the one without which all the others would only be fragile toys with which to go to sleep on the edge of the abyss; God, as we believe that we have sufficiently proven, has revealed himself to the Selenians, with the result that after having enjoyed their planet, the Selenians have the hope of enjoying an even superior felicity in the bosom of the Creator; and it seems that, in order to heighten in their estimation that unappreciable advantage, God has placed beside them a miserable race, given to a criminal idolatry, of whose terrible punishment the Selenians are aware.

"And yet, in spite of all these means of happiness, the general impression resulting for us from our long observations is that the Selenians are not happy. We have often seen one isolating himself in space and staying there for a long time; then the details of attitude and physiognomy evident indicate, if not desolating thoughts, at least a profound melancholy. In fact, the life of the Selenians, which leaves all industrial labor to the domesticated Vespertilios, and even all the cares of educating their children, must often be vulnerable to ennui.

"Perhaps that apparent sadness, which we believe that we have seen, was only a pious ecstasy, a hymn of love and gratitude sung in the depths of the heart; it is quite natural to think, however, that the cause of the melancholy comes from an ardent desire that presses the Selenians to arrive at the eternal enjoyment that God reserves for his creatures of predilection, and that it is God himself who has put into the Selenian heart that violent and sometimes dolorous attraction. It is thus that we see among ourselves a few men heaped, by exception, with all the joys that our planet can give, and yet who suffer more than all others in their mystical ardor, so fearful has divine wisdom been that this passage through the worlds might not be taken seriously by its creatures, and in order that they should never forget that the present life of those worlds, however happy its makes us, is merely a road to the veritable life, the eternal life.

"Nevertheless, and in accordance with the conviction that God does nothing without a motive, it is permissible for us to believe that the great discoveries of which we have just provided the prelude will not have the unique result of satisfying a vulgar curiosity, and that they will actively favor the progress of morality and civilization; it is permissible to think that in allowing us to know new worlds and their means of happiness, God has wanted to lead us to a softening of the rigors of our exile.

"That is a hope that might be considered bold, but which does not appear to us to be unworthy of divine wisdom and mercy, which appears to us, above all, to be in harmony with the great and immutable law of progress."

Joseph Déjacque: *The Future World (or, The Humanisphere)* (1899)

> *Mutual liberty is the common law.*
> Émile de Girardin[10]

> *And the earth, which was dry, became green again,*
> *and all were able to eat its fruits, and to come*
> *and go without anyone saying to them:*
> *Where are you going? You cannot go this way.*
> *And the little children picked flowers, and brought*
> *them to their mother, who smiled at them sweetly.*
> *And there were neither poor nor rich, but everyone*
> *had the things necessary to their needs in*
> *abundance, because they all loved and aided*
> *one another as brothers.*
> (Words of a Believer)[11]

---

[10] The journalist and politician Émile Girardin (1802-1881), the pioneer of the French popular press, initially campaigned vigorously for the election of Louis-Napoléon as president of the Second Republic, but became a determined opponent after the coup. His opposition was, however, broadly tolerated, making him the most evident voice of protest, while more radical opponents were ruthlessly suppressed.

[11] *Paroles d'un croyant* (1834) was a collection of aphorisms by Hugues de Lammenais (1782-1854), which denounced the "conspiracy of kings and priests against the people"—a sentiment with which Déjacque agreed, although he had nothing else in common with the author, a conservative Catholic who believed that religion, not anarchism, was the only viable antidote to tyranny.

And right away, the Earth has changed its physiognomy. In place of the marshy wounds that devoured its cheeks shines an agricultural down, crops gilded by fertility. The mountains seem to aspire frenziedly the fresh air of liberty, and sway their fine plumage of foliage over their souls. The deserts of sand have given way to forests populated by oaks, cedars and palm trees, which spread underfoot a thick carpet of moss, a soft verdure speckled by all the flowers fond of cool shade and clear streams. The craters have been muzzled; their devastating eruptions have been silenced, and useful course has been given to those reservoirs of lava.

Air, fire and water, all the elements with destructive instincts, have been tamed, and, now captive under the gaze of humans, obey their slightest whim. The sky has been scaled. Electricity bears humans on wings and transports them in the clouds alongside aerial steamboats. It allows them to travel in a few seconds distances that would require entire months to cross on the backs of heavy marine vessels.

An immense network of irrigations covers the vast prairies, where the barriers have been thrown on the fire, and innumerable flocks destined for human alimentation are grazing placidly. Humans enthroned on machines of labor no longer fertilize the fields with the vapor of their bodies but with the sweat of locomotives.

Not only have the ruts in the fields been filled in, but the harrow has been passed over the frontiers of nations. Railways, bridges extended over straits, submarine tunnels, diving-boats and aerostats, moved by electricity, have made the entire globe a single city, of which one can make the tour in less than a day. The continents are the quarters of the districts of the universal city. Monumental habitations, disseminated in group in the midst of cultivated lands, are formed like squares. The globe is like a park of which the oceans are the water features; a child playing with a balloon can leap over them as easily a stream.

Human beings, now holding the scepter of science, have the power henceforth that was once attributed to the gods in the good old times of hallucinations and ignorance; they can make rain and good weather at will, commanding the seasons, which bow down before their master. Tropical plants bloom under uncovered skies in the polar regions; canals of boiling lava snake at their feet; the natural work of the globe and the artificial work of humans have transformed the temperature of the poles and unchained spring where perpetual winter once reigned.

All the cities and all the hamlets of the civilized world, its temples, its citadels, its palaces, its cottages, all of its luxuries and all of its miseries have been swept away from the soil like ordure from the public highway; nothing more remains of civilization but the historical cadaver, relegated to the Mont-Faucon of memory.[12] A grandiose and elegant architecture, of which nothing that exists today can give a sketch, has replaced the meager proportions and stylistic poverties of civilized edifices.

On the site of Paris, a colossal construction rises up on foundations of granite and marble, its cast iron pillars of a prodigious thickness and height. Under its vast iron dome, outlined against the daylight, and posed like lace against a background of crustal, a million pedestrians can unite without being crowded. Circular galleries, stacked one atop another and planted with trees like boulevards, form an immense girdle around that immense circus, which is no less than twenty leagues in circumference.

In the middle of those galleries a railways transports people, in light and graceful carriages, from one point to another, picking them up and depositing them where they please. On each side of the railway is an avenue of moss, a lawn; and

---

[12] The reference is to the Gibbet of Montfaucon, the gallows and gibbet of the French kings prior to Louis XIII—a favorite symbolic motif of French historical novelists of the nineteenth century.

then a sandy avenue for riders; and then a flagstoned or wood-en-tiled avenue; and then, finally, an avenue covered with a thick and soft carpet. All along those avenues, divans and rocking chairs with elastic mattresses, silken, velvet, woolen and Persian fabrics are lined up, and also benches and arm-chairs in varnished wood, marble or bronze, bare or garnished with seats, woven or leather-clad, in unified cloth or in spotted or striped fur.

On the edges of the avenues, flowers of all countries, blossoming on their stems, have long white marble troughs for beds. At intervals, light fountains stand out, some in white marble, in stucco, in agate and bronze, lead and solid silver, others in black marble, in violet breccia, in Sienna yellow, in malachite, in granite, in pebbles, in seashells and copper and gold and iron; the whole mixed together or divided with a per-fect entente and harmony. Their form, infinitely varied, is cleverly animated. Sculptures, the work of skillful artists, ani-mate the urns with ideal fantasies; in the evening the jets of clear water are mingled with jets and waves of light, like cas-cades of diamonds and lava that stream through the aquatic plants and flowers.

The pillars and the ceilings of the galleries are boldly and emphatically ornamented. It is neither Greek, Roman, Moor-ish, Gothic nor Renaissance but something recklessly beauti-ful, audaciously gracious, purity of profile combined with las-civiousness of contours; it is supple and sinewy. That orna-mentation is to the ornamentation of our day as the majesty of the lion, that superb mane-bearer, is to the awkwardness and nudity of the rat. Stone, wood and metal concur in the decora-tion of those galleries, and are married harmoniously there. Against backgrounds of gold and silver, sculptures in oak-wood, maple and ebony are outlined. On fields of pastel color or in severe relief, there is scroll-work of galvanized iron and lead. Muscles of bronze and marble divide that rich flesh into a thousand compartments, and link it in unity.

Opulent draperies hang along arcades that, on the inner side, open over the circus and on the external side are sealed against seasonal bad weather by a crystal wall. In the interior, colonnades form verandas supporting at their summit a crenellated entablature, a platform or terrace, like a fortress or a dovecote, and give passage through those architectural openings to visitors who descend or rise up by means of a mobile balcony that travels up or down at the slightest pressure.

These circular galleries, regular with regard to the ensemble but different in detail, are interrupted at intervals by projecting constructions of an even more imposing character. In these pavilions, which are like the links of the chain of avenues, there are rooms providing refreshments and collations, rooms for reading and conversation, games and repose, amusements and recreations, for adults as well as children. In these retreats, open to the variegated crowd of pedestrians, all the refinements of luxury that would be called aristocratic in our day seem to have been accumulated; everything there partakes of a magical richness and elegance.

Those pavilions, in their inner faces, have as many peristyles by which one enters the immense arena. That new Coliseum, of which we have just explored the steps, has its arena like the ancient coliseums; it is a park dotted with clumps of trees, lawns, flower-beds, rustic grottos and sumptuous kiosks. The Seine is an infinity of channels and basins of all forms, running water and still water, flowing slowly or rapidly, resting or snaking through the middle of all that.

Broad avenues of chestnut-trees and narrow pathways bordered by hedges, covered with honeysuckle and hawthorn, furrow it in all directions. Groups in bronze and marble, masterpieces of statuary, decorate those avenues, enthroned there at intervals, or are mirrored at the bend of some hidden pathway in the crystal of a solitary fountain.

In the evening, little globes of electric light project their timid radiance like stars over the shade of the verdure, and further away, above the most uncovered part, an enormous sphere of electric light pour torrents of solar clarity from its orb. Heaters, infernal braziers, and ventilators, Aeolian lungs, combine their efforts to produce a climate in the enclosure that is always temperate, a perpetual flourishing. It is something a thousand and one times more magical than the palaces and gardens of the Thousand-and-One Nights.

Aerostatic yawls and aerial canoes traverse that free human aviary like flying birds, coming and going, entering and exiting, pursuing one another or crossing paths in their capricious evolutions. Here are multicolored butterflies that flutter from flower to flower; there, birds from the equatorial zones that frolic in full liberty. Children amuse themselves on the lawns with roe deer and lions that have become domestic or "civilized" animals, and make use of them like horses to ride or harness to their wheelbarrows. Panthers domesticated like cats climb the columns or trees, or leap on to the rocky ledges of grottos, and in their superb bounds or capricious affectations design the most gracious curves around people, crawling at their feet, soliciting a gaze or a caress.

Subterranean organs activated by steam or electricity make their sonorous voices heard at times and, like a common concert, mingle their bass notes with the high-pitched chirping of birdsong. Almost in the center of that valley of harmony a labyrinth rises up, on top of which is a clump of palm trees. At the foot of the palm trees is an ivory and oak-wood podium, beautifully contoured.

Above the podium, backed up against the trunks of the palm trees, a large polished steel crown is suspended, surrounded by a blue satin toque proportionate to the crown. Drapery in velvet and grenadine silk, fringed with silver and supported by gold torsades, falls in waves behind. On the front of those tresses is a large diamond star surmounted by a crescent and a plume of bright flame. To either side are two bronze hands, similarly attacked to the tresses, one to the right and the other to the left, serving as clasps, and also as wings to the bright flame.

It is to that podium that people who want to address the crowd go up on days of solemnity. It is understandable that, in order to dare to approach such a pulpit, it is necessary to be something more than our orators and parliamentarians. Those would be literally rushed beneath the moral weight of that crown; they would feel the floor underfoot quivering with shame and parting in order to swallow them. Thus, the people who come to take their place under that diadem and on those allegorical steps are only those who have to spread, from the height of that urn of intelligence, some great and fecund thought: a pearl framed in brilliant speech, which, emerging from the crowd, falls back upon the crowd like dew on flowers.

The podium is free; anyone who wants to can mount it—but only those who want to can. In this world, which is very different from ours, one has the sublime pride of only raising one's voice in public to say something. Icarus would not have dared to try his wings; he would have been too certain of falling. It requires better than an intelligence of wax to attempt the ascension of speech before such an audience.

An ingenious acoustic mechanism permits the millions of listeners to hear all the orator's words distinctly, no matter how far away from him they are. Admirably perfected optical instruments permit them to follow the movements, of both gesture and physiognomy, at a great distance.

Viewed by the eyes of the Past, that colossal carousel, with all its human waves, has the grandiose aspect of the Ocean. Viewed by the eyes of the Future, our academies of legislatures and our democratic councils, the Palais Bourbon and the Salle Martel, only appear to me in the form of a glass of water. That is because humans see things differently according to whether the panorama of the centuries rolls up or unrolls its perspectives. What was utopia for me was quite ordinary for them. They had dreams far more gigantic, which my petty imagination could not embrace. I heard mention of projects so far beyond the vulgar that I could scarcely grasp their meaning.

What a figure, I said to myself, *a civilized individual from the Rue des Lombards would cut in the midst of these people. He could put his head in a mortar, crush it like a peach-stone and triturate the brain, but he would never be*

*able to extract a gleam on intelligence capable of compre-
hending the slightest element of it.*

The monument of which I have tried to provide a sketch
is the palace—or, to put it better, the temple—of arts and sciences, something akin, in the ulterior society, to what the Cap-
itol and the Forum were in anterior society. It is the central
point at which all the radii of a circle terminate, and from
which they spread out to all the points of the circumference. It
is called the Cyclideon—which is to say, the place dedicated
to the circulation of ideas, and, in consequence, everything
that is the product of those ideas; it is the altar of the social
religion, the anarchistic church of utopian humankind.

Among the children of this new world there is neither a
divinity nor a papacy, neither royalty nor gods, neither kings
nor priests. Not wanting to be slaves, they do not want masters. Being free, they have no religion but liberty, so they practice it from childhood and confess it at every moment until the
last moments of their life. Their anarchist communion has no
need of bibles or codes; everyone bears within himself his law
and his prophet, his heart and his intelligence.

They do not do to others what they would not want others to do to them, and they do for others what they would want
others to do for them. Wanting good for themselves, they want
it for others. Not wanting anyone to infringe their free will,
they do not infringe the free will of others. Loving and beloved, they want to grow in love and multiply by love. Human
beings, they render a hundredfold to humanity that which, as
children, they cost the care of humanity, and to their neighbor
the sympathies due to their neighbor: gaze for gaze, smile for
smile, kiss for kiss, and, if necessary, bite for bite. They know
that they have but one common mother, Humanity, that they
are all brothers, and that brotherhood has obligations.

They are conscious that harmony can only exist by virtue
of the collaboration of individual wills; that the natural law of
attractions is the law of the infinitely small as well as the infinitely large; that nothing that is sociable can move except of
its own accord; that it is universal thought, the unity of unities,

98

the sphere of spheres, that is immanent and permanent in the eternal movement; and they say to one another: "Outside of anarchy, there is no salvation!" And they add: "Happiness is of our world."

And all of them are happy, and all of them encounter on their path the satisfactions that they seek. They knock, and all doors open; sympathy, love, pleasures and joys respond to the beating of their heart, the pulsations of their brain, the hammer-blows of their arms; and, standing on their thresholds, they salute the brother the lover, the worker; and Science, like a humble servant, introduces them further forward into the vestibule of the unknown.

And you would want a religion and laws among such a people? Get away! Either it would be a peril or it would be an *hors-d'oeuvre*. Laws and religions are made for slaves by masters who are also slaves. Free human beings bear neither spiritual bonds nor temporal chains. Human beings are their own sovereigns and their own gods.

Myself and my right: that is the motto.

On the sites of today's principal cities, Cyclideons have been constructed, not similar but analogous to the one I have described. That day, there was a universal exhibition in that one of the products of human genius. Sometimes there were only partial exhibitions on a district or continental level. It was on the occasion of that solemnity that three or four orators had made speeches.

In that cyclical of the poetic labors of the hand and intelligence, an entire museum of marvels was exposed. Agriculture had brought its sheaves, horticulture its flowers and fruits, industry its fabrics, its furniture and its decorations, science all its gears, its mechanisms, its statistics and its theories. Architecture had brought its plans, painting its pictures, sculpture and statuary their ornaments and images, music and poetry the purest of their songs. The arts, like the sciences, had put their richest jewels into that casket.

It was not a competition like our competitions. There was no jury of admission and no jury of recompense, no triage by vote or scrutiny, no grand prizes awarded by official judg-es, no crowns, brevets, laurels or medals. The free and great public voice is the only sovereign judge. It is to please that authority of opinion that everyone comes to submit his work, and that is what, in passing before the various works, awards them, in accordance with their particular aptitudes, not toys of distinction but admiration of varying intensity, more or less attentive or disdainful examination.

Thus, its judgments are always equitable, always con-demning the least worthy, always praising the most valiant, always encouraging emulation, for the weak as well as the strong. It is the great redresser of wrongs; it testifies to each individually whether they have followed their part of their vocation to a greater or lesser extent, or whether they have started therefrom—and the future takes charge of ratifying its maternal observations. And all children grow up desirous of that mutual instruction, for all of them have the ambition to distinguish themselves equally in their various works.

On emerging from that festival, I mounted an aerostat with my guide; we sailed through the air for a few minutes and soon disembarked on the perron of one of the squares of the universal city. It is something like a phalanstery, but without any hierarchy, where everything, on the contrary testified to liberty and equality, the most complete anarchy. Its form is almost that of a star, but its rectangular faces are not symmet-rical; each has its particular type. The architecture seems to have modeled in the folds of its structural robe all the undula-tions of grace, all the curves of beauty. The interior decora-tions are elegantly sumptuous. It is a fortunate mixture of lux-ury and simplicity, a harmonious choice of contrasts. The population is between five and six thousand individuals.

Every man and every woman has their own separate apartment, which is composed of two bedrooms, a bathroom or dressing-room, a work-room or study, a small drawing room and a terrace or hothouse filled with flowers and ver-dure. The whole is aerated by ventilators and warmed by cen-

100

tral heating—which does not prevent there also being fireplaces for the delight of the eye; in winter, for want of sunlight, one loves to see a blaze in the hearth. Every apartment also has water and light on tap. The furniture is of an artistic splendor that would put the ragged pretentions of our contemporary aristocracy to shame. And everyone can add to it or restrict it to their taste by simplifying or enriching the details; they only have to express the desire. If they want to occupy the apartment for a long time, they do; if they want to change frequently, they change. Nothing is easier; there are always vacant ones at their disposal.

By virtue of their situation, those apartments permit everyone to go in and out without being seen. On one side, the interior, there is a vast gallery giving access to the park, which serves as the main artery for the circulation of the inhabitants. On the other side, the exterior, there is a labyrinth of small intimate galleries where modesty and amour can glide unobserved.

In this anarchic society, the family and legal property are dead institutions, hieroglyphics that have lost their meaning. One and indivisible is the family, one and indivisible is property. In that fraternal community, labor is free and amour is free. Everything that is the work of the hand or intelligence, everything that is an object of production or consumption, common capital and collective property BELONGS TO ALL AND EVERYONE. Everything that is the work of the heart, everything that is of intimate essence, sensation and individual sentiment, individual capital, corporeal property, everything, in sum, that is human in the proper sense of the word, whatever one's age or sex BELONGS TO THE INDIVIDUAL.

Producers and consumers produce and consume as it pleases them, when it pleases them and where it pleases them. *Liberty is freedom.* No one asks them: Why this? why that?

The children of the rich, in the hour of recreation, taking from the toy basket a hoop or a racket, a ball or a bow, amuse themselves together or separately, and change their comrades or their playthings as the whim takes them, but always solicited to movement by the sight of others and the needs of their own turbulent nature; so too do the children of anarchy, men or women, choose in the community the tool and the labor that suits them, work in isolation or in groups, and change tools or groups in accordance with their caprice, but always stimulated to production by the example of others and the charm they experience in the collective enjoyment of creation.

Again, at a dinner of friends, the guests drink and eat at the same table, taking as they choose a morsel from one dish or another, a glass of one wine or another, without any of them abusing with gluttony a delicacy or a rare wine; so too do the people of the future, at the banquet of the anarchic communion, consume in accordance with their taste everything that seems agreeable to them, without ever abusing a toothsome delicacy or a rare product. They are more likely only to take the smaller share.

In a restaurant, in civilized countries, the traveling salesman, the businessman, the bourgeois, is coarse and brutal; he is unknown and he is paying; that is legal morality. At a meal of selected individuals, the man of the world, the aristocrat, is decent and courteous; he wears his name blazoned on his visage, and the instinct of reciprocity commands him to civility. Who obliges others obliges himself. That is free morality. Like that victim of commerce, legal liberty is coarse and brutal; anarchic liberty has all the delicacies of good company.

Men and women make love when it pleases them, as it pleases them, and with whom they please: full and entire liberty on one part and the other. No convention or legal contract binds them. Attraction is their only chain, pleasure their only rule. Thus, amour is more durable and is surrounded by more modesty than among the civilized. The mystery with which they are pleased to envelop their free liaisons adds an ever-renewed charm to them. They regard it as an offense against the chastity of mores and a provocation to jealous infirmities to unveil to public view the intimacy of their sexual amours.

Everyone, in public, has affectionate gazes for one another, the gazes of brothers and sisters, the warm radiation of lively amity; the spark of passion only gleams in secret, like the stars, those chaste glimmers, in the somber azure of the night. Happy amours seek shadow and solitude. It is from those hidden springs that limpid joys are drawn. There are sacraments for hearts smitten with one another that ought to remain unknown to the profane.

In the civilized world, men and women pin up at the Mairie and the church the notification of their union, and display the nudity of their marriage to the light of a fancy dress ball, in the middle of a quadrille, with the accompaniment of the orchestra: all the glare and bacchanal desired. And, scandalous custom of the nuptial brothel, at the prescribed hour, the vine-leaf is snatched from the lips of the bride by the hands of matrons, and she is prepared ignobly for ignoble bestialities.

In the anarchic world, one would turn away, blushing and disgusted, from that prostitution and those obscenities. All those men and all those women sold, that commerce of cashmeres and notaries, of cotillons and feasting, that profanation of human flesh and thought, that crapularization of amour...if the people of the future could form a image of it, they would shiver with horror, as we shiver, in a dream, at the thought of a horrid reptile strangling us with its cold and deadly coils and inundating our face with its warm and venomous drool.

In the anarchic world, a man can have several lovers, and a woman several lovers, without any dubiousness. Temperaments are not all the same, and attractions are proportionate to our needs. A man might love one woman for one thing, and love another for something else, and reciprocally. Where is the harm, if they are obeying their destiny? The harm would be in violating it, not in satisfying it. Free love is like fire; it purifies everything.

What I can say is that in the anarchic world, inconstant amours are very small in number, and constant amours, exclusive amours, amours *à deux*, are very considerable in number.

Vagabond amour is the search for amour, it is the voyage, the emotions and the fatigue, not the goal. Unique amour, the perpetual amour of two hearts confounded in a reciprocal attraction, is the supreme felicity of lovers, the apogee of sexual evolution; it is the blazing hearth to which all pilgrimages tend, the apotheosis of the human couple, happiness at its zenith.

At the moment when one loves, is not doubting the perpetuity of one's love crippling it? Either one doubts, in which case one does not love, or one loves, in which case one does not doubt.

In the old society, love was scarcely possible; it was never more than a momentary illusion; too many counter-natural prejudices and interests were there to dissipate it; it was a fire extinct as soon as it was lit, and which evaporated in smoke. In the new society, love is too vivid a flame, and the breezes that surround it are too pure and gentle, such sweet and human poetry, for it not to be fortified in its ardor and not to be excited by contact with all those breaths. Far from impoverishing it, everything that it encounters serves as an aliment.

Here, the young man and the young woman have all the time needed to get to know one another. Equal in education as in social position, brother and sister in arts and sciences, in studies and professional labors, free in their steps, their gestures, their speech and their gazes, free in thought as in action, they have only to seek in order to find. Nothing is opposed to their meeting; nothing is opposed to the modesty of their first confessions, or to the sensuality of their first kisses. They love one another not because it is the will of their parents, the interests of trade, or by virtue of genital or cerebral debauchery, but because nature has disposed them toward one another, because it has made twin hearts of them, united by the same current of thoughts: a sympathetic fluid that reverberates all their pulsations and puts their two beings in communication.

Is the love of the civilized—the love of naked forms, public love, legal love—really love? There is a savagery in it, something like a coarse and brutal intuition. Love among the harmonized, love artistically veiled, caste and dignified love, although sensitive and passionate, anarchic love: that is natural and human love, the ideal realized, its scientification. The former is animal love, the latter hominal love. One is obscenity and venality, the sensation of the brute, the sentiment of the cretin; the other is decency and liberty, the sensation and sentiment of human being.

The principle of amour is one and the same, for the savage as for the hominal, for the humans of civilized times as for the humans of harmonic times: it is beauty. Except that beauty, for the anterior and inferior humans, for the fossils of humankind, was sanguine and replete with carnality, or deformed and variegated envelopment, a luxury of meat or crinoline, ribbons and ostrich or seabird plumes, the Hottentot Venus or the drawing-room doll. For the ulterior and superior humans, beauty is not only in the carnal fabric, but also in the purity of forms, the grace and majesty of manners, the elegance and choice of adornments, and above all in the luxury and magnificence of the heart and the brain.

Among the perfectibilized, beauty is not a privilege of birth or the reflection of a golden crown, as in savage and bourgeois societies; it is the daughter of its endeavors, the fruits of its own labor, a personal acquisition. What illuminates the visage is not the exterior reflection of an inert metal, so to speak—a vile thing—but the radiation of all that there is in human being of ideas in effervescence, of vaporized passions, of heat in motion, a familiar gravitation that, having arrived at the summit of the human body, the skull, filters through its pores, flowing in a stream of impalpable pearls, and, as a luminous essence, inundates all external forms and movements, consecrating the individual.

What is, in the final analysis, physical beauty? The stem of which mental beauty is the flower. All beauty comes from endeavor; it is by endeavor that it grows and blossoms on everyone's forehead, an intellectual and moral crown.

Essentially, carnal amour, the amour that is only instinct, is for the human race merely the indication, the root of love. It vegetates, opaque and devoid of perfume, buried in the filth of the soil and delivered to the embraces of that mud. Hominalized amour, the amour that is above all intelligence, is, in the corolla of transparent flesh, the corporeal enamel from which embalmed emanations escape, a free incense of invisible atoms that cover the fields and rise up to the clouds.

To Humanity in seed, filthy amour
To Humanity in flower, the flower of amour.

This square or phalanstery I shall henceforth call a Humanisphere, because of the analogy between that human constellation with the grouping and movement of the stars, an attractive organization, a passionate and harmonic anarchy. There is the simple Humanisphere and the composite Humanisphere—which is to say, the Humanisphere considered in its individuality, or embryonic monument and group, and the Humanisphere considered in its collectivity, or harmonic monument and group. A hundred simple Humanispheres grouped around a Cyclideon form the first ring of the sequential chain and take the name of a "communal Humanisphere." All the communal Humanispheres of the same continent form the first link of that chain, and take the name of a "continental Humanisphere." The combination of all the continental Humanispheres forms the complement of the sequential chain and takes the name of the "universal Humanisphere."

A simple Humanisphere is a building composed of twelve wings joined together and simulating a star—the one, at least, whose description I am undertaking here, for they come in all forms, diversity being a condition of harmony.

One part is reserved for the apartments of men and women. Those apartments are all separated by walls that cannot be pierced either by gazes or voices, partitions that absorb light and sound, in order that everyone might have privacy and can laugh, dance, sing, and even play music—which is not always amusing for the obligatory listener—without inconveniencing their neighbors and without being inconvenienced by them. Another part is disposed for children's apartments.

Then come the kitchens, the bakery, the butchery, the fish-processer, the dairy, the vegetable-processer; then the laundry, the machines for washing drying, ironing, and the underwear-store; then the workshops for everything related to the various industries, and factories of all kinds; the food-stores and the stores of raw materials and manufactured goods.

In addition, there are stables for a few animals of pleasure, which wander freely by day in the interior park, and with which children or adults play, as riders or as drivers. Next are the garages for vehicles of whimsy; after that come the saddlery, the tool-sheds, and the hangars for agricultural locomotives and apparatus. Here is the landing-stage for large and small aerial vehicles. A monumental platform serves as their dock. They drop anchor there on arrival and raise it again on departure.

Further away are the study-rooms for all tastes and all ages—mathematics mechanics, physics, anatomy, astronomy—the observatory; the chemistry laboratories; the botanical hothouses; the natural history museum; the galleries of painting and sculpture; and the main library. Here there are rooms for reading, conversation, drawing, music, dancing and gymnastics. There is the theater, the concert hall, the display halls; the arenas for dressage and equitation; the firing range; the billiard-room and accommodation for other games of skill; the playrooms for little children; the young mothers' hearth; then the large meting-rooms, the refectories, etc., etc.

Then, finally, comes the place where people assemble to discuss questions of social organization. That is the little Cyclideon, the club or forum particular to the Humanisphere. In that parliament of anarchy, everyone is their own representative and the peer of the others. Oh, it is very different from those of the civilized; there one does not perorate, one does not debate, one does not vote, one does not legislate, but everyone, young and old, men and women, confer in common regarding the needs of the Humanisphere. Individual initiative grants itself or refuses itself the floor, depending on whether it is useful to speak or not. In that enclosure, there is an office, as is appropriate; but in that office there is no authority but the book of statistics. The Humanispherians find that it is an eminently impartial president, very eloquent in its laconism, so they do not want any other.

The children's apartments are large rooms in series, illuminated from above, with a row of bedrooms to either side. They are reminiscent, but on a larger scale, of the lounges and cabins of magnificent transatlantic liners. Each child has two connected rooms, a bedroom and a study, in which are placed, according to age and taste, books, tools or toys of predilection. Surveillance is maintained night and day by men and women occupying cabinets of vigilance in which there are camp-beds. Those watchers contemplate solicitously the movements and the slumber of all the young human shoots, and provide for their needs and desires.

That guardianship is entirely voluntary, taken up and abandoned freely by those who have the greatest sentiment of paternity or maternity. It is not a chore commanded by discipline and regulation; in the Humanisphere there is no other discipline and regulation than the individual will; it is an entirely spontaneous impulse, like the glance of a mother at her child's bedside. It is for those who testify the most love to the dear little beings, and who enjoy their infantile caresses the most.

Thus, the children are all charming; mutuality is their humane educator, which informs them of the exchange of mild manners and makes them enthusiasts for cleanliness, generosity and kindness, which exercises their physical and moral aptitudes, which develops in them the appetites of the heart and the brain, which guides them in their games and studies, and finally, teaches them to pick the roses of instruction and education without scratching themselves on the thorns.

Caresses are all that anyone seeks, child or adult, in the prime of life and in old age. The caresses of science cannot be obtained without brain work and the expenditure of intelligence, nor the caresses of amour without the work of the heart and the expenditure of sentiment.

Human children are rough diamonds; friction with others polishes and cuts them, forming them into social jewels. They are, at all ages, pebbles of which society is the mold and individual egotism the lapidary. The more contact they have with others the more impressions they receive therefrom, which multiply the passionate facets in the head and in the heart from which the sparks of intelligence and sentiment fly. A diamond is wrapped in an opaque and rough crust; it only really becomes a precious stone, shows itself to be diaphanous and shines in the light, when that crust has been removed. Human beings are like precious stones; they only pass into the state of brilliance after their crust of ignorance, their harsh and filthy virginity, has been worn away in every sense, and by means of every sense.

In the Humanisphere, very young children learn to smile at those who smile at them, to embrace those who embrace them, to love those who love them. If they are surly to those who are amiable to them, the privation of kisses soon teaches them that one is not surly with impunity, and amiability is returned to their lips. The sentiment of reciprocity is thus engraved in their little brains. They teach one another to become humanely and socially human.

If one of them tries to abuse his strength against another, he immediately has all players against him, is put under the ban of juvenile opinion, and the neglect of his comrades is a punishment more terrible and far more efficacious than the official reprimand of a pedagogue. In scientific and professional studies, if there is one of them whose relative ignorance casts a shadow in the midst of scholars of his own age, that is a fool's cap heavier to wear than the paper one inflicted by a Jesuit of the seminar or a universitarian, so he makes haste to rehabilitate himself and strives to regain his place at the level of the others. In authoritarian education, the cane and impositions might well bruise the bodies and brains of pupils, degrading the work of human nature, and giving rise to acts of vandalism, but they will not model original humans, specimens of grace and strength, intelligence and amour. For that, the inspiration of the great artist whose name is Liberty is re-quired.

Adults almost always supervise the accommodation of children during the night. It does happen, however, albeit rarely, that if one of them, for example, spends the evening with his mother and stays late, he remains there until morning. The apartments of adults being equipped, as noted, with two bedrooms, they can be shared, if that is convenient for the mother and child. That is exceptional; the general custom is to separate at the hour or sleep; the mother remains in her apartment and the child returns to the dormitory.

In the dormitories, moreover, the children are no more compelled than adults always to keep to the same compartment; they change them at will. Nor are there special places for boys or girls; they make their nests where they wish, only attractions decide. The youngest generally accommodate themselves pell-mell; the older ones, those approaching puberty, generally group themselves by sex; an admirable instinct of modesty draws them apart by night.

No inquisition, in any case, monitors their sleep. The watchers do not do that, the children being big enough to look after themselves. They can find the water, fire, light, syrups and essences of which they might have need without leaving their dwelling. By day, girls and boys meet one another again in the fields, the studies or the workshops, reunited and stimulated to work by those common exercises, taking part in them without distinction of sex and without regular fixity in their places, always acting in accordance with their own caprices.

As for the lodgments, I have no need to add that nothing is lacking there, neither comfort nor elegance. They are decorated and furnished with opulence but with simplicity. Walnut, oak, marble, waxed canvas, rush mats, striped cotton curtains in various colors or monochrome twills, oil paintings and varnished paper screens form the furniture and decoration. All the accessories are porcelain, earthenware, sandstone and pewter, and a few in silver.

For the youngest children, the main room is sanded like training-ring and serves as an arena for their vacillating evolutions. Everything around them is thickly padded and leather-clad, stuffed and framed in varnished wood frames. That takes the place of paneling; above a certain height, in panels divided into compartments, there are frescos representing the scenes judged most capable of awakening the imagination of children. The ceiling is crystal and iron. The daylight comes from above. There are, in addition, openings in the sides. During the night, candlesticks and candelabras spread light.

In the accommodation of the older children, the floor is covered with waxed cloth, mats or carpets. The decoration of the walls is appropriate to their intelligence. Tables set in the middle of various rooms are laden with albums and books for all ages and all tastes, boxes of games and necessary tools—in sum, a multitude of playthings serving for study and items of study serving for play.

In our day, many people—especially those who are partisans of large-scale reforms—are inclined to think that nothing can be obtained except by authority, whereas the opposite is true. It is authority that is the obstacle to everything. Progress in ideas is not imposed by decrees; it results from the free and spontaneous education of people and things. Obligatory education is a contradiction in terms; whoever says education says liberty; whoever says obligation says servitude. Politicians and Jesuits might want to impose instruction; that is their business, for authoritarian instruction is the obligatory imposition of stupidity. But socialists can only want anarchist study and information, liberty of education, in order to have the education of liberty.

Ignorance is the most antipathetic thing there is to human nature. Humans, at all the moments of life, and especially children, ask for nothing better than to learn; it is solicited by all aspirations. But civilized society, like barbaric society and savage society, far from facilitating the development of aptitudes, can only be ingenious in suppressing them. The mani-

111

festation of faculties is imputed to crime, for the child by paternal authority and for the adult by governmental authority. Deprived of enlightened care, of the vivifying kiss of Liberty—which makes a race of beautiful and strong intelligences—a child becomes an adult stagnating in original ignorance, allowing in the mire of prejudice, and, dwarfs with regard to the arm, the heart and the brain, reproduce and perpetuate, from generation to generation, the uniformity of deformed cretins who have nothing human about them but the name.

The child is the ape of humanity, but the perfectible ape. He reproduces all that he sees done, but with varying degrees of servility, depending on whether the intelligence of the man is more or less servile, more or less child-like. The sharpest corners of the virile mask are what strike his understanding first. If a child is born among a warrior people he will play soldier; he will like paper helmets, wooden cannon, petards and drums. If he is among a people of navigators, he will play mariner; he will make boats with nutshells and will push them on the water. Among a people of agriculturalists he will play gardener, amusing himself with forks, rakes and wheelbarrows. If he has a railway before his eyes he will want a little locomotive, carpenter's tools if he is near a carpentry shop.

Finally, he will imitate, with a similar ardor, all the vices and all the virtues of which Society gives him the spectacle. He will acquire the habit of brutality if he is among brutes, urbanity if he is among polite people. He will be a boxer with John Bull, utter savage howls with Jonathan. He will be a musician in Italy, a dancer in Spain. He will grimace and gambol at al harmonies, mark his face and his movements with the seal of industrial, artistic and scientific life if he lives with laborers in industry, art or science, or with the imprinted of profligacy and idleness if he is only in contact with idlers and parasites.

Society acts upon the child and the child then reacts upon society. They move together and not to the exclusion of one another. It is therefore mistaken to say that to reform society it is necessary to commence by reforming childhood; all reforms must march in parallel.

The child is a mirror that reflects the image of virility; he is the zinc plate on which, under the radiation of physical and moral sensations, the features of the social being are daguerrotyped. And those features are reproduced all the more emphatically in the one if they are in greater relief in the other. A man may say to his child, like the curé to his parishioners: "Do as I say and not as I do," but the child will take no account of what the man says if what the man says is not in accord with what he does. In his limited logic, he will attach himself above all to following your example, and if you do the opposite of what you say, he will be the opposite of what you have preached to him. You might then succeed in teaching him to be a hypocrite, but you will never make him a good man.

In the Humanisphere, the child only has good and beautiful examples before his eyes, so he believes in goodness and in beauty. Progress is taught to him by everything that falls under his senses, by voice and by gesture, by sight and by touch. Everything moves and gravitates around him in a perpetual effluvium of knowledge, a stream of enlightenment. Everything exhales the sweetest sentiments, the most exquisite perfumes of the heart and brain. Every contact there is a sensation of pleasure, a kiss fecund in prolific sensuality. The greatest enjoyment of human beings, work, has become there a series of attractions, by virtue of liberty and the diversity of labor, and reverberates from one to another in an immense and incessant harmony.

How, in such a milieu, could children not be laborious and studious? How could they not love to play at science, the arts, industry, and not try, at the most tender age, to bring their productive forces into play? How could they resist the innate need to know everything, the ever-new charm of education? To respond other than in the affirmative would be willfully to misunderstand human nature.

Look at the children of the civilized, the children of the hat-maker or the grocer; watch them, as they emerge from their home to go for a walk, when they perceive something of whose existence they were unaware or whose mechanism they do not understand: a windmill, a plow, a balloon, a locomotive. Immediately they interrogate their conductor, they want to know the name and purpose of all objects. But alas, often, in civilization, their conductor, ignorant of all the sciences or preoccupied with mercantile interests, cannot or does not want to give the explanations solicited. If the children insist, they are scolded, threatened with not being taken for a walk another time. Their mouths are closed; they are muzzled; the expansion of their intelligence is violently halted—and when children have been docile all along the way, remaining quiet, and have not annoyed Papa or Maman with importunate questions, having allowed themselves to be led hypocritically and idiotically by the hand like a dog on a leash, they are told that they have been very good, very well-behaved, and to reward them they are bought a gingerbread man or a toy soldier. In bourgeois societies that is known as forming a child's mind.

Oh, authority! Oh, the petty family! And there is no one on the heels of that father or that mother to cry: "Murder! Rape! Infanticide!"

Under the wing of liberty, in the bosom of the great family, in the contrary, children, only finding among their elders, men or women, educators disposed to listen to them and reply to them, quickly learn to know the why and how of things. The notion of the just and the useful thus takes root in juvenile understanding and prepares equitable and intelligent judgments for the future.

Among the civilized, human beings are slaves, children writ large, rods that lack sap, poles without roots or foliage, aborted intelligences. Among the Humanispherians, the child is a free human being in miniature, an intelligence that is growing and whose young sap is full of exuberance.

Very young children naturally have their cradle in their mother's house, and every mother nurses her child. No woman in the Humanisphere wants to deprive herself of the pleasurable attributions of maternity. If the ineffable love of a mother for the little being to whom she has given birth is insufficient to determine her to be a nurse, concern for her beauty and the instinct of her own self-preservation also bids her to do so. In our day, there are women who die of having dried up the source of their milk, and all of them lose something of their health thereby, something of their ornamentation.

The woman who causes her teat to abort commits an attempted infanticide that nature reproves as much as the one who causes her organ of generation to abort. The punishment follows not far behind the sin. Nature is inexorable. Soon the woman's breast becomes etiolated, withers and testifies by a hasty decrepitude against that crime committed against organic function, a crime of lèse-maternity.

What is more gracious than a young mother giving her breast to her child, lavishing it with caresses and kisses? If only for the sake of coquetry, every woman ought to breast-feed her child. Then again, is it nothing to follow, day by day, the phases of development of that young existence, to aliment with the nipple the sap of that human sprig, to follow its continuous progress, to see that human bud grow and embellish under the rays of maternal tenderness, like the bud of a flower in the rays of the sun, eventually opening more and more, until it blooms on its stem with all the grace of its smile and the purity of its gaze, in all the charming naivety of its first steps? The woman who does not understand such enjoyments is not a woman. Her heart is a lyre whose strings are broken. She might have conserved human appearance, but she no longer has its poetry. Half of a mother will never be more than half of a lover.

In the Humanisphere, every woman has the vibrations of amour. A mother, like a lover, quivers with sensuality at all the breezes of human passion. Her heart is a complete instrument, a lute in which not one string is missing; and the smile

of the infant, like the smile of the beloved man, always awak-
ens sweet emotions there. There, maternity really is maternity,
and sexual amours veritable amours.

In any case, that work of breast-feeding, like all other
maternal tasks, is more of a game than a punishment. Science
has destroyed the most repugnant aspects of reproduction, and
it is steam engines and electricity that take charge of all the
heavy work. They wash the linen, clean the cradle and prepare
the baths. And those iron slaves always act with docility and
promptitude. Their service responds to all needs. It is by their
care that all ordure and excrement disappear; it is their indefatigable mechanism that takes possession of them and delivers
them as pasture to cast-iron conduits, subterranean boa con-
strictors that filter them and digest them in their tenebrous
circuits, and expel them subsequently on to workable land as a
valuable fertilizer.

It is the same maid-of-all-work that takes charge of everything concerning the household; she it is who makes the
beds, sweeps the floors, dusts the apartments. In the kitchens,
she it is who washes the dishes, scours the pans, peels or
grates the vegetables, carves the meat, plucks and guts the
poultry, opens the oysters, scrapes and washes the fish, rotates
the turnspit, saws and splits the logs, carries the coal and
maintains the fire. She it is who transmits the food to the domicile or the common refectory, who serves and clears the tables. And everything is done by that domestic machinery, by
that slave with a thousand arms, the breath of fire and muscles
of steel as if by enchantment. Command, she says to humankind, and you will be obeyed. And all the orders she receives
are carried out punctually.

If a Humanispherian wants his dinner to be served in his
private dwelling, a signal is sufficient; the service machinery
goes into operation; she has understood. If he prefers to go to
the refectory, a carriage lowers its footstep, an armchair extends its arms, the rig moves off and transports him to his destination. Having arrived at the refectory, he takes his place

wherever he likes, at a large or a small table, and he eats according to his taste. Everything is there in abundance.

The rooms of the refectory are elegant in their architecture, and have nothing uniform in their decoration. One of the rooms was decorated in embossed leather, framed with an ornamentation in bronze and gold. The doors and casements had oriental curtains with a black background and horizontal stripes in bright colors. The furniture was sculpted walnut wood, garnished with fabric matching the curtains.

Suspended in the middle of the room, between two arcade, was a large clock. It was both a Bacchante and a Ceres in white marble, lying in a hammock of polished steel mesh. With one hand she was tickling a little child who was standing on her with a sheaf of wheat, and in the other she was holding a cup at arm's length above her head, as if to dispute it with the mutinous child, who wanted to take possession of both the cup and the sheaf at the same time. The woman's head, crowned with vine-branches and ears of wheat, was tilted back on a porphyry cask that served her as a pillow; golden sheaves of wheat lay beneath her loins and formed a litter. The cask was the clock-face, on which two ears of wheat marked the hours. In the evening a flame spread from the cup like a burning liquid. Bronze vine-branches climbed up to the vault and along the ceiling darted flames in the form of vine leaves, making a cradle of light above the group and illuminating all its contours. Clusters of crystal grapes hung down through the foliage, scintillating in the midst of that undulating brightness.

On the table, porcelain and stucco, porphyry and crystal, gold and silver contained the host of dishes and wines, and sparkled with reflected light. Baskets of fruits and flowers offered their taste and scent to everyone. Men and women exchanged words and smiles, and seasoned their repast with witty conversation.

When the meal is over, everyone passes into other rooms, no less splendidly decorated, but more elegant, in which they take coffee, liqueurs, cigarettes or cigars: salon-cassolettes in which all the aromas of the Orient burns and fumes: all the essences pleasing to the taste, everything that caresses and stimulates the digestive functions, everything that oils the physical gears and, in consequence, accelerates the development of mental functions. Some savor, in groups or alone, the vaporous puffs of tobacco and capricious reveries; others imbibe, in the company of two or three friends, odorous gulps of coffee or cognac, and fraternize, clinking glasses of softly fizzing champagne, using without abusing all those excitations to lucidity. Some talk science or listen, pour out or draw out, in a group, the nutritive distillations of knowledge; others collect artistically, in a little circle, the delicate flowers of conversation, criticize one thing, praise another, and give free rein to all the emanations of their melancholy or cheerful humor.

If it is after lunch, everyone soon goes, alone or in groups, to their work, some to the kitchens, others to the fields or various workshops. No regulatory constraint weighs upon them, so they go to work as to a pleasure activity. Does not the hunter, lying in a warm bed, get up of his own accord to go ride through woods replete with snow? It is the same attraction that causes them to get up from the sofas and guides them, through fatigues, but in the society of valiant and charming companions to the rendezvous of production. The best workers consider themselves the most fortunate. What distinguishes them among the most laborious is that they furnish the most beautiful strokes of the implement.

After dinner, one passes from the coffee-rooms to large conversation rooms, either to small intimate meetings or to various scientific courses, or rooms for reading, drawing, music, dancing, etc., etc. And freely, voluntarily, capriciously, for the initiator as for the follower, for study as for instruction, they always find teachers for pupils and pupils for teachers. An appeal always provokes a response; a satisfaction always replies to a need. Man proposes and man disposes. From the diversity of desires, harmony results.

The rooms for courses in scientific study and those for artistic study, like the spacious meeting rooms, are magnificently ornate. The lecture rooms are constructed as amphitheaters, garnished with velvet-upholstered benches. To each side is a room for refreshments. The decoration of these amphitheaters is in a severe but rich style. In the leisure rooms, luxury sparkles in profusion.

Those rooms communicate with one another, and could easily contain ten thousand people. One of them was decorated thus: paneling, cornices and pilasters in white marble, which ornamentation in gilded copper. The hangings in the alcoves were in damask silk, solitaire in color, with a silver strip for an interior rim, on which were placed, in the guise of gilded nails, a multitude of fake diamonds. A field of pink satin separated the border from the pilaster. The ceiling was compartmentalized, and from the bosom of the ornaments, jets of flame emerged, which figured designs and completed the decoration while serving for illumination; arabesques of light also sprang from the middle of the pilasters.

In the middle of the room was a pretty fountain in bronze, gold and white marble; the fountain was also a clock. A bronze and gold cupola served to support a group in white marble representing an Eve lying limply on a bed of leaves and flowers, her head applied to a rock, raising a new-born child in her arms; two doves perched on the rock were pecking one another. The rock served as a clock-face, with two golden hands modeled as serpents making the hours. Behind the rock, a golden banana tree was visible, whose branches, laden with fruit, were leaning toward the group. The bananas were formed by jets of light.

An artistic fireplace in white marble and gold served as a stand for an immense mirror; mirrors or fine paintings were also suspended in all the panels amid brown silk drapes. The doors and windows in that room, as everywhere in the Humanisphere, did not open by means of hinges or from bottom to top, but by means of grooves and springs; they moved from right to left and left to right into the walls, disposed to that effect. In that fashion the battens did not inconvenience anyone, and doors and windows could be opened as widely or narrowly as one wished.

Several times a week there is a spectacle at the theater. Lyrical works, dramas and comedies are performed there, but all very different from the poverties presented on the stage in our day. There is, in magnificent language, a critique of tendencies to immobilization, an aspiration toward the ideal future.

There is also a gymnasium where feats of strength and agility are attempted; the arena where riders of both sexes compete in grace, vigor and excellence in guiding, standing on their rumps, the horses and lions bounding round the circuit; the rifle and pistol shooting-ranges; and the rooms where players of billiards or other games exercise their skills.

If the weather is good there are also walks in the splendidly illuminated park; concerts under the stars, rural amusements, distant excursions into the countryside through the solitary forests, plains and mountains, where one encounters at measured intervals grottos and chalets where one can refresh oneself and have a snack. Aerial vessels or railways carriages carry swarms of excursionists wherever their caprice takes them.

At the end of the day, everyone returns home, some to summarize their impressions of the day before going to sleep, others to wait for or go to find someone beloved. In the morning, lovers separate mysteriously, exchanging a kiss, and resume, each according to their taste, the route to their multiple occupations. The variety of enjoyments excludes satiation. Enjoyment is for them perpetual.

About once a week, approximately, when it is necessary, people assemble in the conference hall, otherwise known as the small internal cyclideon. They discuss major projects that are to be carried out. Those most versed in the specialized knowledge in question take the initiative of speaking. The statistics, projects and plans have already appeared in printed sheets in the newspapers; comments have already been made in small groups; their urgency has been generally recognized, or rejected by each individual. Thus, there is often only one voice, the unanimous voice, to acclaim or reject it. They do not vote; the majority or the minority never makes the law. If a proposal brings together a sufficient number of workers to carry it out, whether the workers are a majority or a minority, the proposal is carried out, such being the will of those adherent to it.

More often than not, it happens that the majority rallies to the minority or the minority to the majority, as in an excursion to the country, some propose to go to Saint-Germain, others to Meudon, one to Sceaux and another to Fontenay, opinions are divided; then, in the end, each one cedes to the attraction of being with the others, and they all take the same route by common accord, without any authority than pleasure having governed them. Attraction is the entire law of their harmony. At the point of departure, however, as on the route, everyone is always free to abandon themselves to their caprice, to form a separate group if that suits them, to rest on the way if they are tired, or to turn back in they are bored. Constraint is the mother of all vices, so it is banished by reason from the territory of the Humanisphere. Egotism—intelligent egotism, of course—is too well-developed there for anyone to think of compelling his neighbor; and it is by virtue of egotism that one exchanges good deeds.

Egotism is human; without egotism, humans would not exit. It is egotism that is the motive of all actions, the motor of all thought. That is what makes people think about self-preservation, and self-development—which is also preservation. It is egotism that instructs an individual to produce in order to consume, to please others in order to be pleased by them, to love others in order to be loved by them, to work for others in order that they will work for him.

It is egotism that stimulates ambition and excites people to distinguish themselves in all the careers in which they exercise their strength, skill and intelligence. It is egotism that raises them to the heights of genius; it is in order to grow, to enlarge the circle of their influence, that people raise their heads and look into the distance; it is with a view to personal satisfactions that they march to the conquest of collective satisfactions. It is for themselves, as individuals, that they want to participate in the lively effervescence of general happiness; it is for themselves that they dread the sight of the suffering of others. It is for themselves, too, that they are emotional when someone else is in peril; it is to themselves that they are bringing help in bringing it to others.

Egotism, incessantly spurred by the instinct of progressive conservation and the sentiment of solidarity that links people to their peers solicits perpetual emanations of one's own existence into the existence of others. That is what the old society called, inaccurately, devotion, and which is nothing but speculation, speculation that is more humanitarian the more intelligent it is, the more humanicidal the more imbecilic it is. Humans in society only reap what they sow, malady if they sow malady, health if they sow health.

Humans are the social cause of all the effects to which they submit socially. If they are fraternal, they will effectuate fraternity on the part of others; if they are fratricidal, they will effectuate fratricide on the part of others. Humans cannot make a movement, an action of the hand, the heart or the brain, without the sensation reverberating from one to another like an electric commotion. And that happens in the estate of anarchic community, the estate of free and intelligent nature, as in the estate of civilization, the estate of domesticated humankind, of nature enchained. Except that in civilization, humans, being institutionally at war with other humans, can only be jealous of the happiness of their neighbors and howl and bite to their detriment; they are tethered dogs crouching in their niches gnawing their bone and growling with ferocious and continuous menace. In anarchy, humans, being harmoniously at peace with their fellows, are only able to compete in passions with others in order to arrive at the possession of universal happiness.

In the Humanisphere, a hive where liberty is queen, humans only collect perfumes from other humans, and only produce honey.

Let us, therefore, not curse egotism, for to curse egotism is to curse human being. The compression of our passions is the sole cause of their disastrous effects. Humans, like society, are perfectible. General ignorance has been the fatal cause of all our woes, universal science will be the remedy. Let us therefore educate ourselves, and spread education around us. Let us analyze, compare, meditate, and, moving from induction to induction, and deduction to deduction, let us arrive at the scientific knowledge of our natural mechanism.

In the Humanisphere, there is no government. An attractive organization takes the place of legislation. Sovereignly individual liberty presides over all collective decisions. The authority of anarchy, the absence of any dictatorship of number or force, replaces the arbitrariness of authority, the dispositive of the sword and the law. Faith in oneself is the whole religion of humanispherians. Gods and priests, religious superstitions, arouse a universal reproval among them. The Humanispherians do not recognize any kind of theocracy or aristocracy, but individual autonomy. It is by their own laws that everyone governs themselves, and it is on that universal self-government that social order is based.

Interrogate history, and see whether authority has ever been anything but individual suicide. Will you call "order" the annihilation of humans by humans? Is it order that reigns in Paris, Warsaw, Saint Petersburg, Vienna, Rome, Naples and Madrid, in aristocratic England and democratic America? I tell you, myself, that it is murder. Order with the dagger or the cannon, the scaffold or the guillotine; order with Siberia or Cayenne, with the knout or the bayonet, with the watchman's stick or the guardsman's sword; the order personified in the homicidal trinity of iron, gold and holy water; the order of rifle-shots, Bibles and banknotes; the order enthroned on cadavers and nourished thereon, is perhaps that of moribund civilizations, but it will never be anything but disorder and gangrene in societies that have the sentiment of existence

Authorities are vampires, and vampires are monsters that only inhabit cemeteries and only walk in darkness.

Consult your memories and you will see that the greatest absence of authority has always produced the greatest sum of harmony. Look at the people from the height of their barricades and say whether, in those moments of temporary anarchy, they do not testify by their conduct in favor of natural order. Among the men who are there, bare-armed and black with powder, there is certainly no lack of ignorant natures, men scarcely rough-hewn by the scraper of social education, and capable, in private life and as the heads of families, of many brutalities toward their wives and children. Look at them, then, in the midst of the public insurrection and in their quality as men momentarily free. Their brutality has been transformed as if by enchantment into mild courtesy. If a woman passes by they have only decent and polite words for her. It is with an entirely fraternal urgency that they will help her across the rampart of paving-stones. Those men who, while out walking on Sunday, would have blushed to carry their child and would have left the entire burden to the mother, take in their arms with a smile of satisfaction the child of a stranger in order to help her over the barricade. It is an instantaneous metamorphosis. In the man of the day you would not recognize the man of yesterday. Let Authority be re-edified and the man of tomorrow will soon revert to the man of yesterday.

Again, recall the day of the distribution of flags after February 1848. There was no gendarme or agent of public force in the crowd, larger than it had ever been at any fête; no authority "protected" circulation; everyone was, so to speak, their own security. Well, was there ever more order than in that disorder? Who was trampled? No one. Not one blockage. It was up to them to protect one another. The multitude flowed, compactly, through the boulevards and the streets as naturally as the blood of a person in good health circulates in their arteries. In humans it is malady that produces swelling; in multitudes, it is the police and the armed force; malady then bears the name of authority. Anarchy is the state of health of multitudes.

Another example:

It was in 1841, I believe, aboard a frigate of war. The officers and the commandant, every time he presided over the maneuvering, swore and raged at the sailors, and the more they swore, the more they raged, the more the maneuver was executed poorly. There was one officer on board who was an exception to the rule. When he was on watch, he did not say four words, and always spoke with an entirely feminine softness. No maneuver was ever better and more rapidly carried out than under his orders. If it was a matter of taking a reef in the topsails, it was done in the blink of an eye, and as soon as the reef was taken, as soon as the topsails were hoisted, the pulleys were fuming. A fairy could not have acted more promptly with the flick of magic wand. Even before the command was given, everyone was at his post, ready to climbs into the shrouds or slacken the halyards. They were not waiting for him to give the order but for him to permit the maneuver. And there was not the slightest confusion, not one knot forgotten, nothing that was not rigorously executed. There was enthusiasm and harmony.

Would you like to know the magical secret of that officer and the manner he adopted in order to operate the miracle? He did not swear, he did not rage, he did not command; in a word, he let things happen. And that was the best thing to do. Humans are like that; under the lash of authority, the sailor only acts as a brute; he goes stupidly or leadenly when he is shoved. Left to his anarchic initiative, he acts as a man, he operates with his hands and his intelligence.

The example I am citing took place aboard the frigate *Calypso* in the Oriental seas. The officer in question only remained aboard for two months; the commandant and officers were jealous of him.

So, the absence of orders is the true order. The law and the sword are only the order of bandits, the code of theft and murder that presides over the division of booty and he massacre of victims. It is on that bloody pivot that the civilized world turns. Anarchy is its antipode, and that antipode is the axis of the Humanispherian world

Liberty is their only government.

Liberty is their only constitution.

Liberty is their only legislation.

Liberty is their only regulation.

Liberty is their only contract.

Everything that is not liberty is external to mores.

Liberty, total liberty and nothing but liberty: such is the formula engraved in the tales of their consciousness, the criterion of all their relationships.

Is there a shortage in one corner of Europe of the products of another continent? The newspapers of the Humanisphere mention it; it is inserted in the Bulletin of Publicity, the monitor of anarchic universality; and the Humanispheres of Asia, Africa, America or Oceania expedite the product requested. Is there, on the contrary, a European product of which there is a lack in Asia, Africa, America or Oceania? The Humanispheres of Europe dispatch it. The exchange takes place naturally and not arbitrarily. If one Humanisphere gives more one day and receives less, what does it matter? Tomorrow it will doubtless receive more and give less. Everything belongs to everyone and anyone can change their Humanisphere as they can change their apartment. What does it matter, in the universal circulation, if something is here or there? What difference does it make? Is everyone not free to go wherever he wishes and bring to themselves whatever they want?

In anarchy, consumption aliments itself by production. A Humanispherian would no more understand a man being forced to work than a man being forced to eat. The need to work is as imperious in humans as the need to eat; a human being is not all stomach; he has arms and a brain, and obviously, it is to enable them to function. Manual and intellectual labor are the nourishment that enable him to live. If a human being had no more needs than the needs of the mouth and the stomach, he would no longer be a human being but an oyster, and then, instead of hands and the attributes of intelligence, nature would have given him, like the mollusk, two halves of a shell.

"What about indolence? What about sloth?" you shout at me.

O civilized, indolence is not the child of liberty and human genius, but of slavery and civilization; it is something filthy and unnatural that can only be encountered in old and modern Sodoms. Sloth is a debauchery of the arm, a torpor of the mind. Indolence is not an enjoyment, it is a gangrene and a paralysis. Only decrepit societies, doddering worlds and corrupt civilizations can produce and propagate such scourges. The humanispherians satisfy the arm's need for exercise as naturally as they satisfy the stomachs. It is no more possible to ration the appetite for production than the appetite for consumption. It is for everyone to consume and produce in accordance with his strength and his needs.

By curbing all human beings under a uniform retribution, one starves some and causes others to die of indigestion. Only the individual is capable of knowing the dose of labor that his stomach, his brain or his hand can digest. A horse in the stable is rationed; the master grants a domestic animal a fixed amount of nourishment; but at liberty, the animal rations itself, and its instinct offers better than the master what suits its temperament. Untamed animals scarcely know disease; having everything in profusion they no longer battle one another to pull up a sprig of grass. They know that the prairie produces more pasture than they can consume, and they graze it in peace alongside one another. Why do humans fight to snatch consumption from one another when production, by means of mechanical forces, could furnish more than they need?

Authority is indolence.

Liberty is labor.

Only the slave is indolent, rich or poor; the rich man is the slave of prejudice and false knowledge; the poor man is the slave of ignorance and prejudice. Both are the slaves of the law, one for submitting to it, the other for imposing it. It would not be the same for the free man. Would it not be suicidal for him to condemn his productive faculties to inertia?

An inert human is not human; he is less than a brute, for a brute acts in accordance with its means, obedient to its instinct. Whoever possesses a particle of intelligence can do no less than obey it, and intelligence is not indolence; it is fertile movement; it is progress. The intelligence of humans is their instinct, and that instinct says, incessantly: labor; put the hand and the head to work; produce and discover; production and discovery is liberty. Who does not labor does not enjoy. Labor is life; sloth is death; die or labor!

In the Humanisphere, property not being divided, everyone has an interest in being productive. The aspirations of science, thus rid of the fragmentation of thought, invent and improve communally machines appropriate to all purposes. By means of all the activity and rapidity of labor, an exuberance of production bursts forth around humankind. As in the earliest ages of the world, humans have no more to do than to reach out their hand in order to seize a fruit, no more to do than lie down at the foot of the tree to have shelter, except that the tree is now a magnificent monument in which all the satisfactions of luxury are found; the fruit is everything flavorsome that that the arts and sciences can offer.

That is anarchy, no longer in the marshy forest with miry idiocy and umbrageous bestiality, but anarchy in an enchanted garden, with limpid intelligence and smiling humanity. It is anarchy, no longer in weakness and ignorance, the nucleus of savagery, barbarity and civilization, but anarchy in strength and knowledge, the trunk and branches of harmony, the glorious blossoming of humanity in flower, of free human being, in the regions of the azure and under the radiation of universal solidarity.

Among the humanispherians, a man who can only handle a single implement, whether that implement be a pen or a file, would blush with shame at the mere thought. Human being wants to be complete, and is only complete on condition of knowing a great deal. The man who is only a man of the pen or a man of the file is a castrated individual, whom the civilized might well admit or admire in their churches or their factories, their workshops or their academies, but he is not a natural man; he is a monstrosity who would only provoke avoidance and disgust among the improved humans of the Humanisphere.

A human being ought to be simultaneously a thinker and an actor, producing by means of the hand as well as the brain. Otherwise, he sins against his virility, he forfeits the work of creation, and, in order to obtain a falsetto voice, he loses all the deep and moving notes of his free and vibrant instrument. A man is no longer a man then, but a canary.

A Humanispherian not only thinks and acts simultaneously, but exercises different métiers on the same day. He sculpts an item of jewelry and digs a plot of land; he passes from the graver to the spade, and from the kitchen oven to the music-stand. He is familiar with a host of tasks. An inferior worker in one, he is superior in another; he has his specialty, in which he excels; and it is exactly that inferiority and superiority of one toward another that produces the harmony.

It costs nothing to be submissive to a superiority, I do not say officially, but officiously, recognized, when a moment later, in another phase of production, that superiority becomes your inferiority. That creates a salutary competition, a benevolent reciprocity destructive of jealous rivalries. Then, by means of those various labors, humans acquire the possession of more objects of comparison, their intelligence is multiplied, like their arms; there is a perpetual and varied study that develops all physical and intellectual faculties, from which they profit in order to improve themselves in their actions of predilection.

I repeat here what I have noted previously: when I speak of human beings it is not only half of humankind that is in question but humanity entire, women as well as men. What applied to one applies equally to the other. There is only one exception to the rules, one labor that is the exclusive prerogative of woman, and that is childbirth and nursing. When a woman is accomplishing that work, it is perfectly simple that she can scarcely occupy herself actively with any other. It is a specialty that separates her momentarily from the plurality of general attributions, but, once her pregnancy and nurture are accomplished, she resumes her functions in the community, identical to those of all humanispherians.

At birth, a child is inscribed under the name and forename of the mother in the book of statistics; later, he takes of his own accord the name and forenames that suit him, keeping or changing those given to him. In the Humanisphere, there are neither disinherited bastards nor privileged legitimates. Children are the children of nature, not of artifice. All are equal and legitimate before the Humanisphere and Humanispherity.

So long as the external embryo is still attached to the teat of the mother, as the fetus is to the internal organ, it is considered as only being one with its nurse. Weaning is for the woman a second delivery, which is operated when the child can come and go independently. The mother and child can still remain together, if such is their wish, but if the infant, who senses the pressure of his petty will, prefers the company and the dwelling of other children, or if his mother, weary of a long brooding, does not care to have him constantly with her any longer, they can separate. The children's apartment is there, and no more lacking in care than any other, for all the mothers meet up there.

If, in the permutation of deaths and births, it happens that a new-born loses its mother, or a mother loses her child, the young woman who has lost her child gives her breast to the infant who has lost its mother, or the orphan is given the teat of a goat or a lioness. It is even customary among nursing

130

mothers to give a puny infant the milk of a vigorous animal to drink, such as that of a lioness, as it is among the civilized to give the milk of donkeys to consumptives.

(Let us not forget that in the era in question, lionesses and panthers are domestic animals; that humans possess flocks of bears as we possess flocks of sheep today; that the most ferocious animals are ranged, submissive and disciplined, under the human pontificate; that they crawl at human feet with a secret terror and bow down before the aureole of light and electricity that crowns the human head and imposes respect upon them. Humankind is the sun around which all the races of animals gravitate.)

The nourishment of men and women is based on hygiene. They adopt for preference the aliments most appropriate to the nutrition of the muscles of the body and the fibers of the brain. They do not have a meal without eating a few mouthfuls of roasted meat, whether mutton, bear or beef, and a few spoonfuls of coffee or other liquids that stimulate the sap of thought. Everything is planned so that pleasures, even those of the table, are not unproductive or injurious to human development and human faculties.

Among them, every pleasure is labor, and all labor a pleasure. The fecundation of wellbeing is perpetual there. There is a continuous spring and autumn of satisfactions. The flowers and fruits of production, like the flowers and fruits of the tropics, grow there in all seasons. As the banana tree is the little humanisphere that provides shelter and pasture to the negro child, the Humaniphere is the vast banana tree that satisfies the immense needs of free human beings. It is in its shade that they fills their lungs with all the gentle breezes of nature and, raising their eyes to look at the stars, contemplate all their radiations.

As one might imagine, there are no physicians—which is to say that there are no maladies. What is it that causes maladies today? The pestilential emanations of one part of the globe and, above all, the lack of equilibrium in the exercise of human organs. Human beings exhaust themselves in one unique labor, one unique enjoyment. One writhes in the contortions of hunger, another in the colics and hiccups of indigestion. One occupies his arm to the exclusion of his brain, the other his brain to the exclusion of his arm. The frictions of the day and the worries of the day to come contract the fibers, inhibit the natural circulation of the blood and produce interior cloacas that exhale withering and death. The physician arrives; he has an interest in disease, just as the advocate has an interest in crime, and he inoculates the veins of the patient with mercury and arsenic; of a temporary indisposition he makes an incurable leprosy that is communicated from generation to generation. One is horrified by a Brinvilliers,[13] but what is one Brinvilliers compared with the poisoners named physicians? La Brinvilliers only attacked the lives of a few of her contemporaries; they attack the life and intelligence of all men, including their posterity. Civilized, civilized, have academies of torturers if you wish, but do not have academies of medicine! Men of amphitheaters or scaffolds, murder the present if you must, but at least spare the future!

Among the humanispherians there is an equation in the exercise of human faculties, and that leveling produces health. That does not mean that they do not occupy themselves with surgery or anatomy. No art or science is neglected there. There is not a single humanispherian who has not studied them. Those laborers who profess surgery exercise their knowledge on an arm or a leg when an accident occurs. As for indispositions, as everyone has notions of hygiene and anatomy, they medicate themselves; one takes a spoonful of exercise, another

---

[13] The Marquise de Brinvilliers (1630-1676) was convicted of conspiracy to murder her father, on very poor evidence, and was widely rumored to have poisoned other people, on the basis of no evidence at all. Her conviction launched a scandal in which several other people were charged with poisoning and witchcraft, in the absence on any evidence whatsoever. Naturally, she became famous and is featured in numerous literary works based on fanciful renditions of her legend.

a draught of sleep, and the next day, as often as not, all is said and done; they are the most predisposed people in the world.

Contrary to Gall and Lavater,[14] who have mistaken the effect for the cause, they do not believe that humans are born with absolutely pronounced aptitudes. The lines of the visage and the contours of the head are not things innate in us, they say; we are all born with the seeds of all the faculties—save for rare exceptions; there are mental infirmities as well as physical ones, but monstrosities are summoned to disappear in Harmony—and external circumstances act directly upon them.

According to whether those faculties are or are not exposed to their radiation, they acquire a greater or lesser growth, shaped in one fashion or another. A person's physiognomy reflects their penchants, but that physiognomy is often quite different from the one they had as a child. The craniology of a man testifies to his passions, but that craniology often has nothing in common with the one he had in the cradle.

In the same way that a right arm exercised to the detriment of the left acquires more vigor, more elasticity and also more volume than its counterpart, to the extent that abuse of that exercise might render a man hunchbacked on one shoulder, so the exclusive exercise given to certain passionate faculties can, by developing the organs, render a man's skull bumpy. The furrows of the visage, like the bumps of the skull, are the blossoming of our sensations on our face, but are not original stigmata. The environment in which we live and the diversity of the points of view at which humans are placed, which means that they do not see things in the same aspect, explain the diversity of craniology and phrenology in humans as well as the diversity of their passions and aptitudes.

The skull in which the bumps are equally developed is assuredly that of the most perfect human being, but how many people in the present world are proud of their bumps and their

---

[14] Franz Gall (1758-1828) and Johann Lavater (1740-1801), the pioneers of physiognomy and what later became known as phrenology.

horns! If some learned astrologer in the name of that pretended science were to say that it is the sun that is escaping its radiation, not its radiation that is escaping the sun, trust me, he would find civilized persons to believe him and sub-professors to discuss the matter. Poor world! Poor educational bodies! Inferno of humans! Paradise of spice-merchants!

As there are neither slaves nor masters there, neither chiefs nor subordinates, neither property-owners nor disinherited, neither legality nor penalization, neither frontiers nor barriers, neither civil not religious codes, there are no longer any civil, military or religious authorities, nor abdicates, bailiffs, solicitors, notaries, judges, policemen, bourgeois, lords, priests, soldiers, thrones, altars, barracks, churches, prisons, fortresses, pyres or scaffolds; if there are any, they are preserved in alcohol, mummified in natural grandeur or reproduced in miniature, all arranged and numbered in some back-room of a museum, as objects of curiosity and antiquity.

Even the books of French, Russian, German and English authors, etc, etc. lie in the dust and the store-rooms of libraries; no one reads them; they are, in any case, written in dead languages. A universal language has replaced all those national jargons. In that language, one can say more in one word than could be said in ours in a sentence. When, by chance, a humanispherian takes it into his head to cast his eyes over pages written in the times of the civilized and has the courage to read a few lines, he soon closes the book with a shiver of shame and disgust, and, thinking about what humankind was in that epoch of Babylonian depravity and syphilitic constitutions, he senses a blush rising to his face, as a woman, still young, whose mouth has been soiled by debauchery, blushes after being rehabilitated, at the memory of her days of prostitution.

Property and commerce, the putrid affection for gold, the usurian malady, the corrosive contagion that infests contemporary societies with a virus of venality, and metalizes amity and amour: that scourge of the nineteenth century has disappeared from the bosom of humankind. There are no more sellers or sold. The anarchic community of interests has spread purity and health in mores everywhere. Amour is no longer a filthy traffic but an exchange of tender and pure sentiments. Venus is no longer the immodest Venus but Venus Urania. Amity is no longer a market trader caressing the purses of passers-by and changing honeyed words into abuse depending on whether one accepts or refuses his merchandise; he is a charming child who only requests caresses in exchange for his caresses, sympathy for sympathy.

In the Humanisphere, everything that is apparent is real, appearance is not a travesty. Dissimulation was always the livery of valets and slaves; it is required among the civilized. The free human being bears frankness, the escutcheon of Liberty, over the heart. Dissimulation is not even an exception among the humanispherians.

Religious artifices, the edifices of superstition, respond among the civilized, as among barbarians and savages to a need for the ideal for which those populations, not finding it in the world of the real, go in search in the world of the impossible.

Women especially, the half of the human race even more excluded than the other from social rights, and relegated, like Cinderella, to the corner of the household hearth, delivered to catechismal meditations and unhealthy hallucinations, abandon themselves with all the impetus of the heart and the imagination to the charm of religious pomp and spectacular masses, to all the mystical poetry of that mysterious romance of which the handsome Jesus is the hero and divine love the intrigue.

All those songs of angels and saints, that paradise filled with light, music and incense, that opera of eternity of which God is the great maestro, the decorator, the composer and the leader of the orchestra, those azure pews in which Mary and Magdalen, the two daughters of Eve, have places of honor; all that phantasmagoria of sacerdotal physicians cannot fail in a society to impress the sentimental fibers of women, compressed and always quivering, forcefully.

Their bodies chained to the kitchen oven, the shop counter or the drawing from piano, they wander in thought, without ballast or sail, without tiller or compass, toward the idealization of human being in the spheres, strewn with reefs and constellated with superstition, of the fluidic azure, in the exotic reveries of the paradisal life. They react by mysticism, rebel by superstition, against the degree of inferiority in which men have placed them. They appeal from their terrestrial abasement for celestial ascension, from human bestiality for divine spirituality.

In the Humanisphere, nothing similar can happen. A man is nothing more than a woman, and a woman nothing more than a man. They are both equally free. The urns of voluntary education have poured their streams of knowledge over their heads; the collision of intelligences has leveled their course. The flood of fluctuating needs raises that level every day. Men and women swim on that ocean of progress, linked to one another. The lively springs of the heart spread their heady and burning passions into society and make a flavorsome perfumed bath for the ardors of men and women alike. Amour no longer has anything in it of mysticism or bestiality; amour has all the voluptuousness of physical and mental sensation; amour is that of humanity purified, vivified and regenerated, humanity become human.

As the ideal is on Earth, present or future, why would you want to seek it elsewhere? In order for the divinity to float over the clouds of the imagination, there have to be clouds, and within the humanispherian cranium, there is only sunlight. Where light reigns, there is no darkness; where intelligence reigns, there is no superstition. Today, when existence is a perpetual maceration and claustration of the passions, happiness is a dream. In the future world, life being an expansion of all the passionate fibers, life will be a dream of joy.

In the civilized world there is nothing but masturbation and sodomy, masturbation or sodomy of the flesh and masturbation or sodomy of the mind. The mind is a sewer of abject thoughts, the flesh a cesspit of filthy pleasures. In present

136

times, men and women do not make love; they serve their needs. In the future there will be no need for them but that of love! And it is only with the fire of the passion of the heart, and with the ardor of the sentiment of the brain, that they will unite in mutual intercourse. Sensualities will no longer operate in any but the natural order, those of the flesh as well as those of the mind.

Liberty will have purified everything.

After having visited in detail the buildings of the Humanisphere, where everything consists of workshops of pleasure or salons of labor, storehouses of sciences and the arts and museums of all productions; after having admired the machines of iron powered by steam or electricity, laborious mechanisms which are to the humanispherians what multitudes of proletarians or slaves are to the civilized; after having witnessed the no-less-admirable movement of that human mechanism, that multitude of free laborers, a serial mechanism of which attraction is the sole motor; after having observed the marvels of that egalitarian organization whose anarchic evolution produces harmony; after having visited the fields, the gardens, the meadows, and the rustic hangars whose roofs serve to shelter the flocks wandering the countryside and whose lofts serve for the storage of grain and forage; after having traveled all the railways lines that furrow the interior and the exterior of the Humanisphere, and having navigated in the magnificent aerial steamers that transport people, products, ideas and objects with the flight of an eagle from one humanisphere to another, from one continent to another and from any point of the globe to its extremities; after having seen and heard, having palpated with the fingers and thought all these things, how can it be, I said to myself, on returning to the civilized, that one can live under the Law, that Knout of Authority, when Anarchy, that law of Liberty, has such pure and mild mores? How is it that one regards that intelligent fraternity as something so phenomenal, and this fratricidal imbecility as something normal?

137

Oh, phenomena and utopias are only phenomena and utopias in relation to our ignorance. Everything that is phenomenal for our world is something quite ordinary for another, whether it is a matter of the movement of planets or the movement of people; and what would be most phenomenal for me is if society were to remain perpetually in social darkness and not awaken to the light. Authority is a nightmare that weighs upon the breast of human beings and stifles them; let them hear the voice of Liberty, let them emerge from theirs dolorous slumber, and they will soon have recovered the plenitude of their senses and their aptitude for work, for amour, and for happiness!

Although, in the Humanisphere, the machines do all the heaviest labor, there are, in my opinion, some labors that are more disagreeable than others, and there are even some that seem to me unlikely to be to anyone's taste. Nevertheless, those labors are carried out without any law or regulation constraining anyone. *How can that be?* I said to myself, having only as yet seen things through my civilized eyes. It was, however, quite simple.

What is it that renders work attractive? It is not always the nature of the work but the conditions in which it is carried out and the condition of the result to be obtained. In our day, a worker goes to exercise a profession; it is not always the profession he would have chosen; hazard more than attraction has decided it thus. If that profession procures him a certain relative ease, if is salary is high, if he deals with a boss who does not make his authority felt too heavily, that worker will accomplish his work with a certain pleasure. If, subsequently, the same worker labors for a churlish boss, if his salary diminishes by half, if his profession no longer procures him anything but poverty, and he will henceforth only do with disgust the work that he formerly accomplished with pleasure. Drunkenness and indolence have no other cause among workers. Slaves at the end of patience, they throw in the towel and, rejects of society, wallow in the lees and the dirt, or, if they are elite characters, they rebel to the extent of murder or martyrdom, like Alibaud,[15] like Montcharmont,[16] and lay claim to their human rights, iron against iron, face to face with the scaffold. Immortality or glory for them!

In the Humanisphere, the few labors that appeared to me to be repugnant by nature nevertheless found workers to carry them out with pleasure, and the cause of hat was the conditions in which they were exercised. The different shifts of workers were recruited voluntarily, as the men at a barricade are recruited, and are entirely free to remain there as long as they wish, or to pass on to another shift or another barricade. There is no entitled or appointed leader. The person who has the most knowledge or aptitude for that work naturally directs the others. Everyone takes the initiative mutually, in accordance with his recognized capacities. By turns, each of them gives advice or receives it. There is an amicable understanding, there is no authority. Furthermore, it is rare for there not to be a mixture of men and women among the workers in a shift Thus, the work is done in conditions too attractive, however repulsive it might be in itself, for there not to be a certain charm in carrying it out.

Then there is the nature of the result to be obtained. If the work is, in fact, indispensable, those who find it the most repugnant and who abstain from it will be delighted that others have taken charge of it and will subsequently render them, in affabilities and laborious attentions, compensation for the service that has been rendered to them.

It ought not to be thought that among the Humanispherians, the heaviest labors are the share of inferior

---

[15] Louis Alibaud (1810-1836) was a soldier guillotined for attempting to assassinate Louis-Philippe, and was hailed by radicals as a martyr.

[16] Claude Montcharmont (1822-1851) became famous as the "poacher of Morvan" when his execution for two murders was initially botched and had to be rearranged, briefly becoming the focus of protests against the death penalty by Victor Hugo and others.

intelligences; on the contrary, it is the superior intelligences, the luminaries of science and the arts, who most often take pleasure in shouldering those burdens. The more exquisite the delicacy of a man is, the more developed his moral sensibility is, and the more apt he is, at certain moments, to rude labors, especially when those labors are a sacrifice offered to the love of humanity.

I have seen, during the June transportation, at the Fort du Homet in Cherbourg, delicate natures who would have been able, in return for a few coins, to have a co-detainee take their turn on fatigues—and it was filthy work empting the buckets of ordure—but who, to give satisfaction to their moral enjoyment and internal testimony to their fraternity with their fellows, preferred to do that work themselves and spend at the canteen, with and for their shift-companions, the money that could have served to free them from it. The veritably human man, the egotistically good man, is happier doing something for the benefit it procures others than dispensing with it in view of an immediate and entirely personal satisfaction. He knows that it is a seed sown in good earth, from which he will sooner or later obtain an ear of corn.

Egotism is the source of all the virtues. The first Christians, those who lived in community and fraternity in the catacombs, were egotists; they placed their virtues at usurious interest in the hands of God in order to obtain the premiums of celestial immortality. The humanispherians place their good actions in an annuity with Humanity, in order to enjoy, from birth to death, the benefits of mutual assurance. Humanly, one can only purchase individual happiness at the price of universal happiness.

I have not yet talked about the costume of the humanispherians. There is nothing uniform about it; everyone dresses as they wish. There is no particular fashion. Elegance and simplicity are its general characteristics. The distinction is primarily in the cut and equality of the fabrics. A blouse, with pagoda sleeves, linen for work, woolen or silk for leisure; Breton culottes or trousers, wide or tight-fitting but always narrow at the bottom, with boots lined above the trousers or light buskins in varnished leather; a round felt hat with a simple ribbon or a single feather, or a turban; the neck bare as in the Middle Ages; and the decorations of the chemise protruding from the blouse at the neck and the wrists: such is the costume most commonly adopted.

The color, the nature of the fabric, the cut and the accessories are essentially different. One person allows the blouse to float, another wears a sash around the waist, or a pouch in leather or cloth suspended from a steel chain or a leather strip, dangling over the thigh. In winter, one man envelops himself in a cloak, another a burnoose.

Men and women wear the same costume indifferently, except that women generally substitute a skirt for the trousers, ornament their blouse or tunic with lace, their wrists and neck with artistically sculpted jewelry, and devise hairstyles that show of their facial features to their best advantage—but none of them think it graceful to pierce their nose or their earlobes order to pass gold or silver rings through them or attach precious stones thereto. A considerable number wear long dresses whose multiplicity of forms is infinite. They do not seek to imitate one another but to differentiate themselves from one another.

It is the same for the men. Men generally wear a full beard and long hair with a parting on top of the head. They find it no more natural or less ridiculous to shave the chin as the head; and in their old age, when the snow of age has blanched their head and blurred their sight, they no more pull out the white hairs than they pluck out their eyes.

They also wear many variant costumes, those of the Louis XIII era among others, but none of the masculine costumes of our era. The balloons in which the women of our day navigate are reserved for the aerial steamers, and the stovepipes in linen or black silk that serve as head-dresses are the prerogative of chimneys. I do not know that there is a single man among the humanispherians who would want to make himself ridiculous in a frock-coat or bourgeois suit, the livery of the civilized. There, one wants to be free in one's movements and that a costume should testify to the grace and liberty of its wearer. The majesty of a simple and lose pleat is preferred to the puffy stiffness of a crinoline ad the epileptic grimace of a frock-coat with the head of a cretin and the tail of a cod.

The habit, a proverb says, does not make the monk. That is true in the proverbial sense, but the society makes its habit, and a society that dresses like ours denounces, like the chrysalid in its shell, its ugliness as a caterpillar to the light of the eye. In the Humanisphere, humankind is far from being a caterpillar; it is no longer a prisoner in its cocoon; its wings have grown and it has donned the ample and graceful tunic, the charming coloration and the elegant wingspan of the butterfly.

Taken in the absolute sense, the envelope is the man; the physiognomy is never a mask for whomever knows how to interrogate it; the moral always pierces the physical—and the physique of the present society is not beautiful; how much uglier its morality is!

In my excursions, I had not seen a cemetery anywhere, and I was wondering where the dead went, when I had the opportunity to witness a burial.

The dead man was lying in an open coffin that had the form of a large cradle. He was not surrounded by any funereal appearance. The petals of natural flowers were strewn in the coffin and covered the body. The uncovered head rested on bouquets of roses that served it as a pillow. The coffin was placed in a carriage; those who had known the deceased particularly well took their places behind it. I followed suit.

Having arrived in the country, and a place where an iron machine was standing on granite steps, the train stopped. The machine in question had an appearance similar to that of a locomotive. A drum or cauldron was set on a blazing fire. The cauldron was surmounted by a long piston-cylinder. The cadaver was taken out of the coffin, wrapped in a shroud, and then slid through a drawer-like opening into the drum. The brazier was responsible for reducing it to powder. Each of the witnesses then threw a handful of rose-petals on to the flagstones of the monument. A hymn was sung to universal transformation. Then everyone went their separate ways. The dead man's ashes were subsequently scattered like fertilizer on to agricultural land.

The humanispherians claim that cemeteries are unsanitary, and that it is preferable to sow the dead in fields of wheat than tombs, given that wheat nourishes the living and marble crypts can only impede their regeneration. They do not understand funerary prisons any more cellular tombs, the detention of the dead any more than the detention of the living. It is not superstition that makes the law among them, but science. They have only reason, and no prejudices. For them, all matter is animate; they do not believe in the duality of the soul and the body; they only recognize the unity of substance—except that the substance acquires thousands upon thousands of forms, more or less coarse, more or less purified, more or less solid or more or less volatile.

Even if the soul were distinct from the body, they say—which everything denies—it would still be an absurdity to believe in its individual immortality, in its eternally compact personality, its indestructible immobilization. The law of composition and decomposition that rules bodies, which is the universal law, must also be the law of souls.

In the same way that the heat of the caloric of water vapor condenses in the brain of a locomotive a constitutes what might be called its soul, in the hearth of the human body, the seething of our sensations, condensing in vapor inside our skull, constitutes our thought and sets in motion, with all the electric force of our intelligence, the gears of our corporeal mechanism. But does it follow that the locomotive, a finite and in consequence perishable form, has a soul more immortal than its envelope? Certainly, the electricity that animates does not disappear in the impossible nothingness, any more than the palpable substance in which it is clad disappears—but at the

143

moment of death, as at the moment of existence, neither the boiler nor the vapor can conserve their exclusive personality.

Rust corrodes iron, vapor evaporates; bodies and souls are incessantly transformed and disperse in the entrails of the earth or on the wings of the wind, in as many particles as the metal or fluid contained molecules—which is to say, infinitely, the molecule being for the infinitesimal what the terrestrial globe is for humans: an inhabited world in movement, an aggregation animated by imperceptible beings susceptible of attraction and repulsion, and in consequence of formation and dissolution.

What makes life, or, which is the same thing, movement, is the condensation and dilatation of the substance elaborated by the chemical action of nature. It is the alimentation and ejection of vapor in the locomotive, of thought in the human being, that activates the pendulum of the body. But the body is worn away by friction; the locomotive goes to the scrap-yard, the human to the tomb. That is what is called death, which is only a metamorphosis, since nothing is lost and everything takes on new form under the incessant manipulation of attractive forces.

It is recognized that the human body renews itself every seven years; it replaces us molecule by molecule. From the soles of the feet to the ends of the hair, everything has been destroyed, particle by particle. And one would like the soul, which is nothing but the summary of our sensations, something like their living mirror—a mirror in which the evolutions of that world of the infinitely small whose whole is called a human being is reflected—not to be renewed from year to year, and from instant to instant; that it should lose nothing of its individuality in exhaling itself without, and acquire nothing of the individuality of others in respiring their emanations? And when death, extending its breath over the physical, a finite form, comes to disperse the debris to the winds and distribute the dust in the furrows, like a semen that bear within itself the germ of new crops, one would like—what vanity and absurd inconsequence on our part!—that breath of destruction to be unable to break the human soul, a finite form, and disperse its dust over the world?

In truth, when one hears the civilized boasting about the immortality of their soul, one is tempted to ask whether one is confronted by knaves or brutes, and one ends up concluding that they are both.

We throw the ashes of the dead, say the humanispherians, as pasture to our cultivated fields, in order to incorporate the more rapidly in the form of aliment and this have them reborn more promptly to the life of humankind. We would regard it as a crime to relegate a part of ourselves to the depths of the earth, thus to retard the advent of the light. As there is no doubt that the earth exchanges emanations with other globes, and in the most subtle form, that of thought, we have the certainty that the purer human thought is, the more apt it is to exhale toward the spheres of superior worlds. That is why we do not want what belongs to humanity to be lost to humanity, in order that those residues should pass once again into the alembic of human life, an alembic ever more perfected, acquiring a more etheric property and passing thus from the human circulus to a more elevated circulus, and from circulus to circulus to the universal circulation.

The Christians, the Catholics, eat God for love of the divinity. The humanispherians take the love of humanity as far as anthropophagy; they eat humans after their death, but in a form that has nothing repulsive about it, in the form of a host—which is to say, in the form of bread and wine, meat and fruits, in the form of aliments. It is the communion of human to human, the resurrection of cadaveric remains to human existence.

It is better, they say, to revive the dead than to weep for them. And they activate the clandestine work of nature, abridging the phases of the transformation, the peripeties of the metempsychosis. And they salute death, like birth, the two cradles of a new life, with celebratory songs and perfumes of flowers. Immortality, they affirm, has nothing immaterial about it. The human being, a body of flesh, luminous with

145

thought, like all suns, dissolves when it has furnished its career. The flesh is filtered and returned to flesh; and the thought, light projected by it, radiates toward its ideal, decomposes in its radiation and adheres thereto.

Human being sows human being, harvests it, kneads it and appropriates it by nutrition. Humanity is the sap of humanity, and it blossoms within it and exhales it, a cloud of thought or incense that roses up toward better worlds.

Such is their pious belief, a scientific belief based on induction and deduction, on analogy. They are not, to tell the truth, believers, but seers.

I traveled all the continents, Europe, Asia, Africa and Oceania. I saw many diverse physiognomies, but I only saw one and the same race everywhere. The universal crossing of Asiatic, European, African and American (the red-skinned) populations; the multiplication of all by all, has leveled all the asperities of color and language. Humankind is one.

There is in the gaze of any humanispherian a mixture of softness and pride that has a strange charm. Something akin to a cloud of magnetic fluid surrounds his entire person and illuminates a phosphorescent aureole about his head. One senses oneself drawn toward him by an irresistible attraction. The grace of his movements adds something more to the beauty of his form. The speech that flows from his lips, imprinted with suave thoughts, is like a perfume that he emanates. Statuary could not model the animate contours of his body and his visage, which borrow from that animation harms that re ever renewed. Painting could not reproduce his eyes and the enthusiastic and limpid thought therein, full of languor or energy, mobile aspects of thought that vary like the mirror of a clear stream in its calm or rapid course, and always picturesque. Music could not model his speech, because it could not attain its indescribable melody. He is the idealized human being, bearing in his form and movement, in his gesture and gaze, in his speech and thought, the imprint of the most utopian perfectibility.

In a word, he is a human being become human.

Thus has appeared to me the ulterior world; thus has unfurled before my eyes the sequence of time; thus has harmonic anarchy been revealed to my mind: the libertarian society, the egalitarian and universal human family.

O Liberty! Ceres of anarchy, you who labor the bosom of modern civilizations with our heel and sow revolt there, you who prune the savage instincts of contemporary societies and graft on to their stems the utopian thoughts of a better world, hail, universal fecundatrix, glory to you! Liberty, who bears in your hands the sheaves of tomorrow's crops, the basket of the flowers and the fruits of the Future, the horn of plenty of social progress, hail and glory to you, Liberty!

And you, Idea, thank you for having permitted me the contemplation of that human paradise, that humanitarian Eden. Idea, lover always beautiful, mistress full of grace, houri, enchantress, for whom my heart and my voice quiver, for whom my eye and my thought only have amorous gazes; Idea, whose kisses are the spasms of happiness, of, let me live and die and live again in your continual embraces; let me take root in the world that you have evoked; let me develop in the midst of that human flower-bed; let me bloom among all those flowers of men and women; let me collect myself there and exhale the scents there of universal felicity!

Idea, pole of amour, magnetic star, attractive beauty, oh, remain attached to me, don't abandon me; don't plunge me back from the future dream into the present reality, from the sun of library into the darkness of authority; enable me no longer to be only a spectator but an actor in the anarchic romance of which you have given me the spectacle. O you, by whom miracles are operated, make the curtain of the centuries fall back behind me, and let me live my life in the Humanisphere and humanispherity!

Child, Idea says to me, I cannot grant you what you desire. Time is time, and there are distances that thought alone can cross. Feet adhere to the ground that has seen them born; the law of gravity dictates that. Remain, therefore, on the ground of civilization like a calvary; it is necessary. Be one of the messiahs of social regeneration. Make your speech shine like a sword; plunge it, naked and sharp, into the bosom of corrupt societies, and strike at the heart of the ambulant cadaver of Authority.

Call to yourself the little children and the women and the proletarians, and inform them by predication and example, of the claim they have to the right of individual and social development. Confess the omnipotence of the Revolution, all the way to the steps of the barricade, all the way to the platform of the scaffold. Be the fuse that ignites and the torch that illuminates. Pour bile and honey on the harsh and the oppressed. Wave in your hands the standard of ideal progress and provoke free intelligences to a crusade against barbaric ignorance. Oppose truth to prejudice, liberty to authority, good to evil.

Human errant, be my champion; throw down to bourgeois legality a bloody challenge; fight with the rifle and the pen, with sarcasm and the paving-stone, with the head and the hand: die or...

Human martyr, socially crucified, bear with courage your crown of thorns, bite the bitter sponge that the civilized put in your mouth, let the wounds in your heart bleed; it is that blood of which the sashes of free humans will be made. The blood of martyrs is a fecund dew; let us shake its drops over the world. Happiness is not of this century, it is on the Earth that revolves on its axis every day in gravitating toward the light; it is in future humankind.

Alas, you have yet to pass through the filter of many generations, you have yet to witness many deformed attempts at social reformation, and many disasters, followed by further progress and further disasters, before arriving in the promised land and before all the -cracies and the -archies have given way to an-archy. People and peoples have yet to break and reconnect their chains many times before casting the last link behind them.

Liberty is not a prostitute who gives herself to all comers; it is necessary to win her by means of valiant ordeals, necessary to render oneself worthy of her to obtain her smile. She is a great lady proud of her nobility, because her nobility comes from the head and the heart. Liberty is a chatelaine who is enthroned at the antipode of civilization; there she will convey humankind. With steam and electricity the distance is abridged. All roads lead to that goal, and the shortest is the best. Revolution is laying down its iron rails there; people and peoples, go!

The Idea has spoken; I bow down...

Fernand Giraudeau: *The New City* (1868)

PROLOGUE

Man agitates.

Cruel Doubt!

For more than thirty years, uncertain, tossed and dragged hither and yon, I have been wandering, without knowing my route, over the somber and stormy ocean of politics. What direction ought I to take? Which of the thousand currents that push or pull humankind should one follow? Is it necessary to try to stop in one's course? Is it necessary to go back, or to precipitate more rapidly forwards? Where are the generations headed? Where will these eternal and terrible struggles end?

If I cast a glance over the history of human destinies, how petty the greatest men seem to me! What are they? Not even immortals! How many kings and heroes have filled the world with the noise of a name of which only a worn stone conserves the unknown characters today! The memory of men of genius: pale and feeble glimmers that float momentarily, agitated and capricious, above the great necropolis of people, then to vanish forever!

And what are the peoples themselves? Obscure crowds who are born, multiply, eat and drink, fabricate, sell, fight, make laws and break them, love, believe, pray and are dissipated, bequeathing the earth a few edifices that time takes charge of burying.

That is the spectacle. Where is the philosophy therein? What is the law of these frightful hecatombs?

Theocracies, Oriental despotisms, Republican aristocracies, feudalisms, tempered monarchies, democracies, demagogies: all these ephemeral forms have their goals and rejections by turns; all of them are stages; none is a terminus; none can last—and when the series is exhausted, the indefatigable world retraces its steps and recommences the process. Are we going round in circles? Is the human species subject to an eternal back-and-forth movement?

What is the best of societies? Is it one that marches to grandeur and glory by way of arms, letters, sciences and arts? Is it one that encloses in its bosom the greatest number of materially contented individuals? Or is it the one that tends to make people virtuous and to distract them by religion from the miseries of this world? Perhaps it is all of those at once. Is what is necessary to direct people here or there, or anywhere at all, even by oppressing them, or to let them wander at their whim, even if they will perish sooner? Is the best society the most vigorously constituted, or the one in which the individual is almost disengaged from any obligation toward his fellows?

Is the most civilized the best? Alas, civilization is not indefinite: Egypt and Greece were as civilized as one another, but differently, and they succumbed nevertheless, as we shall succumb. Civilization and progress, alas, are no more the goal of humankind than barbarity and regression: the world belongs to them by turns.

But is one society better than another? Are not all states good, or at least indifferent? Is not the most important thing simply *to be*? Does the manner in which people *are* signify anything?

Yes, *to be*, that is to what humanity appears condemned: incessantly to die and always to live again.

You will always transform and always exist, rocks, trees, humans, societies and stars: such is your destiny.

Why?

Chapter I

The living go quickly.

I feel a finger placed imperiously on my shoulder. I raise my head.

It's Graymalkin.[17]

"Come," he says.

I follow him, and we go downstairs.

Scarcely have I crossed the threshold of my dwelling than I stop, stupefied.

It was no longer my Rue de Ixe. The one in which I found myself did not resemble it at all.

To either side the houses rose up to such a height that, in spite of the width of the causeway, one would have been plunged in obscurity if the gas had not been burning by day as well as by night. That black and permanently damp street, where the sunlight never penetrates, was formed by constructions in bricks and iron that had twenty-five floors. They were all built on the same model, and not a single ornament cheered up their sad façade. Considered as an ensemble, they had the air of an immense barracks or monstrous factory, which made their destination dubious. No simulacrum of an edifice or monument broke the implacable monotony of their long somber mass. They were dirty, and nothing indicated that anyone was responsible for seeing that they were not. Heaps of filth accumulated outside every door, exhaling miasmas. That imprisoned atmosphere was stifling, dense and poisonous, and

---

[17] Grimalkin, or Graymalkin, is an old English name for a cat, apparently first featured in print in William Baldwin's prose narrative *Beware the Cat* (1570), from which the person who wrote the witch scene in the printed version of *Macbeth* (published 1623) presumably borrowed it; because of that usage it became a common appellation for a witch's familiar demon.

the sky seemed very high. At the extremity of the street one glimpsed others exactly similar.

Was that part of the city animated, properly speaking? I cannot say. There was a bewildering movement there, in the midst of a deathly silence. No pedestrians, no horses, no carriages: a multitude of little vehicles moved by steam or some other physical force, carrying one, two or three people, circulating with an almost vertiginous rapidity. To the extent that I could glimpse them in their evolutions, the visages of all the passers-by, among whom there was not a single woman to be seen, were singularly fatigued, wan and thin. The universal expression was that of lassitude preoccupation, worry, harshness and egotism.

On looking into that place—I almost said into the depths of that abyss—at that pale and fantastic light formed by gaslight and the reflection of a few rays from above, on seeing those mysterious shadows hurrying as if drawn by a fatal force, I wondered momentarily whether I did not have before my eyes the damned, accomplishing some strange punishment of which people on earth have no idea.

"Deceptive spirit," I said to Graymalkin, "to what new illusion are you delivering my senses?"

"None, this time," he told me, in his habitual glacial tone. "You've slept for a hundred and thirty years and I've just woken you up. Look and learn."

"I've slept for thirty minutes!" I exclaimed. "And you've made me take some narcotic that has permitted you to transport me I know not where. Where am I?" I added, stamping my foot. "I want to know."

"In the seventh city."

"What's the seventh city?"

"It was once Paris, but nowadays the cities, like the streets and the houses, are designated by numbers. The number one belongs to the most populous city. At present, that's San Francisco; Panama is number two, Montevideo number three; Yeddo is the fourth city."

"That's not picturesque; it's even rather cold."

"It's more *utilitarian*," said Graymalkin, dryly, "than all those baroque names of which no one even knew the meaning."

"And less clear as an appellation; it can vary from day to day or year to year—but no matter. What is New York's rank?"

"It's the twenty-second city."

"Impossible! What's the fifth, then?"

"Port Said."

As I was about to ask what extraordinary series of events had caused the greatest cities to fall to that extent, while others had overtaken them, Graymalkin took me into a kind of untidy office, at the door of which a man was standing, handing out announcements to the passers-by. He was the telegraph clerk. His functions were limited to counting the clicks of the apparatus that the sender of the dispatch transmitted himself, and collecting the money. He did all that with his ears and one hand, while he was distributing with the other. Time is precious. It was also in application of that maxim that he was operating with one foot I know not what machine, at the summit of which a poor child about four years old was perched, pale and unsteady, and working with difficulty.

I might perhaps have made that the subject of observations to the clerk, but Graymalkin, who had sat at the apparatus and was making it function, was speaking to me.

"I'm telegraphing," he said, "to person 85, number 4, street 26, city 3, nation 2—which is written 85, 4, 26, 3, 2."[18]

"What!" I said. "Friends are numbered too!"

---

[18] Author's note: "The author coincides here with a recently-published ironic article. Between the two images there is, however, the essential difference—not to mention others—that one represents the mania for numbers as a monarchic excess, whereas, on the contrary, it is one of the ridiculous tendencies that are appropriate to popular regimes and is beginning to carry away certain Republican States; thus, in New York, the streets to not have names, but bear numbers."

"Everything is numbered."

"Like veal-calves?"

"There are no more names today; there are a hundred numbers, from 1 to 100. Everyone has a number, and no forenames."

"Only a hundred names? But that must give rise to inextricable confusions."

"There's sometimes a little confusion, but that doesn't matter; it's simpler. It's more *utilitarian*."

"Oh yes?"

The dispatch had gone. Graymalkin took a piece of paper from his pocket, which he said was worth 320 francs, the price of the telegram."

"It's America, then, the second country?"

"No, it's Germany."

"And that costs 320 francs?"

"That's not much."

"Damn!"

"One the one hand, money is worth four times less than it was in your time, and objects of acquisition cost four times as much; things are therefore eight times as expensive.[19] On the other hand, the telegraph companies have an understanding, and it's take it or leave it, because they're free to fix their prices and I'm free not to send dispatches."

"Free, free! If there are no other companies, and if they have the right to raise their tariff infinitely, why has the State given them the concession…?"

"There is no concession. We're all free; everyone does what they want."

"Or what their neighbor wants, when there's no competition."

"Haven't I just sent my dispatch myself? That's liberty."

"Of course. You're perfectly correct."

---

[19] The fact that Graymalkin does not say sixteen might well be attributable to diabolical arithmetic.

He was getting up in order to pay when a man raced into the office, knocked him off his chair, sat down in his place and started the apparatus going, without worrying in the least about what harm he might have done. I was indignant.

"Monsieur," I said, moving closer to him. "I desire to know whether you knocked my friend over deliberately."

No response; impassively, he continued to click away. I grabbed his arm, in spite of the intervention of Graymalkin, who seemed desirous of letting the matter drop. Jabbing his elbow into my stomach, the boor sent me sprawling in a corner, and said to me at the same time, without turning his head: "Imbecile foreigner. Broken arm? Dislocation? Bumped head? Will pay."

All that was accomplished in less than a minute, and yet Graymalkin had had time to pick me up and prevent me from leaping on the fellow.

"You don't understand," he said.

"What! I don't..."

"No. He's in a hurry, that's all."

"Of course! I don't doubt it."

"Well, it's necessary to make way for him. If he's injured us, he'll pay."

The man in a hurry had finished his dispatch. He paid for it and ran outside, shouting: "17, 15, 3."

"That's his address," said Graymalkin. "There's nothing to say."

"Nothing to say! You'll see,"

And I ran after Monsieur 17. But he was already far away. I stopped, and Graymalkin, having caught up with me, explained that what had just happened was not contrary to custom, and that similar things happened every day to everyone, because time is money.

Besides, he added that I was free to do as much to anyone else. "We're all free."

"By the way," I said, "What proof do I have that that clown is really citizen 17?"

"It's embroidered on his hat. Every citizen has to have his name and address on his hat."

"Has to? That's not liberty."

"It's order."

"Ha! Liberty has its limit, then? Liberty is sometimes sacrificed to order here? That's no mistake."

Graymalkin shoved me under a hangar filled with the mechanical vehicles I saw in the streets. He chose one of them, climbed into it and made me sit down beside him, received a ticket bearing the address of the hangar, had his own address inscribed there by the clerk, along with the time at which he was taking the smashall—that is the name of the vehicles—and we left. Graymalkin explained to me that when we arrived at our destination we would return the smashall to an office of the company and pay on presenting our ticket. There were smashall offices at every street corner.

We slid over the ground with a speed equal to that if locomotives, and I was admiring the dexterity with which everyone steered their vehicles, and sureness of eye with which they avoided one another, when a loud scream rang out. It was ahead of us; one of the smashalls in front of us had run over a child.

To my great surprise, no one stopped. The smashall driver who was the author of the accident had continued on his route without slowing down for an instant, and those who separated it from us contented themselves with making a detour as they approached the unfortunate child, who, with both legs broken and his head injured, was writhing bloodily on the ground, making vain efforts to get up.

That indifference revolted me; I told Graymalkin to stop, and that I wanted to help the poor child. He increased speed and laughed at me, saying that it was not customary, and that it was the concern of the child, and his mother at most. I nearly hit him. I contained myself, however, resolved to discharge my anger on the person who had done the damage. I seized the handle of the smashall and, launching it at top speed, found myself, after turning a corner, level with the ill-fated vehicle.

"Since there are no police in this street," I cried, leaning out of my seat and seizing the individual by the collar in spite of all Graymalkin's efforts, "I'll arrest you myself."

I then received a furious punch, but as I had not let go, counting on the scuffle assembling the passers-by and attracting a policeman, a regular battle commenced. The two smashalls stopped; we got out and boxed in earnest.

After a few minutes, during which no one paid the slightest attention to us, being equally weary of having obtained no result, we concluded a tacit armistice in order to catch our breath.

My adversary immediately took out his wallet and inscribed therein the numbers borne on my hat, which was still in my vehicle.

"Good day," he said, then. "Seized by the collar; forced to stop for quarter of an hour; forced to box. Damages and interests. Dirty, dirty. Good day. Are we continuing?" And he put himself on guard again.

I did the same—but Graymalkin addressed my adversary. "Imbecile foreigner," he said, indicating me.

"Imbecile foreigner! Thought sent by competition to cost me business. No matter: will pay, will pay. Dirty, dirty."

He bounded into his smashall and departed like an arrow. I was unable to follow him.

Then I turned against Graymalkin, and asked him what he meant by "imbecile foreigner." He told me that the designation was not personal, but that in this country foreigners were despised to such an extent that they were always thus designated.

We resumed our route, and he explained to me on the way that in the seventh city, like all the rest, no one occupied himself with anyone else's affairs, because one had enough of one's own, and because everyone was responsible for his own actions. An accident only concerned the person who was its author and the one who was its victim. "The damage is charged to one or the other, according to the share they had in it. The law regulates all that. There's a tariff; it's so much for a contusion, so much for a blow that draws blood, so much for a fracture, so much for a punch, a blow with a stick, a stab with a knife. There's a fixed price."

"As among our ancestors the Franks, so renowned for the advanced state of their civilization."

"As for the child," Graymalkin continued, "If he has no one interested in him, to whom does it matter whether he's wounded, suffers or dies? It only concerns him; it's therefore up to him to get himself out of it. On the other hand, it's absolutely certain that the citizen whom you molested so ardently has thrown his number to the child; with the consequence that, if the accident was his fault, he'll indemnify the latter. As for you, as he said, you lost him a quarter of an hour with no reason. And you struck him. You'll pay, pay, and are dirty, dirty."

"Well, you've brought me to a nice society! So that child might remain there until another smashall runs over him?"

"Perhaps."

"Great God what about the police? Aren't there any?"

"Very few. There are as many as are needed to carry out judgments. You keep forgetting that we're free, and want to stay that way. It's our strength, our superiority, our pride and glory. Oh, we're a very great people."

"Thank you. And who apprehends thieves?"

"Pooh! Thieves!"

"Why *pooh*?"

"What does that have to do with the State? If you're robbed, it's your fault. Either you're carrying precious objects on your person and, as innocent as an imbecile foreigner, have forgotten the risks you're running and haven't taken precautions in consequence, or you've come out without having locked your door securely enough, or without having locked your valuables in a strong enough, complicated enough, heavy enough safe—how do I know? One is always the accomplice of one's thief. You're not five years old, damn it! Why should anyone protect you? You ought not to be in tutelage; make arrangements; defend yourself. We're free and responsible; that's what makes our grandeur."

"Under the law of the revolver, then? And what about murderers—does anyone occupy themselves with them? Would it be in poor taste to inhibit the liberty of their industry, or make observations to them?"

"Pooh!"

"Pooh again! Oh, it's too much. One is the accomplice of one's murderer, then? But in truth, in truth..."

"Calm down. You haven't seen anything yet."

Chapter II

Nothing any longer differs from liberty
but absolute liberty.

In the depths of the black streets of the seventh city, by the dreary gaslight, I did indeed see many other things.

The boiler of one of the steamboats traveling along the Seine exploded and a hundred people disappeared into the river; I was told that it was not necessary to budge, that it was their affair; and that there is, in any case, a rescue company that has an interest in helping the victims of the frequent accidents of that sort. They have a very simple manner of proceeding; they haul you half way out of the water and tell you the price that it will cost you to be pulled out entirely; if that price is not agreeable to you, they let go of you and go to make the proposition to someone else.

"And those murders are tolerated?" I protested.

"Those suicides are certainly tolerated. It's necessary to respect the liberty of transactions."

The river is spanned by twenty bridges covered in twenty-five story houses; in their great funereal shadow the water seems to flow like ink or bitumen. If an arch collapses with a dozen houses, do you think that anyone moves a muscle? No. No one says: "Poor people!" Everyone chants: "It's their own fault; why were they living on a bridge? Why did they rent rooms in houses under threat? Doubtless because the rents were cheaper by virtue of the danger, so they accepted the risk. The chances for and against what happened have their weight in the subsequent deliberation into which the tenants decide to enter, and the discussion of prices that takes place with the landlord. Everything therefore happens very fairly."

"And the police don't enquire as to whether the houses are tottering on their foundations?"

"No. We want, and we have, the least government, the least administration and the fewest police possible. That's our adornment."

However, I saw one man being dragged away by agents of the public force. *That*, I said to myself, *must be a great criminal; he's done more than commit murder.* I asked by what sin he was soiled. The reply was that he was a pauper. Paupers are virtually the only criminals that are pursued here. Poverty only results from idleness or incapacity; the man who is poor out of idleness has doubtless weighed up the balance-sheet of the advantages and inconveniences of working or not working; he has made his choice; that is his business, but society owes him nothing. If he is incapable, as he is useless, it rejects him.

"But there are intelligent and willing people who can't find work."

"No, if they can't find any, it's because they don't know how to look for it, so they aren't intelligent."

"But what about the infirm?"

"Oh, you can understand that it's not my fault, as an individual, or ours, as the State, if some citizen is missing an arm."

"What about charity?"

"Suppressed."

"Fraternity, then?"

"Oh as to that, it's a joke—a hollow word with which people wanted to replace charity. One doesn't replace a sentiment, one kills it; that's what we've had the glory of doing; it was neither virile, nor rational, nor utilitarian. No sentiment is, in fact; they're all absurd; they're all contrary to the reason that ought to guide us."

"So be it. What do they do with those unfortunates?"

"Take them to the frontier—if they get that far, for one doesn't take responsibility for nourishing them on the way."

"So, *starve, dog* is the law?"

"No, it's *useless dog, go starve somewhere else.*"

I soon saw dogs that had been killed.

We went into a factory.

Harnessed to machines that were working relentlessly were young children, boys and girls, and adolescents of both sexes, all in rags. Pale, etiolated, debilitated, dolorously sad and haggard, the wretched creatures were working like automata, without zeal, without intelligence, but regularly; and if one of those specters occasionally made a mistake or stopped momentarily, exhausted, the machine itself, by virtue of a new improvement, showered him with blows that he could not escape.

I asked why the two sexes were together. The reply was that that was liberty.

I asked how long the law permitted those unfortunates to be forced to work. The reply was that the law no longer limited the hours of children's labor, that it no longer protected apprentices, and that that was liberty.

It was added that their mortality rate was high.

Chapter III

*Almost all those who say that they are liberals,
pass for such, and form the party of liberty,
have tyrannical instincts and make tyrannical laws.*

"What is the condition of women in this atrocious country?" I asked Graymalkin as we left.

"They don't work."

"Oh! Much better. Men are sufficient to procure the means of existence of their companions?"

"Pooh! It's forbidden for women to work."

"Damn! But that isn't liberty, is it? No matter; doubtless the legislator wished them to be entirely devoted to the duties of the hearth?"

"Oh, it isn't the hearth that hinders us. The truth is that the labor of women depreciated that of men and lowered the wages of workers."

"But that's abominable! So, a woman who isn't married, or a widow with several children, or the wife of a man who is ill, injured or mutilated, can do nothing to earn bread?"

"No, nothing."

"But then...?" I said, looking Graymalkin full in the face.

"Yes," he replied, with some slight embarrassment. "One resource remains to them."

"Great God! Infamy of infamies!"

"It's dinner time," he replied, coldly. "You can judge the condition of women for yourself."

We went into an immense room, dazzling with electric light and magnificently decorated, albeit in very poor taste. It had the form of a theater, and, indeed, I was in a kind of theater.

Facing me was the stage. Instead of stalls and boxes, there was a series of elliptical steps, broad enough to carry tables all around their perimeter, each accompanied by a padded sofa and a rocking chair, in order that the customer could choose and alternate, and a footstool so that he could stretch his legs. Those items of furniture were upholstered in cerise satin, and the wood was gilded. The room was hung everywhere with cerise satin embroidered with gold, heightened with fringes, torsades and tassels of the same metal.

On every table there was linen, crystal, silverware—what am I saying? splendid gold-plate—and flowers. At each end, a powdered domestic dressed in sumptuous livery stood motionless.

On every sofa a woman in a splendid ball-gown was sitting, resplendent with jewels.

On going in, everyone chose a table.

Everyone arrived at the same time; all business finished at the same time and the spectacle began with the meal.

First there were conjurers, to whom little attention was paid. Then came singers of both sexes, intoning ditties whose lewd words and gestures were welcomed with fervor. Acrobats were applauded, especially tightrope-dancers. Wrestlers attracted serious attention. A fantasy play whose words and music—what music!—were lost in the noise of conversations, for everyone was talking or shouting as he pleased, was a great success because of a singular ballet danced by ballerinas in outrageously short and transparent skirts. But the greatest success, a frenetic success, was for the living tableaux; they were strange groups of men and women in leotards, some clad in waistbands and others only enjoying sashes. I turned my eyes away in disgust.

After that saturnalia, everyone retired with his table-companion; the restaurant-theater was also a hotel and contained an enormous number of regally-furnished rooms.

We finally left, Graymalkin having told me that after the spectacle he would settle up with the women with whom we had dined and that we would go home.

Scarcely had we climbed into a smashall than he exclaimed: "What a life! What a great existence! To empty the cup of pleasures every evening in a single draught! Imagination, amour and the table! And what luxury! What splendor! At the same time, what equality! Did you not see, at the first table to the left of ours, the citizen whose footwear was allowing his dirty toenails to be seen? He was a hat-maker; he's one of the most distinguished citizens. And two tables further on, that jacket with holes at the elbows: he's a millionaire and a former minister."

"Yes," I replied, pensively, "Those fellows had very black hands, a very bad odor, and behaved like street-porters."

"Noble simplicity, my friend, noble simplicity; frank and sincere manners; a casual attitude that puts everyone at ease. Everyone does as he likes; people get up, circulate, talk, lie down, put their feet on the table, smoke, spit anywhere. O Liberty, Liberty! Thou art in our mores and in our laws! What you used to call politeness is only constraint, abasement, degradation and lies. As for costume, you'll encounter tomorrow those you saw so badly dressed today in black suits and covered in golden chains, with three rings on every finger."

"How much did that orgy cost?"

"Three thousand francs all in, my friend—which is about 375 francs in 1868 currency. Oh, damn it, that's why we work so hard during the day; we only live to savor enjoyments."

"And everyone has the means to procure them."

"Many can. They give themselves to it until they're ruined, after which they start making their fortune again."

"And while they're remaking it where do they dine?"

"There are hotel-theaters for all purses.

"No one dines at home, then?"

"No one. Life has become too dear; it's necessary to live communally. Then again, household chores take too much precious time from business."

"What about the family, though? Women and children?"

"The children are brought up by the women, their mothers. As for the women, as you can see, they're not troublesome."

"But what about society and socialites? The rich? The middle class?"

"Oh, my God, there's no more of that. Everyone is rich today and poor tomorrow. Fortunes are made and unmade by the minute. One is only a capitalist momentarily. There are no more private incomes. The heredity of wealth has been abolished."

"So all the women are like those I've just seen?"

"All of them. Obviously, since they can't work."

I uttered a roar. "And no one gets married anymore?"

"In a way, yes. One sees people coming back for months to sit at the same table with the same woman. Some have been seen to keep the same companion for years. That's as if they were married, isn't it?"

"Exactly. Look, shut up, wretch; I don't want to hear another word."

Chapter IV

The houses, all constructed on the same plan, as I said, were rectangular; every floor had only four rooms, two overlooking the street and two on the other side; one penetrated into those fifty apartments, made up of a study or drawing-room and a bedroom, by means of a lift, the cage of which was in the middle of the house and whose compartment had four doors coinciding with those of the rooms on every floor. The elevator went up and down automatically every minute, with the result that any tenant returning home did not have to wait long to reach his apartment.

The elevator's compartment was fitted with divans. It was sitting on one of them that I found myself in front of my door. Graymalkin stopped the apparatus by means of a button that he pressed. We went into my apartment. Graymalkin pressed another button and the elevator continued on its route.

I was not too badly installed from the viewpoint of comfort. A good bed, a good settee, the eternal rocking-chairs, stools, a toilet-commode, a few mushroom-wardrobes, curtains, door-curtains and carpets furnished one of the rooms; in the other was a desk and four rattan chairs; that was obviously the room in which one treated affairs, the other being for repose. Gas lit my lodgings day and night.

Even so, the apartment had something unpleasant about it and I felt ill-at-ease there. The banal character—which is to say, the lack of character—of the furniture, the total absence of taste that I glimpsed in whoever had decorated my abode, was antipathetic to me. There were colors in the wallpaper and fabrics that clashed, designs, lines and forms that offended the eye. There had been no preoccupation with anything but adequacy; the beautiful, the elegant and the agreeable had not been taken into consideration: no works of art, and no ornaments of any kind; no cornice, no moldings, no patterns. One had a clear sense that it was only a pied-à-terre, in which one treated affairs and slept, but in which one did not live.

Such were, however, without exception, the dwellings of all the inhabitants of the seventh city. No one, even multimillionaires, had more than two rooms. In fact, without wives, without children, without friends, without receptions, without meetings, what would anyone have done with a third? In all the houses, on all the floors, the furnishings were invariably the same; what did it matter? Affairs by day and the hotel-theater in the evening—that was the life of these people.

I rediscovered there the same thinking that I had observed in their clothing: no taste, no rules, no formality, no research and no care. One put on the first garment that came to hand, provided that it was comfortable, and warm or cool, depending on the season. Whether it was ugly or beautiful, whether it went well or badly, whether it was new or old, clean or dirty, one did not worry about it. One abandoned it by caprice or kept it until it fell into tatters. One only wore ready-made garments. One obtained complete costumes from stores that sold boots, shoes, hats, caps, shirts, ties, waistcoats, jackets, trousers, overcoats, etc. of all qualities at all prices.

That was what I was told by Graymalkin, who wished me goodnight after having told me that I would have to brush my own clothes the following morning.

Service was organized as follows: a certain number of domestics were lodged in each house; at fixed hours, after the departure of the tenants, the elevator deposited the in the rooms and they "did the housework," as one says. When they came home, the people who possessed two costumes would find their clothing for the following day brushed and their shoes polished. The others took care of it themselves. One never saw those omnibus domestics, whose wages were included in the price of the rent, which was invariably 19,000 francs.

Chapter V

I woke up with the impression that bad dreams had haunted me all night.

After lighting my gas I was taking a bitter pleasure in re-constructing them when I heard my door open. A convention-ally clad individual came straight in, his hat on his head. I was ill-disposed, and was about to make a rather dry observation when he addressed me as: "Imbecile foreigner..."

I responded with a sharp slap that laid him on the floor, after which he got up and we boxed. I soon perceived that I was dealing with a man whose muscles had not received either from labor or gymnastics the strength that exercise provides. The whiteness of his hands confirmed that opinion. It was in conformity with the facts, because I soon mastered my adver-sary. When he had asked for mercy I invited him to sit down.

"Why did you hit me?" he asked.

"Because I don't like being called an imbecile foreigner, and won't suffer it, even though it seems to be a commonly used appellation in your ignoble country."

At those words my visitor seemed struck by amazement; his eyes widened, his mouth opened very wide and his arms fell. I was told subsequently that that extreme astonishment was certainly due to the fact that no inhabitant of the seventh city had ever imagined that his country might not be the object of universal enthusiasm.

I passed on, and, Graymalkin having come in, the con-versation proceeded. I shall mitigate the bizarre language, al-most pidgin, that my two interlocutors spoke.

"What does he want?" I asked Graymalkin.

"Is worker, so does little; wanted to profit from his free time to make grandeur of our institutions stand out to your eyes, to polish you, form you, educate you, to reveal to you what imb...foreigners need to know."

"To form me in his image, the clown? Thanks. Just ex-plain to me what you meant by the words: 'He's a worker, so does little?'"

"Easy. Today, finally, workers content: work very little."

"Oh! He has a meager salary, then?"

"On the contrary. Little work, high wages. Once had ancient laws—of 1863 on coalitions, of 1867 on societies—in virtue of which workers were sure of being paid according to efforts and capability, at the just value of their effort and their time. But that ended up displeasing; just value wasn't enough; more than value, ten times value—that was wanted. What did they do? Had good laws passed permitting them to organize, and organized.

"So, in every workshop, were associated by subscription to oppose employer; all workshops of all industries associated between them; all industries of all cities and all countries, associated together to master employers. All workers of Europe organized with leaders and enormous subscriptions. Result: if an employer refuses to double his workers' salaries when it seems good to them, the leader, by virtue of his discretionary power, secretly condemns him to death and has the sentence executed by one of them.

"If any worker refuses to associate, to demand double salary like his comrades, the leader has him expedited the same way. They've had good laws made to avoid any obstacle to the functioning of that organization."

"But, brigands that you are," I said, turning to the worker, who did not appear to understand me, "if one of your comrades, needy, burdened by children, without any savings, judges that it's in his interest to work for the simple salary, or if he feels that the simple salary is an equitable remuneration for his labor, and that, in any case, to double it would be to make it impossible for his employer to meet his costs, make the withdrawals due to his own personal labor his acquired knowledge and connections, which are anterior labor, and to his capital, which is accumulated labor, and, finally, his risks; if, as I say, one of your comrades understands that, for his employer, after doubling his salary, to have a interest in working, he would have to raise the price of his product, which would result in a reduction in consumption, which might lead to the ruination of his industry; if, satisfied, just, sane and prudent, comprehending his own interests—of which, in any case, he is the sole judge—he refused to take part in your absurd and hideous machinations..."

"To death!" said Graymalkin. "It's not a matter of all, or a majority, being importuned by a minority, or even the converse. It's not a matter of being just. It's a matter of obtaining higher salaries. Besides, have arranged all that. Firstly, children, that's no inconvenience; secondly, doesn't matter whether labor, capital and risks of employer are remunerated, whether sells or not..."

"What! Doesn't matter? But he'll close his establishment and they'll all be out on the street."

"No, by virtue of the new law; no employer may close his establishment; losses or not, he must provide work for his workers, or at least pay them well—very well."

"Then bankruptcy is forbidden?"

"No, but in case of failure, all the assets go to the workers; the other creditors go hungry. When circumstances of that sort occur, most of the time the workers can go for a few months without working, with good money in pocket. Thus have double reason for demanding increase in salary: to receive it and to ruin employer."

I was more astonished than my worker had been a few minutes before. I sought to take account of the new economic situation that was taking shape in my mind.

"But what becomes, in the presence of your organization and your laws," I said, "of the liberty of the individual and the free play of offer and demand?"

"Liberty? Obliged to sacrifice it on these points. No despotism has ever existed more absolute, more energetic, more cruel and more mysterious than that of the leaders of workers' organizations. With regard to them, workers and employers are slaves, and they have the right of life or death over them."

"Another thing: if salaries are exaggerated, the prices of manufactured objects must be too; now, if the prices of all products are raised by fifty per cent, and if salaries are only raised by fifty per cent, the situation of the salaried remains the same; they're no richer, since with the additional money they only but the same quantity of things."

"Are rich," said the artisan, "because, exempt from direct taxes and indirect taxes are reimbursed to us on evidence of consumption."

"Damn! You've maneuvered well! But then, everyone must want to be a worker."

"Yes, but impossible; our corporations don't admit anyone who hasn't been a member for a year."

"One isn't free to be a worker, then?"

"No; our number is diminishing every day, and we're all the better off for it."

"For as long as it lasts. Industry and the other classes of society must find it less satisfactory. Now, let's sum up, and tell me if I've understood correctly. The workers alone fix the level of their salary. The employer complies with their demands under penalty of death. Every worker is obliged to belong to a union and to obey them in everything, under penalty of death. Whether the employer makes a profit or not, he can't withdraw from business. If he goes bankrupt, his assets are divided between the workers alone. The workers are exempt from all taxation. No one can be a worker who hasn't been one for a year."

"Exactly," said Graymalkin. "In addition, the hospitals and other beneficial establishments are now only open to workers. Charitable institutions only exist for them. Long live the workers! I'll add that every worker who has worked for fifteen years receives a retirement pension from the State of ten thousand francs."

"Right—the equivalent of twelve or fifteen hundred of old, that is? So, they've arrived at constituting an aristocracy; they're a determined number of individuals who have invested themselves with the first of privileges and are exempt from the principal social burden. They're freed of all charges without ceasing to participate in the advantages; on the contrary, they have advantages that the rest of the community pays for but doesn't enjoy. And in addition to the question of taxes, in order for them to gorge themselves with money, it's necessary for the mass of consumers to pay exaggerated and artificial prices for everything, which vary according to their whim and their rapacity. In sum, they have the right of life and death over everything that impedes the functioning of the odious abuses they've introduced, and doubtless over everything else that displeases their caprice."

"That's it, precisely," said Graymalkin.

"In that case, accomplice of murderers and oppressor of the people," I said to the artisan, "Go away. I know enough."

And I threw him, utterly astonished, into a passing elevator.

"Oh, I'm not surprised that there are no capitalists here, nor private incomes, no rich class or middle class; if big companies are treated by their employees as the small employers are, what advantage is there in accumulating capital? There's only one thing to do, and that's to devour it; in any case, since there's no more family... But I can't see anything in all this but the acute crisis of a nameless dementia. This state of things can't last a year. Industry, mortally afflicted in its outgoings by high prices, in its production by the idleness and avarice of the workers and the horrible situation of entrepreneurs—only equaled in history by that of the curiales of the fourth century of the Roman Empire—equality destroyed and the people pressured to the profit of a single class, a regime of terror practiced by that class against the others and its own members..."

"That," said a voice behind me, "is only one of the aspects of our social edifice."

"Citizen 3," Graymalkin told me.

I invited the respectable old man in question to sit down, and, the conversation having led us on to that terrain, I asked him to explain to me the situation of the clergy.

172

Chapter VI

It is necessary to worship God or a pebble.

"The situation of the clergy is quite simple," he told me. "You know what it was in the nineteenth century. About 1950, it was decided to apply the formula: a free Church in a free State. The aim was to take away the meager salary that the State gave it; in return, and with a certain justice, it was freed from the interdictions imposed on it. The people who did that were sincere, but their successors were astonished by the results of those measures and soon reacted against some of them.

"The piety of the faithful, taking advantage of the full entitlement that had been returned to them to dispose of their wealth in favor of the Church, had soon endowed it richly by buying the basilicas and chapels back from the State and the cities, and then maintaining them with magnificence; the communities flourished no less. On the other hand, the government had withdrawn from education in favor of more simplicity, and in the name of I don't know what theories of liberty and non-intervention in the affairs of 'private individuals'—as if education were not a matter of public interest—and, the University having ceased to exist, France, almost in its entirety, confided its children to the clergy.

"Now, they accepted the formula as so many propositions, but not, it appears, with regard to its effects. And soon, in the name of liberty, it was forbidden to the rich and poor alike to give the Church a million or a sou; as for that which it already possessed, it was taken away.

"But that would not have mattered if they had not simultaneously forbidden the fathers of families to lead their children to priests or monks, and forbidden Catholics to practice their religion in public—which is to say, anywhere except, as the law of 1978 put it: 'a closed location of which nothing reveals externally the destination.' One no longer even had the right to put a cross on the door of the house of God.

"Alas, in a comparatively short time, that put paid to our temples, resplendent with hangings, paintings, statues, flowers and light, and an immense throng of people. Once, sublime songs celebrated the glory of the Lord, and people prayed with fervor. People believed then; they thought about their salvation; they strove to do good; they were occupied with their neighbor, helped him and loved him; and children were brought up in those views.

"Today, the only kinds of worship tolerated are those of the minority, because no one fears them—but why fear ours? At any rate, they too share our sad condition, and are also being abandoned...

"But no," he went on, animatedly. "We're reaching the end of our troubles; the excess of evil will soon kill the evil itself. The people will not be able to live for much longer in paganism and decadence. Business, money and the theater-hotel are no longer sufficient for them; they'll soon demand the faith of their fathers; they'll be hungry for a Church; the women will resume their place, and their role; wives and mothers will be seen again, hearths and families, and a hundred million French people will render thanks to God in our cathedrals, restored to worship. France was born Catholic, and will die Catholic, if it ever does,"

"God hears you, citizen!" said Graymalkin. "In the meantime, however, it's lanist."

"Indeed," replied 3. "And that's the result of our antireligious laws and our skepticism. Hoping, loving, praying and believing are innate human needs. They require an object. Remove God, and we worship fetishes or korrigans. Our sentiments and our thoughts, gone astray, without a guide or a goal, wander at random, until, fatigued, discouraged, desolate and fearful of the surrounding darkness, we hurl ourselves in pursuit of the first appearance that comes along. With what joy we greet it! How beautiful we find it! It seems to be exactly what we were seeking! It will console us; we shall have a traced path henceforth; the void in our soul will be filled. And who will then be powerful enough to snatch away the chimera that will be doing us so much good? We attach ourselves to it with all the more obstinacy the vainer it is and less acceptable to common sense; for, born from us, or at least only existing by virtue of an effort of our will, we cherish it as a mother loves a feeble and deformed child.

"That is why, in the nineteenth century, when there were already a large number of irreligious minds; magnetism, somnambulism, turning and speaking tables, rappers and spiritism found followers—I ought to say victims, for those unfortunates, limited and debilitated, who allowed themselves to go to those aberrations rapidly fell into the ranks of monomaniacs. That is also why, in our day, the French, prey to a folly of the same nature, are lanists."

"What are lanists?" I asked, after a moment's silence, during which we had both delivered ourselves to the train of our thoughts.

"This is what," he replied, smiling. "Two principles dominate their doctrine. The first is that matter does not perish, but is only transformed. The second is more debatable; there is a bond so tight between the soul and the body, say the lanists, that while one functions the other is modified. Thus, when I walk, my soul enters into a certain state corresponding to that of my body; and when I think, my body is also modified. The latter modification consists of a certain fluid emanating from the head, the seat of thought, or the breast, the seat of sentiments; that fluid, composed of immaterial and material elements, has the property—this is our second principle—of attaching itself by means of its material part to the first material objects that it encounters, and of retaining its immaterial part, which is an emanation of thought or sentiment, there.

"It is also imagined that if certain objects are habitually exposed to the fluid, they will be more apt than others to assimilate it, and to be saturated by it.

"One small accessory law than it is necessary not to neglect is that the assimilation in question is eternal; the part of the object that has received the fluid on the one hand, and the material or immaterial particles of the fluid on the other, will never be separated once united, and however small the particles are into which the object is divided, each fraction will retain the totality of the thoughts and sentiments that the emanation has imparted to the object in question.

"That posited, what are the objects that will first be called upon to receive the nousthymic fluid? Our clothes, evidently.

"Well, let us suppose now that you have in your hands a fragment of the helmet of Alexander or Napoléon I's frockcoat. You have at your disposal a large quantity of the sentiments of one and the other.

"Manner of making use of them: here another law intervenes; nousthymic fluid is transmissible. To infuse yourself with the sentiments of Caesar or Socrates, place a fragment of their coiffure on your head, or a filament of their mantle over your stomach. Isn't that a rather simple discovery of transcendental physiology?

"But, you might say, how can one procure an old section of Louis XIV's braid, or a piece of the lining of Charles V's doublet?

"One doesn't procure them; one encounters them in nature, since matter cannot perish—admire the unshakable logic of that reasoning and the solidity of the conclusion.

"Then, you might say—but there is no question so artful that doctors of Ianism cannot reply to it—how does one know that one is in the presence of a molecule of the mantle of Charlemagne, since it has probably been transformed?

"In only one manner, evidently—everything here is evident; one knows it by virtue of feeling it Thus, you have upon you, combined chemically with the fabric of your overcoat, an atom of the tunic of Ptolemy the Flute-Player;[20] what results therefrom? That the nousthymic fluid, your person and the Ptolemaic atom that is in your overcoat combine; the sentiments of Ptolemy that exist in a latent state in your overcoat

---

[20] The Egyptian king Ptolemy XII Auletes (117-51 B.C.), the father of Cleopatra VII (the famous one).

pass into your heart, and you immediately acquire a liking for the flute. Reciprocally, because all this is mathematical, if you are gripped one day by a passion for the flute, it is because you have some particle of Ptolemy Auletes in your clothing.

"And that," he added, after a pause, "is where we are."

"And why lanists?"

"*Lana*, wool; that is in the clothing most of the time, and in consequence, it is in cloth, in wool, that the thoughts of great men wander."

"Alas," we said, in unison.

Chapter VII

> *It is science that has developed industry,*
> *and has give it power and grandeur;*
> *industry will kill science, and the death of*
> *science will lead to the ruin of industry.*

"Fortunately," I said, "in default of religion, you have science, which must necessarily contain reason in its deviations, and react against the action of simpletons and charlatans."

"Oh, science! Ask the doctor for news of that. I'm expected elsewhere. Adieu."

I escorted Three to the door and hastened to welcome the man who had just come in, and whom Graymalkin introduced to me as Doctor 82.

He was a small man of the most common appearance, with the least intelligent physiognomy. He had deformed and frightfully callused hands. Seeing that they attracted my attention, Graymalkin told me, aloud, that the doctor was also a shoemaker.

"Yes," said the latter, "when I have no visits or consultations, I make boots. It's my principal métier. Furthermore, I've only been a physician for six months."

"What! In six months you've been able to complete all your studies?" *Here*, I thought, *is a man of genius.*

"Studies?" he said, in a puzzled one. "What studies?"

"You've been able to pass your examinations and obtain your diplomas?"

"Examinations? Diplomas? What are you talking about?"

Graymalkin came to his aid. "The profession of medicine is free. Anyone can exercise it from one day to the next. It's liberty: liberty for me to choose that genre of labor; liberty for you to confide or not to confide your health to one person or another."

"Well, that's reassuring. Be ill, then! But how can a shoemaker draw up a prescription? Doubtless he takes one from his bag at random—the liberty of prescriptions?"

"Prescription?" said the doctor-cum-bootmaker. "Here."

And he took a stout book out of his pocket, which he handed to me. It was a kind of dictionary, sufficiently methodically divided. In the first column, under the rubric *Essential Symptoms* I read the words: fever, palpitations, syncope, coughing, headaches, chest pains, stomach aches, etc., inflammation in the eyes, nose, lips, neck, arms, etc., insensibility, insomnia, redness, pallor, etc., etc. The second column and the third were entitled *Complications*, and contained further series of algic manifestations. In the fourth, narrower, column were found the names of the maladies corresponding to the various combinations of symptoms indicated in the preceding columns. To each malady corresponded, in general, four treatments under the rubrics: man, woman, child, old person.

The consultation of a physician and all of medical science consisted of observing one, two or three symptoms, of searching in the book called *Medicine* for the malady to which the isolated symptom or the combined diagnoses responded, and prescribing the treatment—masculine, feminine, juvenile or senile—indicated in its regard. Every word of the book was numbered, in such a fashion that if one had symptoms 921, 453 and 72, that indicated malady number 10,044, which was treatable by the same number and you said: "Have prescription 10,044 made up." After which one sent someone to the pharmacist to ask for remedy number 10,044—and one was cured...or got worse, by the mercy of God.

"So," I said, "that's the whole of the science? No more theories, no more principles, no more research: a formula."

"Exactly," said Graymalkin. "No more verbiage, no more pedantry, no more boring and obscure treatises laboriously engendered by some and laboriously studied by others, no more studies, no more schools—but the result of the experience of centuries condensed in a portable manual of which everyone in the world has the right and the capacity to make use. How simple it is! How practical it is! Oh, it's a great utility! A child could treat two hundred people in a day; he only needs the time to transport himself from one to another. Oh, what a great people we are!

"When I think that all careers are as free as those of bootmaker and physician, that anyone, from one day to the next, without being tyrannically summoned to furnish proofs, without having been enclosed within the narrow limits of a program and an examination, can be by turns, at his whim, a general, a domestic servant, an engineer, a street-porter, a painter, an architect, a cook, a notary, the proprietor of a hotel-theater, a judge, a banker, an acrobat, a gendarme, a writer, dancer or professor, I'm enthused! No more shackles on talent! A universe blossoming. Utilitarianism! Utilitarianism! That's what makes us so great, great, great, great, great!"

"Great! Great! You mean to say greatly ignorant. What! Anyone, if he 's clever, a good talker, if he knows how to impose himself, can contrive to be given responsibility for building a house, provided that it doesn't collapse, or to pierce a railway tunnel, on the same condition. Is there, perchance, also a manual for constructing bridges and highways?" (Graymalkin nodded affirmatively.) "Can one exploit mines by means of a collection of formulae of which the key, the meaning, the scope, the principles and the demonstration have been lost?" (Graymalkin repeated the gesture.) "Can one judge without knowing the law with the aid of a few order numbers whose ensemble is called Justice?" (Again.) "Can one teach if one doesn't know the meaning of the word education?" (Still the same.) "Well, you're following a ridiculous path. Oh, you call that great, great? Servitor.

"What about the scientific bodies? The Observatoire, the Institut, the Facultés? And History, and Philosophy, and Pure Science? Finished, all that, no doubt; suppressed, the books, the great monuments of human thought—paper, paper, isn't it? And you think that applied science can continue to exist without having pure science alongside it, which sustains it every day, animates it, amends it, transforms it, enriches, renews and develops it, which puts it in confrontation every day with new needs that are born every day? You think that Science reduced to practice won't deviate and perish more rapidly? You don't know that the higher the viewpoint, the more one can see? In sum, that one only understands the detail when one possesses the ensemble? You're unaware, finally, that the most elevated theories and laws are the framework of which practices are only the temporary and changing vestments, and that everything crumbles irredeemably if one neglects the interior edifice? Well, you're just barbarians!"

I had spoken. I made a signal to the shoemaker to go away. He informed me first that I had the symptoms impatience and anger, and malady 15,302: cost, 300 francs for the visit.

The empiricist having gone, Graymalkin explained to me, in order to close the incident, that malady 15,302 was one of the two thousand new afflictions that had been added to the ancient ones in the last hundred and thirty years for humans to experience. Those novelties derived from the way of life people led: from the depths, the obscurity and the dampness of the street, to the perpetual glare of gaslight inside and outside houses, to the feverish activity of diurnal life, to the pleasures of the evening and a multitude of inventions that flourished—artificial meat, for existence.

(A word of explanation here: agriculture being much neglected and livestock being in short supply for many years, meat had been replaced in the butchery by a composition of

180

old leather and softened and depilated hides, which were not essentially healthy or nutritious.)

Chapter VIII

Science and rationalism, the full development of industry and industrialism, have killed art and poetry.

The Arts and Letters were not flourishing any more than Science. The description I have provided of the hotel-theater and the amusements that are encountered there, should have given a foretaste of the state in which they are found in the seventh city. An account of a visit that Graymalkin enabled me to make to a factory making paintings and statues and one manufacturing books will complete that summary notion.

The factory making paintings and statues was immense, and to see the multitude of people working there, and the activity they were deploying, one might have thought that one was in a city fanatical about art. That was not exactly the case.

The paintings were manufactured by steam-power, like cloth, footwear and bolts. Powerful machines produced thousand of paintings every day on canvas, wood and textiles of all kinds: silk, calico and batiste for women's dressing-gowns, chemises or handkerchiefs.

Those compositions were all conceived in the same order of ideas. One did not see those great epic pages, of sublime scenes borrowed from Religion, Fable, History or War, which transport the spectator into a superior sphere and put them in the presence of superhuman actions, and divine or heroic characters who elevate, enlarge and purify the soul, at the same time as they console it and extract it from the realities of this base world.

One did not encounter those marvelous combinations of grandiose palaces, dazzling fêtes, magnificent fabrics, golden vases of flowers, men full of strength, women radiant with youth and beauty and children like cherubim, which show us

181

life not as it is but as it might be, which remake our desires at will, which give substance to our most cherished but least plausible dreams and render them verities.

There were none of those vast views of the sea and mountains that show infinity, woods and fields, which bring calm and repose; none of those episodes of spring verdure, foliage reddened by autumn, cheerful streams, melancholy lakes or somber torrents that make one pensive.

The joys of the family were absent too: young mothers did not cradle their infants; laborers did not trace furrows while thinking of the evening to come; there were no oaths of love, betrothals or baptisms.

Even animals were proscribed from that strange domain; the horse, with such elegant forms and its coat so rich in colors; the dog, with its intelligent and noble physiognomy; the ox, whose mass harmonizes so well with the broad lines of the plain; the lion with its warm and tawny hues; the bear with the silvery fur.

No, none of that which, in the ideal or the real, the plastic or the moral, the simple or the complex, once formed one of the innumerable sources, one of the motives, one of the pretexts of art; nothing touched by the magic wand of the imagination, charming and enchanting; nothing had been excepted from the abandonment.

The subjects delivered to commerce by the factory were all borrowed from antiques in the Museum of Naples.[21] And that is understandable: works of art never went anywhere but into the private rooms of the hotel-theaters. As, everywhere

---

[21] The National Archeological Museum of Naples contained in 1868, as it still does, large numbers of objects excavated from the ruins of Pompeii, Stabiae and Herculaneum, which shocked people at the time of their disinterment because of the frequency and flagrancy of their sexual imagery; similar objects presumably in use in all the other cities of the Roman Empire had presumably been "censored" the centuries as standards of decency had shifted.

else, people were only occupied with business, paintings would have distracted them from work and wasted too much time; in the day-time, they were rejected.

The execution was not marvelous. It was well below the level of the Épinal prints that had been the delight of my childhood. The color was brutal and the design gross. By dint of being copied by ignorant hands, the models were deformed and no longer bore any trace of anatomy. The prices varied according to the number and size of the characters. Figures of natural size were the most expensive; those were imprinted on wood cut along the contours and posed on feet like little lead soldiers. That last species of works of art was intermediate between painting and statuary.

The statues did not have the aim of reproducing the real, idealized or typified features of heroes or great men; nor were they designed to recount some great event and perpetuate its memory; they did not even have the objective of the representation of physical beauty. The subjects were the same as those I have just mentioned, except that here, thanks to the round swelling, an attempt had been made to approach nature more closely, and it must be said that if the work had been less imperfect, the illusion would have been possible.

The statues, generally of natural size, were made by galvanoplasty, a procedure that permits the same group to be repeated infinitely; they were also polychromatic, not lightly tinted as was seen in the middle of the nineteenth century—which is to say, sufficiently to remain ideal, but enough to lose the coldness, albeit noble, of marble. Here color imitated flesh very closely; they eyes were in glass with implanted lashes; the teeth were enamel, the nails gelatine, and every head was coiffed with a well-fitted wig. In sum, I had before my eyes something like a Tussaud Museum formed in a lascivious spirit.

I went out hastily in order to go into the book factory, the spectacle of which desolated me in its turn. However, it was only what I should have expected.

In the main, only utilitarian books were fabricated there. Works of science, technical treatises and educational books had been replaced by the formularies that I have mentioned: *Medicine*; *Education* (a teaching manual); *Justice*; *Pontification*, etc. As for philosophy, economics, law, history and poetry, anyone who had had the idea of publishing an old or new work on any of those subjects would not only have failed to sell a single copy but would have got himself imprisoned as an anti-utilitarian.

There was, however, one department of the factory from which works of the imagination emerged. Some were the plays that were performed in the hotel-theaters, simple scenarios with neither head nor tail, which the set-designers filled to their taste, and in which the actors on stage improvised whatever passed through their heads every evening. The others were works of fiction. These were the titles most in vogue—I beg the reader's pardon for reproducing them, and beg female readers to turn the page and pass on to the next chapter, but they are too characteristic for me to remain silent, and in any case, I shall only list four: *The Doting Drunkard*; *The Twenty-Two Rotting Corpses*; *I Rape my Daughter*; and *Incubus and Succubus*.

I shall renounce transcribing, as I had intended to do, a page taken at random from this mire; the French public desires to be respected. I shall only say that, so far as I could judge without remaining any longer subject to the impure contact of those filthy productions, nothing in the form redeemed the subject; on the contrary, they were in perfect accord. There were a series of absurd, flat but revolting episodes emerged without linkage from diseased brains; there was a phantasmagoria of hideous crimes and horrible maladies, photographed in the slightest detail; there was a *danse macabre* of cheats and murderers, of odious characters, monsters of physical and moral ugliness. As for dialogue, written in the language of prisons, it differed little from the style of the book in which the author spoke for himself. Finally, rhetoric and grammar had been abolished, and a lax liberty tempered the rules of

184

syntax and orthography. In brief, they wrote as they spoke, in telegraphic argot.

Here are two of the most intelligible lines, the closest to French and the least cynical—be brave, it's necessary!—from *Twenty-two Rotting Corpses*:

"Wen 15 arived at the seventh rotten corpse, he sat down disapointed for a snak..."

It was the ultimate in filth. But what did I expect? Art had been ruined, books had ceased to be monitored, and most importantly, the family had been destroyed; poisoned mushrooms naturally flourished. Letters deteriorate progressively as the family and taste lose their authority.

Chapter IX

*The social condition that is, for certain "progressives,"
the last word in civilization, is nothing but the
most primitive barbarity.*

On returning home I found a piece of paper informing me that I had to present myself the following day to the judge of the circumscription in order to defend myself against citizen 17, who had a claim for damages to have pronounced against me. I recalled the individual whose smashall had run over a child and whom I had arrested—unduly—at the cost of a fist fight. I answered the summons eagerly, desirous of seeing how justice was accommodated among these savages of a new species.

I went into a low room at the back of which a man with his head covered was sitting on the arm of a chair. Around him, people were jostling fuming, laughing, shouting and asking him questions, to which he responded with coarse gibes. That fellow was a magistrate; he was my judge.

"Let's get on," he exclaimed, after have pulled a citizen's hat down over his ears as a sign of amity after the latter had wittily broken and egg in his pocket. "Midday, let's work. 17 against 42.

185

My adversary and I cut through the crowd, which did not interrupt its racket.

17 spoke; he recounted the facts briefly, and, I must say, with exactitude; then he concluded and demanded an indemnity of a hundred thousand francs.

"To you," said the dispenser of justice. "True or false?"

"My adversary has told the truth," I replied. "However, as a stranger to this country, its laws, its procedure, its jurisprudence, and above all its spirit and its mores, I need to be assisted by a counsel and defended by a voice habituated to judiciary tactics; in consequence, I request a postponement of a week in order to choose an advocate.

"Don't understand a single word," said the judge, while 17 seemed bewildered. "Laws? Jurisprudence? Procedure? Advocate? Postponement? What's all that? If 17 has told the truth, pay the hundred thousand francs."

It was my turn to be surprised, and I was protesting when Graymalkin explained to me that I had been talking about things that had ceased to exist so long ago that the words themselves had been generally forgotten. Civil cases were judged without delay, with no other procedure than a summary assignation and on the simple contradiction of two parties appearing in person; the judgments were all equitable and discretionary, without appeal, to be executed immediately. Having admitted the exactitude of the facts, I no longer had anything to do but contest the level of the demand for indemnity.

I did so, animatedly. I argued that the blows I had struck had not caused any incapacity for work on the part of my adversary; I added that the combat, in which he had given evidence of as much strength as me, had been interrupted without having had the slightest result. In any case, the struggle having only lasted a quarter of an hour, I only owed an indemnity for what 17 would have earned in that space of time.

The judge, having become attentive, had begun by distributing a few blows of his stick right and left, accompanied by a "Shut up, animal!" which had procured me a commencement of silence. Then he sat down on his curule chair, in the fashion of certain compact Egyptian statues, folded in three with his ankles in his hands and his chin on his knees.

"Let's see if true that of equal strength," he said.

We set about that investigation, of a genre new to me, and a profound silence fell in the audience. The fight did not last long, because 17, having an interest therein, allowed himself to be beaten easily. I denounced the ruse.

"Begin again," said the judge who seemed to have taken a keen pleasure in our exercises. "17, if you let yourself get beaten, I'll convict you."

The combat resumed, more seriously, and after a quarter of a hour, when there was a shout of "Enough!" I had not obtained any sensible advantage over 17. My first argument was demonstrated!

As for the second, 17 protested that the fifteen minutes I had retained him had caused him to arrive late at a meeting and miss an affair of 90,000 francs.

"The proof," said Minos.

Two ragged drunkards advanced at a sign from 17. Those gentlemen exercised the profession of witnesses at 16 francs an hour.

"No other witnesses?" said Minos, who knew them.

"No," replied 17.

"42 acquitted."

Scarcely had those words been pronounced than 17, white with fury, approached the magistrate and, waving his fist in his face, heaped him with insults: "Thief, brigand (etc.)...it not enough, then, to have robbed the public when you were a tailor? Three months you've been a judge, and you maltreat us even more. How much have you been given to condemn me? (etc., etc.)"

During this violence, I noticed that the tailor gradually extended his limbs, uncoiling, as it were, like a snake waking up. First, he had silently placed the palms of his hands on the edge of his seat, then put one foot on the ground, and then the other. Suddenly, he stood up and knocked 17 down; then he seized his stick and lashed out forcefully at the witnesses, who

187

had intervened. 17 got up; I took a position beside the judge; the public divided into two camps, and a brawl in the Irish fashion was engaged, with brio. A good number of blows was distributed, until the moment when 17, exasperated, took a revolver from his pocket and fired three shots at the judge, which missed, so little mastery did he have of his senses. That incident soon put an end to the fight, and 17 was condemned by the magistrate to pay him ten thousand francs in damages.

I was content enough, if not with the institutions—or, rather, the lack of them—at least with the man who had just give proof of justice, and I thought that there might be some proof in the aphorism that was once cited by such various parties, that the poorest institutions are viable, when applied by certain individuals. I nevertheless said to Graymalkin that in the matter of men, those whom chance had just brought together in the audience had habits and promptitudes as singular as they were unfortunate. He replied with simplicity that all lawsuits terminated like mine, with insults addressed to the judge, a general brawl and the use of a revolver.

"It's for that reason," he added, "that we elect as judges men who are energetic, and above all vigorous. That renders the intervention of gendarmes unnecessary."

"They would not, however, be out of place at those solemnities."

"Their presence would afflict people's noble and proud sentiments of independence."

"I'd prefer their spines to be afflicted. So judges are elected here?"

"In this great country," he replied, proudly, "all administrative functions, military or judicial, are up for election, and revocable from the first day."

"I understand! That's why the tribunal is surrounded by such high consideration. Such an origin, combined with that guarantee of duration, would necessarily lead to that."

"The electors designate to judge them the man in whom they have the most confidence. It's great, great."

"And those who haven't voted for him despise or fear him, and mistrust his verdicts. And they aren't mistaken, for what he has most in view when rendering them is his reelection; then, as a local man, he's necessarily subject to a thousand immediate influences. Well, that's insane; it's necessary that a judge not be appointed by those he'll be called upon to judge; it's necessary that he be appointed by the entire people—which is to say, by the delegation of the people, by the power; then he has independence and authority; he isn't chosen with a view to a paltry and temporary objective, under the influence of an impression of variable rationality. A judge is a social instrument who collaborates in safeguarding one of the great social interest; the locality of a case and his humor ought to be irrelevant; it is a matter of justice…but let's pass on. Anyone can be elected? No preliminary studies, or examinations? It's the same as in medicine, isn't it?"

"All functions are free." As he spoke those words he handed Minos a wallet; it contained fifty thousand francs that he had promised him if he pronounced in my favor.

"And the functionaries are paid liberally, from what I see?" I replied.

"Oh," said Graymalkin, "you disapprove of my recompensing that worthy magistrate! Justice is gratuitous, and, and it follows that it receives no salary; would it be just for him to work for nothing?"

"Why isn't he paid?"

"What! Why? For the same reason that I, who never go to church, ought not to pay taxes to build or maintain that church; those expenses are incumbent on the faithful alone. It's the same for justice; I, who never bring lawsuits, ought not to pay contributions to nourish those who judge them. It's up to the plaintiff to maintain the magistrate. That's evident, evident."

"Yes. Now let's generalize: only merchants ought to maintain the navy that protects them; only travelers ought to subsidize the bridges and highways, etc. It's the destruction of all social bonds; are the French juxtaposed, or a community? And that overt venality is tolerated?

"It's not venality. He renders his judgment in the independence of his soul, and the person who has triumphed compensates him for his labor. Now, in hard cash, as you, this suit might have caused you to lose a hundred thousand francs thanks to him, you only lost fifty. In any case, I was free not to promise him anything..."

"And to lose. But what do the poor do?"

"Bah! The poor, the poor! They're wretches."

"Certainly. Well, to your magistracy, who can be bought by money or the promise of a vote, I prefer qualified lawyers, paid from the budget and unmovable. Alas, in my time, their services were poorly recompensed; I would have liked the most junior, in the era of which I speak, to have an annual income of twelve thousand francs. But people were enraged then against 'high salaries'—which are, however, a guarantee of incorruptibility. That was the opinion in England in 1868, and magistrates whose functions were approximately comparable to President of the Imperial Court of the Seine and President of the Civil Tribunal of the Seine had salaries of 200,000 francs and 175,000 francs; Presidents de Chambre received 125,000 francs. It's true that our magistrates had no need to seek elsewhere than in the elevation and dignity of their sentiments and principles a support against temptation; they were courageous, disinterested and proud."

Chapter X

"Now," said Graymalkin, "let's go to the Slapping Box." That name made me smile. "What's the Slapping Box?"

"It's what you would call the Chambre des Députés."

"By the way, how are you governed here?"

"We aren't; we govern ourselves."

"Bravo! Are you governed well? What is the Constitution?"

"It has a grandiose simplicity. The people have absolute sovereignty. They pass all the laws themselves, by the majority of universal suffrage; all administrative measures are taken and all functionaries are appointed in the same fashion. The vote takes place without scrutiny, in the public square, by acclamation; it is not necessarily preceded by a discussion, but only by the reading of the motion that is the object of the vote. That's the whole Constitution. I can't be any more precise about the dispositions, because outside of those bases, which are a matter of fact and usage, and not written, everything is left to Liberty. Because of those very bases, everything floats incessantly under its vivifying breath; only they are fixed; the rest changes constantly; one never knows what the law will be tomorrow, who will be a Maire or judge in twenty-four hours. All reforms take place suddenly, under the immediate impression of sentiments, needs and the crisis of the moment. I must say, however, that in general, before reforms pass into the domain of accomplished facts, they're submitted to a certain elaboration in the clubs, which absorb a good part of the life of our fellow citizens."

"The clubs take the place of the Conseil d'État?"

"Precisely. Alongside those essential principles there are others that have been maintained for quite a long time. The most important are these:

"1. Only towns, especially large cities, enjoy electoral rights; small villages and rural areas are deemed blind and incapable.

"2. In towns, the votes of workers count double.

"Now, there is still a Chambre, two ministers and a Head of State; but the Chambre doesn't have a very regular existence; it's only when it pleases the people to appoint delegates charged with resolving a question that the assembly is constituted. The Ministers, elected by the people, are the Minister of Finance, and the Minister of the Army and Navy, a simple guardian of State military materiel, since, thank God, we do not have in times of peace a single soldier under arms, nor a single ship at sea.

"As for the Head of State, his only functions consist of rendering himself, in case of war, to the army, to preside over the council of generals and execute its decisions. Outside of that, he's a completely unnecessary mechanism. We keep him anyway—it's the only ancient institution we've respected—out of recognition for the great dynasty of which he's the off-spring. Oddly enough, we, who have expelled and harassed intensively everything that smacks of sentiment, the cult of the past, etc., everything that isn't utilitarian, persistently maintain that family at our head. We even do insane things for them, such as allowing them a civil list; we testify ridiculous regards to our leader, like making way for him in the street and even nodding our heads to him. To tell the truth, these Napoléons—they're also the only ones who have a name instead of a number—are worthy fellows; thus, Napoléon VII spends his life, as an individual of course, since he hasn't even the shadow of power, rendering services to individuals; his house is an advice bureau—and, take my word for it, he gives good advice, and assistance. Outside of that, Napoléon isn't very utilitarian. He thinks, he reads old books, he studies—but no one's perfect!"

"These Napoléons might save you once again."

"Save? From what?"

"From the abject state in which…never mind."

"I'll continue my explanation. As regards administration, every city nominates al the functionaries, tax collectors, judges and policemen for its region, when it pleases them to have any. There are no more départements. The municipalities are as free as individuals—even a little too free, and taxes aren't always forwarded very well, because this is what happens: the collector puts in his pocket all that he can abstract from State funds, and then, with the greater part of what remains, he buys the silence of those who might denounce him—often, the elected individual is only the representative of a group of individuals who have banded together to get him in and who share in the benefits of the election. He buys the judge if he is pursued; and if he's convicted, there's no restitution; that would

192

be entirely opposed to the ideas of the thousand individuals ambitions to replace the concessionary and do as he does.

"Furthermore, it often happens that a city refuses to pay the tax; in that case, as the country is not represented by a central power possessed of any force, the dispute always concludes with a transaction that defrauds the State of a substantial fraction of its due. It has even become a habit among the cities to provoke these conflicts in order to arrive at that solution. Thus, the idea was raised some time ago of investing the leader with the power to compel the communes that don't pay, but it would be necessary for that to organize a national public force, because one can't in this instance have recourse to the municipal militias. Anyway, we shall see.

"In consequence, although we pay enormous taxes, because of the financial organization I've just described, the State only requires very little, given that it undertakes very little. It doesn't pay any clergy, magistrates, diplomats, consuls, functionaries of an administrative order, educational bodies, soldiers, artists, police agents, jailers or engineers. A few employees of the central administration of finances and a few munitions guards in the arsenals are all the personnel maintained at State expense."

"The National Debt must be minimal."

"We don't have one at present; we've just gone bankrupt."

"How casually you tell me that."

"Oh, it often happens."

"That's honest."

"There's nothing dishonest about it; the lenders expect it and fix interest rates in consequence. Besides which, nothing forces them to believe in the engagements we contract with them: that's Liberty."

"Continue your explanation."

"Certain innovators are of the opinion that the regime ought to be modified. They claim that ignorance is profound, that mores are lax, the public money is dilapidated, and that justice is venal. They say that it's scandalous that the old libraries and museums have been left undefended for so long against the spiders and rats, and that the establishments of public instruction have ceased to centralize in order to diffuse intellectual enlightenment everywhere. They claim that works of common interest ought to be executed collectively by the State and not by local stumps.

"They think it would be advantageous if we had a general police force, which, they believe, would succeed in seizing some of the innumerable malefactors who threaten our security and our lives with impunity. Finally, imbued like you with old ideas, they sustain that the only truly independent, respectable and respected functionary is one appointed and paid by the State. They demand the political equality of town and country, that of workers and other citizens, votes that are more regular and les tumultuous, less mutable laws—what do I know?

"They sustain that we ought to have agents abroad that would keep watch on our neighbors and protect those of our nationals who have left their homeland, that armies of volunteers hastily improvised are worthless in the face of a good army fashioned over time by discipline and penetrated by a military spirit, etc.

"These people want to turn the world upside down, for, even though they're supported here and there by just criticisms, what they're pursuing is, after all, nothing but the complete ruination of individual strength, liberty and justice. Only to pay for what one consumes oneself, that's the limit within which social bonds ought to exist. Now the only things that serve everyone without exception are the Ministry of Finance and that of the Army. To govern oneself at the whim of one's caprice, that's liberty. To protect oneself, that's virility. But these innovators are gaining ground every day, and one truly doesn't know where it will end."

As he spoke these words, we had to stop our smashall, a lateral street that we were about to cross being obstructed by a crowd of men who were filing slowly in tightly-packed ranks. They were on foot, all holding on to one another by the flaps

194

of their coats. On their trousers, their arms, their hats and banners that a few of them carried, these words were legible:

HONESTY!!!
THE ONLY NEWSPAPER WORTH READING
400 FRANCS A YEAR
PLUS A STUNNING BONUS
FOR THE FIRST THOUSAND SUBSCRIBERS ONLY
TO WIT:
AN EVENING AND NIGHT
AT THE GRAND HOTEL-THEATER

Those human advertisements, who numbered five hundred, occupied the causeway for an hour and were the cause of an indescribable traffic jam, but that was the object of their procession: forcibly stopping people and making them read their announcement was the best means at the disposal of the publicists of a city whose inhabitants were too hurried to dart even a passing glance at the walls.

That incident led me naturally to talk to Graymalkin about the press. After having defended it against the reproach of immorality that I addressed to him with regard to the singular incentive that *Honesty* was promising so publicly, he said: "Newspapers are as free as books; no more censorship or stamp duty, no authorization, no precaution, no stamp, no special laws for the press. It's simple. One detail: when a newspaper commits an offence against common law, it doesn't go before a judge, but before the jury that exists here in criminal matters."

"So, if you or I commit a crime against common law, we go before a judge, but if a citizen journalist commits an identical crime, he goes before a jury? That's a privilege as iniquitous as it is absurd. Why, in any case, is it established in favor of one profession rather than another? Why to the profit of journalists rather than physicians? And you call this country a land of equality! Another reason that renders the intervention of the jury deplorable is that one set of jurors enthusiastically acquits the same accused that tomorrow's jury would have condemned harshly, justice and its verdicts being no more then than a matter of names drawn from a hat. Go on."

"A newspaper is a trumpet. It has to make a noise, in order that those who have something to trumpet will employ it. It trumpets anything that one wants it to. That, in brief, is the condition of the newspaper. I'll add that the public knows full well what it is, and doesn't seek conviction in newspapers, but only the arguments that one political party or some merchant of hair-lotion wants to put forward. No one is deceived. In any case, it would require a strong dose of naivety to be taken in, for there isn't a single newspaper that doesn't pass from black to white overnight for a reasonable price. Every sheet is for sale, and when in the service of one party, it has harmed another, if that one outbids its adversary, the paper will belong to that one. The politics of newspaper proprietors consists of attacking furiously those they're paid to attack, with the result that they serve those who pay them and have the chance of tiring the enemy and being bought more dearly by him. It's be making those evolutions that they become rich, and in order to be free in their maneuvers they only sign engagements in these terms: 'We promise to insert in exchange for the sum of...whatever might seem good to citizen 1, until the day when an offer superior to that sum causes us to do so for someone else.' All that is perfectly legitimate; it's the liberty of transactions."

"There are things that can't be the object of a transaction; there are things that one doesn't sell and doesn't hire out: one's word and one's pen. In my time, too, there was a distant country where the press was beginning to be organized in that spirit and in those conditions.

"Oh, I can glimpse what a newspaper is. It's nothing but a tissue of vile flatteries. Yes, I see that. In the first column, one celebrates the high value of a simpleton, the services rendered by someone incapable, the virtues of a malefactor; in the second one treats a man of great intelligence as an idiot, one accuses a benefactor of humanity of theft. It's true that the following day, the same rag, via the pens of the same men—who, signatures no longer being obligatory, can hide their ignominy under anonymity, and behave all the more ignobly for being personally unknown—might render justice to the good and attack vice, if the generosity of one has ceased to prevail over the munificence of the other."

"In order to be bought by a public that is, after all, rather indifferent, to make oneself known, to attract people who will buy their services, and in order to make sure that their advertisements and commercial and political announcements are read, the newspapers are marvelously ingenious. First of all, they have ambulant advertisements, as you have just seen, and the promise of incentives. They have incentives that will seduce you on behalf of your domicile in all forms: objects of luxury, fabrics, comestibles, etc., and which the tempter can vary in accordance with individuals. Then the paper lays siege to you from all directions, invades you, and, like it or not, one knows the title, and very nearly the contents.

"One can't buy an overcoat, a hat or boots without finding a newspaper stuck or stitched to them forcefully enough for one to be unable, in the time that it takes to detach it, to be unaware a least of the title. That name is printed on your underwear, traced with a knife on your bread, the shells of our eggs are ornamented with it, and young scamps take charge of writing it on your back in chalk; you take off your new gloves and it's imprinted on your hand; you sit down, feel a pinprick and stand up suddenly, turn around and read the name implacably inscribed on the back of your chair, etc.

"Finally, there's the material composition of the newspaper and the typographical setting, which are designed to attract. The paper is beautiful, sometimes white and sometimes colored; the articles are sometimes printed in golden letters; the titles, above all, are striking, less so by the impression as the wording; headlines in enormous letters announcing the most exorbitant things can sometimes sell a hundred thousand copies of an issue; the entirety of editorial artistry consists of procuring some big news, true or false—especially false—and crowning it with an effective rubric.

"It's the newspaper most fertile in expedients of that sort that is the one most sought-after by lovers of publicity. But here's an issue of *Honesty*. The leading article is the continuation of a polemic directed against the Minister of Finance."

I read:

MURDER
COMMITTED IN 1994
BY THE PRESENT MINISTER OF FINANCE!!!

The truth will always come out and it is rare for a crime to escape punishment. One often sees people deceiving their country with regard to their capability as well as their probity, fraudulently acquiring public confidence. Without intelligence, without talent and without experience of affairs, they have arrived at the summit of power by means of a long series of base actions and villainies; kneaded by vices, they are gorged with gold by the nation, in order to deliver themselves to the most crapulous debauchery. But such scandals do not last. Our Minister of Finance is no longer unaware that at the present moment, the affair of the child murdered by him in 1994 is being brought into the open. It is now known how he abducted the victim from the unfortunate mother who had committed the fault of giving herself to him. It is known where he threw the cadaver after having cut it into pieces. Justice, we cannot doubt, will therefore be done. That is all that we ask. The rumor is going round that the mother, his mistress, has also disappeared, but that rumor, although entirely consistent, does not seem to us to be sufficiently well-founded; we have let it drop. We will only be glad to see a man who has never been able to fulfill them removed from his functions, a vulgar thief dismissed from the State Treasury and condemned, as an abominable murderer deserves to be.

"There are no longer any laws against defamation?" I said to Graymalkin.

"No: the liberty of the press is now absolute. One can write anything about anything and anyone."

I cast an eye at random over the advertisements and read this one, the most extraordinary disposition of which was made to attract attention:

TO YOUNG WOMEN
*who are loved too much
and who fear*
THE CONSEQUENCES.

Citizen 67, ninth street, house 14, in the course of long medical practice and a profound study of the affections of men, has observed that amour fatigues the stomach. His pastilles provide protection from that inconvenience.

N.B. Women who are in an interesting situation ought to avoid these pastilles, which might have the effect of bring a rapid conclusion to their condition, without anyone perceiving it.[22]

"And these horrors," I said, "Are no longer prosecuted?"

"How could they be prosecuted? Citizen 67 warns you honestly of an effect that his pastilles might produce; you avoid or seek that effect at your whim; he cannot be responsible. Everyone is responsible for their own actions. No more tutelage!"

"That's all right. Enough."

So saying, we went into one of the benches of the Slapping Box.

Like all the Chambres of my time, it was a semicircular hall on the diameter of which the presidential chair was situat-

---

[22] Author's note (advertised as "Note by the Editor"): "The advertisement is reproduced almost word for word from a newspaper published in the United States."

ed. What distinguished it from all the others I had seen thus far was the absence of any decoration, a complete nudity and a repulsive state of dirtiness. The floor, not covered by any carpet, had never been waxed, and the divans and the tables that formed the furniture were, the former all in tatters and the latter all broken and covered with a thick encrusted dust.

Shortly after our entry into that hall, into which anyone could go—I mean into the hemicyle itself, no soldier or usher forbidding access—the session began to become animated.

The estimable representatives, mostly in shirt-sleeves, without waistcoats, were sprawling on sofas and smoking enormous pipes, whose clouds obscured the atmosphere. Two or three of them were, however, sitting down. One was combing his hair before a mirror placed on his desk beside a bowl in which he did not take long to make ablutions; the other was pulling apart a roast chicken with his fingers, and throwing the bones away right and left without worrying about where they might fall. I saw one such debris arrive on the paper of a citizen député who was writing; the latter's pen came to a sudden stop; he remained in contemplation for a moment before the object, and then looked around to see where the gift might have come from; having discovered the eater, he got up, approached him and, without saying a word, delivered a vigorous punch to the back of his neck. The other stood up, as if moved by a spring, and a fight began.

Until then, the Chambre had been paying scant attention to the "speech" made by a drunkard who was chanting something from the floor, having rolled under a bench, but torsos suddenly straightened when they became aware of what was happening. Soon, they formed a circle around the combatants and started to lay bets.

Suddenly I heard frightful oaths. It was the President, who was intervening; he ordered the combatants to desist.

He was not obeyed quickly enough, it appeared, for I saw him roll up his sleeves and launch himself from his armchair, foaming at the mouth, in order to administer an energetic correction to both of the pugilists at the same time. The

Chambre applauded enthusiastically, and I learned that Monsieur 5 had just exercised the principle function of the Presidency, and that he had been elected precisely because, being a boxer by profession, he was eminently qualified to fulfill the most frequent and most delicate duties. He had even been recently voted a cudgel of honor by the Assembly bearing the legend: *Hard-hitter*, on the occasion of an advertisement he had applied to one of his députés that had left the latter half-crippled.[23]

They were discussing the proposal of a law whose objective was to have the State furnish the Hotel-Theaters numbering in their personnel the maximum number of pretty women with bonuses, by way of encouragement, distributed by means of a permanent committee of investigation. Opinions were sharply divided. The drunkard opined that the bonus ought to be awarded to the Hotel-Theaters whose wines were the best. The man with the chicken was holding out for the most solid meats.

The citizen with the comb took the floor: "Devil's thunder, citizens!" he cried, from his seat, recommencing his parting for the seventh time. "Devil's thunder! I know the question better than any of you, utter asses that you are. Have you got it into your stupid heads that because you go on the spree in these places you know them? Can't you see, you stupid oafs, that you only see what you're shown, and don't know the underside of the cards. Has that great simpleton who's just been jabbering away in such a tedious fashion been, like me, a hairdresser to all the ladies? And he wants to have an opinion? Oh la la! Woe is me! Get going, you heap of bumpkins! Do what capable people like me tell you to do: the law is good, pass it. And get on with it!" And he resumed work on his parting.

"You're a cretin, you over there, the wig-maker. Me, I run a Hotel-Theater, and I can see that you're talking rubbish.

---

[23] The author adds another note here claiming that this is a reflection of the contemporary political mores of the United States.

Necessary that we not only subsidize for the lovely girls, but for a good table, good wine, for fine spectacles and the lot..."

"Get away, you old thief! You drink the sweat of the people," said a voice from the left.

"Yes, you bloodsucker, you pickpocket," added another.

"Pickpocket yourself, murderer," replied the orator.

"Don't insult my friend," said a fifth legislator, "or I'll give you a beating."

"Come on, then," said the hotelier.

"Are you up to it, good-for-nothing?" said a Hercules. "No, you only have to look at you."

There was a crescendo of insults and cries, which soon expanded into a frightful racket; it was accompanied by the most menacing gestures; and as they were soon close enough to one another I thought a general brawl was going to break out at any moment. I looked at the President, wondering if he was about to leap on his colleagues again. This time, he proceeded differently. Standing on his chair, he caused a forceful cry to resound that was a perfect imitation of a cock's crow. At the same time he waved his forearms in a movement strongly reminiscent of that of the lord of the poultry-yard flapping his wings. Immediately, all attention was fixed on the statesman, who, happy and proud of having been able to deflect a disquieting storm by means of a skillful diversion, soon received congratulations on his talent from the greater number of the members of the majority.

Order having been somewhat restored, the debate continued.

An amiable citizeness whom the political equality of women had brought to the Chambre—"There are no more wives and mothers," Graymalkin had told me, proudly, "there are only citizenesses"—took the floor.

According to her, the subsidy ought to be consecrated to helping women who had done thirty years of service in the Hotel-Theaters.

"What is our position?" she added. "Women like me? I, who was so beautiful..."

A voice from the right: "Have you finished?"

Other voices: "Twenty-four years ago."

Another: "Just look at that head. Shut up, you old mari onette-for-hire."

Another: "Olé, you old bat."

The citizeness representative: "Oh" Wretches! Rabble! Cowards! I'll strangle you like dogs!"

She threw herself upon one of her neighbors, and then stopped, seemingly fainting. Her friends rushed to help her, her adversaries to assure themselves that she was acting. The two camps once again found themselves in one another's presence, with outrage in their mouths, fists clenched and legs braced; this time, the cry of the cock resounded in vain. It was necessary for the President to imitate, successively, a dog, a cat, a donkey and a calf to dominate the assembly. Only the calf prevailed, and it was still necessary for a dancer who was secretary to the Chambre to execute, at the same time, steps of fantastic animation around Hard-Hitter. The influence of the office was sensibly diminishing.

"It's like that every day," said Grimalkin.

"What are the clubs like, then?" I replied, sadly. "I shall never set foot in one of them."

Chapter XI

*Take the Rhine, sire! Strike Russia if she
extends her hand toward Constantinople,
and then give France all the liberties that
are demanded, rightly or wrongly, and your
dynasty will last as long as that of Hugues Capet.*

My soul was overwhelmed by lassitude, steeped in the most profound disgust. The dolorous spectacle of fallen humanity was depressing me.

I seized Graymalkin by the arm.

"Listen," I said, "I no longer believe that I'm prey to a hallucination; I believe that I've slept for a hundred and thirty years; what I've seen afflicts my sight; what I've heard afflicts my ears; what I touch is really beneath my hand. Well, since that's the way it is, I've seen and heard enough. Put me back to sleep, let me die, or I'll kill myself!"

"Decidedly, you don't like liberty."

"You aren't liberty! I know full well what you are. You're the full development of what the society of the United States is. You're the paroxysm of a frantic demagoguery, devoid of genius, devoid of principle, talent, education and intelligence. Ignorant, pedantic, pretentious, vain, haughty, arrogant; insolent, devoid of elegance, mildness, compassion and pity; hideous egotists and gross debauchees, avaricious, greedy, rapacious, devoid of delicacy, honor, dignity, modesty and probity; everything for sale in the public square—that's your fellow citizens!

"Degraded souls, you know nothing but success and force. For you, action is everything; ideas are dead; action is no longer the realization of thought; it's thought that is an instrument for action, and for success by any means.

"You have killed Art; you have killed Letters; you have killed Science, and from the death of that, and many other things, industry and commerce will die.

"Wretch! You have killed Right; you have killed Duty; you have killed the Law; you have killed Charity; you have killed Devotion; you have killed the Fatherland; you have killed the Family; you have killed the Father; you have killed Woman; you have killed Love; you have killed Society.

"Authority is no more; Liberty is no more; Equality is no more. You have summoned Disorganization, Barbarity and Chaos.

"O Lord, how have you permitted so many centuries of effort, labor, suffering, the work of so much virtue and genius, so much progress and civilization accumulated over the ages, to sink into such an abyss?"

Graymalkin smiled disdainfully.

"There exists within the confines of the seventh city," he said, "an old madman with whom you might reach an understanding. I'll take you to his home."

After an hour in a smashall, we arrived at an isolated house, one of the last in the city. The elevator stopped in front of a door that gave us access to a room whose walls were lined with shelves laden with books. At a table covered with maps and papers, an old man was writing, absorbed by his work; the noise we made as we came in did not make him turn round.

Graymalkin put a hand on his arm. He turned round slowly and looked at us, vaguely at first, and then with slight surprise. He was a tall old man with a bald forehead; long white hair hung down over his shoulders, and a long beard fell to the middle of his chest. He must have been handsome in his youth and the prime of life, but the regular features of his face had acquired from the purity of his life and the elevation of the work that he had done a particular beauty and nobility. His gaze, full of fire, was soft and penetrating at the same time. On examining him, I thought that Plato might have looked like that.

He invited us with a sign to sit down, and appeared to be waiting for us to inform him of the object of our visit.

Graymalkin told him that we had arrived from the other world, and how; that I could give him the most exact and precise information about the society of the nineteenth century; and that in return, it would be valuable for me to know how the present society had become what I saw.

"Monsieur," said the old man, after collecting himself momentarily. "I live more in the past than the present; at least, my career has consisted of refastening the chain of time; I am what was once called a historian; today, my work having absolutely nothing about it that is utilitarian, as they put it, I am taken, at best, for an eccentric, perhaps even a madman—at any rate, for a parasite on society; I do not ask, however, for anything whatsoever, and if I have been able to continue working in these last fifty years, it's thanks to the spontaneous aid of a few elevated and disinterested minds who would have regretted seeing the last annalist that the world possesses pass away."

After a pause, he added: "You lived under Napoléon III?"

"Yes, Monsieur."

"Did you know him?"

"I had that honor."

"He not only had a great intelligence..."

"He also had a great heart."

"That is how I imagine him. That tender soul, that good, generous man, was an indefatigable thinker, ardent in the research, pursuit and invention of whatever could develop the wellbeing of individuals, the prosperity of people and civilization. All of his history and politics are there; his profound love of humanity dominated his entire life and determined all his actions."

Me: "Yes, and all the other politics of his time gravitated, sooner or later, whether they liked it or not, around his. He opened a new era. He gave it impulsion and direction. He caused the world to advance rapidly on the path of justice and progress."

The old man: "He founded a new human right. He it was who enabled the right of people to choose their government to triumph, and the right of nations to independence."

Me: "He emancipated the worker; he brought him to life and made him a citizen; he founded democracy."

The old man: "He rid Economics of its wound, Politics. He propagated, in favor of order and calm of mind, the sane doctrines of the one; he reduced the other to his appropriate relative insignificance. He suppressed socialism. He informed the usage of liberty. He did more; he created liberty, which, before him, had never existed anywhere; for ephemeral, troubled and deadly liberties like those with which France was invested under Louis-Philippe and the Republic are not liberty, for there is no liberty without equality and universal suffrage, and neither in antiquity, in Athens or Rome, nor since, in Belgium. Italy, England and the United States, had equality ever

206

existed. Everywhere, in the Emperor's time, aristocracies, there white men, here qualified property-owners, oppressed the helots. But when the tree was shaken, the United States was forced to abolish slavery, England was obliged to draw back the limitations on electoral right, and Russia liberated its serfs.

"He made the peace of the world, for he brought nations closer together by means of the relationships he instituted with the most distant countries; by the piercing of the isthmus of Suez, which, without his firm will would never have been accomplished;[24] by the Exposition Universelle of 1867, of which preceding ones had only been the sketch, and which was the last; by the commercial treaties that reawakened dormant human activity and permitted people, for the first time, freely too enjoy the wealth that nature heaped up for them...

"He resolved all the great external questions. In the Orient, you will remember the Crimean War that saved Turkey, increasing its territory at the expense of Russia, forbade the latter to reconstruct Sebastopol and to have any military maritime arsenal in the Black Sea, limited the strength and number of ships that it could maintain there, neutralizing that Russian lake and removing from the Tsar the exclusive or isolated protection of Oriental Christians, to replace it with the collective solicitude of powers. Those dispositions, rigorous but necessary, constituted one of the finest treaties that France has ever signed.

"Afterwards, in order to adjourn the return of peril, the Emperor took the status quo for the basis of his politics, save for the amelioration of Ottoman institutions and the equitable emancipation of the populations submissive to the Gate.

"That generous work of conservation and progress consisted of fortifying Turkey in each of its elements, consolidating the Ottoman Empire by developing the vitality of all the

---

[24] When the present story was published, work in the Suez Canal was not yet complete; it was only opened in November 1969.

countries that constituted it, making them prosper by enabling them to prosper, to safeguard the interests of the Gate and those of the populations that were dependent on it to a greater or lesser extent, to sustain with regard to all authority the power and the acquired and recognized rights of that State, and, at the same time, to obtain satisfaction of the needs and legitimate desires of its subjects and vassals. That is what the French government strove to accomplish and succeeded in executing.

"Perhaps those Christians and vassals could have been contained with a slightly less complaisant hand, and their sometimes-excessive desires could have been deferred with a less facile benevolence. Perhaps they could have been supported more slowly and resisted more when, after having obtained what justice or utility had awarded them, they allowed themselves to be carried away by the pursuit of chimeras. Perhaps efforts could have been made not to allow them to believe that everything they demanded noisily would be procured for them in the fear that they might make even more noise; perhaps it would not have been bad to convince them that an accomplished fact is not indestructible. Perhaps there was too much condescension when Belgrade was evacuated by the Turks and when a Prussian prince was aided to mount the throne of Rumania. Perhaps there was too much disinterest when the Bulgars were discouraged, who were only waiting for an impulsion to convert to Catholicism, which would have put them under our particular and direct influence. Perhaps it was a mistake not to maintain the Maronites of the Liban under exclusive French tutelage...but no matter. Children spoiled by us, as the Italians had been, the Rumanians, the Serbs, the Montenegrins, in the epoch that commenced at Sadowa and finished with our entry to Berlin, would have taken for weakness the fecund expectation in which France awaited the hour fixed by her leader, and they used a certain familiarity toward us; was it necessary, then, to punish them?

"Questions of detail, moreover, all of that, details of execution; the general progress and the definitive results were excellent; Russia did not gain an inch of territory in the direction of Constantinople, and the prosperity of those populations developed greatly, the Turkish Empire forming, after a certain time, a kind of federation composed of free and sovereign peoples under the suzerainty of the Gate.

"But I'm letting myself go into over-scrupulous developments.

"In Italy, continuing the great traditions of François I, Richelieu and Henri IV, the Emperor was able over time to expel Austria, which, by virtue of the domination it exercised, had become a redoubtable danger to us. But, more of a politician than his predecessors, as sage as he was equitable, he did not follow the example of those French or Teutonic conquerors who had snatched the peninsula during the last eight hundred years and kept it as a prey; he restored it to itself, thus rendering impossible a conflict between France and Austria, since past conflicts had never had any other cause than the possession of Italian soil by one or the other. At the same time, he put an end to the bitter suffering of twenty million people.

"Finally, by founding the French confederation composed of France extended by Luxembourg and the Rhenish provinces on the one hand and Belgium on the other, united in a military, diplomatic and trading communion, he repaired the fault, unequaled in history, committee by his predecessor under the preoccupation of paltry personal considerations and fear: the refusal to accept Belgium. He reassembled the scattered groups of the great French family; he replaced the ancient French equilibrium, so imperfect, so conventional, so artificial, so precarious, always under threat, with an indestructible equilibrium, based on justice and liberty, on the nature of things, history, nationalities, geography, races and the wishes of populations..."

Me: "It's true, then, that you, who are the voice of posterity, judge that reign great!"

The old man: "How could I judge it otherwise?"

Me: "Have you not found traced, in the documents hand-ed down to you, motivated criticisms, radical critiques, and grave accusations? Have you not seen that government stig-matized by the term *personal*? Have you not read that he made enormous expenditures, committed a nameless fault by caus-ing or allowing the unity of Italy? That he was mad to allow the unity of Germany? That he submitted Mexico to an im-mense and irreparable disaster?"

The old man; "I've read all that in the stenography of the sessions of the legislative body. Men whose names are forgot-ten today, although they were not lacking in talent, developed those theses in speeches that are read with a certain curiosity. I've seen several newspapers of the time in which, from the beginning of the reign to the end, all the actions of the gov-ernment, without exception, are examined, debated, funda-mentally attacked with bitterness—which, parenthetically, renders unintelligible the perpetual plaints exhaled by the same papers regarding the oppression suffered by the press. I've had the courage to read a few obscene pamphlets.

"Well, I can assure you that on the impartial man to whom distance from those events leaves all his coolness of appraisal, those epigrams, critiques and attacks produce very little impression, compared with the powerful eloquence of actions, facts and results. One smiles at seeing how the pas-sion of parties agitates in the void, and how little place is taken in the existence of a people, in a movement of humanity by the ambitions and false intelligence of liars. Ultimate failure, and then eternal forgetfulness, was the price of so much effort and so much conflict; that was the term of so much hope. Poor little great men, when will you learn that durable glory is not the lot of orators, but only of those to whom it is given to dis-cern where God is leading the world and who incline under his hand to work for his purpose."

Me: "Let's look closely, however: the government of Napoléon III was personal in the sense that the Ministers were not responsible."

The old man: "The Emperor was. Is ministerial responsibility, then, the essence of liberty? Were the ministers of the United States responsible when that country was a Republic?"

"Me: "No, but a responsible minister would not have done certain things without consulting the country—he would not, for example, have launched France into the war in Mexico."

The old man: "Why not?"

Me: "Because when one is a responsible minister, one dare not take enterprise so far."

The old man: "You astonish me. I have always seen, on the contrary, that in the epoch when parliamentary governments flourished, the great and grave decisions, those of peace and war above all, were taken by the executive, save for posterior ratification by the Chambres. Thus, concerning a distant and adventurous expedition that cost England hundreds of millions, and which was almost contemporary with our expedition in Mexico, the resolution was taken, the projects were settled, the forces were organized and the financial engagements concluded—what am I saying?—the expenditures were made and the troops were in motion when the British parliament was united; which, it must he said to the honor of its patriotism, voted in a single session and with neither shameful bargaining nor futile acrimony the first hundred million requested of it.

"And look: here are documents relating to that parliamentary question. Do you recall how, in 1854, the English parliament was consulted on the question of whether or not to make war on Russia? On the fourth of January, following events in Sinope, Admiral Dundas had received the order to protect the navy of the Gate as well as its territory in the Black Sea—which is to say that the war was irrevocable. Well, it was only on January 31 that Parliament was convened and the Queen announced in her speech that England was to arm. The same day, the government announced that the papers relative to the question would be deposited. That's how the country was consulted in solemn circumstances, and that's why, in the

Lords, the Marquess of Clanricarde complained about the secrecy that had been maintained with regard to the representation of England.

"But isn't that manner of procedure in the nature of things? Can one adopt any other? What—a war is judged necessary and you're going to reveal your intentions, divulge your plans and make your means known, making it impossible for you to act suddenly, giving free rein to all the influences contrary to you, discouraging your chiefs and your soldiers? That is never done! And using it thus would have transformed parliamentary government, which, it seems to me, retains a monarchic element in a republic governed by a sovereign and omnipotent assembly.

"Thus it is understood that a pure parliamentary government, a government according to the heart of the doctrinaire, would have made the expedition of Mexico without consulting the Chambre in advance. I'll add that it's probable that the weakness that is natural to that form would have procured it many other disappointments that he Empire did not suffer. But would the doctrinaires have made that war? Yes, certainly: I can prove it to you; I have curious documents that I shall show you shortly.

"Now, what was the truth about these protests that rose up incessantly in favor of the parliamentary regime? What was that persistence in wanting to introduce into a land of universal suffrage a mechanism that existed nowhere else with universal suffrage, which was only encountered in mechanisms totally different from ours? It was merely a tactic of parties.

"As for 'discretionary power' and 'arbitrariness,' they were used in the early years of the reign; but in practice, that arbitrariness was of a rare mildness and amnesties annulled its effects several times—as you know, the day soon came, under the Empire, when no one was any longer proscribed. Besides, that arbitrariness, after having been worth seventeen years of prosperity to France, which no moral disorder troubled, gradually disappeared, and by 19 January 1867 left nothing standing but the law. Then those quibbles were lost in a regime of full and entire liberty inaugurated by the solemn act of 16 March 1876, the day when the Imperial Prince entered his twenty-first year."

Me: "So be it. But what about finances? How much money spent! What increases brought to the budget and the National Debt."

The old man: "What increases in the budgetary revenues beyond all increases in taxation and even of population! What a development of industry, of commerce, and public wealth and wellbeing! How much labor, how many great things accomplished!

"Would you like figures? I have a few present in memory.

"In 1847, our 'general' exterior commerce with foreign lands and the colonies rose to 2,340 millions, of which 1,290 was importation and 1,049 exportation.

"In 1866, commerce was 8,126 millions, of which 3,845 was importation and 4,281 exportation. The ensemble of operations had more than tripled, and the exportation of our products more than quadrupled.

"In 1847, the maritime movement with the colonies and foreign lands was represented by the entry and exit of 34,928 ships gauging 4,297,000 tons.

"In 1866, 51,509 ships gauging 9,400,00 tons, or more than double, entered and exited from our ports.

"What money spent, you say. But do you think that nothing was obtained or it in the 36 years that reign lasted? To wit:

"Creating and maintaining the innumerable institutions of beneficence, so marvelously organized, which took the child from the crèche, led him to the refuge, to school, and protected him in his apprenticeship;

"Ameliorating the accommodation of workers in the big cities;

"Subsidizing mutual aid societies;

"Founding the asylums of Vincennes and Le Vésinet;

"Subsidizing the treasury of the invalids of labor;

"Etc.

213

"Could the cities have been sanitized and embellished the cities, France equipped with by-roads, highways, canals and railways, and the telegraphic network created without spending hundreds of millions?

"Look, here are some more figures. In 1847 we had 1,830 kilometers of railways; in 1867 we had 15,750. We had 17,235 kilometers of major roads, compared with 164,881 on the first of January 1866; 90,000 kilometers of ordinary by-roads compared with 353,797 in the same epoch.

"Without spending a great deal of money, would it have been possible to make that great and generous attempt in Mexico, of such a noble and far-sighted politics, which brought the opposition down; definitively to pacify the Liban; vanquish with the aid of a handful of men sent six thousand leagues from the fatherland, an empire of more than three hundred million souls, enter the Chinese capital and impose tolerance on the vanquished—the most marvelous expedition that has ever been made, which paid for its expenses, if I'm not mistaken; suppress Algeria permanently, augmenting its exploitation vastly and attracting 700,000 French colonists there; found in Cochinchina an empire that far surpassed English India in prosperity and grandeur; stop Russia in its march on Constantinople; expel Austria from the peninsula; bring the Rhineland into our circle of action; increase our territory by eight départements; create veritable European equilibrium, and even universal equilibrium?

"Would it?

"But from another point of view, far from complaining, it's necessary to rejoice in the borrowings made under Napoléon III. It's thanks to him that the people, the peasants and the artisans associated their fortune with that of the State, and participated in so many enterprises that opened to our country the fields of activity, into which it had not yet penetrated. Now, it's because the people became rentiers and shareholders that socialism died; in fact, the enemy of capital, it found itself one day confronted, not only by a capitalist people, but a people owning the movable property, more destructible than landed wealth, who are essentially conservative. That is one of the great events of the reign."

Me: "My questions are wandering slightly at hazard; tell me about free exchange. I admit that protection is reducible to levying a tax on all to the profit of one; to 'protect' the iron industry is to say to the French: 'You could get this metal of a better quality and at a cheaper price from your neighbor, but I, the government, am opposed to that, and I'm taking measures to force you to buy the product from a few French manufacturers who will sell it to you poorer and dearer, and who, in consequence, will do better business than if competition were established.' That is as absurd as it is barbaric and iniquitous; for, for from protecting industries, that regime ruins them, since it consists of rewarding poor quality, inactivity, idleness, inertia and poor equipment; it's an encouragement to reject new inventions and progress in manufacture. All that is incontestable.

"However, if competition is established, how will the consumers profit from it? When products once prohibited over surcharged with duties have been admitted or freed from tax, instead of prices falling, they have been increased, and the indigenous ones have followed them; all products have becomes dearer."

The old man: "Some of them for causes external to free exchange. It was thus with butchery meat, which thousands of people used in that epoch who had not nourished themselves thereon before. Other products were exported in greater quantities—obviously, were could not have the pretention of making a commercial treaty to our advantage alone; it was necessary to sell our wines to the English if we wanted to buy their textiles.

"As for products relieved of duties, competition did bring process down, but in bringing them down, it increased consumption, and did so to the point that the increased consumption caused the prices to rise more than they had been lowered by the reduction in duty. There is even a simultaneity in those two facts."

Me: "Then what advantage does the consumer obtain from commercial liberty?"

The old man: "More wellbeing and enjoyment. He consumes more than before; he consumes more varied products, some of which were absolutely forbidden to him. Competition also forces industrialists to introduce all possible improvements into their manufacture.

"Furthermore, if you had reestablished protection in 1870, while losing those advantages, you would have seen prices stay very high. Firstly, in itself, protection would have caused them to rise; secondly, consumption would have diminished, and although tending to lower prices, would not have lowered them sufficiently to cancel out the surplus they had acquired, because needs had been created that people would have wanted to continue to satisfy at any price. Add to those considerations the continued depreciation of gold."

Me: "You defend the actions of Napoléon III one by one—but what about the errors? He committed some.

The old man: "Great governments are not those that make no errors; none like that has ever existed. They are those which, alongside the errors inseparable from human weakness, have done great things. Bad governments are not those that make errors; they are the ones that do nothing else.

"But let's examine the grievances that were formulated against the one under whose reign you lived. Some people feared that Italy might become a redoubtable neighbor for France; it was, on the contrary, weakened by that exaggerated growth, by the unification that we did not make, and became for a long time another Spain—I mean a Spain like that from 1832 to 1860, for the country recovered thereafter. You saw that when she tried to take Trieste and the Tyrol from Austria, when, drawn by her increasingly crazy ambition, she claimed Nice, the Savoy and Corsica from us; when she lost her senses to the extent of taking up arms against us, the struggle was brief."

Me: "That war was after my death."

The old man: "It was said that France should not have let Germany unite. Strictly speaking, it did not have any more right to impede German unification than to oppose Italian unification. In any case, those two transformations, one of which was the result of the other, were only the final destruction of the treaties of 1845 that had only ever had one goal, to keep France down. Those treaties, which had caused so much bloodshed in Poland, Belgium and Italy, did not constitute any European equilibrium, but merely consecrated our diminution. That is what is fundamental. Thus, when everyone violated them in turn, why should France have defended that dead letter, whose text, spirit and temporary application had been such a heavy burden for us?

"The Emperor did better; he allowed Italian unity and German unity to be founded, and he founded French unity in his turn. If he did not take up arms the day after Sadowa, it is because, under the action of a press whose patriotism seemed troubled in that epoch, public opinion vacillated, went momentarily astray, and voiced the desire in places for peace at any price. Pacific by nature, Napoléon III did no violence to the country, and initially left his sword in its scabbard."

"Me: "But Prussia's war against Germany was a pure war of conquest."

The old man: "Undoubtedly, but for want of conquest, the unification of Germany would have taken place some other way. Then again, we are not the world's Don Quixotes."

Me: "That has been said, though."

The old man: "It's puerile. A great cause and a great idea are always at the bottom of the interests of France; that's the truth—with the result that our most political and most French wars always work to the advantage of the oppressed or contribute to civilization. In any case, Napoléon III had too practical a mind to make wars of sentiment, theory or whimsy. He did not, strictly speaking, make war for the Turks against Russia. With regard to the Turks, he prevented Russia from becoming mistress of the Mediterranean, where we had such considerable interests: Marseille, Algeria, Corsica, Tunis,

Egypt. He did not make war for Italy against Austria, but on Austria on the occasion of Italy, which she had, in fact, conquered, with the result that three hundred years of conflict between her and us had terminated in our radical defeat, and our security was directly threatened. And that is why I willingly exempt the Gate and Italy from any gratitude, even though they owe us a profound amity, born of the community of perils and interests, sealed by blood shed in common."

"Me: "In sum, how was the Franco-German question resolved? How was the French agglomeration formed?

The old man: "By arms and by the will of the populations, honestly consulted. A campaign and a battle in 1869 sufficed. And, in passing, I will tell you that it was high time to make that war.

"In Germany, the work improvised and imposed by Prussia was consolidated; our absolute silence had caused the conquered populations to lose all hope of seeing us come to their aid; they submitted. At the same time, the Rhenish populations rendered hesitant by Louis-Philippe in 1840 became more so every day.

"In France, opinion was labored by an opposition that, fearing nothing more than seeing the government cover itself with glory and fulfill the desires of the nation, enervated the country and strove to shake its patriotism in the name of a ridiculous cosmopolitanism. For in France, opposition always being systematic and antidynastic—it has never hidden that—is only patriotic when the government is not, as under King Louis Philippe; when the government is nationalistic and glorious, it kisses the foreigner's feet, and then, to put its language in harmony with its conduct, it is constrained to affect the most revolting doctrines. Thus, in 1867, one newspaper, which was scarcely of its time, had the indecency to sustain the thesis that the checks that the government and French diplomacy might suffer were of no interest to the country; from there to saying that a battle lost by our armies would be indifferent to us is only a short step. Thus, another rag that did not foresee the future and had nothing nationalistic, provoked Italy with all its might to outrage France by violating a convention solemnly signed with her.

"So, the military spirit was weakened. On the other hand, the Chassepot rifles and Noel cannon could not be kept inactive until the day when some new invention would have sent them to the Artillery Museum as curiosities; victory goes to whoever has the best weapon, that weapon only serves once, and that once never arrives if one keeps the weapon for three years.

"Such were the accessory, political and military motives that combined in the absolute necessary that France was in to make war on the Rhine, under pain of being exposed one day to finding herself in the situation of a second-rate power, or even a nation vanquished without having had the honor of fighting."

Me: "But for what reason did that war break out?"

The old man: "I've indicated to you what rendered it necessary. The motives of right were not lacking either; the Treaty of Prague had been violated as soon as it was concluded in two essential dispositions: the States of Southern Germany that ought to have formed a separate confederation were commercially and militarily part of Prussian Germany, which had imposed on them a customs regime common with the Northern Confederation and offensive and defensive alliances, while the relationships between the South and the North were to be regulated by an ulterior arrangement with Austria. On the other hand, the populations of northern Schleswig, which ought to have been honestly consulted as to whether they wanted to be restored to Denmark were maintained under the Prussian yoke."

Me: "So the Rhine is ours and Belgium is with us! I would never have dared hope for that immense result."

The old man: "In 1858, who would have believed that Sardinia would become mistress of the Milanese? Who in 1865 could have explained how Venice would be Italy's the following year?"

Me: "By the way, what has become of the Pope?"

The old man: "By unanimous accord, the Powers maintained him in his reduced territory. They rose above, if one can put it thus, the question of temporal sovereignty, above the political question, and only wanted to see in his eventual dispossession one more blow against the greatest institution in the world, a disturbance of the most powerful dyke opposed to socialism, materialism, atheism and immortality.

"The Pope is still in Rome, where he governs his petty State in peace, and his crown is the most respected in the world.

"In sum, this is what the reign of Napoléon III produced: internally, peace, security, order, labor, activity, wealth, the relief of poverty, moral and intellectual progress, democracy and all the civil, economic and political liberties; externally, real and peaceful equilibrium, the definitive solution of all the great questions, save for the maintenance of certain provisional ones that are sometimes the best solutions."

Chapter XII

Marcellus lived and reigned.

Me: "Since then what has happened? What series of events has traversed the world?"

The old man: "The first years of the reign of Napoléon IV, who mounted the throne of his ancestors in 1888, were troubled by one of those formidable wars that temper courage, fortify hearts and elevate souls, by exercising the noblest passions: disinterest, abnegation, devotion and heroism. For it must be admitted that if wars are scourges, they are moralizing scourges.

"So, war broke out.

"The ambitions of Russia and the United States, contained by the prestige of the arbiter of the world, were unleashed when he entered eternal repose. There was a kind of universal earthquake; the world tottered; one might have thought that the base of everything was collapsing; the nations were adrift, bewildered.

"People knew what that thirty-two-year-old Emperor was, whose august father had remade Europe and society and whose mother was a saint. He was known to be as brave and firm as he was good and wise. But so what? Not to attempt anything at the beginning of his reign, not to put him to the proof, would have been to renounce old projects forever, to submit forever to the preponderance of France. That could not be.

"The Orient was worked up, exciting the Slavs—who, independent thanks to us, could only lose by any change in the state of things, and ran the risk of seeing their independence in regard to Turkey changed into vassalage with regard to Russia. But people did not understand their interests very well; if it were otherwise, the terms *bad politics* and *adventure* would not exist. So, the Bulgars agitated; the Rumanians, Serbs and Montenegrins armed; the Albanians and Thessalonians engaged in conflict. Then Russia threw away the mask and got ready to intervene militarily. France and England immediately adopted a threatening attitude.

"In that situation, the United States having offered their mediation, which had not been accepted because of the goal to which it manifestly tended—the intervention of America in European affairs, and consequently, the possession of some territory in Europe—a concerted comedy was played out. Russia demanded that the American Republic was appointed as an arbiter between herself on the one hand, and France, England, Austria, Italy and Turkey on the other; the Powers refused; the United States took offense and prepared ostentatiously to attack us.

"It was then that the Emperor proclaimed loudly in the name of all the cis-Atlantic states the 'Doctrine of the Author,' of which the formula was: *Europe for the Europeans*, and whose application consisted of rejecting in an absolute manner the slightest participation of America in the affairs of the Old World.

"It was in the wake of those events that the Tsars were, for the last time, expelled from the Ottoman Empire, and were reduced to the impossibility of ever reentering it.

"The war was brief and terrible at sea and in Europe. It required nothing less than the united navies of France and England to destroy, in three famous battles, one fought in the Baltic, one of the coast of Louisiana and the third in the Channel, the combined fleets of the enemy, and then ships of infernal invention came more than once to bombard our ports. It required no less than 110,000 men to repel the Russian army that suddenly descended upon Bulgaria; it required 200,000 more to take Warsaw and Moscow, and as many to take Cronstadt and Saint Petersburg, and more that 500,000 Germans, English and French acting simultaneously.

"When 90,000 French troops were disembarked in the United States, they fought so well in two encounters with the elite of 1,500,000 American volunteers that they had only to appear before the rest to disperse them as the wind disperses smoke; their machine guns and other engines did not save them. A false idea had doomed them; they had believed, after the Civil War of 1861-66, that improvised armies, who could vanquish volunteers, were capable of withstanding permanent troops fashioned by discipline, imbued with the military spirit—without which there is no army—and proven.

"After that war, the United States were confined to their continent, and no more mention was heard of them. That was justice. Had they not the compensation, in any case, of Cuba, the pearl of the Antilles, Jamaica and the Bahamas, which England and Spain had allowed to be snatched away from them in the struggle? In those conditions, having no more useful allies on this side of the Ocean, and instructed by that lesson, they were not tempted to come back, and signed a solemn renunciation of any mixture in European questions—a renunciation that was, moreover, in conformity with the advice that Washington had given them in his farewell address.

"Russia lost Bessarabia, which was restored to Turkey, and Poland, divided between Germany and Austria, sharing with Pomerania and Galicia a mild domination, the great Slavic empire in Central Europe being, in a way, reconstituted by that plan. Russia was also obliged to raze her places of war and no longer to have in Europe anything but an army and a navy reduced to the necessities of police service. No one threatened her; her forces could only have existed for aggressive purposes. She has reported all her activity since then to Asia, where she has begun to press England closely.

"Thus the question of the Orient was resolved.

"One no longer saw in Constantinople those antagonisms of diametrically opposed politics, those struggles for influence between the powers that had done so much harm to the Ottoman Empire. One no longer saw Russia incessantly raising questions, engendering conflicts, inciting vassal populations against the suzerain. For their part, they understood that well-being for all consisted of enjoying the entire independence of which they were really in possession, and devoting their time and effort to veritable progress. They were no longer seen abandoning themselves to intrigues, allowing themselves to be drawn into foolish enterprises. The Turk, therefore, no longer hesitated to do for them everything in his power, and do so honestly, renouncing the eternal postponements and attenuations, either in concession or execution, which were equivalent to refusals. And the Powers no longer thought of anything but aiding the populations and the governors to persist in that sage community of views; they renounced having any other thought regarding the Bosphorus than that of the amelioration and consolidation of the Turkish Empire.

"That thought had, in any case, been until then the essential feature of French politics, and had entered into that of Austria; they had pursued its realization, if not as a unique goal, at least as a means of saving Turkey from revolt, conquest and destruction. They could persevere in that path, for what had been for them a means of influence and resistance to ambitious projects, and for another State a pretext for dissolving action, became a goal for everyone.

"It was thus that England—once more Turkish than the Turk, more Muslim than the Muslim, and more antiprogressive than him—prefer to an immobility and a fatal inertia adopted on his advice, reforms and a fecund activity inaugurated on ours. England, finally forced to recognize than our politics was absolutely disinterested, no longer put up any opposition, adopted the same object as us, and worked sincerely thereafter to attain it.

"That resulted in such a concurrence of wills that nothing—no hidden agendas, no resistances—any longer opposed it; al the difficulties were soon ironed out as if by magic, and the agriculture, finances and civil and administrative organization of Turkey rapidly caught up with that of more prosperous states.

"That transformation of the Oriental politics of cabinets was all the easier to accomplish because, fortunately, the Egyptian question no longer came up—a question that might have been a new Oriental question whose seat would have been Cairo rather than Constantinople, but whose importance and danger would have been similar, its peripeties analogous, and would have given rise to exactly the same rivalries and political deviations. No one thought of dominating the Viceroy, or, at least, no one dared assume the responsibility of opening such a door to discord; and, no ne having entered that path, everyone limited themselves to maintaining cordial relations with the Prince. It must be said, moreover, that the unity of religion of his peoples, which set aside any pretext for a general and permanent interference; the wealth and abundance of indigenous and foreign activity that determined the movement in Egypt produced by the piercing of the isthmus of Suez; and the excellent organization of the country that soon made it a mighty power, rendered interventions les easy and took away the desire. England therefore limited herself to retaining her possessions in Aden and Perim, without entertaining any more territorial or moral ambitions.

"The same causes preserved from any absorption Rumania and the Slav states south of the Danube; the prosperity and strength they knew after many storms prevented anyone from thinking of conquering them. What would have been more natural, however, than Austria, mistress of so many Slavic provinces and such a large part of the course of the Danube, turning her views and her action toward the sovereignty of the entire river basin? Well, the vitality of the populations to be absorbed had become such that to think of it would have been folly; Austria renounced it with the same sagacity that had made her renounce Italy permanently, as impossible to submit.

"Then was revealed in all its grandeur the Danubian politics of France, whose goal had been to render free and too strong for anyone to attempt to attack them, the Serbs, the Rumanians and the Montenegrins, and to regenerate Turkey itself by reform.

"Everywhere, in Florence, Berlin, Vienna, London and Paris, there was a general renunciation of projects that, in other times, would have been the simple development of new politics based in new circumstances.

"England being disinterested in the affairs of the continent, into which the Oriental question alone had led her to mingle, and from which she had distanced herself as much as possible with that reservation; Prussia, having abandoned any project of expansion, losing all interest in returning beyond the Rhine; France and Italy being satisfied and Russia defeated, a complete equilibrium was finally found that no one any longer had any desire to disturb, and everyone had an interest in maintaining.

"Note once again that the principle of nationalities was not the sole constitutive element of that equilibrium. The equilibrium was normal because it did not repose on that principle any more than on faith in treaties, history, geographical analogies, grouping of interests, etc.—which is to say that all the considerations that can determine the tracing of a frontier, and not one alone, had been put in the balance. And that manner of procedure had been truly wise, for it is as iniquitous and false only to delimit empires under the influence of a preoccupation with nationalities as it would be to regulate the solely on differences of religion. A State is not an abstract and theoretical entity; it is an ensemble of real people and things; it can only live, or at least prosper, on the condition that the elements forming it have more affinities with one another than with neighboring groups; now, when a single link holds them together, it is likely that several attach them to the continuous agglomeration.

"Thus, the peace of the world was founded permanently, and the sword could be transformed into a plowshare. All the peoples disarmed almost completely, even more than they had done after the war that gave us the Rhineland; in that epoch, large-scale disarmament would have been possible because equilibrium had already been established between France, formed from ancient Gaul, Prussia, extending from the Baltic and the Slei to Mayn and Gleichberg, sovereign Austria, suzerain or federal directrice of the majority of territories watered by the Danube, and England, an island power; but the threat of Russian pretentions had imposed a limit on that relaxation of peoples. Once Russian dreams were ruined permanently, Europe could take off its armor.

"After the second Peace of Paris, the temple of war was closed, and politics became a dead science, like alchemy. Henceforth, there were only economic and social questions, and scarcely any but social and economic expenditures. All the strength and activity of peoples was redirected toward economic, intellectual and moral progress. Many institutions founded or projected during the preceding reign were able to attain their full flowering. The great future glimpsed, indicated, pursued, prepared and attained in its principal developments by Napoléon III was realized. Humankind was within sight of its apogee.

"That epoch bears in history the name of 'the century of Napoléon IV.'"

Chapter XIII

The worst of states is the popular state.
Corneille.

After a pause, the old man continued his story in these terms:

"I ought not, however, to pass over in silence the war that broke out in 1960 between Japan and England, in which the latter was submitted to rude proofs and was vanquished rather than victorious. These are the circumstances in which those remarkable events occurred.

"In contrast to China, which had not engaged in politics for centuries, except when incomers put her in a situation in which it was necessary for her to fight and sustain her interests against foreigners, the Japanese, having become unitary monarchists instead of feudal or federal, and having borrowed all their military arts from Europeans—appropriating them with an intelligence and marvelous rapidity, and even improving them—did not take long to expand outwardly. Their commerce came of its own accord to seek in European products in our ports, and their flag was soon floating over all seas. On the one hand it crossed the Pacific and visited San Francisco, Valparaiso and the Antilles, passing through the Panama Canal that linked the oceans; on the other, it traversed the seas of China and Indian and passed via Suez to reach Marseilles.

"That maritime movement caused the Japanese to feel the necessity of having staging posts for rest and reprovisioning, and colonies. They therefore cast their eyes first upon Formosa, which is near the Liou-Tchou islands and linked by them to the large Japanese islands; they remembered that at the beginning of the eighteenth century they had founded establishments in Formosa, and the conquest was resolved.

"Brawls having taken place between Japanese merchants and Formosans that the authorities had supported, and the cabinet in Peking not having given the government the satisfactions demanded, the latter announced its intention to 'occupy'

Formosa until the dispute was settled. Words were swiftly followed by action, and without overmuch noise, but resolutely, fifteen thousand well-armed Japanese, supported by a few armored frigates and two monitors, disembarked at Kiloung, rapidly took possession of the principal points of the country and fortified them.

"England was violently moved by that assumption of possession, which clearly threatened to be permanent, and was surely only the first step on a path at whose end her colonial and commercial interests and her influence might well be compromised, since Formosa controlled the route to Shanghai. She supported the representations of the Chinese government and made her own. It was in vain; long negotiations had no other effect than to permit the Japanese to install themselves strongly in their new territory. England then armed, and, in spite of the pacific offices of France, war broke out.

An Anglo-Chinese expedition attempted, unsuccessfully, to expel the Japanese troops from Formosa. Considerable forces bombarded Yeddo; but at the same time, an armored Japanese squadron suddenly appeared at the mouth of the Thames and sowed fear there.

"England judged that the proportions the struggle was taking were no longer in proportion to the importance of the motive, great as it was, and peace was made under our mediation. Formosa was neutralized, and China, Japan, England and France would have the right to construct identical maritime establishments there. But it was agreed that in case of conflict between Japan and Korea, none of the signatories of the treaty would intervene. Since then, Korea has become Japanese territory. The objective of the Japanese statesmen was not attained, however, and now it is the Philippines that are menaced.

"It remains for me to say a few words about other important transformations that have been accomplished among various peoples.

"Firstly, let's talk about Canada. A long infiltration by people from the United States rendered that territory, originally so French, Anglo-Saxon, at the same time as, by virtue of

228

an analogous fact, corroborated by cunning and violence, Mexico was subjected to the same fate. In that event, England applied the colonial politics that she had commenced to practice in 1863, when she had renounced Corfu; she meekly allowed the link to be broken that united her with her offspring, being of the opinion that there was no more advantage to be gained, by sustaining a formidable and uncertain war in order to keep it in hand, than by peacefully exchanging its products with it and with the great Republic, and importing and exporting merchandise of every sort under the British flag.

"Those various annexations had an expected effect on the Pacific coast; the United States were revolutionized from top to bottom. Radical differences of race, mores, tastes, ideas and, above all, interests, emerged between the North, the South and the West, which had been rapidly populated and enriched. In those respects, the people of each region had almost nothing in common any longer with those of the other two, and the common institutions, laws and measures were ineffective, imperfect and bastardized, either inconveniencing everyone or oppressing one part of the State to the profit of the other two. A double secession took place and three republics were founded. In their turn, too vast to have any need of a central government capable of a certain action, a certain unity of conduct and a certain coherence of views, and the threat of decomposition into elements too small not to produce a general debilitation, fatigued by the excesses of an absolute liberty—which is to say, a theoretical liberty contrary to practical life, apparent, fictitious and deceptive—the three republics were gradually transformed into monarchies governed by princes descended from European dynasties.

"The republics of South America suffered the same fate.

"You know what became of those unfortunate countries: a perpetual mobility of legislation, an insecurity and continuous disturbance, disorders of every sort, a permanent civil war, interrupted by a few brief truces but never by peace—in brief, a bloody anarchy maintained by adventurers ambitious to the point of folly and ferocity: that, in broad, strokes, is the picture formed by the history of those countries since their foundation. Yes, even the War of Independence, for it's necessary not to be seduced by the idea that their existence had its origin in a great act of emancipation. Of one look at that history closely one only sees, from the first days of the struggle, from 1810 onwards, petty rivalries of wretched individuals, cynical egotisms and atrocious and unjustified hatreds; everything is petty and repulsive; patriotism and ideas of independence counted for very little in the movement, to say nothing of the indecisions, the inconsistencies, the incapacities, and the illegality and illegitimacy of actions of every sort, of governments and constitutions.

"What was the superior and essential cause of the duration of that deplorable state? The deadly political regime that had been inflicted upon them: the Republic.

"In fact, the immediate and local causes of the evil were the vastness of the territories, in consequence of which, the cities being situated at enormous distances from one another, the action of government needed to be very forceful in order to make itself felt; the sparseness and incoherence of populations; the antipathy of the juxtaposed races; the rivalry of cities that, by virtue of their desire for particular independence, tended to an infinitesimal fragmentation of States; the traditions of the former regime put in the presence of the most extravagant formulae of European demagoguery; the lack of political education; the effervescence, not to say the fermentation, of personal ambitions; and finally, the passionate vivacity of the Iberian race.

"Now, those principles, which had been mortal for the eight great Latin republics and the five small ones, had not been dangerous in Brazil, the State that, precisely because of its immensity, ought to have suffered the most. That was because it was sheltered by a crown.

"I have to hand an opinion emitted in 1853 before the Brazilian parliament by one Soares de Sousa,[25] if I'm not mistaken, who strove to disculpate the Latin peoples of America. 'Let us not condemn our neighbors,' said the Minister of Foreign Affairs, 'let us not blame them for their condition; let us remember the circumstances that have accompanied their emancipation; let us recall that we would probably have suffered the same fate, that the Empire would have been similarly broken up, that we would have fallen into the same dissensions, of, at the time of our independence, we had not a man born of royal blood here, and with that man a great principle. Let us remember that the same thing could still have happen to us if, at the time of his abdication, Dom Pedro I had not left a child here, and with that child the great principle that has saved us.'

"I will add that the Brazilian constitution, which dates from 1825, is in reality the most ancient that is in vigor in the entire world. For a long time, England's has only been ancient from the historical viewpoint, for in reality, not the slightest fragment of it remaining standing in the nineteenth century.

"But what of Chile? If it was troubled between 1817 and 1830, at least it has maintained a relatively calm and prosperous situation since then. That is because of its geographical configuration: it forms a littoral strip some sixty leagues broad; it was not in one of those conditions that the republic has rendered mortal in all the other States; the population accumulated between the Andes and the sea was much more compact and much more in the hands of the government than any of the populations disseminated in the solitudes that extend from the Rio del Norte to Patagonia; the governmental bond was therefore able to relax with less peril. The Chileans however, have not been sufficiently exempt from sterilizing agitations not to understand the benefits of monarchy.

---

[25] Paulino Soares de Sousa, 1st Viscount of Uruguai (1808-1866).

"As for Paraguay, if, since its emancipation, although a republic, it has found itself, with regard to internal order, in an entirely satisfactory situation, it is because the republican regime was only one in name, while the most absolute monarchy was the reality. Which proves that, outside of the constitutional monarchy exercised by a prince born in the purple, the unlimited despotism of an individual was the sole combination that permitted an American State to escape anarchy. Another proof in support of that assertion is that the brief periods of repose that the Latin republics have enjoyed from time to time have only been due to the energetic action of dictators.

"All those States, therefore, which are now as populous as Europe, have sagely formed monarchies and now enjoy the advantages that are only given by a political organization such that the power is strong enough to do good and prevent evil, liberty weak enough not to hinder the action of government toward good, but strong enough to stimulate it, the authority being the executive, and liberty being the control and the stimulant. The foremost of its advantages is peace, order and security, without which the liberty of labor, the liberty of expansion of all individual forces, true Liberty, does not exist.

"To complete what I have told you about that country—and, as you see, I am taking to you without much order and coherency, as facts and considerations present themselves to my mind—it is as well that you know that Brazil has completely absorbed Uruguay, and that its frontier extends to the Rio de la Plata.

"But let's return to Europe.

"If one disengaged humanity from the various and multiple aspects with which time and place dress it, if, by exploring the route that it has traveled, one turns one's eyes away from the obstacles it has encountered, the ruins of which persist, one is struck by the grandiose unity of its destinies. Almost simultaneously, all the peoples of a region—Europe, Asia, America—undergo the same transformation. To begin with, Greek civilization expands over Italy, Egypt and Asia Minor; everything there, at a given time—arts, letters, sciences, politics—is imprinted with the Hellenic genius. Later, it is Rome, military and juridical, that marks everything with its stamp. Then it is the reign of the Church and feudalism. Then comes the struggle between the lords and the king; unitary power is founded and everything fades away before it. But to triumph over the nobility it was necessary to raise up the commons and find support therein; a day comes when, after having been effaced by the majesty of the sovereign, they reappear, and, strong in their turn, demanding their share of liberty. Combat is engaged; the monarchy succumbs; power passes into the hands of a mixed and median aristocracy. Finally, the petty rise up, universal suffrage is attained; Europe is democratic. And in the principal stages of that long march, all the peoples have found themselves, at the same time or very nearly, feudal, monarchic, bourgeois and democratic.

"Russia, for it's her that I want to come to, has gone through all these phases, like the other nations that live on our continent. Alexander II dealt the final blow to the nobility and emancipated the serfs; he found at first, among them, submission, gratitude and support, but when they no longer had anything to fear from the boyars, when they had received the benefits of their independence, when a large number of them had become rich tradesmen and important proprietors, when a middle class, previously unknown in Russia, had formed, it wanted, as it had an interest in it, to count in the State, and it was necessary to open the doors of power to it; an aristocracy of money was constituted, the true principle of which is broadly, if not radically, democratic, since nothing is more mobile than riches, and yesterday's beggar might perhaps be tomorrow's millionaire. Eventually, and rapidly, pure democracy replaced it.

"Russia, and with her England, Prussia, Austria, Italy, Spain, Turkey, Egypt and Persia thus became, like France, and shortly after her for the most part, monarchies based on universal suffrage, on equality and liberty.

Chapter XIV

Vox populi...

"Now you'll ask me how, from so high, we have fallen so low?

"We slid down a gradual slope.

"But before acquainting you with the social history of Europe, before retracing the events that have led all the peoples to that condition in which you find us, I want to tell you a little about the internal history of France. That way, I shall detach from my story one of its particular aspects, and we can proceed from the particular to the general.

"1789 was a political and social revolution; it destroyed both the absolute monarchy and political and civil castes.

"The Empire consecrated its work while sacrificing the liberty of which the country as weary, by which it was horrified because of the crimes committed in its name.

"The hazard of battles overthrew the Empire; the Bourbons returned to France in the bloody footprints of the allies and remounted the throne of their forefathers under the protection of the bayonets of those that France had been fighting for twenty-five years.

"Certainly, Europe had not made war on us with the objective of restoring them, and had little enthusiasm for placing the crown of France on their head; but the mere coincidence of our defeat and their reinstallation left no room in the hearts of the majority of Frenchmen for the slightest favorable impression. Almost forgotten for ten years, accept with mistrust after the first impulse of joy the change brought and above all caused by the prospect of peace, suffered with impatience and anger, the Bourbons did not take long to be hated. France could not be reconciled the idea that the scepter of the man who had covered it with glory, for whom so much blood had been shed, and who had been the incarnation of the revolution and the people, could be in the hands of those who had cursed our victories and the revolution. They were considered as enemies, as foreign conquerors, as oppressors. The presence of the Bourbons, a monument to our defeat, was a permanent outrage.

"The foreign habits and mores of the émigrés, their pretentions, their arrogance, their passions and their foolish threats aggravated those sentiments. And no matter what Louis XVIII, an arrogant but clever prince, did, conceding fairly considerable liberties, especially at the emergence from the imperial regime, containing and discontenting the Court and the Vendée, every day saw France's aversion for its former dynasty increase.

"The situation soon became impossible. The liberties demanded were only pretexts for attacks; the liberties conceded were only weapons in the hands of the Bourbons' enemies. There were conspiracies everywhere; they could not live with liberty. They tried reaction, which had no greater success. No, in addition to an incompatibility of humor, tastes and ideas that separated the people from the royal family, and above all its entourage, there was on the side of France an absolute, preconceived antipathy, ardently maintained, which it was impossible to cure. Those unfortunate princes could have given everything and it would have been deemed insufficient; people only wanted one thing: that they should go. Charles X issued his orders and was expelled; if he had not done so, if he had surrendered all liberties, he would still have been expelled. The July Revolution was a revolution of blind passion, a revenge taken by deeply wounded national sentiment—a grave fault, involving many dangers, which might have led liberty and France to ruin, if the era of revolutions had not subsequently been closed in time.

"And in those manifestations of sentiment, what odious injustices! Was the Restoration not accused, still because of the circumstances in which it had been made, of humiliating France before foreigners? Well, that was false; the Restoration was very proud, and, as much as its situation as a vanquished power permitted, very independent. Louis XVIII, at the Congress of Vienna, and later Charles X , were veritable Kings of

France with regard to foreign cabinets, and not for a single day did they conduct themselves other than as Kings of France.

"The war that was waged against the Bourbons was extremely disloyal. The politics of the opposition often consisted of preventing the government from taking liberal measures, in frightening the Court with ultra-liberal amendments, in rendering the collaboration of the government and the Chambre impossible, and in precipitating a *coup d'état* by disturbing and agitating the country.

"I will show you shortly a monument to the infamy of a certain opposition party in that epoch: an article in *Le Globe* of 24 October 1830, which sets out with an odious cynicism the shameful means of which use was made to wage war against the fallen government.

"When the revolution was made, a question arose. It had been accomplished in the name of certain liberties; it was necessary to institute them; that they would be instituted was not open to doubt. But what government would replace the former monarchy?

"The Republic had few adherents; Napoléon II was a prisoner in Austria; to whom should great France be given? It did not have time to interrogate itself; it was hoodwinked.

"There was, among the number of the most cunning and most active conspirators whose work had just come to fruition a prince belonging to a house whose founder had been famous for his perpetual conspiracies and for the facility with which he had abandoned his accomplices; the last head of that house had extended a regicidal hand toward the crown. It was his son, ambitious without grandeur and without dignity, who was suddenly made king by a few friends that he had inserted into the bosom of the liberal party. Two hundred and twenty-nine députés modified the Constitution without a mandate, pronounced the fall of one dynasty and erected a new dynasty in a single session lasting seven hours! And those députés, elected under the empire of a charter that they remade at their whim, under the reign of a man whose family they proscribed, awarded the crown of France as they would have voted a regu-

236

lation, and went to fetch their candidate without even waiting for the assent of the Chambre of peers.

"Assuredly the choice was singular. The Bourbons were overthrown and replaced by a Bourbon; they were rejected because they had re-entered France 'on the ammunition-wagons of cossacks'—that was the conventional expression and their throne was given to a prince who, an émigré like them, had returned like them, the same time as them, and with them, on the cossacks' ammunition wagons. They were re-proached for having borne arms against their country, and if he had not fought against us, that was not his decision, for he had gone over to the enemy with weapons and luggage in the company of Dumouriez, but the enemy had peremptorily re-fused his services. His proclamation of Tarragona, the com-mandment in chief of the army of Catalonia that was given to him by the governmental junta of Cadiz, and the withdrawal of that commandment on Wellington's orders, are indestructible facts.

"How did France let that happen? Two things allowed that improvised king to pass. He had made himself a reputa-tion as a liberal, and he was known to be an enemy of his el-ders. There were, therefore, points of similarity between him and the country. Finally, and above all, the tricolor cockade, the imperial cockade, covered the merchandise.

"What proves that in advance is the first proclamation of the Duc d'Orléans: 'As I enter the city of Paris I wear with pride these glorious colors that you have taken up again, and that I have worn for a long time.' There are also these words, which Monsieur Boinvilliers addressed to him on 30 July 1830: 'Supposing that you become king, what is your opinion of the treaties of 1815? Take note that it is not a liberal revolu-tion that is being made in the streets; it is a national revolution. The sight of the tricolor flag, that is what had excited the peo-ple, and it would certainly be easier to push Paris toward the Rhine than over Saint-Cloud.'

"Whatever the principle and causes were of the July Revolution, and the double usurpation of the man who profited from it—a usurpation to the detriment of his family and to the detriment of France—it briefly took on the appearance of a transformation and a partial progress.

"It was only for a moment. That deceit, which stained the debut of the reign, characterized it from one end to the other. It was one long duel with discourteous weapons between the government and liberty; the government was often the victor; every time, and as much as he could, he tied the hands of liberty; but liberty ended up being the stronger and by killing the government, the king and the dynasty.

"Louis-Philippe had failed in his mandate. Raised to the throne—or, to be more exact, accepted, more or less—on condition of combating reaction, of developing liberty and repairing the defeats of 1814 and 1815, or at least holding the flag of France high, he had combated liberty and humiliated France before the powers. All the internal and external politics of Louis-Philippe gravitated around his preoccupation with dynastic interests; always fearful that cabinets might oust him, he let them do anything; the fall of Laffitte in 1831 had no other cause than the secret and individual politics of the king with regard to Austria, politics contrary to that of the Council. It was in those paltry endeavors that the maladroitly clever prince, too fecund in expedients, incapable of broad vision, who mistook knavery for politics, used himself up,

Let us now consider the first fifty years of the nineteenth century from the special viewpoint of the rights of the people in general and democracy.

"A distinguished historian has said, and I share his opinion, although I do not admit the consequences that he has drawn from his assertion, that the reign of Louis-Philippe was the triumph of the bourgeoisie over the monarchy, over the aristocracy and over the people. Under the Restoration there was a real, if not very apparent, struggle between the debris of the aristocracy, which wanted to reconstitute itself, and the crown; at the same time there was a real, if not very apparent, struggle between the crown and the bourgeoisie; finally, there was a struggle between the aristocracy and the bourgeoisie.

The aristocracy defended the crown, but at the same time wanted to diminish it to its advantage; the bourgeoisie wanted very nearly the same thing; 1830 was the triumph of the bourgeoisie over the crown and the aristocracy—but in all of that, where were the people?

"I accept that theory, and I recognize that the people began to become something in 1848. But universal suffrage, precarious then, led, by an accident in which, I must admit, the people had not played any part, the fact coinciding with the institution of a government antipathetic to the country, on which it had been imposed in the most insulting fashion, which did not really exist, did not pass into the realm of right and legality, and was only consecrated and guaranteed on the day when it became the basis of the sole veritably legitimate government that France had had, along with those of the Consulate and the Empire, to the election of Prince Louis-Napoléon to a decennial presidency.

"I emphasize this point: the revolution of 1848 came as a profound surprise to the bourgeoisie. There was, alongside it, a smaller bourgeoisie that wanted its share of power and had demanded reform; suddenly, a revolution emerged therefrom.

"On the other hand, who had demanded the Republic? Who had consulted the country in order to establish it? That form of government, antipathetic to our genius, to our historical past, to our religion, to our mores, was imposed on France by a small group of wayward individuals. And that is so true that, on the day when the people were consulted, when they could finally express their sentiment and their opinion, in spite of the maneuvers of the parties, in spite of the energetic action of the existing power, they proclaimed the monarchy by summoning to the presidential seat an imperial pretender. That day, the people took their revenge, and repudiated the bloody, insane and grotesque Republic that had emerged behind the muddy paving-stones.

"Again the people rejected that wretched government—whose short existence had also been sent struggling against liberty, exhausting itself withdrawing or limiting the impracticable liberties that it had inflicted on the country—when from all parts, almost unanimously, with an indefatigable persistence, ardently and proudly, they told the man who held the destiny of France in his hands to save it from the ruination with which it was threatened. They insinuated to him, they counseled him, they begged him, they rejoined him, and they summoned him to action. And, detested and scorned as it deserved to be, the Republic fell like a rotten fruit under the finger that pushes it. In this case, the pushing finger was that of the people.

"A Head of State who senses an entire people behind him, who hears their supplications, their universal incitements, who has measured the extent of the danger by which the people are menaced, who knows that he is able to save them but who does not do so is the greatest of criminals. By what evils the world would have been overwhelmed without the second of December! How far and for how long would civilization have been held back in Europe!

"For a third time, the people trampled the Republic underfoot when, consulted again, it consecrated by the glare of a solemn vote the great action that had been carried out. It did so once by demanding the reestablishment of the Empire, and again in voting for it.

"Such were the ordeals through which France passed before becoming the France of Napoléon III, the last form of which was a democracy invested with all the liberties and only having for a counterweight the Crown and the Senate. Such is the route that the people—which does not mean only the poor classes but the whole ensemble of citizens—traveled before arriving at the democratic monarchy, before being, in security, their own masters.

"At the succession of Napoléon IV, quasi-unlimited liberty had been founded for twelve years; already the acts of 24 November 1860, 19 January 1867 and 16 March 1876, among others, had had the result of disorganizing the parties, reducing them to impotence and causing them to fall into oblivion. What could they demand, in fact, and what remained to prom-

240

ise them? What could the pretenders—who were relived of their exile with the accession of the prince—have brought as a dowry to free France, the France of universal suffrage, to France the mistress of the Rhine? One of them, in any case, the most august, had died without noise and without lineage, and all the old French nobility had immediately rallied *en masse* to the Empire, only recognizing after the legitimacy of divine right the legitimacy of the rights of the people.

"Under Napoléon IV, therefore, there was no longer, either in the Chambres or in the press, any constituted, permanent and, in consequence, systematic opposition, ever-ready to form a coalition, and having only one goal, the overthrow of the dynasty, or at least the rise to power. There were no longer anything but momentary and partial oppositions based on real interests put in question, agitated because a projected measure affected them; when the debate was over, those oppositions dissolved of their own accord, to be replaced by others whose objective was entirely different. There were public questions and opposition, no longer political questions and opposition.

"The political history of France since then has been entirely comprised in the social history of Europe, which I shall trace for you briefly.

Chapter XV

If it is true that individual interest ought to be subordinate to that of society, it is no less true that it is an essential interest of society that the individual should be respected and independent.

"I said just now that the French Revolution, which has become the universal Revolution, was both political and social. The spirit of the Revolution was essentially Christian; it was equitable and charitable; it was an aspiration toward human happiness. *Télémaque*, which is the most ancient of our revolutionary monuments, is nothing else.

"Later, Montesquieu, Voltaire and Rousseau modified that spirit in the direction of philosophy and right, but fundamentally, it remained the same.

"The memoranda of the Estates General, which are the definitive formula of the wishes of the new France, and the acts that realized those wishes, tended above all to the amelioration of the civil and social condition of individuals. Suffering had been traced back to abuses; the abolition of the abuses tended toward wellbeing.

"But the struggles that were produced from the very beginning of the Revolution had the effect of giving the first place to politics, and questions of wellbeing were almost forgotten. The warrior workers of the Empire also lost sight of them.

It was only in peace that the chain was reconnected; Fourier and Saint-Simon took it up. Their doctrines rested on two completely false bases: one was the very folly of their projects, the other that the first illuminate who comes along has the right to exterminate society, if he has the strength, in order to apply he formulae that have emerged from his lucubrations: a detestable and deadly principle that was emitted and practiced by the Convention and had long hung over Europe.

"That hideous doctrine of public salvation has led many people astray in the pursuit of human wellbeing, in making the seek absolute formulae that they do not despair of applying some day by means of force and the aid of the guillotine; whereas, without the precedents of the Republic, they would have limited themselves to inventing practical means of relieving general suffering. From that comes the communist and socialist constellation that does so much harm, alarming minds and exciting resistance to useful and just reforms that are confounded with chimeras, awakening unrealizable hopes and desires, deceiving intelligences and hearts, exciting evil passions, advocating systematic depredation and murder. Hence, a considerable delay in the solution of questions and the foundation of economic liberties, which, presented in several works of the school, at the same time as new political organizations from which they show them as inseparable, were thus subordinated to extravagances with which, however, they had no connection. Hence, in brief, the slowness of economics to make itself plain.

"It finally triumphed. The Republic of 1848 permits the judgment of almost all those projects of radical reorganization; several were applied and for the others, their authors made them well-known; the effects of both could be seen in the street, at the barricades.

"Fortunately, order having been rapidly reestablished, nothing remained of that bad dream but the fact that they had been close enough to the edge of the abyss to measure its depth. The peace that reigned under the Empire, in the cities as in souls, permits the discernment of what good there might have been in the dangerous plans that had nearly wrecked society, and to separate the politics from the economics. Then, socialism, having been by turns feared, hated and ridiculed, fell into the domain of forgetfulness, and, alongside their labor of external and internal politics, governments and peoples devoted themselves to a permanent investigation of the suffering and wellbeing of the masses, and the means of attenuating or making the former disappear, while developing the latter.

"Everything, moreover, concurred with that movement. The Revolution became scientific. The progress of science, its marvelous applications, communications of all kinds rendered so facile, the borrowings of very kind that peoples were able to make from one another, the softening of mores produced by the multiplicity of relations founded commercial liberty in a few years, caused individual liberty to take full flight, and, thus permitting everyone to give all that they could, also led, in general, to everyone receiving everything they needed.

It is necessary to recognize that, in the époque we have now reached, under the reign of Napoléon III and his contemporaries, especially at the beginning of the fourth quarter of the nineteenth century, governments were practicing a little socialism. That is what they were doing when they took from the pockets of all the taxpayers in order to help a particular

243

class of citizens—the workers, for example—charging some in order to compensate others. That is what they were doing when they exempted the poor from direct taxation. Undoubtedly, it was charity, and well-placed charity; undoubtedly, political reasons motivated that privilege, and I'm not taking about the argument that consists of saying: 'Let's satisfy the people, stuff them and corrupt them, and they'll shut up.' No, there were in measures of that sort a nobler political reason, which was this: 'Let us help those who are weak, in order that none of society's strength shall be wasted.'

"Undoubtedly, that was not to constitute a caste, for in a democratic society everyone can be great one day and petty the next; but it was to constitute a privilege in favor of a condition. Undoubtedly, it was not a principle, a general system that was being followed; it was, on the contrary, an exception, a detail, whose application was secondary and the inconvenience light for those on whom it fell, and of which the benefit was enormous for those who profited from it. But fundamentally, rigorously, theoretically, it was an imposed charity, an injustice and an action stained by socialism, in a measure of which no one ever thought of complaining, so excellent was it in practice and so much did the idea present itself naturally to the mind. Let us therefore pass over that purely incidental point.

"The state of affairs in 1876, therefore, gave the maximum possible satisfaction to everyone; it procured the greatest sum of possible good for the greatest number. It lasted for some time.

"But there is one law that takes precedence over all the other laws to which the destinies of humankind are subject. It is neither good nor evil of which the reign is established, although, over time, one can observe that the domain of good extends little by little. It is movement, it is transformation, that is the supreme law.

"Happy as that epoch was, it was bound to change its manner of being, and then, evidently, that could not be for the better. The summit had been reached, it was necessary to descend. Everyone was as happy as it was possible to be without hindering others, but they wanted to be even happier, and that was to the detriment of one another. The liberty of all was eroded to the profit of some.

"The less rich classes wanted to ameliorate their relative situation; now, perfect liberty and equality being founded in principle—for, as I've said, they had already been slightly transgressed in favor of the poor—to want more was to seek privileges. They entered into that path, and did not emerge from it again. Governments were unable to stop the minds drawn into a false route, and became the instrument of deadly measures.

"The best institutions were the first denatured.

"In France, the councils of industrial arbitration—which, reorganized in 1853, had given such admirable results for many years that in 1865, out of 42,978 disputes, only 11 had not been settled amicably—instead of being a neutral terrain to which employers and workers could come to reach an understanding, were again, toward 1890, delivered to the latter; the pernicious decree of 1848 that had temporarily destroyed those councils, was reestablished after ninety years, and it resulted in a new abandonment by the employers of that tribunal of conciliation, which had changed into a court in which the same interests were judges and shared, and war broke out with the workers.

"It was subsequently resolved to forbid employers to form coalitions, while that legitimate right was maintained for the workers. The excellent law on 1864 on coalitions, which had had the magnificent effect that, from the second year after its promulgation, not one of the coalitions formed in Paris gave rise to pursuits, was modified. Everywhere, equality and justice were replaced by privilege.

"Then insensate salaries were demanded. Industry suffered therefrom; there is a sum of salaries beyond which an employer no longer has an interest in working, in that the sum leaves him little or no profit margin; many factories closed; industries were displaced. It happened one day, for instance, that all silk ribbons came from Berlin; the ribbon-manufacturers were dying of hunger for having wanted to earn more than was possible.

"On the other hand, as salaries were rising everywhere, the worker's expenses increased in all their elements; if the shoemaker had himself paid more for his work, the tailor had to pay more for his shoes, and was obliged to sell his clothes more dearly.

"Remedies were only sought in strikes and monstrous associations whose purpose was to oppress the employers—which is to say that, in order to remedy the evil, it was aggravated. Strikes were formed not only between the workers of a single factory but all the workers in a city—which was opposed to the free discussion of salaries, which can only take place in a serious manner between one employer and his own workers, and which was pure oppression of the master by strangers. Then there were départemental strikes, regional strikes, national and international strikes; there were universal strikes; one day, not a single silk hat was manufactured in all of Europe.

"In sum, a secret, powerful, irresistible and frightfully tyrannical organization brought together all the European workers in a monstrous group. On a word of order sent from who knows where, the workshops closed from Saint Petersburg to Madrid. And woe betide the artisan who refused to be part of the society; woe betide the man who, burdened with children, did not pay the weekly subscription by means of which the formidable strikes could be sustained; woe betide the man who did not find the subsidy the society paid him during the strike sufficient to allow his family to live, and resumed work without receiving the order. The first time, his tools were stolen; the second time he was mutilated by a mysterious bullet; the third time, his house blew up, along with him and his family. The members of several cooperative societies who, thanks to the small number of their associates and the constitution of a capital anterior to their functioning, had succeeded, were trapped and lost in that system of terrible oppression. It was a new form of slavery, a new reign of terror. The worker was powerful in the sense that he belonged to a powerful organization, but with regard to that organization he was nothing but a slave. Individual liberty was lost.

"It went further. The International League of Workers resolved to dominate in politics as it did in industry. There were terrible struggles, and politics once again became one of the country's occupations; it was soon the principal one, and Europe divided almost all of its time between the newspapers, the clubs, meetings, elections and the Chambres, where the League members ended up being the masters.

"From that day on society went rapidly toward its ruin. An absolute centralization, a necessary instrument of the occult tyranny that oppressed it, replaced the municipal and regional liberties that people had enjoyed, and the measures most destructive of society, its vitality, its activity, its wealth and its happiness were adopted in turn and imposed on populations incoherently.

"Those events, which occurred in all the countries in Europe, were accomplished here at the end of the reign of Napoléon V, who, born in 1877, mounted the throne in 1936 and died in 1957. Under Napoléon VI the fatal work was completed, and made France what it is today, the sovereign losing almost all his power and being reduced to a vain nominal authority.

"Thus," he added, an in melancholy tone, after a moment's silence, "God, in his impenetrable designs, only raises people and kings to cast them down!"

Chapter XVI

Grande quidem dedimus patientiae documentum.
Tacitus.[26]

As he spoke those words, we heard a great noise in the street, the confused murmur of an agitated crowd, and soon clamors and cries; then, lending an attentive ear, we distinguished the distant roll of drums.

I descended in haste and arrived on the threshold of the house at the moment when a considerable troop of citizens, formed in dense columns, was going past in god order. They seemed to be prey to a keen animation, and an energetic resolution was painted on their faces. From time to time a formidable shout went up, of which I only grasped the meaning imperfectly:

"Long live Napoléon VII, governing emperor!"

I could see that something extraordinary was happening. So, slipping into the ranks, I started marching with the troop, which paid no attention to me, and seemed to take me for one of their own.

After some time, I dared to ask my neighbor: "Where are we going?"

"To the Tuileries, to beg the Emperor to reorganize the country and the government, to render us the civilization, religion, laws and liberty of our forefathers. Long live Napoléon VII, governing emperor!"

And the crowd repeated that cry, enthusiastically.

I understood. I was witnessing a revolution! Except that the struggle seemed to me to be far from being engaged, since I could hear neither the sound of cannon nor that of musketry,

---

[26] The citation is inaccurate, presumably intending to refer to the passage "Dedimus profecto grande patientiae dctumentum...." [Certainly, we showed a magnificent example of patience (as a former age had witnessed the extreme of liberty, so we witnessed the extreme of servitude).]"

and I could not see any weapons anywhere, nor any dispositions announcing any resistance, not any tumult, nor any trace of discontent, or even surprise, in the physiognomy of the spectators.

Meanwhile, we advanced, and as my curiosity was growing with every step, I gained ground, and ended up in the first rank of the column, marching at its head.

I had before me a group of two hundred people at the most, whose external dignity, intelligent faces and respectable age enabled me to recognize them as considerable individuals. They were, in fact, the delegates of the various territorial divisions and principal cities of France. They represented them with a simple and sympathetic majesty.

As I drew level with them I perceived that we had entered into the courtyard of the Tuileries, leaving the mass of the cortege outside the gates. I thus found myself in the ranks of the delegates. I made no protest, and prepared to do as they did.

They negotiated briefly at the door of the Pavillon de l'Horloge, the service inquiring as to what they wanted, after which we were shown into a waiting room when the Emperor was informed.

We soon went up, and, the Emperor being seated, the doyen of the delegates addressed him in these terms:

"Sire, the delegates of the cities and rural areas of France, all duly and unanimously elected by all the citizens, voting in conformity with the principle of equality—which is to say, each having a single vote—have come to you in order to fulfill the mission in view of which their election has taken place.

"Sire, the genius of France is indestructible: France is egalitarian, liberal, Catholic, tolerant, and loves letters and the arts. For fifty years, all the goods that are the most dear have been denatured and destroyed. There are citizens who enjoy unique privileges. Equality has been suppressed to their profit; they vote twice while others have no vote at all, and it is their

249

elected representatives who make the laws. They are exempt from taxation. They are the tyrants of industry and commerce.

"Catholics or protestants, it is not permitted to us to practice the religion of our forefathers. Our letters and arts, Sire, you know them! We have come to beg the Emperor to render us the happiness that France enjoyed under his illustrious great-grandfather.

"Take back the Empire, Sire. At least reign, if you do not want to govern. Render us the constitution of 1852, which, after the modifications of 1860, 1867 and 1876 is the only practical formula of perfect equality and liberty. Render us the civil laws of the same epoch, which are the consecration and the guarantee of general prosperity. Above all, replace woman in her rank in society; reconstitute the family. And as a sign of our return to existence, render us also the names of France and Paris, which your dynasty was able to make so great.

"Sire, it is the entire nation that invites you and implores you; there is no resistance anywhere. Here are the delegates even of the privileged who have just given up the advantages with which bad laws had invested them."

At these words, a man emerged from the group and placed himself to the right of the orator. He was tall; he seemed to be about forty-five years old; courage, firmness, honesty and good will were painted in his physiognomy. He said:

"Sire, privilege is more deadly to those who have it than those it despoils. The workers have had that dolorous experience for a long time. That is why, by my voice, in the name of justice, in the name of equality and in the name of democracy, they have come to deposit the harmful advantages they have usurped on the altar of the fatherland.

"In the future, let all the citizens, rich or poor, be equal, civilly and politically. Let employers enjoy the same liberty as the workers. Let the workers play taxes like all other citizens, and be subject to the same community charges, according to their means. Let the workers be electors with the same entitlement and the same force as their fellow citizens, but not more. Those are the wishes, Sire, that the dignity, the honor and the courage of the so-called working classes desires to formulate, and request the Emperor to realize."

The Emperor replied:

"Messieurs the delegates of the cities and rural areas, Messieurs the delegates of the workers, by the fact of your election, your presence here and the words that you have just addressed to me, a pacific but immense revolution has just been accomplished: a revolution that will count among the most memorable and the most fecund in god effects that our history will record. By virtue of it, and thanks to you, thanks to the good sense and generosity of the country, the equilibrium of our social institutions, which had taken so many centuries to found, momentarily troubled, is finally reestablished.

"You can indeed consider your wishes as realized, for you are the sovereign people, and I, charged with executing your decisions, will not hesitate to undertake to do so in these grave circumstances.

"There is, therefore, on the present question, a unanimous concert of reflective determination that will guarantee immediate and absolute success.

"I shall form a Council of State similar, to the extent that it can be, to the one that, under my ancestors, played such an important and useful role in the elaboration of laws. I shall submit a Constitution similar to that of 1852, completed by the developments that it attained successively until 1876, appropriating what was good from the mores of the day. You shall have a conservative Senate, a Chambre de Députés elected by the suffrage of all the French, invested with equal rights. You shall have the freedom of the press, the freedom of the right of association, religious liberty, the liberty of education—in sum, all the liberties that have been abused. Of which experience has taught us the perils, and of which, thanks to the political education so dearly acquired by the country, public spirit will prevent from being abused in future. A solemn plebiscite will approve or reject these measures.

"Messieurs the delegates, I thank you for the confidence that you have in me, for the expression that you have brought me of the memory that the people have retained of the efforts that my dynasty has made for the prosperity of France. I shall continue to devote my life to following in the footsteps of my ancestors.

"Now, Messieurs the delegates, let us go to Notre-Dame to thank God for having granted France this day."

To cries of "Long live the Emperor!" repeated twenty-one times, Napoléon VII, followed by his commissioners, went out.[27]

---

[27] The next page of the text is missing from the available version. It might not contain any text at all, but if it does, the missing passage cannot amount to more than two hundred words, and might well be considerably less. The remainder of the published volume consists of a series of reprinted documents supposedly given to the narrator by the old man to illustrate and support the claims he has made about the reign of Napoléon III.

Paul Adam: *Letters from Malaisie* (1898)

A Spanish diplomat with whom I had the honor of making friends once, in the vicinity of Biarritz, has written a series of letters to me from the Philippines. They reveal a curious historical and social accident. Perhaps I shall not recall uselessly, for the explanation of the phenomenon related below, the success achieved in 1842 by the publication of Cabet's *Voyage en Icarie*. People entirely gripped by reading that communist utopia followed the author to Texas, and then to Illinois, where the realization of the economic theory was attempted under his auspices. No one is unaware of the painful result. Thus, it is hardly surprising that a dissident rival of Cabet attempted a similar realization in Malaisie.

The epoch comprised between 1830 and 2 December 1851 will remain conspicuous for the effervescence of socialism. Born in 1772, Fourier, having seen the French Revolution, judged it as it deserved, harshly. Henri de Saint-Simon, his contemporary, similarly deemed the Jacobin project of scant worth, if its program were not combined with the suppression of inheritance and the civil equality of the sexes. He instructed Auguste Comte and Blanqui, one of whom magnified his thought and the other his action. In 1840 those ferments of socialism agitated minds greatly, no less than in the present day.

In 1832 Fourier founded his periodical *Le Phalanstère*; in 1840 Proudhon cried: "Property is theft." Napoléon's ashes were transferred to the Invalides; the column of the Grande Armée was erected at Boulogne. The Attila of the Revolution was officially recognized as a hero. In 1841 Proudhon launched his *Avertissement aux propriétaires*; at almost the same time, the law of expropriations was promulgated. Interned since 1839 for the skirmish in Boulogne, at the fort of Ham, the future Napoléon III wrote his *Extinction du paupérisme*. 1842 saw the appearance of the law relating to the employment of children in factories. For the first time, the Authority attempted to inhibit capitalist exploitation and protect laborious lives. A royal decree authorized the construction of great railways lines. Economic evolution took a considerable step forward.

People read Cabet's *Voyage en Icarie* and were impassioned for that trial, amid the reformist fervor that prepared the revolution of February 1848, the Ateliers Nationaux, the ideal of the "Right to Work," drowned by General Cavaignac in the blood of twelve thousand proletarians. The bourgeoisie thus trained the suffrage of the people to prefer, as President of the Republic, Louis Bonaparte to the mass-murderer of June.

The Spanish diplomat's narrative cannot, therefore, astonish us overmuch. A competitor of Cabet led to the islands of the Indian Ocean a few simple individuals enthused by the fashionable utopia. A rival and personal enemy of the Icarian, he directed his expedition to the Far East while the other led his to the West.

That is all that it seems indispensable to remember, before reading what follows.

P.A.

N.B. The naïve mind of my friend, a worthy man of limited intelligence, judges rather maladroitly and his style lacks ornamentation. It is necessary to excuse the administrative habits of a diplomat.

Furthermore, it will very easily be seen that THIS IS NOT AN IDEAL.

LETTER I

Celebes Sea, aboard the Novio,
in dock at the city of Amphitrite,
20 September 1896.

My dear friend,

You will doubtless pardon me for having left you abruptly in Saint-Sébastien, when I tell you that an order came from the Ministry obliging me to leave immediately for the Philippines, where the insurrection had suddenly taken on a deplorable importance because of the new calamities that had fallen on unfortunate Spain. Woken up in the middle of the night by an agent, now without anxiety for the *basquina*—whose sister must have satisfied you, I imagine—I embarked two hours later on the *Novio*, the sleek white cruiser that was stirring up the water in the harbor. You cursed the bellowing of her siren often enough. My telegram ought not to bewilder you less than her voice when you awake.

Abominable crossing. I hardly quit the cabin. The sea was crashing down on the deck. I rendered my stomach's accounts to the indispensable utensils. The joys of the Career!

First of all it's necessary to tell you that the agent handed me an envelope containing orders. They gave me the mission of discovering what strange and powerful ideas were disturbing, in the colony, the loyalty of our planters and traders, and the placidity of the indigenes.

Certainly, neither party was acting solely in the confidence of their own strength. To attack the government of the metropolis they had to believe themselves supported. The Cubans had that of the United States. Having reached Manila, I commenced enquiries. I immediately had reason to think that the political megalomania of Japan was not abstaining from encouragements in favor of the insurgents.

I convinced myself, however, that that influence was not the principal one; for if Japan is thinking of conquering the large islands of the Indian and Pacific Ocean and creating an insular power analogous to that of Britain, its diplomats are not unaware of the difficulties of such a task. To despoil Spain and Holland of their Malaysian possessions today would not be easy. Europe, whose federative union is being sealed by recent events, would rise up against young Asia. In brief, it was important to discover another efficient cause. I shall spare you the summary of the steps I took.

Several of the senior functionaries in Manila entertained me, on disembarkation, with a fable much in credit among the people. For ten years, European aeronauts had been arriving from the sky in the interior cities of the colony. On many occasions, these travelers would enter into communication with our indigenes, and some colonists. They would exchange watches, tools and gold ingots for several kinds of seeds, pigs and sheep. I was shown one of these ingots: a perfect little rectangle bearing the stamp of a heraldic escutcheon whose origin is certainly Byzantine.

On traveling along the coasts in the *Novio*, the Malay pilot drew my attention to a distant projection of the central plateau in the insular mountains of Mindoro, and to a kind of lattice-work column thereon, quite similar to your Eiffel Tower, which, constructed by those mysterious explorers, served as a landing-stage for their aerial ships. Others were pointed out to me, perceptible from the coast, on the peaks of the central massif, on the large island of Mindanao, and on the isles of Iebu and Negros. All those stations are situated at the top of summits rendered inaccessible by the mountainous nature of the terrain, the impenetrability of virgin forests, the pestilence of marshes and our general ignorance of the topography of the region. You know that in Borneo, the Celebes and the Philippines, Europeans occupy a few coastal provinces; they affirm a nominal protectorate over the populations of the almost-unknown interior.

Now, Borneo is two hundred square kilometers larger than France, and the other groups of islands, including Luzon, Mindanao, Sumatra and Java, are collectively immense. My compatriots in Manila suppose that in the center of these little continents, energetic Occidentals might have established a secret civilization attested by the passage of these aerial ships, which have the form of large birds with vast wings, and carrying a sail analogous to that of our sloops.

A few prisoners of the insurrection were interrogated in my presence. They were asked about the provenance of printed papers found on them. Those documents established their allegiance to the flags of revolt. They seemed to be formulae, in Spanish, of a revolutionary diploma. Something that struck me was that the exergue represented a crowing cock perched on the helmet of a lector carrying his ax. I remembered having seen identical emblems in Paris on French stamps produced in 1849. Dare I believe, my dear friend, that you are beginning to excuse the length of this missive? Does that interest you, specious French anarchist? It is your brethren who are exciting our Malaysian subjects against the old Castilian monarchy.

I'll go on, because this will please you. For ten years all the governors of the Philippines have been addressing occasional reports to Madrid on these indications. They develop therein the logical hypothesis of a center of French "aerial pirates" developing on the inaccessible high plateaux of the large islands. The ineffable assurance of our ministers criticized these reports. Their authors were told to cease making jokes scarcely compatible with the character of their functions. One obstinate individual was subjected to disgrace; his successors maintained a silence favorable to their future glory.

One, however, wanted, without metropolitan authorization, to clarify the matter. A detachment of marines sent to the island of Mindanao attempted to reach one of those tall latticework columns. It was necessary to fray a path through the jungle, carve out a path, blow up rocks, shoot tigers and crocodiles. Of the entire expedition, only three men returned. They related that when they had almost reached the top of the mountain, terrible explosions had annihilated the detachment. The tower was defended by a ring of torpedoes hidden underground.

As you can imagine, the governor did not breathe a word about his audacity. He reported that the marines had been massacred in an ambush by natives, and then sent the three survivors to an unhealthy post where fever and death sealed their lips.

In spite of the objections of the central government, I resolved to pursue the investigation. My first telegraphic report only mentioned the Japanese intrigues. But it happened that a young Batavian insurgent betrayed the adventure in order to avoid the death penalty passed on him by the court martial. The arms, munitions and money came from Borneo; he confessed that. Malays skillful in slipping through the jungle, knowing secret paths, reached the base of the columns, where one of these pirates gave them the necessary instructions and gold. Junks then went forth by night in quest on some islet out at sea, of crates deposited there by the aerial ships shortly before the time prescribed in the letters.

Pushed to the limit, even subjected to a kind of instruction that our ancestors the Inquisitors excelled in rendering useful, my Batavian ended up confessing the existence of a little harbor in a creek on the island of Borneo, hidden by reefs. Very narrow, the passage was never attempted by the captains of European vessels, uninspired, in addition, by the abrupt and deserted appearance of the cliff. From a distance, all that was perceptible was lines of breakers and a sea whitened by the surf of submerged rocks.

To persuade the Batavian to identify an indigenous pilot capable of guiding the *Novio* through the pass, it was necessary to employ all the genres of coercion. You, a Frenchman and a humanitarian, attach an excessive value to human existence. Personally, I think that the interests of an entire nation are worth many lives of imbeciles. My Batavian, a kind of merchant who poisons the indigenes by means of ignoble alcohols and sells them the caresses of syphilitic girls, was of scant interest to us. He had joined the revolt after the police had shut down his dive after a murder committed before his eyes. I extracted profitable information from that vile matter, by forceful means.

I learned that on two or three occasions, the junks of the insurrection had received, in the little harbor of a city hidden in the bosom of the cliffs, their cargoes of rifles and several artillery pieces. It was necessary for me to be taken there. Without losing any time, a pilot was discovered, arrested and skillfully interviewed in prison by a traitor in our service, who asked for a plan of the pass, wanting, he said, in order to fulfill in the detainee's place the dangerous insurrectional duty during his incarceration. He, he assured him, would be released that evening for lack of evidence. He was.

The *Novio* put to sea immediately, under the double plume of its funnels.

With great difficulty, we found the pass on the south-east coast of Borneo. Several times in the night, we saw immense shadows soaring above our heads, at incalculable heights, while the beam of an electric searchlight suddenly illuminated the deck of the ship, the furious white water, the sounders' launch prudently going ahead of our prow through the reefs. I dreaded the fall of a torpedo that might have smashed the ship to smithereens. The *Novio*'s captain shared that apprehension.

I can assure you that we lived twenty-four joyless hours in that sinister region. Several times, a hail of grapeshot landed on the deck, as if the aerials wanted to alert us to the precision of their aim and were thus inviting us to retreat—but I am a descendant of conquistadors. That bravado simply enraged me, and I threw a negro stoker who manifested too much fear into the sea. He was fished out again.

The day before yesterday, at dawn, we finally crossed the last line of breakers and penetrated into more placid waters.

Immediately, above the height of the cliffs and between the tips of the summits, five aerostats appeared. We could observe them at our ease because they were circling slowly, at a good height, around a center that was the zenith of the *Novio*.

Two wings of between a hundred and fifty and two hundred meters sustained each of them in the air. They seemed to be thick. We thought that they formed two flat envelopes containing gas, that they assisted them, most of all, to glide. It was rare that any movement agitated them. At the extremities of an axle subjacent to the ship, two enormous helices, one at the prow and the other at the stern, were spinning horizontally in the air. Between them was a deck where mechanics and observers were moving. We followed their movements. They were photographing the *Novio*. Born of the gyration of the helices, a wind was making their clothing flap. They were fastened to the rails of the gangway.

Three meters above them the framework of an oblong terrace pierced by a trap-door received a minuscule stairway. The terrace seemed no thicker than a solid plank. It supported a mast and the sail of a sloop, serving to steer the ship. The immense thick wings were attached and articulated to its flanks. We succeeded in distinguishing light, subtle machines on the oval of that terrace, the wheel of a dynamo, a tent, and a crew consisting of eight men at the most. We also saw that the mast was maintained by numerous complex stays anchored to the edges. The flight of the ship differs little from that of buzzards, eagle-owls and other birds of prey.

All day long the squadron hovered, describing circles around our center. At certain moments we perceived the noise of the helices, a formidable throbbing, if one of the vessels tilted toward us. The crewmen presented the sail to the air current, steering by that means. They seemed to be admirable topmen.

In the middle of their circles, we were like a poor grouse watching a flock of voracious hawks. It was necessary for me to rally the courage of our men. Incessantly in the shadow of the ships gliding over our decks, we nevertheless headed into the creek. It commences a kind of shallow fjord, hollowed out between two sheer mountainous rock faces bristling with brushwood and firs.

Toward midday we perceived, after having doubled a little interior cape, the whiteness of the city named Amphitrite.

The semaphore signaled to us to stop, announcing a boat and a message. We obeyed.

The city is nicely installed in stages on the flank of the mountain. The low quays do not seem to be designed to welcome large ships. That is explicable, aerostats replacing the navy. Electric beacons border a boulevard. The low houses have stone arcades, under which a crowd circulates, in costumes in the French style of the seventeenth century. Its members examined us from a distance, without surpassing a kind of ideal limit, even though no police agent appeared to me to be holding them back. We saw several large automobile carriages. A delightful carillon preceded the chiming of the hour. The rising sun revealed the gilded or silvered facades of the houses, and porticoes in blue faience, under which jets of water danced, springing from fountains. Trees and vegetation screened much of the view.

A launch emerged from a dock. It advanced, moved by a covert but powerful force; its astonishing rapidity surprised us. On the prow, the figure of a chimera cleaved the water with its breast of green faience scales. We scarcely had time to hoist the Spanish flag. A large shadow veiled the sky above our heads, and we saw an aerostat descending between the walls of the fjord, brushing them with its enormous wings. From the inferior deck, hanging over us on the end of a chain, was a monstrous torpedo. The copper tip of its detonator was gleaming.

It was under that sword of Damocles that I received the magistrate of the launch at the gangway port.

He climbed the stairway briskly in spite of the seventy or eighty winters that had blanched his short trimmed side-whiskers. A small, thin old man with shaven lips, he saluted me with his musketeer's hat rather impertinently, allowing a momentary glimpse of the snowy toupet surmounting silky hair swept back from the temples before covering himself again. Behind him, five men surged forth in royal blue uniforms, hoisting several ensigns, one of which was a golden cockerel with extended wings, another the Byzantine arms already inscribed on the rectangular ingots of their money, and a third two hands, one gold and one iron, interlaced between two palms. They terminated scarlet poles.

I considered my minuscule interlocutor, his ample Louis XIV coat in gray silk, is broad culottes disappearing under his white-dotted waistcoat, his little legs impatient in tawny morocco gaiters buttoned up to the knees.

"Monsieur," he said to me in French, "You are doubtless unaware of whose abode you are in. For fifty-three years no European has been admitted to this bay. For you, the torpedoes that reinforce the line of breakers were neutralized. The time seemed to have come to make known to someone the dispositions of our colony. This little book that I am giving you will instruct you regarding the origins of our work.

"We are Frenchmen who expatriated ourselves to flee a regime of iniquity and tyranny. Disciples of Fourier and Saint-Simon, and friends of Proudhon and Cabet—I hope those illustrious names are not unknown to you—we wanted to realize here an existence in conformity with sound phalansterian logic. What Cabet attempted in Icaria, we tried out in this fertile country. Monsieur, the mild Virgil has said: '*O fortunatos nimium sua si bona norint Agrocolas!*' We have therefore resolved to know our happiness.

"Long enough and too long we have been able to experiment the *sic vos non vobis* of the swan of Mantua, and we murmur with the Latin: *quandoque, o rus, te aspiciam!* Here, we finally enjoy nature. Be welcome to this land of fraternity, Monsieur. You will undoubtedly soon be able to enumerate its felicities to your compatriots, when you have returned to the lares of your ancestors. And perhaps you will say then, like the eloquent Chrysostom, *Mataïotes, mataïotélôn, kaï, panta mataïotes*; vanity of vanities, all is vanity, when veritable amour does not preside over the destinies of great peoples.

"In this envelope, Monsieur, you will read the conditions that our government imposes in case the desire to visit our cities and fields solicits you. As to the diplomatic affair of which you will stir up the grave problem, it is only in our capital, before the council of the Dictatorship, that you will be able to obtain a solution. For myself, Monsieur, I am only a humble servant of our people, the seneschal of this province. I am glad, Monsieur, to have been the first of our nation to salute here the envoy of a noble land."

I tried to reply, but the dried-up little old man turned his back on me and descended precipitately into the launch with his flag-bearers. As rapidly as it had come, the boat departed.

I read the opuscule and the papers handed to me by the seneschal of Amphitrite. They confirmed the hypothesis of the government of Manila. A colony of Saint-Simonians and Fourierists, disembarked here in 1843, had prospered clandestinely on the high summits of the interior where it was initially necessary to take refuge as a precaution against the ferocity of the autochthonous populations. Gradually, the territory had extended, after a long and hard period of wars. Now it occupies, in the interior of Borneo, an area a third as large as France. In spite of the singular conditions imposed on travelers by the official communiqué of the Council of Dictatorship, I shall penetrate into the country. My diplomatic mission, in any case, constrains me to do so.

I thought, my dear friend, that I might obtain forgiveness, in writing to you these curious reasons, for the rudeness of my abrupt departure from Saint-Sébastien. Will you excuse me?

I am your very devoted...

LETTER II

Minerve, September 1896
Palais des Voyageurs.

My dear friend,

I expected that news of my incursion into this land would have reached you by way of the newspapers. Official correspondence has reached me from Manila that indicates the designs of my government. They oppose the revelation of the

discovery. As you know, the interests of the State coming before all else, it might be that some misfortune deprives our
contemporaries of my presence when I return to friendly territory. The example of a community that has prospered thanks
to the entire abolition of the family, capital, competition,
amour—and liberty—might be fatal to the prestige of the
Powers of Europe.

Do you recall that evening in Biarritz when we imagined
the future tyranny of Marxism imposing on millions of agriculturalists, scientists and artists laws only to the liking of the
minority of workers? The most rigorous of our predictions
have been surpassed here. Now, as the lure of liberty sanctifies
the entire European system, I'll wager that the monarchs and
demagogues will make alliance to put a lid of silence on my
story, perhaps even before I have succeeded in publishing it.
This, I am making you the depositary of my secret, in order
that its immediate divulgence, even though partial, might render the measures of force futile.

This explains to you the sending of several manuscripts.
I beg you to forgive me.

I would certainly have liked to use, for that, the means of
correspondence that satisfies the people of this nation, but,
taking into consideration all the trouble you would have in
finding a phonograph in Paris, the sums it would be necessary
to disburse to acquire one, and the probable defects of the apparatus, I would rather make use of ink.

In the Palais des Voyageurs in this city of Minerve, every
room possesses its phonograph, its electric lamps and its taps
of hot and cold water. Several iron plaques embedded in the
wall redden if one turns a switch that dispenses powerful electric currents. The heat expands in proportion to the number of
turns of the switch, and a thermometer indicates the sum of the
degrees obtained by that manipulation.

The room in which I am writing to you has walls of orange faience, a floor of opaque glass, a stucco cupola, and an
arched window overlooking the perspectives of the great curve
of the streets. I can see the city, and its houses: blue, crimson,

yellow, gilded, silvered or the color of iron. It's raining. The water from the sky is making the enamel of the facades glisten. Trams are gliding vertiginously under the light footbridges that pedestrians hooded in gray rubber are crossing. No sounds of hammering, no songs and no hoofbeats trouble the uniform murmur of pedestrians shod in muffled soles, who are borne along by moving sidewalks rolling alongside the ground floors.

Between the columns that succeed one another in the square, where there would be shop windows in our cities, tables support beverages whose composition does not include any alcohol. Coffees, beers, teas, creams, sorbets, ice-creams and chocolates regale the repose of the stroller momentarily extended in his rocking-chair, lending a distracted ear to the news recited to him by the phonograph, its intonations breathed by an actor.

These people no longer take the trouble to read. Enclosed in a kind of mechanical piano are albums indented with various holes, into which fit the protrusions of gears of a dimension corresponding to the capacity and shape of the whole. Louder than a normal voice, a voice announces accidents, the temperature and declaims a chronicle or a story. Nothing is more bizarre than hearing the thousand phonographs under the arcades. Each of the "stations" carries a sign indicating the nature of the recitations. The lovers of news stop under the *Voice of Events*; people fond of literature sup tea under the *Voice of the Poets*. Those who like to relive ancient times drink within range of the *Voice of India*, the *Voice of Rome* or the *Voice of Greece*. The marine murmur of those confused voices causes a kind of anguish.

From Chaldean inscriptions and those of Egyptian steles to modern imaginations, the testimony of the humanity of old rains down within the city. One listens to the Idea, the One Idea, the Mother Idea, sounding in its marvelous transformations. It floats over the innumerable cupolas of multicolored faience, over the sound of the high jets of water that spring forth decoratively at the corner of avenues, surpassing the tops of the houses and crowning the city with splendid liquid plumes.

That is what I can hear in this room and what I can see through the window.

Think of the total of labor, effort and activity required for that result!

As soon as dusk falls, there is music. The sounds engulf the city, rising up and floating. Organs cry; invisible orchestras strive. Sometimes, it's a mass by Palestrina, sometimes a work by César Franck, sometimes Wagner, Beethoven, Gluck or Chopin. Machinery alone replaces virtuosos. One can perceive a slightly annoying stiffness of execution, but only in certain passages. The sensation is brief. A surge of perfect harmonies drowns the awkward note.

I obtained the privilege of knowing these things by giving the seneschal of Amphitrite my word of honor to observe certain conventions. I must not, during my journey, buy or sell anything. All my entitlements have been given to me at the offices of Amphitrite. I have been told that, as a guest of the Dictatorship, I shall not have any expenditure to make. It is forbidden for me to make or receive gifts. All circulation of money, all commercial exchange, is forbidden on the territory of the Dictatorship, and in order to forearm me against human weakness, I was taken to a store, dressed in a coat similar to that of the seneschal, in a kind of somber silk, culottes like those of our cyclists, and knee-length boots in raw leather. A felt hat was adapted to my head. An entire outfit was folded up in a valise, and I was confided to the care of two individuals whose intonations alone denounce that they are women, their costume not differing from that of men, nor their hair, cut roundly up to the ears with a fringe over the forehead, like the pages of the fourteenth century.

I asked in vain for permission to bring my box of cigars. My guardians declared that alcohol and tobacco had no right of entry into the country. I feel a malaise at that deprivation.

The train that brought us from Amphitrite to Minerve, in six hours, travels at a speed twenty-five or thirty per cent greater than our expresses. The carriages are vast rooms equipped with large glass bays, where the entire perspective of an equatorial country files past, imbued with heavy vapors that emanate from marshy regions. Profound divans garnish the walls. The system of lighting and heating by the red electric plaques renders the hours comfortable.

At the stations, people board without any supervision. They are similarly dressed. They speak very little, understanding one another by means of signs; they seem grave and collected. The women are almost entirely virilized. Hands in their coat pockets, legs crossed, they meditate. From time to time the voice of a phonograph announces some item of news. At each station the train's conductor collects a series of plaques, which he slides into the apparatus.

As in London, the women and men do not seem to desire one another. They do not undress one another with their gaze. Their eyes do not mark any connivance. The women put more sugar in their tea, the men blow their noses into their handkerchiefs more loudly. No distinction of gestures, no coarseness of manners places one or other in evidence. Equals in education as well as in costume, one cannot say that there are inferiors among them. The strong stand aside before the weak, the big before the small, men before women; that's all.

No one talks to the train conductor or the employees with impatience, but rather making use of the humblest formulae of politeness. During dinner, my companions helped the waitress with an entirely fraternal kindness, and she treated familiarly, making amusing remarks to them. My different manners appeared to shock everyone around me, especially when I asked the waitress to pick up a napkin. She blushed deeply, obeyed, and turned away, not without evidence of her scorn and indignation. My companions made excuses for me, in my capacity as a foreigner.

One does not see fat people or thin ones, nor lame individuals, nor people who are excessively old or children excessively young, nor mothers accompanied by restless infants, nor sick people, pale and coughing. When I expressed my astonishment, my companions informed me. They told me that the first efforts of Jérôme the Founder were aimed at the installation of gymnasia. Scarcely had he driven back the Malay tribes and cleared the fertile land on the High Plateau, and protected them with a ring of forts, than he had nine large wooden edifices constructed on the banks of the River Coti: the Maternity, the Nursery, the School, the College, the Lycée, the University, the Presbytery and the Hospital. Separated by distances of about thirty kilometers, those buildings immediately received their inmates.

Every woman known to be pregnant was taken to the Maternity. Cares of every sort were lavished upon her. The best game from the hunts was reserved for her, the most beautiful fabrics, the most comfortable seats, and all the honors. None of that has disappeared from mores in fifty years. The mother remains the sacred individual, above all. In place of the primitive wooden buildings, palaces have risen up, filled with statues and paintings. She lives there, dispensed from work during the entire period of pregnancy, that of nursing and that of primary education. For her, Chinese cooks of considerable science prepare feasts; choirs of young women sing and make music; the best troupes of actors perform the masterpieces of known literatures; gardeners complete marvelous flower-beds and the paths of vast parks.

"It is," my companion told me, "a year of royal triumph. Nothing similar is accorded to our inventors or our physicians, who are nevertheless honored in imitation of historic emperors. Jérôme the Founder has judged that nothing is more beautiful than producing a thinking being. You will doubtless see corteges of matrons going by in their ivory and silver litters. The law obliges everyone to prostrate themselves before them. Our heroes, our inventors and our doctors, wallow in the mud as they pass by, while a seneschal or the dictator himself is only saluted by the crowd, whose members affirm themselves his equal.

"Have you enjoyed those honors?" I asked.

"Twice," she replied; "at fourteen and a half and at twenty. Look, for that I wear two gold plaques in my buttonhole."

"And your children?"

"I had news of them ten days ago. The elder, who is now thirteen, is finishing her choreographic studies. I was shown her painting. She is collaborating in a large painting that will ornament the Temple of Iron. The picture represents the triumph of our aerial ships, on the day when they were finally able to take flight, after fifteen years of fruitless attempts. At this moment, my daughter ought to be in the country for the autumn sowing. Physical labor is very good for her. Last year, after the beet harvest, she was definitively rid of her migraines. I hope that the doctors will think her strong enough to be transferred to the city of Diane next year, for it's better to approach the male early; that way, one avoids the exhaustion of unslaked imagination."

I knew that the family and marriage no longer existed in the nation, but I had a great deal of difficulty hearing at young mother talk like that, with her legs crossed and her frail hands choosing pastilles for her mouth.

She went on: "My second, a boy, is eight years old. He seems a little slow for his age. I think it's my fault. His father, so far as I can tell, was a poor old man who came from France in his youth with Jérôme the Founder. Still victim of your illusions about sentiment, he loved me, as you put it. He seemed so unhappy that I didn't refuse him my body. It's necessary to be kind, isn't it, to all weaknesses? I imagined that his semen would be infertile—on the contrary. The child seemed puny, a trifle stupid. He had to be inscribed in the instructors' section. He was crammed by all mnemonic techniques, with grammar, history and geography, and will doubtless spend his life reciting it into scholarly phonograph."

"And now," I asked, "are you not hoping for another maternity?"

"As you can imagine, in this country the hope of many women is pregnancy. There are fortunate ones who don't spend ten months outside the Mothers' Palace; every intercourse fecundates them. But for the greater number, the facility of amour renders them sterile. Thus, personally, I was taken at fourteen, after the second embrace. That happens to the majority. The conditions of the first encounters are so special. When we leave University, and are truly women, we're transferred to the city of Diane. There we live in the Maidens' Palace.

"Every day we perform dances; we put on sumptuous costumes appropriate to emphasize our beauty; we listen to phonographs reciting erotic poems and stories. After a few weeks, there's a great festival to which males of thirty are invited, selected from among the most handsome and robust. They come in silk leotards. In the morning there's a service in the Basilica. The archbishops file past at the head of processions. One is intoxicated by incense and the sound of organs.

"Afterwards there's the admirable cortege of Mothers, who go past on litters with great sheets of precious fabrics. A feast brings the sexes together. They mingle. After that, in front of the assembly of men, dressed in ballet costumes, the virgins dance certain long, very beautiful dances, in which we're educated from the age of six at college so that we can perfect them at the lycée and the gymnasium. When the dances are over, everyone accepts an intoxicating beverage and goes to lie down in her lodge, on cushions, amid flowers. The man comes in. One devotes oneself to reproduction for two weeks, either with the same man, another or several.

"The festivals are prolonged. Almost everyone, in the following month, becomes pregnant and leaves the city of Diane."

"They never return there?"

"Never. There's another city, Venus. Similar ceremonies are held there for those who emerge from the Mothers' Palace after their little one is weaned. You'll doubtless witness one of those Festivals of Reproduction. Before then, we'll have the great Festival of Locomotion at the Temple of Iron, in the city named Vulcan. That's held every spring, on the anniversary of the day when, for the first time, the aerial ships were able to

270

sustain themselves in the transparency of the air. A week after that is the Festival of Nutrition, the celebration of the earth, shortly before the rainy season. Those three great Festivals mark, for our calendar, the end of the annual labor, at the epoch of your winter solstice."

"But," I said, excited by the description of the Festivals of Diane, "outside of these amorous ceremonies you mention, the taste for passionate things doesn't seduce souls?"

"The taste for that pastime has certainly lost its prestige if you consider it with your European illusions. Here, a woman doesn't refuse a man her flesh, any more than she would refuse to return a greeting among you. It's a politeness that we grant quite graciously, without attaching any more importance to it."

"But what if an old man solicits you, or an unpleasant man?"

"For one thing, old people live in the Presbyteries, for the most part. They go in at the age of forty. The deformed don't frequent the milieu of the beautiful and the healthy. They live in particular places reserved for their distress. Thus, we only encounter individuals of admissible appearance and stature. Then again, to accomplish that very simple function, we have no need of so much choice or circumlocution. Nothing in the laws or habits opposes the exercise of an instinct useful to the expansion of the race. One reproduces when one has the desire, with whoever proposes it, just as one eats in the company of a passer-by in the refectory of the train or travels in a vehicle with a driver."

"What about the ideal?" I said.

My two companions smiled.

I considered them. Brunettes, evidently imprinted with Malaysian blood, they had languid eyes with long lashes and mat eyelids with delicate corners. Their slightly flattened noses did not spoil the sad sensibility of visages striped by blood-red mouths. In the folds of silk vests their liberated breasts did not vanish to such an extent that they could not be divined to be form and full. They also had broad hips under the vast tails

271

of their jackets, svelte calves within their gaiters, and pointed feet. The more loquacious of the two was named Théa , and the other, who had thus far only said anything by means of smiles, was named Pythie. Although she was younger, three medals indicated the number of her children. I complimented her on the grace of her figure after several births.

"It's for the doctoresses to receive those flatteries," she replied. "The art of obstetrics has reached a high degree of perfection, for the greatest recompenses are reserves for those who discover the means of embellishing and ennobling maternity."

"What recompenses?"

"Exemption from labor, for one, two, three years, or for life. Thus, three times a mother, I'm dispensed of work for nine years. I'm not accompanying you by virtue of function, but out of amity for Théa , in order to help her in her task. In any case, I declare myself doubly glad of that friendship, which has offered me the joy of knowing you, Monsieur."

I bowed. That Pythie seemed very charming. She even pretended to look at me seductively. Something akin to a golden stripe bordering her iris illuminated her thick lashes. I gazed rather fixedly at her breasts. She perceived it, smiled, and, turning toward me, unbuttoned her waistcoat, in such a way that I could perceive brown skin inflated by respiration.

"Thank you," I murmured.

"That gratitude is sincere," said Théa , whose hand insinuated itself, for a natural observation toward the most excited part of my flesh.

I felt some shame at that undissimulated gesture, but the other three passengers in the salon did not appear to pay any heed to it.

"To Lucine, two male children have just been born; well constituted," cried the shrill voice of the phonograph at that moment. It continued: "Four ships have departed for the province of Cavite. Spanish troops have been defeated at Luçao. Our allies have burned the plantations of Altavila and Notre-Dame del Pilar... The calculation of the harvest is concluded.

The reserves appear sufficiently furnished for us to hope for a reduction in agrarian labor of five hours a week during next year's toil... The ninth group of engineers has concluded experiments with the glass-blowing machine. It is thought that the fabrication of bottles will cease to require human breath in six weeks..."

A blast of a whistle signaled the end of the phonographic communication.

"There's a fortunate conquest of matter," said the traveler sitting opposite us to his neighbor. "I rejoice in it, for I've been blowing glass for four years and I'm a little weary of it."

"You have broad shoulders," she replied, "which denote lungs capable of supporting that fatigue."

"Certainly, but I'll adapt very well to another kind of work, and I confess to you that I shall take advantage joyfully of my trimestrial leave."

"You're going to Minerve?"

"Yes, I'm undertaking some very interesting work on the variations of Aryan idioms. Only in Minerve are the libraries sufficiently well furnished to permit me to carry that curiosity through."

"How can you succeed in interesting yourself in philology, Monsieur," I asked him, "while blowing glass?"

"My God, it's easy. My section works from six o'clock in the morning until midday. By four in the afternoon I've strolled sufficiently. It's necessary to kill the hours before bedtime. By chance, my comrades have very similar tastes. One operates on the Chaldean languages, another on the Egyptian, two others on the Celtic. We thus have a common subject to group our minds and our conversations."

"Monsieur is European, and is visiting the Dictatorship as a guest of the Council," said Théa .

"Well then, Monsieur. I'm glad to wish you welcome," replied the bottle-blower. "The phonograph informed us of your voyage. I understand that it astonishes you to hear such words, but why? Do you not have compulsory military service in Europe? Are you not obliged, at times, to play the cavalier second class in a barracks? As a stable-hand, you clean out the filth, polish the saddles and bridles, you groom the horses. That doesn't prevent you, in the evening, from reading a literary magazine. We do social service for twenty years, as you do military service for three, that's all. It's no more brutalizing, and the art of Production elevates the mind, whereas the art of Destruction debases it. Every trimester we enjoy a fortnight's leave. I'm going to utilize my leisure in Minerve."

"I admire you," I said, a trifled dazed.

"Don't admire me. I'm one human being among thousands. Bear in mind that from the age of seven, at college, I learned the mysteries of glass-working at the same time as my Latin declensions; that I was able, in the same month, to translate Sophocles with an open book and blow a bottle of two-thirds of a liter; that at the lycée I learned about the caloric transformation of sand into glass, the chemical and physical reasons for that transformation, in the same epoch when I was initiated into Sanskrit, trigonometry and the rules of river-boating; that at the gymnasium I learned the history of the glass-working industry concurrently with those of philosophy and equitation; that at University, the social adaptations of glass to greenhouses, interior paving and the construction of telescopic lenses were taught to me by the same professors preaching the principles of astronomy, the theorems of general economics and the psychology of crowds, without, for that, it being permissible for me to neglect the firing range, nor the maneuvering of sails, nor the amorous initiations that the reestablished young mothers dispense to adolescents in our city of Venus."

"That's a complete education!"

"Ha ha! It's not yet divine, but in fifty years, the country has succeeded in installing in mores the truth that pleasure is Knowledge, that honor is Production and that shame is Destruction. We've taken a few steps."

"Have these ladies received the same instruction?"

"Not absolutely," Théa replied. "Our literary and esthetic knowledge is particularly developed, to the detriment of the pure sciences. We know how to paint, sculpt, construct the plan of an edifice, write a faultless symphony, play comedy and tragedy, and dance in accordance with ancient traditions and the art of modern ballet. We possess several dead languages better than men. The fine arts have devolved to us."

"Do you learn métiers?"

"Oh, yes. Our social service includes bureaucracy. There's no bureaucratic man. We also exercise the direction of the national esthetic. Women compose the décor of cities, and also occupy themselves with agriculture and gardening, according to their aptitudes."

"But there are many mixed functions in which men and women compete," Pythie declared. "Medicine, for example, agriculture too, and gardening. The two are confused. We're weavers, telephonists and telegraphists. In studying philology, Monsieur is encroaching on our domain, and it's not forbidden to any of us to preoccupy ourselves with mechanics or artillery, even though those fields of investigation are usually male preserves."

"What about the law?" I asked.

"Every work group," Théa replied, "judges the fault of one of its members. The convicted individual can appeal the verdict to other groups. If he's convicted of a crime, he's punished. There's only one crime: contravening the law of labor. Whether a man kills or refuses to work conscientiously, the crime is the same and the punishment similar. The convict is enrolled in a regiment for life. Having wanted to destroy social Harmony, he's sentenced to destruction and murder in perpetuity. If the mothers who produce life are heaped with honor, soldiers are heaped with opprobrium. People turn away when they go past."

"So you punish the theft of a loaf of bread and the murder of ten people in the same way?"

"No one steals bread. Anyone who is hungry goes into a refectory and eats until his appetite is sated, and drinks until his thirst is slaked, forty times a day if it pleases him. With the means of intensive culture, we can make land render four and a half times as much as it requires to stuff the entire people with nourishment."

"In Europe," said the bottle-blower, "you could nourish five times your population if, instead of letting your peasants scratch their fields with the implements of savages, you used common culture and scientific methods of renewing the soil, plowing it and inseminating it. Your goal isn't to nourish but to possess, to overproduce and to sell. Here, we don't sell anything; we consume everything. There are no poor people, nor thieves of bread—nor thieves of gold, since one can't do anything with gold, no one being able to buy anything."

"And what if someone wants to make a gift of it?"

"No one can possess anything. When our clothes are dirty we change them. Even our underwear doesn't remain in our hands; and we never know whether we'll go to bed in the evening in the same room as the night before."

"I suspect that a perpetual espionage watches you."

"Yes, but it's not inconvenient. No one has anything to hide. Like Gil Blas, one carries one's entire fortune on one's back. Who would want to steal, if there's nothing to steal, everything belonging to everyone?"

"Who are the criminals, then?"

"The wrathful, who kill or try to kill in a quarrel, or insult a contradictor gravely. The idle, who refuse to work. The smugglers, who attempt to introduce alcohol or tobacco. Those are the principal criminals. The bulk of the army is composed of people who calumniate, insult or do violence to a woman."

"And you don't fear a revolt of the armed men?"

"No, because the aerial ship and its torpedoes is always over their camps and their columns on the march."

"It isn't soldiers who form the crews of the aeronautical crews?"

"No, scientists."

The conversation petered out. The train was speeding through the humid shadow of infinite forests with the crazy velocity obtained, not by steam or electricity, but by the continual explosion of detonated gas. We were traveling through a deafening thunder.

Théa went to sleep. Night was about to fall. The bottle-blower turned the switch controlling the lights, which dimmed, and settled himself in order to go to sleep. His neighbors were already breathing more heavily. Pythie drew closer to my fever, seized my hand and drew me through the connecting corridor into another compartment of the train. There was a little lodge passed with poppy-red silk. The carpet was something soft, like an eiderdown; there was no other seat.

"You ought," she said, "to have treasures of amorous ardor, and not to be blasé, like the men here, whose satiety our bodies no longer seduce."

Without any further oratory precautions, she raised her lips toward mine; the viper of her tongue slid between my teeth. Her skillful hands, full of intention, half-undressed me. The effect of her caress was manifest; she shivered all along her spine on perceiving it.

Thus we reached the city of Minerve, in a few voluptuous hours.

LETTER III

Minerve, September 1896
Palais des Voyageurs.

My dear friend,

Nothing, among the impressions that assail me here, astonishes me more than the deviation of socialist ideas. The principle of liberty seems to have been denied immediately upon the descent of Jérôme the Founder in this land. Militarily and tyrannically, he led the revolutionaries to their ideal. In any case, it is sufficient to consider his statues, in which he appears in a martial attitude, his gaiters up to his knees, his hair in the wind, his side-whiskers rough and short, his eyebrows joined, his lip curled and shaven. On the plastron of his frock-coat with a folded skirt, a meager chest justifies the

277

bronze pleats. A historic gesture launches the first seeds into the air. The other hand clutches the handle of the plow like a weapon. The feet are embedded in the soil. Deeply sunk in the shadow of the eyebrows, the eyes are small and watchful. The heavy nose overhangs the cleft of the sneering mouth. Those characteristics of the effigy design the rudeness of the soul sufficiently.

His work, in the beginning, was, in any case, entirely warlike. The Malay tribes were disquieted by those men, who arrived without merchandise, from the coast facing China where the British commercial ailing ships had left them. Scarcely had they disembarked from the junks than they knew the treachery of ambushes during the long marches through the humidity of the forests. Five years it required, step by step, to fray a passage, remounting the course of new rivers, which drowned temporary camps with sudden floods; and those men, fleeing Europe because of hatred of injustice and social war, found, on the threshold of the anticipated paradise, battles, and then the cruelty of Asiatic tortures for prisoners and laggards.

The imminence of peril thus constrained those libertarians to the strictest discipline. Around them prowled the sanction of death. It was necessary to forget all the claims and all the hopes of solitary individuality. When the high plateaux had been conquered, and access to them forbidden, a salubrious country finally discovered, with propitious waters, deposits of oil and metals, a fertile humus, and the ears of the first crop ground, that sense of obedience occupied the reason of everyone. Jérôme only had to promulgate his laws.

Had that son of a Picard horse-dealer nursed the vulgar ambition of generals and nourished the stupid desire to return triumphantly to Paris, nothing would have been less difficulty for him. He did not want that wretched privilege. On the contrary, during the French expedition in China, he issued severe decrees forbidding any imprudence capable of revealing the mysterious and already prosperous empire. Such was his authority that no one transgressed the prescriptions or attempted to return to Europe spontaneously. Emissaries were sent there

278

several times for the public interest, without their speech betraying the secret.

Perhaps the Asiatic climate, favorable throughout the course of history to the success of absolute autocracies, modified the character of the pioneers; perhaps the infiltration of autochthonous races was able to insinuate into the conquerors the respect for destiny that imposes the will of a king on millions of human beings. At any rate, a singular languor persists in the eyes and the allure of people. Their eyelids seem weighed down by resignation; their smile wanders with indulgence and skepticism. Few things move them. If people in the streets couple on stone divans installed in the depths of the arcades bordering the numerous squares with fountains, or even if the momentum of a tram cuts the body of an impudent person in two, that is not sufficient to deflect them greatly from their internal reverie. An expression of disdain is scarcely sketched on their faces for the former spectacle; and for the second, the face they pull is more because of the disgust procured by the bloody mess than commiseration for the victim.

I cannot tell you the extent to which that character grates upon our impetuous habits of participating in all the manifestations of existence in others. Théa and Pythie, my companions, have ended up desolating me. I feel almost ready to hate them. If I talk to them about our arts or our politics, they listen to me without responding, evidently bored. They don't fail to satisfy my requests for information, but without their speech becoming animated to extol the marvels of their inventions or to denigrate abuses. They aren't delighted by being able to cross distances with so much celerity, not in enjoying the beautiful décor that the cities possess. They don't complain about the excessively overt life that obliges them to leave their clothes at the door of the bathroom preceding the dining rooms in order to put on others, new and unfamiliar, imposed by the administration. Everything comes to them on the dot, the sense of struggle is lost. They don't desire anything with sufficient violence to act in hope. Life seems to them denuded of value. Once I risked a fatal fall at the exit from an elevator.

279

It didn't even make them blink. Although the intimate connections of sexuality bind me to both of them now, they don't confide to me their enjoyments or their fears. We remain as much strangers as at the second hour of our meeting. Here, everyone remains a passer-by to everyone else.

Can you imagine that this Pythie almost impassions me? The intelligent charm of her silence, the cruelties of her debauchery and the superiority of her scorn dazzle me. Her fatigued body emits odors that stun, enlacing you with sweetness and warmth. She reads all the secret covetousness in your eyes. Théa and I are devoid of mystery before her. If speech ceases, for a few seconds, to stir our lips, Pythie suddenly starts laughing at what we are thinking, and describes the thought that is capable of amusing her. She's rarely mistaken. We estimate ourselves inferior at every moment. She sees it too clearly to attempt by her manner to make us feel it.

Before the triple maternity that exempts her from social service, Pythie taught history to the girls to the gymnasium. Her memory knows all the works of the erudite, the compilations of diplomats, the secrets of archives, the anecdotes of annalists, the sentimental causes of wars, and the virtues and weaknesses of cities. When she decides to speak, she reveals the origin, the development, the apogee and the decadence of a social idea expressed in the actions of peoples from century to century. She follows the idea on its travels. She shows it departing from the Orient for the Occident with the migration of races, and then returning, magnified, from the Atlantic toward China with the new European tide, which is recommencing the migrations of the cycle of Ram. Her voice generalizes the efforts of the planetary soul, which has peoples for its vital organism and the human individual for the unity of its cerebral cell. Pythie doesn't waste time counting the exploits of conquerors or the amours of kings like our professors in Europe. She aims for higher endeavors.

When I listen to her I understand the superiority devolved by fifty years of such an education on the virile age of this young people.

Minerve is the city of bureaucracies and libraries, and of printing. The feminine schools, the colleges, the lycées and gymnasia occupy the burgs surrounding the city at various distances within a radius of twenty-five or thirty kilometers. It is also the city of ministries and ministrations. A league from its limit, in the middle of a very beautiful forest, the University raises its sumptuous monuments, at the end of channels of water and severe hornbeam hedges.

The masculine element is present in limited numbers in the city. It is made up of inventors or workers on leave who come to the libraries in order to perfect their knowledge of scientific indications. So the Palais des Voyageurs is vast in its proportions. The women of the bureaux fill the avenues with their capacious black coats, their white cravats and their hard felt hats. At all the windows of the high edifices one sees them traversing the interior, papers in hand.

In groups, they enjoy the sunlight under the arcades of slender iron that cover the greenhouses preceding the edifices of the Laboratory. Those greenhouses protect hypertrophic flowers against the all-too-frequent rain: inconceivable orchids; monstrous chrysanthemums, and also delicate graminae; corollas that one might believe the crazy wings of minuscule birds. On paths of scarlet sand the ladies walk, two by two, with neither laughter nor outbursts of voices, eyes lowered.

In the public refectories they eat with pleasure, but hastily. They are vast greenhouses too, full of flowers and bushes and scarlet sand. The tables occupy arbors of a sort. They have two, three, ten or twenty place-settings. Through the ceiling of yellow and red glass the daylight spreads, traversed by white canopies. Mechanical organs sing in the basements, and their great voices are transmitted through series of slender metallic columns clad in faience where enamel birds parade.

There is always silence, smiles, a murmur, no loud speech. The frankness of the light allows all the little afflictions of age to appear on the women's faces, inasmuch as none seem to use powders or cosmetics. Their stiff hair, swollen by hygienic lotions, is rather delicately perfumed, but pimples spoil their rough, dark skin. Few blondes have survived the mixture of races over three generations; but one encounters manifestly Chinese faces with malicious eyes, prim lips and narrow dimensions, and slow and sly Malays. The members of this society stretch nonchalantly in large armchairs made of bamboo and woven rushes.

The male and female domestics are only distinguished from the diners by their costume. They bring the food in closed dishes, the beverages in simple pitchers. The diners drink from crystal glasses a kind of honeyed water, heady beers, cold tea and liquid sorbets. From metal vessels similar to gold, they eat exquisite pâtés, cold meats, jellies and poultry. To avoid the odor of sauces the kitchens prepare nothing hot. The nostrils of these people have become very susceptible. No one tolerates the slightest emanation. The effluvia of grilling and roasting that we enjoy nauseate them; but they partake with appetite of salads, tomatoes, spices and a great variety of fruits that the climate favors on espaliers. No cooked vegetables. The pâtés, poultry and roast meats are therefore served in containers known as "mouth assistants." Far from the cities, in the depths of isolated farms, a decried class of people prepares and cooks those victuals. Soldiers provide the service in abattoirs for which no honest people would take responsibility. The kitchens, from what I understand, are a kind of prison for women.

Above the restaurant, on the upper floors, simple and rapid mechanisms take hold of the plates, present them to jets of boiling water, swiftly turn them upside down, and slide them into driers, room which they re-emerge clean and bright, a beautiful metal similar to gold. Two overseers operate lavers with porcelain handles and switches, and the cleaning of several hundred plates is accomplished automatically in less than an hour without dirtying a single maidservant's fingernail.

Oh, I'm a long way away from our European family, its hearth, the good odor of soup and our dishwashers. The modest and simple, slightly dirty, existence of our old world is

282

finished. Here, the servers receive us as polite comrades. It isn't permitted to address any observation that might offend them directly to them. One writes one's choice of dishes and one's protest against a smudged glass on pieces of paper.

In the evening, the work groups meet up in the theaters.

Don't imagine that the theaters resemble ours. Immense edifices with cupolas and basements, they are slightly reminiscent of winter gardens, ballrooms and brothels. The principal one in Minerve possesses a façade in porcelain, very artistically enameled with clusters of men and women who seem to be descending from the sky. It is not unlike the *Last Judgment* that Michelangelo created. Each of the figures represents passion of a type due to a national literature and they are falling, it seems, through the starry profundities of the firmament along the immense gleaming façade that is not pierced by any window. It is a miracle of art much admired here, where there is no lack of beautiful works. Eighteen young women composed it in the decoration studios of the city of Diane. It took three years to complete.

With Pythie and Théa I went, at dusk, through the low and wide portal of the place, into a vestibule in iron and silver mosaic. Indicative gestures separated us for the bath that precedes every important action in this hygienic land. A Chinaman introduced me into a circular chamber in which a meter and a half of warm water covered the blue faience of the floor-tiles. Soaped and massaged, hair and beard equalized by scissors and doused in perfumes, I was also crowned, like an effigy of Caesar, with red headbands and a double palm. The servitor fitted me with boots of supple red silk laced all the way to mid-thigh and put over me a kind of blue chlamys with black stripes, which a brocade belt secured to my figure. Forewarned by my companions, I was not astonished by that festival costume.

A few moments later, I was on the threshold of an edifice higher than the largest Gothic cathedrals. The rows of long columns sustained on the palms of their capitals five cupolas of orange glass. The voice of invisible orchestras rose up from the ground. A cheerful light expanded through pink and green canopies, tinting a crowd dressed like me in chlamydes in various fabrics, long red boots with thin and muffled soles, each member coiffed as I was in a double imperial palm, perfumed like me with delicate and penetrating odors.

The bare beasts of Théa and Pythie, and a thousand other women, trembled as they walked beneath the transparency of the fabric. One sensed flesh close to flesh, odor within odor. Enervating music was perpetuated, covering the sound of water-jets falling into the pools of fountains between the columns. Divans covered with furs, colored woolen carpets and silk cushions welcomed all attitudes. With pretty cries, a hundred free-flying birds moved through the nave, fluttering among verdure bristling on the walls. A murmur of joy rippled through the audience. The eyes of women responded to one another. Many lay down, entwined, their lips joined; and then, in front of us, a fresco representing the cortege of Bacchus sank beneath the turquoise floor-tiles. The stage appeared.

Its scenery prolonged agrarian perspectives extending toward a landscape of gilded mountains, a marine line of violet waters, evoking a pleasant beach of Hellas. Laburnums bordered a stream. Goats were browsing laurier-roses. A satyr with silvery fur was blowing into a panpipe a melody that repeated the laughter of the stream, the whisper of the wind and the quarreling of warblers.

He was an old faun. His curly beard was as gray as his wooly hair, pierced by two golden horns, and the pelt of his belly was a little blacker. An extraordinary virtuoso, he was blowing into his seven-holed flute the song of total nature. Delighted sighs around me revealed the satisfaction of the auditorium.

We made a long voyage with him; we confronted the tempest on the mountain; we descended beside the cascade, by means of a path of sonorous pebbles. We encountered beasts, the rustle of their flight through the bushes, the gallop of herds. Eagles cried over our heads; then there were more familiar voices, those of finches and cuckoos, the caresses of the breeze in the light foliage, the trotting of horses, and the running of humans. Later, the water of the river splashed against the banks, the cries of infants appealed; then the confused voices of virgins, young women. Matrons, old women... Silence again; the fall of an apple into the grass; the flight of doves...

At that moment, the timidity of a nymph parts the bushes. She inspects the scene, but does not perceive the faun, who is crouching down treacherously behind the laurier. A ballerina, the nymph enters cautiously, listening. The flute resumes the quarreling of warblers. A second nymph comes through the bushes, a third...five...twenty...and there they are, listening to the dispute of the birds.

I shall not retrace the phases of the spectacle for you, my dear friend. Imagine that immense stage, gradually foiled by the quadrilles of the dancing girls in leotards clinging to their nudity. The cortege traces marvelous figures. The faun resumes on his flute the symphony of the overture, amplified by all the means of a powerful invisible orchestra, with a savant artistry, the dancers become themselves the natural forces that he is singing. They fly like clouds before the wind; they unite and imitate water, with the swell of their hips and breasts. They are the cascade and the river; then the hinds of the frightened herd, then the children, the girls, the women, the voices on the bank of the river.

Suddenly, the faun surges forth; the nymphs flee, come back, surround him. A dialogue is engaged. He shows the power of his art as best he can, blind and without mobility, but visiting, by means of suggestion, the most beautiful aspects of the world. Now he extracts from his flute the sound of a kiss. They laugh; they quiver. They represent to him that he is too old, too ugly. He tries to embrace one. The others extract her from that desire. Then he takes up his flute again and draws therefrom the imitation of all that amour has of resounding kisses, murmurs, nervous laughter, sighs, gasps, hiccups and cries.

On hearing that, the nymphs mock him at first, then are astonished, and then become exasperated. One embraces another, and another phase of the ballet begins, in which bodies embrace and writhe, in which passions is slaked in postures. Other fauns come running, the priapic folly takes hold, full of cheerful speech, witty and delicate repartee. Those nymphs and those fauns know the rationale of the world. They foresee the ridiculous effort of the peoples who will succeed them on the terrain of Hellas. From their amours, humans will be born, who will abandon the joy of nature in order to dominate or serve...

The second act presents a ring of rocks, the wild man, the chief of the horde, who returns home brings his prisoners, the weak: adolescents, women, old men. With his bloody ax, he obliges the old men to repair his weapons, the women to satisfy his lusts, the adolescents to build for him. He founds the family, killing those who resist, and when he leaves, having taken away the tree that serves as a bridge to cross the abyss, a chorus of lamentations weeps.

The third act shows the lair of the hero, at the summit of a hill that serfs in rags are laboring. Clad in his armor, the faun, the man, is sitting under the oak of justice, leaning on his sword. On his knees, the vanquished renders him homage, and to seal the peace gives him his daughter in marriage, gold, horses and silver reliquaries, arms, dowry and booty. Enslaved, the woman lies, deceives. The serf sins with the chatelaine.

In the following acts, all the avatars of amour are represented, from epoch to epoch, race to race. Oedipus wanders, Othello strangles Desdemona, Romeo and Juliet cherish one another, Antony stabs. Armed with religion and the law, the husband replaces the chief of the horde, the wild man, but with no less ferocity.

Thus the spectacle continues, traversing the series of the centuries. The relevant scenes of amour are mimed every time, all the way to the most humble of the denouement; and it finishes with the return of the faun and his cortege of nymphs. He

286

takes up his flute again. He recalls the cries heard in the pangs of eternal passion. He represents the actions of the world unfurling and unraveling around the divine Phallus, and the ballet recommences, the living tableaux completing it with a magical eroticism.

Other performances that I have seen summarize thus passion through the ages. That justifies marvelous and various settings, from act to act, multiple fashions of dialogue, heterogeneous studies of mores. A drama unfolding, as among us, in accordance with the unities of time and place, would not please. The far more synthetic intelligence of the crowd likes that negation of time, that search for the transformation of an idea, an instinct, in the course of successive societies, and that content of enchantment, lyrical drama, sentimental comedy, farce, priapism and sumptuous dances.

It was after one of those spectacles that I observed the strength of my inclination with regard to Pythie. As the members of the audience stirred, looked at one another and greeted one another in the glare of a thousand electric flowers that suddenly lit up on the trees of iron that formed the fabulous vegetation of the columns, a man approached her, a smile in his beard. She recognized him, they held out their hands to one another. She made him take his place alongside her on the fur of the divan. They did not take long to start laughing and whispering, and it was necessary to anticipate, from the kisses they prolonged with closed eyes, imminent intimacies.

Doubtless the alteration of my face alerted Théa to my pain. She told me to go with her into the basements, where the celebrations were continuing. I obeyed, not without turning round again, before going down, to savor the dolor of seeing the gilded beard of the intruder against Pythie's face, his crown of palms united with her crown of palms, and his powerful musculature imprinted on the softness of her undulating lines. A physical anguish afflicted my body. I had difficulty breathing. My hand became limp in Théa's. The veins in my temples swelled. Very slowly, I recovered my energy, which had fled.

At that moment, my friend, I remembered what you had said to me in Biarritz about passionate torture. Yes, the dolor of seeing oneself abandoned causes physical distress. It is not only our pride that weeps; it is our fibers, our bones, and our blood. I sensed it then, and was frightened by my condition.

The contemplation of the subterranean rooms settled me somewhat. Their mirrored walls seemed illuminated by multi-colored flowers, whose pistils were luminous flames. I saw without pleasure women and men clinging together in the depths of dark lodges, over the openings of which the folds of painted curtains fell back. I tested with insipid lips the golden beverages that Chinese children poured into cups. The spright-ly delirium of music struck my ears with futile sounds. Alt-hough I had consented to those sensualities, the caresses, by turns bestial, light and nervous, of a woman with firm breasts and clenched fingers, although they shook my body with un-expected spasms and caused my mouth to cry out, did not ef-face the image of Pythie in the other's arms, nor the anger that her indifference left me. In vain Théa made me drink the lips of a serpentine Malay woman and the breasts of a fleshy Chi-nese woman; in vain she enveloped my loins with the embrace of a blonde with the scent of warm milk. I acquired bodily fatigue therein without obtaining the lassitude of my anguish.

We quit the mattress of violet silk that garnished the lodge and remained under the raised curtain. Behind us, in the glimmer of the red night-light, the blonde, exhausted by pleas-ure, was asleep. The octagonal rooms converged, with their mirrored walls, on the intersection where we were.

Intoxicated by the golden liquor we had drunk, obviously aphrodisiac, women were running in a farandole, breasts trembling, naked to the girdle that retained their loosened clamydes. Toward the signs of men, too few in number, they slid under the door-curtains of the open lodges in the corners of the octagonal rooms. Mirrors multiplied the vermilion laughter of their mouths, the brightness of their teeth, the white or brown gestures of their arms, the rhythmic dancing of their legs in scarlet stockings. Ten ventilators were blowing out gusts of perfume over the murmur of the excited crowd.

Momentarily, one admired the science of a dancer who was reanimating the vigor of men by miming with the spasms of her belly a rage of desires. Later, a group of women, white and brown, entwined themselves together; sighs swelled the ivory of bosoms; the mauve and pink tips of breasts kissed. Slender girls swung on trapezes, rotating, offering to the eyes the taut lines of their arid haunches.

Moaning, howling, furious and joyful, women crushed one another, knocked one another down and raised themselves up to reach the loins of a ephebe mounted on a stool, who promised himself to the most alert. For a second, it seemed to me that I saw Pythie among them, her ripe breasts, her hairy armpits, her broad rump. But Théa covered my face with her face, and pushed me back into our lodge, letting the painted curtain fall back over the light of the blazing flowers.

We found ourselves back in the red penumbra, on our knees on the silk of the cushions. Other women had slipped in there, gasping. An odor of burning flesh, a perfume of ether and roses, choked me. Hands took possession of me. Mouths were stuck to my skin. I fell into arms. Embraces were sealed.

There was black fire in eyes, breath, the crawling of velvet skin, the clawing of cruel hands, the biting of dry mouths, the ebb and flow of flesh against my flesh, the suction of cupping lips, soft breasts flattened against my hands, extraordinary kisses, the friction of tresses.

Strangled by dolor or joy, a female voice was moaning lamentably. Warm women were drowning me. I was choking. My body was bent like a bow. I was afraid of dying; I struggled; I pushed that vermicular mass of bacchantes away; I extracted my body from hands, arms legs; I reached the curtain and drew it aside.

Everywhere, the lust of shapeless couples was groaning, and in front of me, a child stuck to a mirror misted all over by her warmth, was sobbing voluptuously against her image.

I completed her dream with my strength.

Up above, in the hall with the cupolas, one rediscovers the beat of the music, laden tables, and fortifying beverages. One grasps the measure of things again. One calms down before the architectural harmony of the infinite naves, before the colors of the glass flowers in which electricity shines.

Ceremonies of that sort take place once a week.

I can well understand how, compared with such lusts, the petty stupidities of sentiment appear negligible. Go talk about moonlight, eternal passion and twin souls to women sated like that once a week. They look at you as they would a silly child. But it reduces passionate dramas to a minimum. The communism of erotic sensations destroys the desire for property over the lover. One remains free to offer kisses to whomever one likes, without a first connivance creating any obligation to future connivance.

Amour does not occupy, here, the place that it occupies in the old world. And yet, I assure you, one is better able to profit from the pleasures it involves.

Thus, sentimental novels do not attract anyone's attention. Women as well as men seek in libraries works on history, linguistics, geography and science—hence the extreme intelligence of everyone. No longer having to equip themselves for the combats necessitated among us by the conquest of amour and bread, the peoples of Jérôme the Founder spend their leisure time fortifying their souls with knowledge. They talk about problems of science as Europeans gamblers talk about problems of baccarat, chess or écarté. They amuse themselves by competing in knowledge.

You can easily imagine that in the wake of the weekly orgies that exhaust their sexual instincts in the theaters, neither men nor women plan rendezvous in the intervals between those fêtes. If they grant favors, it isn't with fever, but out of politeness.

You will not hear anyone here taking pleasure in narrating the details of those common adventures, just as you never hear anyone in Europe harping on the menus of their meals. There is, in this country of Malaisie, a people with sated instincts who no longer have any covetousness, except for intelligence.

In a future missive, I shall tell you about the education received by children; you will see with what artistry the instructresses and the professors give them the taste and avidity to know more.

LETTER IV

Jupiter, October 1896,
Palais des Hôtes.

...I remember you telling me about someone who, during the school vacations, persisted in spoiling the hours by the number of his questions relative to the problem of three fountains, or the encounter of two locomotives departing at different times and traveling at different speeds. He tested your knowledge with interrogations about the longitudes and latitudes of islands, or the classification off insects. Like that relative, the people here only distribute pedantic propositions. The beauty of natural scenery only excites them to quantify the value of pigments, the curvature of lines, the radiation of heat and light.

A cloud passes over. If I say: "There's a cloud." Someone replies to me by estimating the approximate density of its vapor and calculating its velocity. Someone else overbids him, communicating a hypothesis regarding the formation of winds. Five or six theories overlap. There is an outcry. Someone resolves the problem by means of algebra. Texts are cited. The shrill voices of women pierce the quotation of figures. I remain bewildered by my ignorance amid that racket of contradictory methods.

Their scientific institutions do not, any more than their political institutions, establish perfect accord between their souls. In the city of Diane, I am assured, a group of female workers avid to know astronomy has commenced by proving that the Earth and the Sun remain motionless, and movement

291

in general is only an illusion of the senses. You can imagine that I shall not report in this letter the reasons advanced by the young women, but they seem to have rapidly conquered a multitude of believers. Oh, that poor planet! Before Galileo, it was the Sun that bounded above her, from Orient to Occident; since Galileo, it is she who waltzes around the star. Tomorrow it will be demonstrated that neither one of them dances, and that by the practical adepts of the positive philosophy that basis itself on the immutability of knowledge.

Thus, here as in Europe, struggles, competition, rivalries, acrimony and hatred are not hidden by the scruple of history. Only the motive has varied. People do not tear one another apart for the conquest of women, for lust, nor for ambition, but the intellectual need for certainty acts as harshly on covetousness as our material needs. The government falls when a new discovery belies by its evidence the theoretical assertions it sustained.

In this city of Power, Jupiter, oligarchies succeeded one another quite rapidly. Their average duration is less than a year. Less the cruelty, their fashion of ruling the State recalls that employed by the Council of Ten in Venice. As soon as an invention, a book or a work of art gives prominence to a group of creators, that group becomes, without asking to be or being able to avoid the duty, a candidate for the succession of the reigning Oligarchy, which hopes to resign. For, of all social service, that of government is reckoned the least agreeable. No honor is rendered to those supreme "clerks." Their task is considerable. It demands work much harder than other métiers, without any compensating advantage.

Initially limited to twenty members, the Oligarchy was expanded to thirty and then fifty. Today its fifty employees accomplish their task painfully, the principal part of which consists of listening to phonographs reciting complaints, criticisms and advice addressed by some work group or other. It is necessary to classify those documents, summarize their claims on a daily basis and to spell out the official logic that admits them or rejects them. Nothing obliges the Authority to satisfy a demand by citizens, even if that demand is unanimous, but it must explain its reasons clearly. If the public persists, the Oligarchy asks to resign. The citizens grant or refuse the resignation. In the former instance, a different group succeeds it

Not one work of science, art or letters is recognized as the result of a single personal effort. If a man writes a book, his whole group signs it. To all of them, it seems evident that if he was able to write the book, it is because his comrades' words and the observations of which they were, for his intelligence, the object, made an infinite contribution to that effort.

Imagine France governed, in successive series, by several oligarchies, one composed of scientists attached to the Pasteur Laboratory, another of writers revealed by *Les Soirées de Médan*,[28] a third of General Négrier and his general staff, a fourth of Francis Magnard and the editorial staff of *Le Figaro*, a fifth of Claude Monet and the Impressionists, a sixth of Monseigneur Hulst and his clergy, etc.[29]

Evidently, among us that system would soon collapse. Each coterie coming to power would strive to destroy all the work of the preceding coterie, stupidly. It is not the same here. Less barbaric, people consider themselves too skeptical to want to be sectarians. If an oligarchy of chemists arrives in government, it does not worry about undoing what the ethnographers established before it. It occupies itself above all in applying the benefits of its chemical knowledge to the univer-

---

[28] *Les Soirées de Médan* (1880) was a showcase anthology of writers connected with the Naturalist Movement. Émile Zola had moved out of Paris to Médan, and hosted a limited salon there, mostly consisting of writers who used to dine with him in Paris.

[29] François de Négrier (1839-1913) distinguished himself in several colonial campaigns, including the Tonkin campaign of 1884-5. Francis Magnard (1837-1894) was editor-in-chief of *Le Figaro* until his death. Maurice Le Sage d'Hauteroche d'Hulst (1841-1896) founded the Catholic University in Paris and served as its rector from 1880 until his death.

sality of things. It transforms simultaneously the charges of torpedoes, culinary recipes and the composition of perfumes. If an oligarchy of mechanics follows, it ameliorates the machine-tools in the factories, the arms of the soldiers, and the smooth movement of the trams. If a group of artists replaces it, the buildings are embellished, corteges better adorned, and the streets are decorated. In sum, the State always remains a building under construction through which the various bodies of artisans pass successively. Politics does not exist. Let us agree to praise that absence of conflict, in practice.

Thus, and perhaps because of laxity, the people almost never insist on obtaining a reform if the authority has demonstrated its inconveniences. Even less does the latter refuse unless the trial appears absolutely impossible. The battle is fought in the domain of ideas. When a theory has produced its masterpiece, it is its adversaries who bear the men and women supporting it to power.

Jérôme the Founder inculcated that way of thinking into his soldiers from the outset. The proof has been made in the subject of religion. Some exalted atheism, others professed deism. In order to lay low the spirit of triumph, Jérôme decided that official education would be religious, even though the deists were certainly in the minority—except that he included the heresies propagated by Mani and the Gnostics, invoked interpretations due to cabalists like Fabre d'Olivet,[30] and enlarged the Catholic dogma once established according to the needs of barbaric minds in accordance with the curiosities of ignorance, and subsequently become too naïve for the requirements of modern intellectuality.

---

[30] Antoine Favre d'Olivet (1767-1825) was a historian and linguist whose interest in and translation of neo-Pythagorean writings made them available to grateful nineteenth-century occultists, but also made significant contributions to Biblical hermeneutics and produced an unorthodox interpretation of *Genesis*, some of whose elements are echoed in the author's invented catechism.

Before quitting Minerve, during my visit to the girls' gymnasium, I had the opportunity to understand how the opinions of the race are formed. This is how it works:

The scene is set in a room looking out through arcades upon the richness of tropical vegetation. A hundred Chinese, Malay, European and mulatto adolescents, a few blonde but the majority brunette, are sitting on a series of steps. A quadragenarian dame in a Trissotin costume,[31] the instructress, is interrogating a dainty little Japanese with slender hands.

"What is God?"

"The ensemble of Forces," stammers the shrill and musical voice.

"What is a force?"

"That which creates movement, heat, electricity, all the states and aspects of nature, and in consequence, the universal physical laws, the attractive relationships of heavenly bodies, nebulae, suns, planets, vapors, seas, waters, vegetation, plasmatic cells, mollusks, fish, amphibians, quadrupeds and humans.

"Did God, then, create humans?

"Yes, through the series of the three kingdoms, and in order that humans, in their turn, in accordance with the evolution of races, would know and adore the harmony of Forces."

"What do you know about Adam and Eve?"

"Adam is the red Earth, the incandescent Earth before the gradual cooling of the planet. Eve is Aïscha, or the volitional faculty, the energy that permits the evolution of life, from the humblest cell of vegetal plasma to the scientist and the hero. Because of that, the priests taught that Eve was taken from Adam's rib—which is to say that human intelligence was extracted by the evolution of cooling matter."

---

[31] Trissotin is a character in Molière's *Les Femmes savantes* (1672), a satire on academic pretention and female education; the reference is malicious.

"According to you, then, Mademoiselle, Adam and Eve are therefore the origins, or the parents, of all humankind? Tell us how they were expelled from Eden."

"Adam and Eve lived in bliss so long as they did not concern themselves with judging. They accepted as a splendor the equilibrium between life and the death that engenders life by its fertile corruption. They admired and adored. But the serpent Nakasch, their instinct, counseled the will of Eve, and praised the precellence of life over death. 'For,' it said, 'in prolonging individual life, Eve and Adam will prolong egotistical enjoyment, and life will be good, and death will be evil,' Adam and Eve lost all confidence in death, when they had tasted the fruit offered by the lie of the serpent, their instinct. They immediately lost the happiness of admiring the Harmony of the World. They restricted their views, their admiration and their concerns to themselves. They perceived their paltry reality, their nudity, their weakness, and they hid themselves with fig leaves, in order that the other Forces would not make them ashamed. The preoccupation with existing longer as individuals caused them to lose the sense of eternal and divine life in which the forces intersect, collide, are transformed and perish, without ever dying. In order to defend their lives, they admired hatred. They distinguished God from Evil: that which helped them from that which harmed them. Adam and Eve lost the felicity of paradise."

The young child of fifteen years repeated the lesson without too many faults, her eyes attached to the blue stucco that covered the ground.

"Is it unnecessary to fear death?" asked the instructress.

"It unnecessary to fear death," replied the hundred voices of the disciples in chorus, in a joyful tone.

"Why is it unnecessary to fear death?"

"It is unnecessary to fear death," replied a plump little blonde, indicated by the mistress, "because ideas are immortal, and our consciousness, made of united ideas, is immortal."

"Is the soul immortal, then?"

"The soul of humankind is immortal," replied the hundred joyful voices of the children, in chorus—and their hundred little hands traced a hundredfold sign of the cross."

"How do you explain that ideas are immortal?"

"The positivists of our time are merely continuing the evolutionism of the sages of Ionia, the *perpetual becoming* of the Greeks. Through the races, ideas grow, from century to century. They express themselves by means of the human voice, the development of cities, the social amour that multiplies the presence of humans in cities, for reasons of war and those of social conflict. The Idea is God."

Rising to their feet on the steps, one after another, the girls continued: "The Father is the unknown cause of causes, the egg of universal laws, the center that extends to the utmost limits of the sphere. He is the center and the periphery, the beginning and the end."

"What is the Son?"

"The Son is the recognition of God in the human soul in accordance with the processes of planetary evolution. Thus, he was engendered of the race of David, who descended from Adam, the red Earth, as the Scriptures say."

"Do you know several incarnations of the Son?"

"All the Gods of all the religions. The Son is the Word, the speech of the world."

"Is the Word God?"

"Yes, for the Word alone is real. We do not know whether the vocables correspond to realities. For example, the mother qualifies as red, before her offspring, an object that he might perhaps see as green. Throughout his life, that child will name red things perceived green by his organ. No one will contradict him. In fact, other disciples, if they perceive yellow the object that the educator qualifies as red, or if they perceive it as black or blue, they will all call it red, as the authority of the master indicates. Perhaps, since the origins, no one had perceived the colors in a fashion identical to another, but by virtue of tradition everyone names different sensations by means of the same word. Daltonism proves that some people cannot distinguish cherries from foliage by their color. The errors of the senses are innumerable, as science reveals. As the proverb says, 'It is necessary not to argue about tastes and colors.' so much does it seem that my soul knows the world especially. Everyone's universe is different, and the philosophies of the epochs indicate the uncertainty of relationships between names and objects. No philosophy can say whether the external world corresponds to what we think about it. Humans perceive within the prison of the senses. They follow the fatality of the Word blindly. The Word is God."

"Are the Cause, the Word and the Idea the three distinct persons of the one God, One and Triple?"

"One is the center; two is the periphery of the sphere; three is the relationship between the circle and the center. One is the Father, two is the Word, three is the Evolution, the Spirit that radiates from the Father to the Son: from the Original Force to the human being who recognizes it."

"In the name of the Father, the Son and the Holy Spirit."

"So shall it be."

The instructress made a gesture. The adolescents quit their steps and spread out through the arcades of the cloister, chatting. They leap in their gaiters; the short blonde or chestnut curls and the wiry wisps also leap toward the fresh gleam of their eyes.

They assembled in the sun and turned in a circle, holding hands.

I made enquiries of the mistress about that abstract religion.

"Monsieur," the lady replied, "that is the supreme stage of religious instruction. When very small they learn the ordinary responses of the catechism. From class to class explanations are added that render the Christian dogmas acceptable. On Sunday they take communion. When absorbing the host, I believe that not one doubts the Real Presence. At that moment they will think that, made of wheat, the fruit of the Sun, itself fecundated by the Harmony of Forces, the definition of God, the host contains the Real Presence of the God who sanctifies the sacrament of the Holy Altar. I inform them, therefore, that Abel incarnates centrifugal force, the chemical dilatation of substances, the impulse of the amplified soul toward pure verities; that Cain embodies centripetal force, the cold that shrinks, the tendencies of egotism leading the mind only to conceive the immediate good of instinct."

I contemplated the round-dances, the pretty gestures of the adolescents, their games.

"Certainly," the instructress went on, "if we only counted European pupils, the teaching of Christianity would have had no result. Jérôme the Founder sent emissaries to collect the children of unfortunate families from China and the islands, mingled the overly mobile minority of Occidental souls with ten times the number of Oriental minds capable of grasping abstractions. The desire to match one another animated those young intelligences, and the mutual commerce of their ideas fashioned a median mind very capable of being interested in our lessons, hard as they might seem to you.

"On the other hand, pedagogy here is founded on an amusing system. It differs from your Roman disciplines. By means of grammar, declensions, conjugations, syntax and a thousand numbered and rebarbative rules, your professors put children off from the start. By force, under pain of impositions and detentions, you oblige them to learn by heart, without their being interested, the avatars of the past participle. By contrast, we begin by amusing the pupils. We read them history. We tell them how rain is formed and storms, and why ink stains their fingers. They immediately like the adventures of Romulus and those of Noah. They call their dolls Cleopatra and their puppets Caesar. By means of history they learn geography, which is no longer a tedious enumeration of subprefectures but the evocation of places where people fought.

"Later, we add to historical certainties the classification of dates, those of social economy, the presentation of the philosophical ideas by which governments and their adversaries were inspired, and, finally, the languages that the great peoples spoke—but all of that is framed by objective facts. Our programs never include things analogous to your themes and Latin discourse. Grammar is only taught to the adolescent, like mathematics, when the child's mind, awakened by stories of history, spontaneously seeks an exact measurement of that knowledge.

"Thus, philosophical, mathematical and grammatical abstractions are not intimidating. They complete anterior notions. They come to satisfy a curiosity, a veritable desire—whereas your pupils, bewildered too young, deterred by declensions, syntax and exemplars, only find at the end of their courses, in philosophy and science, a summation of past ennuis. They learn poorly, mechanically, stuffing their memory with a view to examinations; they acquire forever a hatred of the sciences, of which they do not want to know anything after college. They no longer read anything but novels and newspapers. Our pupils retain for life the avidity to increase their intelligence. It's a pleasure."

In fact, when the break was over, the pupils returned to the steps without any reluctance.

"What is the second mystery, after that of the Trinity?" asked the dame.

"The mystery of the Incarnation."

"Explain it."

"Mary contains within her two contradictory principles, virginity and maternity. If we cannot conceive something as Being and Not Being at the same time, and in the same frame, that comes from the weakness of the human mind. By the mystery of the Incarnation, God informs us that the pure Phenomenon, the absolute, exists outside those two forms of conception. The Virgin Mother engenders God, or the absolute, by the operation of the Holy Spirit, for intelligence can succeed in making the Pure Phenomenon of Being conceivable, beyond its temporary appearances of existence and non-existence, life and death, good and evil. Thus the Holy Virgin conceived without sin because she conceived, thanks to the Spirit, without differentiating being and non-being, in the same state in which Adam and Eve, substance and will, thought before the original sin. Mary's virginity denies the existence within her of God and her maternity affirms that existence. Because of that, she engenders the absolute, the Man-God, the identity of the microcosm and the macrocosm."

"What is the original sin? Is it true that we bear its punishment?"

"Adam and Eve having differentiated life from death, all their weakness became manifest to them and hatred was born. By atavism, we continue to know that weakness, to fear death and to hate."

"Explain the mystery of the Redemption."

"The macrocosm, or the greatest expansion of God, is identified with the microcosm, the planet of which humankind is the cerebrality. God is made human. Unlimited, he accepts limits. Eternal, he dies on the cross. Universal life, Jesus suffers individual death, and departs from Life. He redeems humankind from fear and science in reestablishing, by means of the torture of Calvary, the identity of being and non-being, of the infinite and the limited. Whoever dies for the triumph of eternal life, for the glory of the immortal idea, recommences the sacrifice of Jesus and redeems the sin of Adam. He becomes unlimited in eternity."

"What is the cross?"

"It is the Center, the point at which the radii of a circle meet; it is also the sign of fecundity, the phallus, the horizontal jod, traversing the vertical kteis,[32] the origin of all life; it is the Cause, or the Father. Thereon the Son died, by the operation of the Holy Spirit. The Trinity of God, the world, was brought back to the single point of the One, the Center."

"What was Mary?"

---

[32] Following the syncrectic policy of this catechism, *jod* (the Hebrew-derived Cabalistic term for the phallus) and *kteis* (the Greek-derived Gnostic term for the vagina), are drawn from different and perhaps incompatible sources; whether that deliberate disjunction is significant, and, if so, of what, is for the reader to decide.

"The form or the appearance of things, the illusion, mother of the Word. Like Isis, Mary is the sensible world that engenders the Word, which disappears on the cross absorbed in God..."

A bell rang. The church was summoning its faithful. The disciples arranged themselves in two files, intoned a canticle, and we followed them along the paths of the garden.

In the image of Byzantine naves, the basilica supports several cupolas. Under the sky of the largest, a central Virgin is painted, gigantic, with mountains, rivers, cities, seas, animals and peoples on her robe. All the way to the iconostase, lateral chapels to the right and left contain, in accordance with the banal eclecticism of pantheons, several elevated altars, one to the Buddha in a Japanese décor, others to Mohammed, in a Moorish décor; to Siva, in a Hindu décor; to Isis, in an Egyptian décor; to the gods of Olympus in a Hellenic décor; to Astarté, Moloch, the gods of Mexico and Peru, to Mani. That would give the impression of a bazaar were the proportions of the edifice not imposing in their immensity.

The organs play. The iconostase opens. A Catholic altar appears, where a priest in a chasuble officiates. The service of the mass does not differ significantly from ours.

One savors the odor of incense, the freshness of choral voices. I thought I remarked a sincere attitude of meditation among the girls kneeling on little padded cushions.

LETTER V

Jupiter, November.
Palais des Hôtes.

Under a heavy sun, reflected in the glass panels of roofs, domes, bays and greenhouses the village is in fête.

Long sheets of violet, red and white silk quiver along the facades. Gods are painted on many of them. The large figure of the Virgin with her robe full of cities and peoples on the march recurs incessantly. On the surface or her metal eyes, engraved ships float. The milk flowing from her nipples contains the names of Noumena, mingled with creatures of the three kingdoms, and Jesus, sitting on her lap, bears maxims that summarize the speculations of philosophers inscribed all over the nudity of his body. Generally, behind her, the two directions of the cross traverse one another. Painted or sculpted, they reproduce the emblemature of ethereal currents. The planets seem to be drawn there in a descending and remounting horizontal course that circulates them, combining them with comets, suns, the nuclei of nebulae and hordes of stars.

With one wing, the Holy Spirit touches the summit of the Cross; the other attains the head of Christ. The pinions of that sacred fowl, as vast as those of our archangels, envelop the Son and the Virgin Mary with the same almost-white protection, even though each septenary of plumes bears the hues of the prism. In sum, the triangle of the Trinity frames the complication of the symbol luminously.

That is repeated everywhere, on the silk sheets as tall as the facades, on the litters where the clergy caries them in groups of metal, ivory and wood. The statue of Mani and that of Buddha also ornament the temporary altars. From tripods garlanded with fresh flowers—roses, violets and dahlias—perfumes swirl.

The tram carrying my two friends and me does not run on wheels but slides on a kind of steel spindle encased in a single rail. The cushions are soft. We move rapidly through the joyful murmur of the avenues. Corporate uniforms are assembled under porticos around nymphaeums: black scribes, crimson factory-workers, the Chinese of the public services in national costume, the Malays of the highways carrying canes, with yellow miters on their heads. We glide between the indefinite edifices, all open, allowing glimpses of assemblies in their halls.

Naturally, the organs glorify the day. The insurgents of the Philippines have just beaten our Spanish troops, and the oligarchic Dictatorship is celebrating that victory, which it calls that of Liberty against Tyranny. Here is the procession, similar to all Catholic processions, except that the costumes and the objects of worship are indescribably luxurious.

On horseback, a hundred beautiful young women in violet stockings, torsos bare, their heads crowned with enormous flowers, precede the Holy Sacrament, swinging golden ciboria. From their hips to the undersides of their breasts they wear corselets of fabrics garnished with jewels, composing in their assembly the form of fabulous plants. Their long hair spreads out from a small bonnet in silver mesh. Large rubies scintillate at the tips of their breasts. Short skirts of black and green strips, terminated by hollow golden buckles, float over the velvet saddles. Holding on to the horses' bits are ephebes, similarly naked from the nipples to the white satin trunks on which a sun and precious stones illustrate the location of the penis. Supple boots in white leather cover their calves and thighs. Their right hands are holding a thyrsus or a caduceus. Surmounted by the closed wings of doves, little helmets coif their hair.

Others, mounted on black horses, are blowing slender trumpets. Robust women march beside their stirrups. Their breasts are supported by crimson networks, their robes made of black canvas into which fresh yellow roses are fitted. On their heads they wear tiaras of myosotis.

Then come giant men with undulating beards strewn with spangles. Royal crowns consecrate them. The hair on their torso is jaundiced with henna. They display all the beauty of virile vigor. They are holding back the impatience of greyhounds on leashes, mastiffs, lion cubs, antelopes and deer. Some carry spades, other shiny pickaxes, some levers of furbished copper, others gilded hammers, while others hold up set-squares and trowels at the end of scarlet poles. In a low chariot that they are dragging, a red metal machine advances. Its flywheel and its polished steel piston-rods shine more coldly against the other metal, which retains the somber gleam of incandescent iron. In their crimson vestments, the factory-workers file past like an army behind the chariot. They all have a green branch in their hat and a wooden caduceus on the shoulder.

The scribes, clad in black, follow, and then the Chinese in brown silk robes, and two hundred girls on foot, with tame birds on their fingers, ivory canes, white trailing tunics and crowns of laurels in their hair. Then come a thousand ballerinas, in swarms, who are dancing, each with a different step, their slender hands agitating sistrums and clicking cymbals. Some, in scaly sheaths, writhe like snakes, and silver wigs shiver against their cheeks. In the midst of violet wings, others bound on vigorous legs, their breasts passed through the oblong openings of blue corsets. Corollas on green legs, flowers spin. An entire squadron represents minerals. Idols of diamond, topaz and sapphire go by; living statues in granite, malachite and bright marble. With one girl of gold, one of silver, one of iron and one of copper, the metals shine. Adolescent simulate aquatic creatures, algae and fish; their slow choreography marks the indolence of floating bodies.

Oh, that army of dancing-girls! It unfurls for a whole hour. Out of the colleges, the lycées, the gymnasia, all the girls of some beauty had come to the parade. Over the nudity of their limbs a kind of make-up put a miraculous sheen, with the result that no fault of the epidermis was evident. Their flesh seemed to have a bright, slightly varnished freshness. Perfumes that would escape you in their gestures, and you, flowers, flowers, flowers thrown, flowers of costumes, flowers of tiaras, flowers of garlands, flowers of bouquets, innumerable colors of flowers!

Between the enameled facades, the squadrons of dancers fill the avenue. With their evolutions march white elephants, bearers of towers on which domesticated eagles frolic at the summit. The spindles of many tall chariots slide along the rail, the file of which successively presents the gods of all known religions, with their priests and priestesses in sacerdotal costumes officiating at the altars. The palanquin of a Mother oscillates on the shoulders of a dozen virgins in striped silk leotards. Among the white and yellow veils the pregnant woman lies, under the canopy, and he movement of fans shows a pale face banded by a diadem. Around her, dancers spin, choirs sing a hymn and litanies; cymbals resound and harps vibrate. Stretchers of flowers, drapes of heavy cloth illustrated by embroidery, canopies of white brocade, the palanquins succeed one another between the chariots of the gods, the battalions of dancing-girls, and the choirs of children in red robes.

Finally, the colossal image of the Virgin terminates the center of the cortege, behind a clergy of bishops, deacons, bonzes, lamas, muftis, softas, bayaderes surrounding the white highness of an old man who, as Pope, holds up beneath a red metal canopy the Monstrance, image of universal cycles and the great Vedic fire.

Over her mantle, blue as a distant mountain, the hair of The Mother is a forest of minuscule trees. Her knees are two cascades. The miracle of a perfect mechanism launches luminous bubbles of star, suns and comets into the tall glass cross behind her.

After that come more cavalries of beautiful girls on white stallions. They are sounding long slender trumpets. And now, there are more throwers of flowers, Mothers' palanquins, ballerinas, harpists and sumptuous choirs of children.

And that goes on and on. I can't tell you everything. My eyes, in any case, grew weary. I looked at Pythie and Théa. They seemed to me to be in ecstasy, those creatures who manifested an unbearable coldness and scorn toward everything! I questioned them.

"You don't understand," they told me. "Those harmonious bodies, the play of the combined shades of the folds of the robes, those symbols of religions evoke such simultaneously subtle and universal ideas in us. The total history of Evolutions is readable from gesture to gesture, group to group. For us, the cortege is a volume unfurling. The immense poem of Forces is sung in the splendor of antelopes, eagles, ballerinas and males. We sense God in Everything. A vigorous semen spurts in our imagination, fecundating it. The point, the center, the i, the jod, the phallus and God penetrate us at that instant, and makes us whinny and prance for memorable enjoyments. Evidently, with your European education, you only see naked women and the passage of animals borrowed from a zoo; for us, its harmony that is passing, the jet of creation in fusion. Don't say anything more. Leave our Spirits to pant, we beg you..."

I stood up to look down from the height of the vehicle. Then I saw the whole of the file. It extended through the curve of the avenue, extending and moving in accordance with the form of the creative phallus, two or three miles long. Groups of statues eternalized the visages of inventors gazing down from the height of their pedestals around their bronze machines, at that monstrous passage of Life.

The great voices of phonographs alternated with that of organs, declaring strophes. The choirs in the cortege responded, and then the lyres, the trumpets and the dances.

Stupidity or good sense, I confess to not enjoying myself as much as my companions or the other people amassed in the vehicle. It all seemed to me to be very obscure, very pedantic, and not a little pornographic. In spite of everything, the heart of an honest man revolts at these spectacles of nudity. No matter how broad a mind one can claim, it is not appropriate to approve of debauchery when it poses as the principle of government and religion.

The next day, at the audience granted to me by the Dictatorship I could not prevent myself from saying so to the oligarch who was reproaching me for the obsolete practices, once employed by the Inquisition and reestablished in the province of Cavite by our General Blanco in order to punish the Philippine insurgents.[33]

---

[33] General Ramón Blanco (1833-1906) was Governor-General of the Philippines from 1893-96. Although his approach in confrontation with the independence movement was generally conciliatory he placed eight provinces, including Cavite, under martial law. Repression, including the use of torture, gradually intensified even before Blanco was sacked for being too soft.

A tall woman, dressed like a white musketeer, the oligarch smiled at my accusation and changed the subject. I was received in a vast, extremely simple room. The stucco walls only astonished me by the fact of elevating a dome of blue glass at their summit. The oligarch examined me with little eyes like particles of quicksilver. She was sitting in a white velvet armchair, and behind her, against the wall, the State banner was unfurled, half black and half red.

"And what if," she said to me abruptly, "we were to use our technological superiority to descend upon Europe, annihilate its armies with the aid of projectiles launches from out aerial frigates, and impose upon it what we believe to be Intelligence, Harmony and the Better Fate?"

"Bah!"

"It could happen; it would be our duty..."

The tall woman rose to her feet and started marching back and forth on the rubber floor. She had colorless and wiry hair, a face that had lost its freshness, dead lips and bony hands.

A sudden anger inflamed her flat cheeks. She came back toward me, exclaiming: "Yes, yes, the time has come. You, the Spaniards, with the cruelty of ancient ages, are stimulating the haste of our projects. Don't think that our soul saw without passion your justice crushing Cuban ardor thirty years ago, shooting the anarchists of Xérès and Barcelona, reinventing the instruments of the Inquisition for the Philippines. The blood spread over the world fumes as far as us, and our strength trembles with impatience. The veil of hypocrisy will be harshly ripped from the face of the world. The immortality of Power is becoming too great everywhere. It was not merely for us to rejoice and cease to suffer that Jérôme the Founder brought our race to this land and sowed the truth in the minds

---

At the time the present novel was published he was Captain-General of Cuba, where he introduced "reconcentration camps" and helped to provoke the Spanish-American War, which he then prolonged by his refusal to surrender.

of its decadence. He created duties for us too. Three hundred thousand Armenians perish, slaughtered, and the Christian Powers, by virtue of an ignoble avidity and an ignoble mutual suspicion, threaten with war anyone who might dare to close the sluice-gate of the blood of the weak. Never, in any time, has that been done. History cites the Crusades. For what example?"

"Europe would be very glad," I said, ironically, "if the Dictatorship could prescribe a means of terminating those massacres without opening European conflict."

"Could Belgium and Switzerland not act in the name of Christian Concert, and then establish a Byzantine Confederation on the example of the Helvetic Federation, with the small Balkan States, Greece…? But let's leave it there. The note that has been given to the Dictatorship, on your behalf, demands an explanation for the aid given to the libertarians of the province of Cavite. Our Oligarchy is composing the reply at this moment. I fear that it will not be of a nature to satisfy the ministers of Spain completely."

"Ah!"

I stood up. A sign from the tall woman caused me to sit down again. She continued to march, maintaining an irritating silence. From a distance, she appeared to me reminiscent of an ostrich with white wings and red legs—her morocco gaiters were that hue. Multiple small steps made her gait staccato. She reached the wall and came back toward me rapidly, her hands extended, like an angry chicken.

"Yes, yes, it's better to say everything," she went on. "Know this, then. Three years ago, our predecessors prepared a plan for the conquest of Europe and the gradual extinction of social justice. I won't talk to you about military projects, but I can indicate the general principles that were to guide the conduct of our strategies following our victory."

"That would interest me greatly," I said.

"In a year or two it will interest you even more," she cried, harshly, in her shrill voice, and an echo threw the sonority of her prophecy from one corner of the room to another.

I allowed a smile to animate my lips. The madwoman became exasperated, more and more reminiscent of an ostrich in a zoo whose provender had been stolen by a turkey.

Tumultuously, she declared: "Suppose this for a moment. Our aerial squadrons are hovering over Paris. They have crossed all military lines, reduced forts, artillery dumps, arsenals, barracks and prisons to smithereens, sparing the lives of soldiers as much as possible. The terror produced by the material effect of our explosives masters opinion. Around the city, our torpedoes fall once again on inhabited areas, hollowing out hundred meter craters in the ground, breaking all the windows in the city with the noise of their detonations, which, perturbing the atmosphere drown the country with rain. Resistance has evidently become impossible..."

"Might surpasses right!" I pronounced, appositely.

"Yes, since people only recognize the evidence of might; since, without the terror of greater force, they will not alleviate the fate of those that their own force crushes. What are a majority and a minority? Two armies in confrontation, of which the weaker numerically, too cowardly to attempt the contest, renounces it immediately. What triumphs in that instance, except stupid numerical strength, without which the vanquished minority will obtain nothing of its hopes? Yes, we shall be the strength of minorities, the brute force of minorities finally victorious. We shall throw into the lighter pan of the scales enough weight for equilibrium to be established in a stable manner. Know that..."

The ostrich flapped her wings comically before me. Saliva leapt from her beak with the words...

"What do we have to fear in imposing our force?" she went on. "Crushing intelligence and spirit? No, truly. There are diplomats that our European newspapers praise, that your Academies invite as notable minds to sit among them. Having the honor of representing Christian thought before the world, they applaud all the massacres and all the injustices of the Powers. Diplomats make arrangements to allow the Turks to slaughter, gut and disembowel at their ease, opposing them

310

with phrases of absurd elegy. One obtains by that genius the protection of Greeks and Armenians in words without protecting them in fact, while delivering them to the sword of the bachibouzouk, without approving of the crime of which they are the evident accomplices. Sinister slyness wins them the flattery of letters, arts and nations. Do you think that by crushing intelligences of that sort our force would be crushing a veritable thought, a veritable honor, a nobility of soul? Yes, we would be brute force against their base ideas, but our force would kill fewer people than they massacre..."

The ostrich stopped, out of breath. She took a handkerchief from her pocket and fanned herself.

"There's one thing," I said, "that I don't understand. You carefully close access to your country to others. How do the telegrams informing you of the physiognomy of the world reach you?"

"We have a house of correspondence in Hong Kong, and a submarine cable. In certain inaccessible massifs of the Alps, the Himalayas the Urals and the Rocky Mountains we have posts that communicate with the telegraphs of cities and our aerial ships."

"And no indiscretion?"

"We pay well enough for trusted consciences to remain unbribable."

"So, if that expedition had been made, and Europe, vanquished by the explosives of the aerial frigates had sued for peace, the Dictatorship would have made a *tabula rasa* of our Latin institutions, from one day to the next?"

"Very nearly, but not immediately. Your hosts are still so deprived of altruism and energy that they would not tolerate the operation of a *tabula rasa* without perishing in civil wars. Our plans accommodated a transitional period, yes. If it interests you, I can have you shown one of the printed posters that would have been stuck to the walls in Paris during the preliminaries of the armistice."

"I'd like to know the tenor..."

The lady promised to send one.

"You'll see," she added, "that we would have made use of the army, the only organization functioning well, and put it to work for some time for the first applications of the new regime. For the military army we would simply have substituted, without disruption, the agricultural and industrial army. The exercises would have changed, that's all."

"So," I continued, "nothing of the mission that my government has given me appears likely to succeed?"

"You must excuse me, Monsieur. The Dictatorship cannot respond definitively. Yesterday, in Cavite, eight insurgents were shot. The governor of Manila twists the truth in his dispatches, like his colleague in Cuba. Even Japan is moved by these injustices and is preparing to lend the insurrectional movement effective aid. Circumstances are becoming aggravated. Diplomats require prudence."

The audience was about to conclude. The nervous lady sat down again in her white armchair, fanned herself with her handkerchief, chewed a pastille and, with one of those mental leaps familiar to her sex, asked me whether the frequentation of my companions, Pythie and Théa was satisfactory to me. I praised them highly.

She told me then that her normal social function was that of telegraphist in a railway station. Her group had found a means of simplifying telephonic and telegraphic transmission, and had been put in candidature for the Oligarchy. The receivers of the apparatus are being replaced everywhere, and that is an enormous task, all the more so as public petitions are demanding the placement of telephones in every room of all habitations.

The lady got carried away by her telegraphic theory, not without the disobliging pedantry that seems to infect all the people here. Even so, I succeeded in taking my leave.

The city of Jupiter does not include anything particularly remarkable. It possesses a theater similar to the one in Minerve, greenhouse-restaurants, curved avenues, edifices with glass cupolas, nymphaeums, enormous docks, facades with enamel images, and a rather rich temple where the colossal image of the Virgin Mary that serves to ornament processions is usually housed.

In the streets, the white garments of the oligarchs do not attract the respect or salutes of anyone, nor the irony. They are passers-by, like all the rest. I have neglected to see the interior of the theater and to take part in the weekly festival, so true is it that the practical liberty of pleasure wearies you and renders you virtuous.

The number of statues of groups is a curious feature of the city. At the corners of all the avenues, in the squares and in countless smaller spaces, there are pedestals on which ten or twenty figures of men and women wearing the costume of factory workers stand. These images are very realistic, even too much so. One could believe that one is looking at skillful molds taken of the people. Generally, the bodies and clothing are bronze, the heads and hands in a paste of colored glass. In the middle of the group stands the model of the object that invention created. Several fountains spring from the pedestal.

I have learned, moreover, that the splendid costumes of the procession will not be seen again in Jupiter. They will appear successively in all the cities of the Dictatorship for a similar ceremony and will then be destroyed. For each fête the artists imagine a new decoration of creatures and chariots. They are never used again. That provides an illustration of the crazy richness of social production.

When I expressed my amazement, Théa said: "Here we produce joyfully to consume ourselves. You produce sadly in order to sell. How can you expect that our labor would not be a hundred times more productive than yours?"

To estimate what a similar cortege would cost in Europe with the system of salaries and commerce, one quickly attains a figure of fifty or sixty millions. Neither Holy Week in Seville nor your Parisian Mardi Gras can compare with it—but is such labor useful for such a mediocre joy? I know that I have pronounced the word "useful" and that Pythie laughed in my

313

face with utter impertinence. They both consider me to be an incorrigible imbecile. I almost detest them.

You will find attached a fragment of the poster printed in advance that the commanders of the aerial ships would have struck on the walls of Paris after it was taken. I've removed the preamble.

After the signature of these preliminaries, the government of Paris will act as follows:

Article I. It will pronounce the dissolution of the Chambre and the Sénat. The present members will be replaced as follows:
1. For the Chambre des Députés:
A hundred will be chosen from among scientists and inventors; a hundred from among writers and philosophers; a hundred from among plastic artists; a hundred from among advocates, professors and bishops; a hundred from among industrialists and agriculturalists; and a hundred from among historians, geographers and physicians.
2. For the Sénat:
A hundred will be chosen from among generals; fifty from among admirals and engineers; fifty from among magistrates; fifty from among diplomats; and fifty from among financiers.

Article II. These new functionaries will not have to deliberate over the laws. They will be charged with collating the petitions of commoners, without discussing them.

Article II. Civil marriage is abolished.

Article IV. The imputation of paternity being illusory and not reposing on any natural certainty, new-born children will take their mother's name in the registers of civil estate.

Article V. The sole legal heritage is that of the mother to her children.

Article VI. That heritage will be transmitted in the following conditions:
A. An expert evaluation will be made of the movable and immovable property bequeathed. The heir will be inscribed for a corresponding sum in the Great Ledger. The income at a tariff of three per cent will be paid to the heir for life. That income will not be transferable.
B. Other legacies to third parties will only be valid by virtue of testamentary clauses. They will be subject to the same formalities; but the State will impose a levy of fifty per cent on the tariff of the income and the sums raised by that levy will be added to the budget of public education.

Article VII. Every woman with reason to believe that she is in a state of imminent maternity must declare her condition at the Mairie of the arrondissement. She will be immediately hospitalized in a maritime town in a mild and salubrious climate. The time of that hospitalization will be counted from the third month of pregnancy until the weaning of the nursling. At that time the child will be admitted to an establishment of public education in order to be raised and educated at the expense of the Nation.

Article VIII. The general mobilization of the French armies is decreed.

Article IX. The army will cultivate the soil of the fatherland, sow, till and harvest, care for flocks and herds, exploit the wealth of mines, produce in factories and workshops, construct edifices and divide and distribute between the citizen the wealth of the nation.

Article X. The State factories and those requisitioned for that usage will immediately manufacture agricultural equip-

ment in conformity with the progress of the sciences, including steam-powered plows, threshing-machines, seed-planters, harrows, etc. That equipment will be delivered within three months to the military stewards.

Article XI. A committee of agronomists and engineers, half of the members chosen by competition and the other half elected by their qualified colleagues, will direct the work of the social army in order that the rendition of the soil will be maximized.

Article XII. The courses at the École de Saint-Cyr and the École Polytechnique will be extended to five years. During that period the pupils will add to the knowledge required thus far those necessary for the general application of scientific principles to ameliorate the cultivation of the soil and the production of industry.

Article XIII. Whoever shall import, manufacture, sell or buy alcohol will be prosecuted in conformity with the laws on a charge of attempted murder. The State will provide the needs of laboratories of chemistry and pharmacy, with regard to the production of alcohol.

Article XIV. Any individual convicted of theft, murder, arson, bankruptcy, abuse of trust, fraud, whatever the facts thus qualified might be, giving proof of the desire for conquest, will be incorporated for at least five years into the colonial armies. The colonial armies will play the same role in their military territories as the regular armies on the metropolitan territory.

Article XV. By way of the decease of the holders, all immovable property will become the property of the State, the sole legal possessor of land.

Article XVI. The colonies are submitted to the same transitional social regime as the metropolis.

Article XVII. The system of direct government by the people is substituted for the system of parliamentary representation.
A. Every Sunday, in a register deposited for that purpose in the Mairies, the citizens of the commune will inscribe the text of petitions concerning the subjects that they judge useful to the general interest.
B. The following Sunday, the citizens of the commune will vote on the texts, yes or no.
C. The officers of the legislative body will classify the communal petitions by analogy, indicating the number of votes expressed, for or against.
D. Within a period of six months at the most, the Authority will make known via the Communal Bulletin the reasons that it believes ought to favor or oppose the principles of the petitions.
E. After a further communal vote, and the sanction of the Council of State, those petitions will acquire the force of law, but their dispositions will only be applied in the communes where they were originally drafted.
F. Nevertheless, if other communes claim that application, it will be granted to them.

Article XVIII. Men and women will enjoy the same civil and political rights.

Article XIX. Every woman between twenty and forty-five years of age owes social service to the State.

Article XX. The working day is six hours.

Such, my friend, is the law of the conqueror, which I fervently pray to God to spare you.

317

LETTER VI

March.
Fort des Quatre-Têtes.

After the train had crossed indefinite terrains lugubriously clad in dense forests, and plunged into the gorges of violet-
tinted mountains, it reemerged the following morning in a
region of lakes. Over the extent of the vast waters, many small
islets were mirrored in bouquets. Ships glided between two
wakes, without smoke, without noise and without masts, rapidly. We traveled over a median causeway where the waters
ended. Gradually, that causeway broadened out. The tropical
flowers invaded the ballast, soon defended by means of a trel-
lis against the thorny plants and shrubs of the brushwood.
Then an entire countryside spread out, almost entirely covered
by the tall glass edifices of agricultural greenhouses. Thickly
painted with colors, the panes protected the cereals, fruits and
vegetables from burning by the sun. Those colors were various, according to the nature of the vegetables. A long explanation by Théa educated me with regard to that kind of medica-
tion by colored light.

Many greenhouses were open. We perceived automobile
plows tiling by themselves, and elsewhere, seed-planters distributing the grain. In a third location rollers were flattening
white-tinted soil stuffed with artificial fertilizer. Here, the seasons do not collaborate. Mechanics and chemistry replace the
care of nature, with a multiple activity.

The agricultural greenhouses are gigantic. They cover
whole areas. The Galerie des Machines in Paris gives some
idea of the least of them. Under the edifices of glass dynamos
set the apparatus in motion. A few men supervise. There are
vineyards bearing the grapes of the Promised Land, wheat-
fields whose overly heavy ears require stays, and rice-stems
three meters high—but the potatoes remain minuscule because
their taste accommodates better to that dimension. As large as
walnuts, they are, browned, crunchy and cold, a delight for the

mouth. In the same way, the Lilliputian strawberries enthuse the palate, whereas the flavorsome monstrosity of pineapples and pears renders the soul blissful for hours.

"Yes," Pythie declared, "our stomachs are the most pampered in the world. As it is unnecessary to sell inferior products cheaply to the poor, our agrarian groups eliminate from culture everything that does not seem to attain succulence. The study of the conditions that favor it permits them to be reproduced to the benefit of all the fields, and you've been able to see manual works eating victuals at the tables of the public refectories that are only served in Europe to millionaires, kept women, great criminals and kings. Honest people enjoy good sensations here..."

That is the bitter tone incessantly employed in my regard. You will appreciate, my dear friend, the petty torture caused to me by the presence of that woman beloved by my passion, very welcoming for the folly of my senses, and conspicuously disdainful of my person.

"To think," Théa said, "that with your enormous population, you could make the soil of Europe render the same felicities, on condition of shaking off the tyranny of money. Instead of that, you continue to compete, hate, vanquish, enslave and debase...after nineteen centuries of Christianity!"

"But it seems to me that we're reaching the military zones," I announced. "Are those not the rectangular terrains of the defense: fortifications at ground level, a steel cupola scarcely emerging from concrete embankments that mask those artificial slopes and that plantation of small trees? That's evident proof! In truth, you desire neither to hate, nor vanquish, not enslave...and the Dictatorship has invited me to follow a expedition of your troops against the Malay tribes, to whom you will certainly express love at the point of a bayonet, as our Weyler[34] did to the Cubans."

---

[34] Valeriano Weyler (1838-1930), replaced by Blanco as Governor-General of the Philippines and, subsequently, as Captain-General of Cuba.

No, not at all! We're making war on a kind of indigenous tyrant who cuts off heads to decorate his feast, who impales, pillages, rapes and kills in order to relieve the monotony of his days. The majority of his slaves desert and come to us. He is demanding that those lives are rendered to his bloody caprice. We refuse. He has ambushed and murdered our sentinels, derailed two trains and caused eight hundred deaths. Even so, the Dictatorship has offered to make peace with him. He wants his victims; his honor demands it! And he prefers to be buried under the ruins of his palace rather than permit his fugitive subjects an easy existence."

"He's not alone in sustaining that principle of honor, however."

"No; ten or fifteen thousand men are armed for that."

"For the honor of the fatherland, which they judge superior to the material wellbeing of the individual. I don't find that ugly."

"Your race approved for a long time of the frenzy of Inquisitors who preserved the paradisal eternity of crowds by removing, by means of massacre, the contagion of heresies. It doesn't astonish me that you applaud a war sustained for the honor of causing people to perish, at the whim of one alone."

"For the honor of the fatherland and for the laws of the fatherland. In any case, are you not arming yourselves very patriotically in order to avenge your fellow citizens killed in railway catastrophes?"

"No, we're defending productive life against destruction. We're arming ourselves in order to protect life."

"A certain way of life, as the Malays are arming themselves in order to protect another way of life, which they judge superior to yours."

"They know full well that it is inferior to ours."

"Why?"

"Because, proportionately to the number of the population, there is much less death among us, and we produce much more. That is the sole criterion of superiority or inferiority between peoples."

"Then the races afflicted by a high mortality, who produce little, ought in consequence to renounce the laws of their fatherland and their traditions, and adopt the legislative formulae of states...

"Where life and production are multiplied the most."

"And that without taking account of the atavisms of race, or mores, or the personality of the fatherland, or the principle of nationality."

"But my dear friend, you're saying sentimental things, uttering the commonplaces of rhetoric; you're not reasoning. Cite us then, in Europe, one fatherland that is the exact representation of a face or a nationality. Your Spain, for example, contains Basques whose language is foreign to all Latin dialects, and Celts in Galicia who are closely related in their mores to the people of Wales and Scotland, and play the same bagpipes. It includes Andalusians of Moorish blood and Castilians who are sons of Iberians and Visigoths. In the times of Charles V your nationality also included Italians, Germans, Burgundians, people of Flanders and Picards. Your neighbor France is almost as well supplied with a mixture of races. It is, therefore, puerile to sustain that the principle of nationality corresponds to a homogenous assemblage of souls. Geographic nationalities such as Italy seem more acceptable.

"In sum, your fatherland exists by virtue of the peninsular figuration of the land. Nationality is, therefore, purely a definition of the atlas. It is to misunderstand all of history only to attribute its origin to the personal ambitions of leaders, kings and emperors, the proprietors of territories whose views were limited to the increase of the serfs of their domain.

"The real fatherland, the corner of land where a race exits speaking the same language, employing the same mores, is always tiny. The Basque country would be one fatherland, Provence another, Brittany a third. The Walloons of the century of Louis XI would form a fatherland. Germany, save for the Polish provinces, represents a fatherland where homogeneous races are assembled in the same region. After the Zollverein, however, it does not constitute a nationality. At what moment was Rome a fatherland? In the epoch of the kings, that of the Republic, that of the twelve Caesars, or of Byzantium? If it was in one, it was not in the others. In the time of the Republic, its spirit was Hellenic, and Asiatic after the Antonines. Only the Armenians maintain the unity of Byzantium. How, then, to define the Roman fatherland, the most complete and best-known historical phenomenon, from its origin to its dehiscence?

"In the beginning, the fatherland designated the territory of the people. The tribal leaders, out of need or ambition, attempted to increase their property. They conquered, they enslaved. When the vanquished are numerous, a contract is imposed by the victor. Laws form the first bond of nationality, which can grow without limit by means of successive annexations. The desire for property drives the chiefs of a strong people to multiply their resources in men—producers and soldiers—and in fertile soil.

"Nationality, therefore, defines a temporary agglomeration of races living in the same territory and regulated by the same laws. That does not represent anything stable or tangible. On this point, history expresses only one thing: the general law of sociology shows that the tendency of human societies is for each one to progress from the smallest fatherland to the greatest, without distinction of races, mores or climates. It is therefore a matter of seeing that clearly, and of dissolving nationalities as far as is possible into one, which, by uniting them, facilitates communication between provinces and the altruism of individuals. At that task, the civilizations of Chaldea, China, India, Egypt and Rome labored. In modern times, England has recommenced the work of unifying the world. By comparison with that gigantic labor, what do patriotic concerns matter?"

"So," I replied, "you forbid by means of torpedoes and aerial bombardment the intrusion of strangers into the domain of the Dictatorship..."

"Because we do not want anyone to come here to corrupt weak souls, neither to sell nor to buy."

"Nor to violate the customs that constitute a fatherland and a nationality of which, if I'm not mistaken, these are the defenders."

I pointed to a troop on the march. Coiffed in low helmets in black leather, clad in brown dolmans and breeches like those of zouaves, also brown, long gaiters and light brown shoes, the soldiers, carrying haversacks that were evidently not very heavy, were marching briskly with a long stride, in quintuple file. They were singing a rather beautiful hymn. The infantrymen were the tallest and the cavaliers the shortest of men. I was astonished by that.

"It's quite simple, though," said Théa. "The tall, solid fellows are better able to march and carry sacks. On the contrary, men of short stature fatigue the horses less by their weight. Thus one obtains the maximum mobility in both corps. There are military women who drive the regiments' vehicles, the ammunition trucks and the ambulances. Look!"

They only differed from the men in their uniforms. I also saw some who were marching in infantry companies. I was told that they were employed occasionally on long marches, but they make up the artillery units of the fortresses, and the railway troops who guard the tracks and defend the stations, and the sedentary regiments in garrison in the forts. They are administrative soldiers, secretaries to the general staff, and furnish all the elements of the catering corps and the sanitary service. They do not appear to be any less nimble than our graceful female cyclists.

The column disappeared around a bend in the road.

"There," said Pythie, "are the forces that bear the best fate in the world."

"By iron and fire." I added.

My companions disdained any response, somewhat indignant that I had divined in their altruistic souls the crude dream of all conquering nations, with a slightly different apparent motive.

As one approaches Mars, the carriages suddenly plunge underground, descending the slope of a tunnel, where an unin-

323

terrupted glass tube contains incandescent electric wires. Vast in extent, that tunnel contains stations served by elevators. They command complicated branches. From time to time a shaft pierces the thickness of the terrain and allows smoke to escape.

That subterranean part of the line shields the trains from projectiles launched by a possible invader. It permits the arrival of munition trains until the moment of a very restrictive investment. In fact, Mars occupies the strategic center of a system of mountains that closes the territory of the Dictatorship to any incursion coming from the sea by means of the only approachable coast and then through the valley of the only river that gunboats torpedo boats and lighters laden with supplies could follow upstream.

We traveled for nearly two hours through that resplendent tunnel. The phonograph cried the news. Pythie and Théa read, embraced one another and mocked me. In order to thwart them I pressed the switch of a music box and an entire mysterious orchestra played a piece by Schumann, to which they ended up listening silently.

Retuning to real daylight, les agreeable than the light of the broad tube, our track combined with others on which wagons were rolling filled with livestock—sheep, cattle and pigs—heading for the mass of the city huddled behind its ground-level fortifications.

"Where are those animals going?" I asked.

"To the abattoir. All the animals destined for the alimentation of the entire country are killed here. That cloud of dense smoke covers the culinary factories where the cooked and seasoned meats are put into terrines, which depart on other trains for all the parts of the provinces."

"It's the city of butchers and cooks, then?"

"It's the city of Death. The soldiers cut the throats of the sheep and pole-ax the cattle in order to familiarize themselves with bloody work. The veterans whose declining strength exempts them from service are employed in the culinary factories. They confect the pâtés whose flavor your taste-buds appreciate in our restaurants."

"Look over there: those blue domes are the crematory ovens."

"And there, in that blue train, a cargo of human cadavers going to the definitive fire."

"Look there, after the verdure of the great woods, those edifices…do you see them? They contain the ashes of our fellow-citizens, sealed in a million little boxes."

With a fearful rapidity, the blue train passed by, leaving in the nostrils a strong pharmaceutical odor. In the lattice-work wagons the cattle were bellowing, the pigs squealing and the sheep bleating. The sounds of military trumpets burst forth from all directions, while a perfume of cooking and grilling reached our sense of smell.

The train circled around immense parks. There, herds of cattle were fleeing the prods of cavaliers in uniform under the command of some sort of captain in tan boots. Elsewhere, sheep were galloping too. An ocean of pink pigs was swarming in limitless mire. Afterwards, we recognized a military esplanade, artillery batteries, gun-carriages, automobile haulage vehicles, armored wagons surmounted by metallic cupolas split by the emergence of long gun-barrels. Not far from there, companies were being briskly drilled, with low helmets of black leather, armed with small double-barreled rifles, very military in their bearing by virtue of their gaiters, broad canvas trousers, and short gray dolmans with brown piping. The artillery, however, wear a flame-colored uniform, because their weapons, operating at a long distance, do not denounce themselves to an enemy by the scarlet color of their costume.

We disembark. Here there are patrols, battalions, drums. The facades of high buildings are red. Made of bronze skeletons raising electric searchlights over their heads, street-lamps border the sidewalks where an armed and helmeted crowd circulates. Sabers resound on the flagstones. We see the blue train again, crossing a viaduct that spans the avenues. The pharmaceutical odor spreads. The smoke of the crematory fires and culinary factories has difficulty rising up because of the heat of the heavy atmosphere. Sealed trams pass by, coming from the abattoirs. Their bloody spindles slide within the rail. The insipid odor of butchery emanates.

In a restaurant hall devoid of plants, the faces of soldiers, similar to those of our European butchers, astonish me with their low brows, and their sanguine and adipose flesh. The seal of crime is revealed on almost every face. I'm not unaware that military service replaces fines and prison here.

"Almost all these people," Théa told me, "are smugglers who attempted to introduce alcohol, tobacco and other poisons. Many were sent to the regiments for crimes of passion after their anger had afflicted rivals of either sex, those who would not accept their sentimental domination, who wanted to limit the free practice of amour as counseled by law. Jealousy is punished harshly because that base pretention of property over the life of another hinders fecundation and maternity, the maximization of the source of life, and hence the maximization of production. In spite of the severity of the judgments though, those sorts of crime encumber the statistics."

In order to exasperate my grievances against her, Pythie continued: "It's hard to lose the habit of old injustices, difficult to renounce the ludicrous privilege that renders two beings slaves to their reciprocal caprices for life because they've confounded their spasms for an hour, in accordance with the hazards of instinct."

"Really?" I replied. "Have there never been among you, then, two beings who cherish one another to the extent of creating a single soul and a single body with their two forms, and perpetuating that new being in contemplating it with all their joy?"

"There are some, certainly. No one opposes their mania."

"Are there not also women among you who refuse men, in order only to cherish one?"

"There are a few."

"And what of them?"

"Their desire is respected. Our laws first warn and then punish anyone who attempts to enslave a woman by obsession or brutality. The group tribunal watches over the repose of each individual. Here, in the course of a year, a considerable number of fellows with an overly active instinct are enrolled.

With her eyes, Théa designated a trio of infantrymen who were staring at both of them without dissimulating an erotic covetousness. I felt ill at ease, all the more so as Pythie, as a game, did not refrain from smiling at the colossi.

Women came in wearing red dolmans trimmed with black. They were coiffed in the same flat helmets, Save for the lightness of their step they were scarcely differentiated from young men. A few of them, in their forties, had faces like those of our priests, but imprinted with a rare impression of cruelty. Their baked and fleshy lips were projected in a disdainful moue. From the nostrils to the chin, the pleat of flesh marked the effects of hatred and rancor.

The men and the women quickly exchanged filthy remarks. The abjection of our European populations was manifest in mouths affecting kisses and their obscene gestures. Couples immediately form. Everyone quarrels, kiss, hug. There is no longer the silence or pedantic speech of other cities. Pythie is amused by the sight of that shameful grunting. One soldier having insinuated his hand into the dolman of a female comrade, our friend stands up and approaches the couple to request her share of merriment. The brutal satisfaction of the two ruddy-faced and drooling individuals tempts her. Théa has to address a reprimand to her in order for her to come back, laughing, and follow us into the street.

"So," I said, a trifle angrily, to Pythie, "this social condition represents the realization of all the desires of your ideality?"

"Certainly not," said the music of her voice. "I don't pretend to sustain such a stupidity. I even affirm that such an opinion doesn't exist in any of those still alive who disembarked in his latitude with our Jérôme. They possessed a notion of society and human beings very different from what the actual results of their efforts produced. Logically, however, what happened in this country, over fifty years, is what is bound to become of a conflict between a pure ideal and characters, instincts and survivals. Certainly, the Dictatorship has not succeeded in transforming the citizens into gods, as Jérôme and the socialists of 1840 expected, and as Kropotkin and the anarchists expect, as a matter of faith. Everyone runs toward the ideal according to the impulsion of their material needs. It's not magnificent, but it's better than what there was before.

"Nothing of what the reactionaries of Europe predict today, in glimpsing the advent of the social era, has occurred. Very few people refuse to work. There has even been a commencement of competition to collaborate in the public good. The majority of alcoholics renounced drinking; some died of it, and with heroism. Jérôme's companions fought for five years, weapons in hand, against the indigenes suffering the heat, disease, thirst and hunger, to lay down the roads, channel the rivers, dig wells and mines, and created an enormous stock of equipment. In almost all of them, Jérôme encountered the devotion that Napoléon was able to expect from his soldiers and the Mahdi succeeded in obtaining from his dervishes.

"When the heroic times were past, the cities built and ease came, weaknesses became much more numerous. The population of Mars multiplied, and our army comprises nearly a fifth of the citizens. But the education of the colleges is amending the minds of all. You'll perceive few young soldiers here. The enrolments go back seven or eight years. We're even studying means of warding off the diminution of our military forces, which are reduced from day to day by the falling crime rate. In the early days, people sacrificed themselves to the ideal of universal ease for the same obscure reasons that counseled Napoléon's soldiers to risk death with a view to a vain glory that they scarcely enjoyed, or for the benefit of a fatherland that nourished them poorly. It was not their minimal pay that excited the grenadiers of Wagram to combat, nor the hope of becoming maréchals, since the vast majority of them were unaware that they were carrying the baton of command in their kit-bags.

"The belief that money and ambition alone guide effort is a simplistic faith. The movements of enthusiasm among crowds obey mysterious influences much more difficult to define. Your European bourgeois advanced stupid arguments when they showed, the day after the general revolution, weakness overcoming effort. Nevertheless, I think that Jérôme was wise when he instituted the sanction of enrolment and military exile against the abetters of social disharmony. I also think that in a century, perhaps before, that sanction will have become unnecessary, or nearly so. The intelligent egotism of each individual will have progressed to the point of always wanting to act with a view of the general good whose spectacle delights him, whereas its injury would hurt him. Thus, in your Europe, the intelligent egoistic father of a family working for the ease of his daughters and sons, redoubles his effort in order not to encounter hostile faces when he returns home. We are going toward egotism, properly understood."

"Slowly," I added.

In fact, a brawl was assembling gawkers in front of us. Two women were hitting one another, scratching and tearing one another's hair out. Between the tatters of their scarlet dolmans their flesh was visible, exciting the crapulous reflections of soldiers with the muzzles of murderers. One took hold of the dangling breast of the other and twisted it. The screech of a strangled cat split the air. Outside of that claw, the violet summit of the breasts was bleeding. Then the ten fingers of the wounded woman clutched at that fist, which stopped squeezing. Voices encouraged the fighters. The victim hurled herself at the victor, clamping her jaw on her adversary's mouth. Blood spurted again, but neither the claws of the one nor the teeth of the other let go. We even saw by the movements of her throat that the woman with the twisted breast was drinking the blood of the cut mouth...

It was ignoble...for, while the hatred in their faces and their arms united them, it seemed that the perversion of instinct mingled their kegs, which entwined in spite of the large rents in the canvas breeches, drawing their bodies together.

I was certainly not the only one aware of the dual impulse of those amorous enemies, for the warmth of Pythie, suddenly leaning against me, came to penetrate me while the secret research of her hand obliged the emotion of Théa, plastered against her.

Around us, couples and trios were uniting. Hands were disappearing into the vestments of others. Toward the brawl, the crowd with warm cheeks and panting breasts agglomerated, sniggering, gasping, and became quieter. Sweat ran down faces; gleams striped blinking eyes...

Glad expirations revealed pleasure.

The two women continued their fight and their game; they ended up by falling into the dust, rolling around there, remaining there, shaken by cries and spasms, until a police patrol, running with bayonets raised, parted the crowd. Seized by rough hands, brought upright, gripped, they were marched off, faces bloody, one with a split and torn lip, the other supporting a breast blue with contusions with her free hand. She was sobbing...

The rest of the crowd dispersed by the patrol took refuge in the gardens of nymphaeums, under the arcades that veiled the bushes and the water jets.

"Those people offend the sense of smell," said Pythie. "It's a pity, because they'll fill the arcades and stone divans, and I'd really like to soothe my nerves, with the aid of your complaisance."

"Me too," said Théa."

Her eyes searched for a solitary spot. We didn't find any. Two enormous edifices enameled in red displayed facades with large bays, through which we could see women writing. Down below, the reading rooms and refreshment rooms were full of those tumultuous individuals.

We continued on our way, uneasily.

By way of caryatids, the houses have images of Perseus brandishing the Gorgon's head, David decapitating Goliath,

Hercules slaying the hydra, and similar exploits. Celebrated battles are depicted on the ceramics; one can see Bonaparte at Arcole, Attila in the Catalaunian fields, the cuirassiers of Reischoffen charging through the streets of the Alsatian village, the elephants of Pandjavana crushing the heads of twenty thousand Parsees,[35] Hannibal at Lake Trasimene, the battle of Actium, and a thousand other polychromatic images of times of war. From one façade to the next they follow one another, in historical order. Slaves of an outré realism, strongly influenced by nearby Japan, the artists have painted beautiful routs with the cadaverous faces of those fleeing, the grated teeth and haggard eyes of their pursuers, the lividity of sabers in the air, the panics of cavalry, the earthen fists of the moribund. There were pitched battles. To the right and the left, the blood of the images splash the enamel with flowers. There are grimacing heads on the end of pikes, bellies cut upon to let out floods of entrails...

Between those facades swarms a mocking, vulgar population, girdled with belts and brandenburgs. It jeers, abuses, makes obscene gestures and performs ignoble mimes. All the faces are shaven; the lips make violet buttonholes under big noses Brown and sickly after the double projection of the cheekbones, Malay faces glide among the others like the heads of snakes.

We mingled with the flow of pedestrians. To hear their noisy speech, I could have believed that I was in a Parisian faubourg on a holiday. Without having taken any alcohol, all those people were drunk. They affected an ignorance more base than it really was. They called to one another, insulted one another, replied with other fraternal insults. The scarlet

---

[35] The name Pandjavana does not appear to exist outside the present text, but the intended reference might be to the Battle of al-Qadisiyyah in 636, between an Arab army and a Persian army, in which elephants were employed; it resulted in the conquest of Persia during the Muslim Expansion.

dolmans of women contrasted sharply with the gray and brown uniforms of the soldiers.

We arrived at a large blue portico fabricated in the Chinese fashion. Before the drawbridge, the entire crowd stopped. They lined up, and then fell silent.

Then we heard, as at our entry to the station, the bellowing of livestock behind the walls whose ceramics represented hunting scenes, and we knew that these were the Abattoirs.

An officer came to collect us, and to guide us. We reached a kind of low triangular tower where an entire general staff was seated.

We witnessed hecatombs.

To the west of the plain in front of us the trains were disgorging nations of cattle, ewes and pigs, immediately released into immense muddy meadows. Companies of soldiers armed with prods surrounded the mass, harassing them and driving them toward areas surrounded by low walls, increasingly narrow, until the animals pricked by the lances of the cavaliers, riding on the other side of the low wall, reached a short tunnel. At the exit, they received on the back of the neck the blow of a bone mallet driving in a blade fixed at its center. Several colossal soldiers were operating that instrument of death with vigor and promptitude from the summit of the portico at the issue from the tunnel.

The ox falls in a mass on a wagon whose surface prolongs the floor of the tunnel and which, as soon as it is released, slides down a slope toward a vast courtyard where squadron of men and women welcome them, equipped with knives, saws, hammers and bowls. They fall upon the animal, decapitate it, slice it up, open it up, holding out the bowls to trickles of blood, detach the fry, the heart, the viscera, saw through the bones, strip off the hide, disarticulate the feet, split the skull, remove the brain, wash away the flowing grease and then roll up the intestines, stir the blood with a pole, collect the fibrin on rods and, in less than ten minutes, all that remains of the ox is a dozen pieces of butchery, all fuming, but rectangularly sectioned, tied, wrapped and ready for another wagon that carries them away, to the rattle of its wheels, toward the culinary factories situated to the east of the plain.

Immediately, the squadron in red aprons races to the death-throes of another animal sent down from the porticos, and reduces it to the same comestible state.

There are a hundred and fifty tunnels, which end in the same number of corridors, and terminate in the same number of porticos, above each of which stand two colossal soldiers equipped with bladed mallets.

For the sheep and the pigs, the tunnels and the porticos are not as high.

That abattoir service seems to furnish the people with pleasure. Merrily, the women and men fall upon the felled beasts and cover them like flies on ordure. Clouds of cries and laugher swirl over the blood. In the distance, the companies driving the still-living beasts toward the corridors and porticos launch glorious clamors toward the heavens. Around the slayers, on mounds and crests, companies of the line cheer the artful blows if the beast falls in a mass into the mobile wagon, immediately detached. Young women gambol around the hides while their companions scrape the interior, up to their knees in viscera and slime.

Toward the north, in the middle of vast esplanades, the schools of the battalion are drilling. The captains' horses race; batteries go through firing exercises. The infantrymen study dispersed order, service in the field and battle formations; the columns file past to the muffled rhythm of a thousand cadenced footfalls. The cannonade rumbles; the automobile caissons flee to the horizon in the stridency of their wheels and the trepidations of drivers. That does not prevent the drums and clarions from battling in the fields, not the bands from exciting hymns of majestic ferocity.

"How can you," I said to Théa, "by reducing the duties of war to the work of the abattoir, inculcate your soldiers with the sentiments of honor and courage that their function necessitates? Here, from what I can see, the prison camp and the army are confused. Here, as in Europe, you allow the subsist-

333

ence of prison, forced labor, disciplinary punishments, the authority of leaders. And there, above our heads, an aerial ship is circling, whose great wings cast the shadow of an exterminating archangel over the camp, for one can make out the chaplets of torpedoes suspended from the gangway. In truth, I don't understand this organization at all."

"Why not?" said Théa. "We enroll in the army those who manifest their appetite for conquest by theft, their appetite for death by the thirst for alcohol, their appetite for destruction by disobedience to the laws of production. Far be it from the State to have the idea of punishing them. They are simple assimilated to the métier that seduces their temperament the most.

"What better soldier is there than a brute, a thief, a drunkard, a smuggler or a murderer, since his social duty is to vanquish, to conquer, to intoxicate himself with rage in order to kill, to use cunning in order to deceive the enemy, to put the weakest to death? Except that we prefer that those sick individuals exercise the virtues of their energy against the peoples menacing social harmony.

"In the army we count one general who remains one of our most fertile scientific minds. He wanted to kill his mistress and his rival. His group designated him to command troops. He has brought back victory after victory for ten years. He invented a strategy. He has charged at the head of his cavalry in a battle that recalls the statues in the squares of arms. His wrath and his jealousy serve the cause of civilization admirably.

"You're astonished to see the abattoirs constructed on the drill-fields. On the contrary, that habituation to giving death, of seeing blood flow, of not softening at the sight of a gasping, sliced up, boned and skinned victim prepares our military personnel in a marvelous fashion not to fear wounds or to be astonished in battle. We develop the desire to kill by all means, the habit of killing and the instinct of victory. Listen to those clamors of joy!

334

"Look—the bladed mallet falls on a pig, half-decapitated by the force of the blow. The blood spurts in two fountains; the bewildered beast grunts and agitates; it splashes the hedge of gawkers with red spittle and they amuse themselves by offering their faces to the jet of blood. How can those people be frightened later if the enemy decapitates their comrade of equal rank alongside them?

"Look to the left at those young women pursuing an escaped sheep. What agility, what grace and what rapidity in their course! Now they've about to reach it. The tall redhead is brandishing the knife. The little black-haired one is trying to overtake her in order to strike first. A third gallops up. She's gaining ground. Can you hear them laughing? Can you see them pouncing. That's that—the black-haired girl has seized the beast. The blade flashes. Bang! She rolls on the ground with the sheep. Look: all those blades plunge into the bleating life; they get up again red. Oh, the little one holding by the fleece the severed ovine head, from which a rag of flesh hangs down! Behold the warrior spirit in all its glory. Listen to the laughter of the intoxication of victory..."

Pythie sniggered. I felt sick and asked to leave. We drew away.

Everywhere, one encountered men and women stained with large red spots, with hair and viscous clots on their gaiters. As inebriated as if they had been drinking, they were staggering, singing, talking feverishly, kissing one another, coupling randomly on the ground, insulting one another among their gasps of joy.

A tram took us far away from that ignoble phantasmagoria. A crown of fire circled my head. Nausea stirred my stomach. Pythie made me sniff smelling salts.

"But why that diatribe?" she replied to my exclamations. "Is it not logical to divide the forces of citizens into productive and destructive, according to individual temperaments? Certainly, Jérôme's companions hoped, like the present day anarchists, for a people composed exclusively of excellent and benign souls. It was necessary to retreat from it. The better

335

compromise has been adopted, of parking the instinctive and the stupid in the army, where their brutality becomes merit, honor and glory. As they aren't permitted to leave the military territories, they don't corrupt the minds of the pacific. They don't molest them and don't summon either a riposte or a struggle.

"It's only at the price of an absolute separation that intelligence has been able to increase to such an extent in Minerve, Jupiter and Mercure. These in Mars are our physical vigor, our redoubtable physical vigor. Of these soldiers, the majority don't even think about the difference between living and dying. They eat, they fornicate, and they kill. Giving death appears to them to be a good joke. Thus, for a little girl, it seems amusing to pinch her younger sister. They put malice and slyness into it in a puerile spirit of play. They don't understand pity or sensibility, any more than your soldiers understood it in Cuba, or Manila, or the Turks in Armenia. Except, here, we have the frankness not to make magnificent deities of courage and murder named Glory, Honor, Abnegation, Patriotism, etc..."

The tram took us to the culinary factories. They are unremarkable: ten thousand cooks, male and female, shredding, seasoning, cooking, grilling, organizing into terrines and packing, in immense edifices of blue iron and white ceramic. Clad in the fashion of our European scullions, in immaculate cotton, those people, quadragenarians for the most part, operate in front of monstrous cooking-pots.

Then we visited the tanneries and the curreries, where the soldiers' haversacks and belts and leather harnesses are made. As everywhere, the workshops are vast, the enamel walls represent subject appropriate to the industry of the place. Men and women work in common at neat benches. There is none of the filthiness habitual to our Occidental factories. The ventilators project perfumed air. Jets of water fall back into bowls. The workers are seated in good capacious armchairs. An organ plays pleasant tunes, for the rule of silence is admitted and observed by everyone.

That excursion concluded with a trip to the crematoria.

In the middle of a dense wood, the mystery of the Temple receives visitors with its long and monstrous columns in blue ceramic. Trains bringing cadavers from all points in the Dictatorship stop behind the buildings in a special station. Steeped in phenol, embalmed, coated with odorous wax, the dead do not stink. Before the voyage all are subjected to a scrupulous autopsy before delegates of the group to which the defunct individual belonged. After the cremation, the ashes are analyzed chemically. Thus, no death occasioned by a crime can pass unperceived.

The blue ceramic cupola covers a rotunda in which two hundred ovens are open around an electric hearth developing a temperature of a thousand degrees. Hoisted into its compartment, the naked corpse is immediately exposed to the radiation of that destructive heat. A lucid strip of mica permits the process of cremation to be followed through the ocular of a telescope. When we went in, past the blooms of the celestial flower-beds we were subjected to the curiosity of a military audience whom the spectacle of cadavers inflated by the heat amused greatly.

The young women laughed at the horrible pustules swelling on the bellies, the tumors that quickly deformed the blue faces with a violet gleam. In a coffin of sparkling plates with a quasi-solar glare, the corpse very quickly takes on the appearance of an enormous blister blown up by the bellows of a forge. That swells, undulated, rises, stretches, bursts, collapses, flows, dries up, cracks and crumbles. After ten minutes, nothing remains but a white powder.

Then the operator turns switches. The five faces of the coffin sink, reddened and blackened. The mica ocular is closed, to the great disappointment of the gawkers, who protest. The ash, placed in a casket, is transmitted to the laboratory for analysis.

That spectacle delights the audience. The same interjections that salute the masks of the carnival in our streets bid adieu to the absurd rictus of the deceased, to green lips pulled back over tarnished teeth, to eyes that have become, by decomposition, larger than hens' eggs and protruding from ripped lids.

All that populace sniggers, insults, writhes with joy. Childish remarks excite unanimous laughter. While we were there, a young woman unfastened her dolman and pretended to reanimate the corpse of an old man, already boiling, with the sight of her charms. The heat caused a pustule to grow on the cadaver, which grew and stood up. The entire society, seized by delirium, carried the slut away in triumph.

LETTER VII

Camp of the Red Forest.

We quit the railway three days ago. It was necessary to leave the automobiles yesterday; the road came to an end. Now we're in the bush, an expanse of red and green thorny plants into which the cannons sink to their wheel-hubs. And above it weighs a sky charged with storms, an insipid air. In front of us, the cavalry is burning the grass and the thickets to fray a route for the caissons and the columns. One rides over warm ashes. Sometimes sparks blow up when the wind blows. Overhead, the aerial squadrons make a noise as they fly; the great wings of the ships cover us with shadow. Some of them seen to tilt, cleaving the thick air with the profile of their gray sail. The chaplets of torpedoes gleam under the inferior gangway. A wheel three meters in diameter spins at the rear with a velocity that causes the image of its pokes to vanish. That wheel surrounds the singular apparition like a halo when it overtakes you.

Advance parties, the aerial squadrons have just bombarded the woods and villages held by the enemy. The infantry and the cavalry units only operate in their wake to occupy the positions and complete the victory.

As far as the eye can see the black helmets of the regiments are progressing. The absolute silence demanded by rigorous discipline reveals nothing of that march. Even the women of the artillery are not chattering. Seated on the banquettes of the prolongations following the guns, they remain mute and meek, chin-straps tight, hands on the knees of their broad canvas breeches, like those of your zouaves.

At the halt, everyone scatters, lays vast cloaks on the ground, sits down and cook.

In every squadron two men carry a can of oil in his knapsack; when the lid of the cylinder is unscrewed, three thick wicks appear that are lit. Springs push up a metal disk. That is the hotplate. A mess-tin full of water is placed on the disk.

The soldier's sack is not, like that of his European colleague, a heavy and formidable thing destined to reduce his agility, reinforce his fatigue and render him weary and useless. That pocket of thin rubber contains a few small packets of compacted rice, a tin containing a kind of liebig,[36] a uniform of rolled cloth, and a packet of brushes and needles. That's all. On the exterior one doesn't see the heavy cooking apparatus that overwhelms the European soldier. The catering corps cooks all the meat and vegetables behind the lines. When they make camp, if the caterers can catch up with them, as if usually the case, the soldier finds his ration prepared and seasoned. He can warm it up or eat it as it is. Thus, the meat doesn't arrive stinking, for having been piled up in the wagons, not blued by commencing corruption. If the caterers cannot succeed in reaching the camp, he soldier cooks his rice with meat extract on the bivouac. One of the oil cylinders aids that cooking. The other serves to heat water, into which coffee essence is tipped, filling the dosages of a metallic flask.

The soldier also carries two pouches; the one on the left contains bread; the other, on the right, contains cartridges. In a gourd he had water slightly alcoholized by mint. All the weight is thus not concentrated on his back and the man can

---

[36] The chemist Justus Liebig (1803-1873) founded a company to manufacture meat extract products; the one sold in the form of cubes was subsequently brand-named Oxo.

march upright, run and defend himself without the hump beloved by European general staffs.

The rifle supports, along the barrel, another cylinder of
aluminum, which is simply the tube of a telescope extending
from the butt to the sight. That telescope brings the silhouette
of the enemy very much closer and facilitates the shot. The
mechanism of the back-sight raises it or lowers it. The artillery
pieces are provides with an analogous telescope of astonishing
power.

The miracle of that equipment is the mantle. Imagine a
cloak similar to that of cavalry officers, Light, coated with
gum, the fabric protects against the most tropical rainstorms. It
covers the soldier from the helmet, under which the collar fits,
to the gaiters. There it tapers, and the rain runs off it like the
slope of a roof. At the camp, the mantle is spread on the
ground. It is a round carpet that protects the sleeper from
dampness in the ground and paludal miasmas. A comrade sets
his up like a tent of which a rifle planted by the bayonet forms
the support. Carpet and tent constitute a warm impermeable
shelter in which two men can repose at their ease. It would be
difficult to perform gymnastics therein, but one can sit up or
lie down. Ingenious dispositions seal the hut hermetically or
leave it open, according to the caprices of the sky.

Another advantage: those low gray huts seem almost invisible in the bush. Ten thousand men can camp without being
perceived before encountering the sentinels. The gleams of the
oil cylinders do not shine in such a fashion as to denounce the
presence of troops for three leagues around, like our bivouac
fires and their smoke. It is indispensable for an army having to
undertake a campaign in regions devoid of villages, to possess
a system of discreet encampment.

Vast and supple, the mantle does not hinder the movements of the shooter if, having donned it again, he meets the
enemy. Two large slits at shoulder level permit him to pass his
arms trough and move them freely. I think of the poor French
troops of 1870, whom the Prussians so often surprised occupied in drying their capes laden with rainwater, and who were

obliged to put on damp uniforms, heavy and rough, in order to fight. Here, no soldier is attained by a drop of rain. Under his cloak, he remains dry and agile.

On the first evening of the march we camped at the bottom of a valley protected by a plateau covered by patrols and lines of sentinels. The cavalry had sounded the woods eighteen kilometers ahead; the security was therefore absolute. When the meal was finished, as the cool of the tropical night descended upon us, the soldiers organized dances in order to warm themselves up. That, in this immoral land, concluded with gallant fellows coming to visit the camp of the artillery and sanitary service, where women are numerous. Nothing happens with noise or fury, but familiarly.

"Why," I asked Pythie, "does discipline not forbid these satisfactions? The unfortunate women might chance to become pregnant in the course of the campaign, and that would diminish the strength."

"Pregnant! But all these people are sterile. As soon as the groups designate a member of either sex to be incorporated, the new recruit is directed to the hospital in Mars. There, the fomenter of social disharmony is anesthetized by the surgeons. An ablation of the ovaries is carried out or the atrophy of the testicles provoked, according to the sex. Thus, atavism cannot perpetuate its tendency to destruction in future time. They are condemned to definitive sterility. We protect the race against the shame of destruction."

"Are those operations not dangerous? Are there no patients who remain in the hands of the doctors?"

"Very few," Théa replied. "Our surgery is very expert in that regard, because, as soon as the cities were established, Jérôme the Founder obliged our gynecologists to perfect that kind of intervention. Whoever sins by hated or covetousness can no longer reproduce."

"That's terrible," I said. "What are you doing to liberty, to personality? You're creating a race of numbers devoid of character, devoid of passion."

"Pure minds."

"What if intelligence is precisely the result of conflicts between the passions and altruism, between the instincts and pity, or the spectacle of those conflicts..."

"Who can tell?" said Pythie. "It was certainly necessary to attempt the experiment...

"In any case, if the personality of each individual is effaced, won't the character of the race acquire the most admirable unity? The goal of an effort like ours is precisely to substitute the person of the race for the person of the individual. That will run into the characters of other nations, contemplate the struggles of other nations, and its collective intelligence will augment as a whole by virtue of the spectacle of those general conflicts, in the wake of those conflicts, as individual initiative diminishes.

"We shall be the only body of seven, ten or thirty million similar souls, and that body will grow in force, as the force of an electric battery increases as a result of the parity and number of its elements."

"So be it. But in that case, that race having to struggle against the simple appetites of other races, which are the extension of property and the desire to vanquish, will soon find itself, by the necessity of having to fight with equal weapons, returned to the purely warrior condition—which is to say, brutal, pure egotism; which is to say, to the quality contrary to the one you claim to be attaining…ah!"

Pythie welcomed by objection with a smile.

"We won't have to fight with equal weapons, since ours are superior..."

At that moment, a clap of thunder split the air. Then formidable detonations sent back echo after echo over the expanse.

"The aerial ships are commencing the torpedo drop," said Théa.

From then on it was impossible to hear one another. The sky was falling on the earth, smashing it, crushing it. Everyone who was asleep woke up. The horses whinnied and panicked. It was necessary to run to them in order to calm them down.

The vibratory waves struck the temples and bones of the skull dolorously. The soldiers put on their helmets, furnished with little cushions, which the chin-straps stuck to the ears.

Almost immediately the order came to resume the march. The tents were dismantled, the mantles rolled up and slung over shoulders, gaiters buckled, dolmans refastened, ranks formed; and in the interval between explosions we heard, against the thickets, the bite of scythes and large sickles pushed forward by columns of slender locomotives, in order to complete the work of burning and flattening the tracks.

The army moved off toward the night of the great woods...

LETTER VIII

Mercure, Palais de Coupoles Astronomiques.

The most recent cities of the Dictatorship are, like this one, planted in the middle of forests. Lively waters whisper around the buildings. Swans swim on the shade. Pink ibises meditate standing on one foot. The electric trams bear graceful sculpted figureheads on the prow, projecting like those of antique ships, which hold the headlight in their hands. Automobiles with the form of attenuated hippogriffs run on the roads covered by vaults of verdure furnished by the foliage of tropical trees; the half-closed wings enclose the hood while the monster's swollen neck and bulging breast terminate the anterior trunk. Crowning the hippogriff's head, six ornaments are electric bulbs; and when night falls, those beautiful beasts of dark lacquered wood are seen gliding vertiginously, crowned with light.

In one of those vehicles we have gone along the masonry dyke that sustains and elevates the monstrous telescope three kilometers long and proportionately stout. We have circled the lakes of reagents in which the scientists study the warfare of substances; we have circulated for hours between the glass domes in which, vacuums having been created, odic currents

343

and the moist subtle fluids undulate and float, alive, revealed by diaphanous shimmers and sometimes by brief blue flashes; we have scaled the crystal paths of the magnetic hill from which a spray of glaucous essence darts on certain evenings, toward which innumerable drops of yellow, green and blue light flow through space, and lightning zigzags continually.

This is the region of scientific miracles. As soon as the sun sets, the people light up, because of a phosphorescent preparation that dyes their garments. Then the brightness of pedestrians illuminates the streets in a soft and charming fashion. The shadows fill with brilliant phantoms who talk as they glide two by two or three by three. The hidden organs sing. One perceives a close relationship with the hypothetical beings inhabiting the myriads of planets in suspension in the profundities.

In truth, enthusiasm has conquered me this time. How can I explain the secret of the wellbeing I sensed? Does it relate to the speech of the scientists who explain the composition of worlds with mystical voices? Does it come from the air impregnated with suave effluvia, or the faces embellished by an honest adoration of the Harmony of Forces that all of them name God? Here, no pain is legible in any gaze. One does not encounter anyone who laughs, but one does not encounter anyone who is sad.

"Listen," Pythie sings to me. "Listen, if your ears are capable of it. Can't you hear the sound of the invisible life of Ideas around our limbs? Don't you feel as if the vigor of Great Beings is fortifying you, in this place? Can't you taste the delightful confidence of knowing minuscule organs of the Planetary Person? I don't know whether you can perceive, as I can, the sweetness of losing oneself in a form more total than our human individualities. I don't know whether the sense of being diluted in the immense current of the Gnosis transports you outside your carnal sheath as it transports me. Everything flows out of me that isn't thought. A magnetism discorporates mentality here. Doesn't it seem to you easy to conceive what each of these strollers hopes, glimpses and contemplates in the mind? Oh, you talk to me about love, souls in communion, distinct beings reassembled into a single being; you recommend the fusion of our two sentiments into a single passionate ardor…this is what fulfils your desire. All the inhabitants of the city live in the same soul, which strives to know more of the secret of worlds, and the rest is abolished before their desire to seek the veritable God…"

Certainly, the atmosphere of the city is special. One enjoys a calm intoxication in the magnificently colored gardens.

Have you not, my dear friend, on certain days, been subject to the driving force of the crowd in the streets of a capital? Doesn't the indignation or mockery that animates it before spectacles of brutality or disgrace grip you, in spite of the advice of reason? Mingled with the popular crowd, have you not acclaimed the sovereign who passes by, jeered the quarrelsome drunkard, applauded the heroine of a stupid vaudeville or pursued the thief who has just stolen something from a shop's display?

At least, if you have not gone as far as action, you needed, at such times, a victory over the inclination, a resistance to the appeal of the multitude. The contagion of the example is maddening, when the crowd is numerous. The preoccupation of the incident suppresses the sum of other concerns in the members of the crowd. The entire will of each is concentrated in participation in the general emotion, playing a part therein. Angers, mockeries, furies, hopes of victory and bestial desires unite above the human residues and compose a single omnipotent force whose effluvia intoxicate. Instincts are excited to paroxysm; they flood bodies, and their external mixture creates a collective being of which individuals become the servile limbs.

That anger or joy of the street can give an approximate impression of what I feel in the environment of this city. I have become a docile member of a collective idea of existence. The fury of scientific pursuit is drawing me away with the crowd of people frenetically avid to participate in it. My attention is augmented in a phenomenal manner. Without knowing anything about physics, chemistry, mathematics or cosmography except the rudiments learned at school, I see the evidence of phenomena, laws, formulae, calculations and solutions revealing itself. Between others and myself there is a continuous endosmosis of knowledge. In gazes and smiles, as much as in speech, I read the certainty that it is appropriate to acquire, as I run with the crowd to the hunt for the truth. Nothing can resist that driving force.

"That's it, that's it...I love you," Pythie said to me this morning. "You've just clarified the rationale of the rhythms that regulate the formation of substance in the imponderable ether, and my mind espouses yours, adores it in admiration... O dear lover, dear lover, who makes the force of your intelligence manifest; you've understood the emotions of the world, the motives of its genesis, and creation is palpitating on your eloquent lips. Take my body, and, for good measure, my, hands, my breasts and my mouth, and the rest of me...."

We had a divine embrace...

Théa has not accompanied us to the city of Mercure. She has gone back to Jupiter, to which her office summoned her. We are walking alone, Pythie and I, through the miracles of the scientific city.

Pythie is full of charm. Light and magnificent, in her blue costume, above her light brown gaiters, she goes forth. The mat gold of her visage radiates around her profound and ironic eyes; but her smile has gained ineffable indulgences.

The palaces smile with their colored ceramics at the end of arbors united in the air by roofs of lianas and wild vines. Clad in blue, people walk with the allure of a grave happiness. There are paths of scarlet sand; fountains of violet, crimson, orange and mauve water; grouped statues of noble individuals gazing at the stars with passionate eyes, or whose gesture in marveling before the minerals hatched in the transparency of a retort. An exceedingly fine metallic mesh encloses in the sylvan perspectives the running of red deer, fallow deer and roe deer. The beautiful animals wander between the trees. Pheasants peck the ground. Peacocks spread their tails, perched on the edges of fountains. After the dark verdure of the thickets, pink flamingoes are bathing their filigree feet in a pool constellated by enormous flowers.

The strangest place in the city is a hollow like a gigantic Byzantium Hippodrome. In that valley, negroes and Malays live in solitary fashion, each in the shelter of an arcade closed by grilles. Many artificial cascades impregnate the streets serves in facades with freshness. Bushes and blinds propagate shade.

Those prisons form a kind of triangular avenue, the base of which is a stage of a vast theater. The right-hand line on the angle is inhabited by women, the left-hand line by young men. Odorous flowers ornament he hair of both. Their bodies emit a heavy perfume. One sees them incessantly in the hands of masseurs. Voluptuous music visibly enervates the languor of their eyes. Within the reach of their arms, tables are laden with fruits, beverages, certain succulent and spiced preserves and singular sauces drowning ruddy purées.

In melodious voices, phonographs recite certain Malay rhapsodies that seem to interest the reptilian allures of domestic jaguars, cats and panthers brushing the rose-bushes. Those animals stretch, creep and then yawn. They rub along the bars or mewl at the sky, which sparkles, ringed on the circular crest of the valley by the quivering of the forest.

There are times when the theater is populated by Javanese dancers. Their copper tiaras shine above black tresses. Their erotic hands agitate and cleave the air left the fins of fish cleaving the water. Often, a horde of howling negresses imitates the obscenities of amour. It is the habitual representation of the theaters of this land, but with something more bestial, with savage music, alternately frenetic and lugubriously slow.

It makes the jaguars wail. They pursue one another. They mewl. The tomcats also become nervous and fight. Claws are bloodied. Their anger coughs. Lying on their backs, showing their white bellies and there rows of pink nipple, female panthers appeal to the males, which, in order to surge forth, cut through the bushes, where the petals of mature flowers fall like snow. Then, frantically, the animals bite one another and couple. A warm odor of wild beasts corrupts the air.

Bands of somber silk unfurling along masts swell up softly in the breath of artificial winds.

One perceives the solitaries stirring behind their silvered grilles. Eyes and teeth illuminate the brown physiognomies beaten by the thick fringes of eyelashes.

The narrowness of the angular avenue only maintains a minimal distance between the men and the women. They consider one another, stretching themselves. Gazes declare the mutual covetousness of flesh. Pensive, the young women press against the bars of their arcade and contemplate the lust of the jaguars and cats. Nervous frissons shake their shoulders and their breasts while the spectacle and the music go on. The flowers shine in colors against the blue-tinted hair of the captives. The perfumes of bodies emanate more powerfully. One begins to groan. Other plaints respond. All the faces are plastered against the silver bars; the brown hands clench. Staccato hysterical laughter unites with the frenzies of the orchestra. The men also yawn dolorously and twist their arms in the grilles.

"They're suffering," I said to Pythie, the first time.

"Yes," she replied, "they're suffering. Those foodstuffs, the fruits, the sauces, the preserves, of which you've tasted samples, are powerful aphrodisiacs that stimulate their desire or their instinct to paroxysm. Soon they'll be leaping on the spot, spurred by the delirium of the flesh that the music and the dances are still exciting. And yet, no one will open the silver grilles between whose bars they're passing their arms, thighs and dolorous mouths."

"And why this torture?"

"Aha! You understand! This is the reason. These two hundred barbarians in the flower of strength and youth, thus saturated with desire, are in the state in which their nerves disengage the greatest force of will. They're projecting their fluids, their soul, their psychic vigor, outside themselves. They're trying to spring forth from their bodies to join the forms of the opposite sex, just as electricities of different de-nominations project themselves from the tips of spikes in or-der to unite in the brief joy of a blue spark. Our scientists es-timate that something similar is occurring with regard to these savages. Their voluntary fluids spring from the points of their bodies—hands, legs, mouths—to attempt to join up and fuse.

"If the hypothesis is justifiable, that narrow angular ave-nue contains a quantity of psychic force, human fluid, that is accumulating invisibly. One can thus infer that a healthy per-son momentarily bathed in that flow will attract a part of the static force, and, being neutral, will be charged with fluids of contrary denominations. The deneutralization, as it occurs, will occasion a state such that, for a moment, at least, the bather will be able to contain the paroxysm of the psychic force emitted by those two hundred savages.

"Imagine a scientist, penetrated with the importance of a capital problem, who suddenly senses that the solution is im-minent. He enters this avenue. He walks, eyes closed, through that accumulation of fluids. Fasting, a bath, and preliminary copulations have prepared him in such a manner as not to be sexually stimulated. His mental power will thus be increased by a considerable fluid sum borrowed from the special atmos-phere. It will be concentrated more vigorously; it will expend, more forcefully, an effort multiplied a hundredfold. There are a thousand chances to one that our thinker will find the result of his problem in that immersion.

"Look: a glass ceiling in two parts is lowering progres-sively over the avenue. The fluids are going to be condensed by the pressure of a gas recently created for that purpose. How the air is thickening before the grilles—can you see it turning blue? At the extremities of the hands and legs, minuscule sparks are emerging. That's how one distinguishes the psychic waves. Currents are acting in layers, in opposite directions. Ah! The cats and the jaguars are beginning to moan. Good, all the hysterical laughter is bursting forth. What a racket!

"Look how the poor brutes are pressing against the bars…and that one, tearing her robe, pushing her flesh into the interstices of the grille…and her rictus, and her hair standing up between the crimson flowers. So many male and female odors emerging from the epidermis in sweat are suffocating. Notice also the safety belts that preserve the captives from any artificial relief. For another hour the desires and deliria will be exasperated in their bodies. Oh, how high that panther leaps! One's beginning to feel ill at ease. The phosphorescences are dangerous to look at. My torso's twisting on my hips and my breasts are hurting. Let's go out for a while. We'll come back in an hour."

When we returned, the spectacle was repulsive. Like lianas and ivy wrapped around trees, the bodies of the captives were still knotted around the silver bars. Almost all of them were voiceless from howling. Tongues were twitching in their open white mouths. Several, in pressing against the bars, had left their flesh bruised and bloodied. There were young women who were writhing on the ground, weeping, men who were lying on their bellies, panting. The jaguars, cats and panthers, huddled in corners, among the bushes, no longer moving, were mewling faintly.

In the middle of the angle, sitting on a throne, was a motionless veiled figure. We saw that the veins were swollen in the old man's hands. The dense air had red, violet, mauve and blue zones, and the currents were acting in rapid waves in its phosphorescent thickness. The frenzy of the music had fallen silent. Shadow filled the theater. The closed glass ceiling trapped a colorless mass of gas in an atmosphere under pressure. At the silver bars the solitaries were still extending hands and lips, banging their foreheads, with their raucous sighs and their fiery eyes.

The form of the scientist did not move at all for an hour, insensitive to the plaints of the tortured. Suddenly, he uttered a cry of triumph, and quit the throne in order to run to the exit.

"He's found it," said Pythie.

At the same moment al the grilles turned on their hinges, opening outwards, and the solitaries surged toward the open arms of the women, toward the quivering bodies and the

350

bruised breasts. Scarcely had they stood up, however, than they tottered. Neither the women nor the man could cross the narrow avenue. Bodies sank on to the rose-bushes, from which the jaguars fled. A great sob resounded once more. Desire had abolished the strength to realize the embrace.

Gently, the ceiling was divided. The two glass sections we re-raised. The air escaped through the fissure, whistling. We left.

Outside, the phonographs were proclaiming the miraculous discovery obtained by the patient of the twelfth mathematics group. A celebratory cortege was forming at the crossroads of the gardens.

LETTER IX

Vulcan.

Humming violently, the wings of the airship lifted us up yesterday. The city shrank. The fields lost their colors. The roads diminished. The ground seemed to fall into the luminous abysms of the world, and the clouds enveloped us for a time.

It is difficult to get used to the tumult of the air where the helices spin and the mechanical wings beat. Human speech is inaudible. We're wearing thick leotards that did not give the wind any purchase. It's necessary to walk holding on to tringles and cords. Above our heads, the sail that regulates the progress inflates and causes the ship to veer in direction. Placed at the rear, an enormous mizzen plays the role of rudder, supported on the wind; it's the tail of the artificial bird that is carrying us through the lukewarm mist. The rigging shrieks. The wheel is spinning so rapidly that one can scarcely perceive a great halo of gray light at the stern. Enclosed in a canvas cabin, the mysterious machines and accumulators of force palpitate with their oiled hum. There is a slow tick-tock. But it's forbidden to approach in order to study the miracle.

"In this," Pythie said, "we possess the power to change the organism of peoples. When the fabrication of our aerial squadrons is complete, when the necessary number of vessels has been constructed, we shall rise up over the Old World in a dense flock, like the armies of titanic archangels with dark wings announced in the Scriptures. Our formidable force will go from south to north. It will soar. It will illuminate the night with new stars. It will furrow the day with its flags and its streamers. Its rapid flight will cut through the air above the frightened crowds and the tocsin of cities.

"To the cannon-fire and fury of the armies united by the masters of Injustice, the enlightening fall of our torpedoes will respond, and formidable explosions capable of annihilating the Babylons. Afterward, we shall disembark plows and seed-planters. The limits will be leveled, the boundary-markers overturned; crops will cover all the land, for the hunger of all the mouths. We shall surround death, distress and despair in their supreme retrenchments...

"Now, it's necessary that no one discovers the mystery of our force before the hour of its beneficence. Abide by the rule that forbids delving into it. Listen to the placid life of the machine at a distance. Do you know that the group who invented the miracle agreed to sacrifice themselves for the fate of the world? Nineteen strong, they departed for the mountain with the secret. In a dismal gorge, separated from other humans, the live in the midst of forges and hasten the labor of the Malays and soldiers. You are going to see the city of Vulcan, the fires of its blast-furnaces. There the next transformation of life is being elaborated in the heart of the summits..."

The ship shook the cotton wool of the last layers of cloud from its wings, and we appeared in the warmth of the sun. Rocks heaped up on the horizon emerged, immense and leprous, over the sea of white mists. We were still rising, and discovered, in the midst of that infinite chaos, the smoke of factories occupying a plateau.

"That's Vulcan," Pythie announced. "That's the city of iron and fire. There's the open head of the metalliferous mountain, and the plain that resounds with human activity;

and there's the flock of new ships circling in the air to practice the strategy of the commandants..."

From all points of the sky, squadrons were soaring, rising and descending over the mask of clouds hiding them from the curiosities of the ground.

I recalled those spring afternoons when, in our Europe, the returning swallows streak through the sky in search of their dwellings. The voices of sirens, the whistle of machines suspended high in the azure, descended distantly, like the cries of birds.

But it was not the placed white facades of our house toward which those efforts were directed. Arcades of iron, low down on the ground, enclosed the din of iron. There were scaffolds for giving birth to the carcasses of ships under construction. Hydraulic cranes were hoisting enormous sections of helices. The foundations of the masts were being fitted with great hammer-blows. On a platform supported by four latticework towers, a few minuscule beings were finishing off the trimmings of completed ships. Vast and light, the aerostats thus maintained spread their wings to either side of the towers. Their shadow, on the ground, protected the labor of many crews.

Our ship began flying in vast circles. The sails inclined. From the tips of its masts, the jibs quivered along the cords. We traced concentric curves in the air, which gradually spiraling inwards toward the platform of the four towers. The wind whirled and vibrated; and we ended up, having grazed the edge of the landing-stage once, settling on it gently.

Elevators took us down to the ground. It's the same city of broad avenues, long painted facades and arcades where comfortable salons open between the glasshouses of refectories, and where phonographs speak. A thousand jets of water rise over the lawns of nymphaeums constructed around statuary groups that perpetuate the memory of inventions. The spindles of trams slide within the rail of the causeways. One hears the voice of the great organs. The multicolored blooming of flowers inebriates the air.

In read jackets he workers of both sexes go about their business. At the entrance of factories stand admirable porticos whose sculpture represents the labor of Vulcan, that of kobolds and gnomes stirring the riches of the earth with their short spades. The racket heard in the distance increases as one approaches the factories. Ingenious hydraulic mechanisms maintain gentle compressions. The iron is crushed almost without noise under muffled pile-drivers. It is a crumb of fire kneaded by a thumb of steel. Ventilators maintain an even temperature. Sitting down, the engineers regulate the effort by pressing numbered keys. Very little burden is put on human arms. A hundred pincers of steel seize the blocks and the bars, lift them, present them, withdraw them and drop them, without human aid.

Metal antennae rise from the floor, along with jointed pincers and articulated claws that work. A few women, with keyboards of force, direct those movements with a brisk drumming of the fingers, which controls a formidable and complicated underfloor mechanism submissive to the currents dispensed by the keys. The energy runs along wires, is launched into the network of rapid belts, sending forth tentacles that bite the molten iron in the furnaces. No human cries, no clamors of metal dropped on metal. Jets of sparks leap in the sunlight coming through the glass panes.

In spite of the promise made, I cannot help wanting to penetrate the industrial mystery.

I think about the peril threatening the world when the squadrons are ready. It is up to me to protect our fatherlands by furnishing them with similar engines of defense. In my heart, all the atavisms of a proud race are stirring, crying out to me to provide protection to Europe by warning it of the danger, and discovering the secret of the constructions.

And there it is: I study with a sly intelligence, I listen to the beating heart of the mechanisms. I sniff the exhalations of gas enclosed in the tubes. I spy on the march of the machines.

"Oh," Pythie repeats, "why allow yourself to be tempted? Think of the Only Interesting Thing. Remember the fables in which the curiosity of the hero brings about his defeat. A sphinx is watching here that will devour your existence if you don't divine the enigma skillfully enough. The destiny of the world is too heavy a dogma not to outweigh one human liberty before those of the Dictatorship who maintain the just balance. I sense your impotence against such a fate. Be careful…you're soliciting the termination of your actions and the annihilation of your strength.

For Pythie is anxious for me.

Truly, since this desire to know the mystery of the imminent cataclysms has animated me, since she has been assuring me of my certain doom, the irony veiled by her eyelashes has diminished; a sure dolor pleats her blanched lips. None of those invitations that she mimes to handsome men any longer express her grave sensuality. She accompanies me sadly through the avenues of Vulcan, under the cool arcades, in the midst of the mute and active machines. She looks at me with her soul through her eyes. There are often sobs in her voice.

Because I am yielding to the need to save my race, my companion softens, saying: "It's because all the old people of the Occident live in you. The force of nationalities rises up in your person, and you are everything that anterior history teaches us. How many races are speaking at this moment in your phrases; how many energies are animating your intention. You are That-which-was against That-which-will-be. The crazy impulsiveness of supreme defenses appears in your gestures; you're drunk on the heroism of those who will succumb... Cease, cease searching for the Forbidden Thing; you will not discover it without disappearing for those who love you..."

I go on, however. I prowl around the factories. I interrogate the workers, the soldiers, the Asiatics with malicious and weary eyes. Undoubtedly, I shall be able to find out.

It will be necessary to reach the chambers of the engineers who are fitting together the pieces constructed in the different studios. Already I'm no longer unaware that the accumulation of force is obtained with the aid of an extremely dense gas agitated by a mechanical means, pursuing the multi-plication if energy included in it. One encloses that gas in tubes made with an amalgam of platinum and diamond obtained after long concoction in an electric furnace, at temperatures surpassing a thousand degrees. But the gas in question owes its birth to the decomposition of particular rare and precious metals that are transported with care in sealed crates under the guard of several men.

I've tried to visit the mines. Access to them has been forbidden to me. Indigenes are spying on me. I sense that I am being followed stealthily at the corners of arcades. They contemplate beside me the chaos of the violet mountains, the unlimited sea of pink clouds above which the city rises like an island harbor over the ocean. They are close to our table when Pythie and I take our daily meals. Not far from the domicile assigned for our sojourn there is one who watches all night long while playing with marbles and mirrors. I've tried to bribe some of them. They remain insensible to promises of gold, the hope of becoming rich in our homelands.

Pythie criticizes my imprudence. She thinks that the people of the Dictatorship are letting me maneuver thus to seduce me into treason, in order to arrest me and enroll me by force in the regiments of Mars. They regret, according to her, having authorized me to visit their estates. They fear that I will inform the world of the existence of their prosperity before the moment when the aerial squadrons can triumph.

Because of all these fears, Pythie's amour for me is increasing. At dusk, we walk along the promontory that advanced into the sea of clouds. The ships return to port with loud cries. They surge out of the sea here and there, rise into the red sky and circle there somberly, with their sails inflated, the halo of the wheel at the rear, the mizzen of the rudder and the chaplet of torpedoes suspended from their inferior gangway. The cries of sirens assemble them. Between the crimson surface of the clouds and the scarlet sky, the ships sail, rigid, pointed at the bowsprit, toward the platforms supported on four iron towers. The searchlights illuminate and swivel, shining in the darkness over the blue spine of the mountains, great mobile eyes, gold, red and green. The sea of clouds floats beneath the stars, slowly appearing in the blue and turquoise sky.

Then, the emotion of the evening puts Pythie's lips against mine. Her entire body trembles against my breast.

"You're going to die," she says. "I sense that you're going to die...and I'm beginning to cherish you for your touching weakness. You can see that. I no longer feel generous to those who are not the sheaths of your soul. I only gaze at the lands that attract your vision. No perfume enchants me any longer if it doesn't please you. I admire the grandeur of your barbarity, which resists the seductions of our favorable and logical life in order to measure your futile effort against that power.

"At first, I was scornful of the need with which you're imbued, to believe yourself the center of the world, to imagine your liberty, your nobility, your traditions, to respect the impulse of your race in yourself. For myself, I only understood the fusion of the individual in the social body, and its contribution to the universal soul in which it loses itself. I only understood that, and I gave myself to all the desires of procreation, to the life of all, to the total instinct of humankind. I lived, proud of respiring through all mouths and thinking with all brains. You came, with your ideas of old, with the follies of the other time, with the puerile arrogance of the savage who likes to think himself incomparable. You assembled everything in yourself. I dispersed myself in everything.

"And here we are, this evening, moved by a similar palpitation, without me having denied anything of my faith, without you having denied anything of yours. I know that you are going to betray my idea. My will doesn't have the strength to vanquish you, and I would allow your caprice to destroy the admirable work...in order to please you; and I would like you to deceive the vigilance of the spies in order to withdraw from the peoples the chance, here concerted, of their liberation. How you've changed me, you! You...you who have made me the enemy of my hopes, my beliefs, of everything that constitutes my being...

"And I can't divine the cause of that change. You're here; I no longer exist except in you...oh, your lips, and the force of your eyes...

To describe the exaltation of my triumph, over that spirit vanquished by the mystery of amour, over the logical and powerful mind, vanquished solely by the mystery of attractions...I don't know how.

We consummate our evenings thus, on the edge of the sea of clouds, while the aerial ships cry out in the obscurity of space...

Such was the last letter I received from my Spanish friend. He has not reappeared in Europe. His family, left without news, made enquiries of the ministry to discover what had become of the diplomat and his mission. A note recently sent by the government in Manila supposes that pirates manning a vessel of Philippine insurgents must have captured the corvette carrying the functionary. Thus far, a continuing administrative investigation has not produced any result worthy of mention.

SF & FANTASY

Adolphe Alhaiza. *Cybele*
Alphonse Allais. *The Adventures of Captain Cap*
Henri Allorge. *The Great Cataclysm*
Guy d'Armen. *Doc Ardan: The City of Gold and Lepers; The Troglodytes of Mount Everest/The Giants of Black Lake*
G.-J. Arnaud. *The Ice Company*
André Arnyvelde. *The Ark; The Mutilated Bacchus*
Charles Asselineau. *The Double Life*
Henri Austruy. *The Eupantophone; The Olotelepan; The Petitpaon Era*
Barillet-Lagargousse. *The Final War*
Cyprien Bérard. *The Vampire Lord Ruthwen*
S. Henry Berthoud. *Martyrs of Science*
Aloysius Bertrand. *Gaspard de la Nuit*
Richard Bessière. *The Gardens of the Apocalypse; The Masters of Silence*
Chevalier de Béthune. *The World of Mercury*
Albert Bleunard. *Ever Smaller*
Félix Bodin. *The Novel of the Future*
Louis Boussenard. *Monsieur Synthesis*
Alphonse Brown. *City of Glass; The Conquest of the Air*
Émile Calvet. *In a Thousand Years*
André Caroff. *The Terror of Madame Atomos; Miss Atomos; The Return of Madame Atomos; The Mistake of Madame Atomos; The Monsters of Madame Atomos; The Revenge of Madame Atomos; The Resurrection of Madame Atomos; The Mark of Madame Atomos; The Spheres of Madame Atomos; The Wrath of Madame Atomos* (w/M. & Sylvie Stéphan)
Félicien Champsaur. *Homo-Deus; The Human Arrow; Nora, The Ape-Woman; Ouha, King of the Apes; Pharaoh's Wife*
Didier de Chousy. *Ignis*
Jules Clarétie. *Obsession*
Jacques Collin de Plancy. *Voyage to the Center of the Earth*
Michel Corday. *The Eternal Flame*

André Couvreur. *Caresco, Superman; The Exploits of Professor Tornada* (3 vols.); *The Necessary Evil*
Camille Debans. *The Misfortunes of John Bull*
Captain Danrit. *Undersea Odyssey*
C. I. Defontenay. *Star (Psi Cassiopeia)*
Charles Derennes. *The People of the Pole*
Georges Dodds (anthologist). *The Missing Link*
Charles Dodeman. *The Silent Bomb*
Harry Dickson. *The Heir of Dracula; Harry Dickson vs. The Spider*
Jules Dornay. *Lord Ruthven Begins*
Alfred Driou. *The Adventures of a Parisian Aeronaut*
Sâr Dubnotal *vs. Jack the Ripper; The Astral Trail*
Odette Dulac. *The War of the Sexes*
Alexandre Dumas. *The Return of Lord Ruthven*
Renée Dunan. *Baal; The Ultimate Pleasure*
J.-C. Dunyach. *The Night Orchid; The Thieves of Silence*
Henri Duvernois. *The Man Who Found Himself*
Achille Eyraud. *Voyage to Venus*
Henri Falk. *The Age of Lead*
Paul Féval. *Anne of the Isles; Knightshade; Revenants; Vampire City; The Vampire Countess; The Wandering Jew's Daughter*
Paul Féval, *fils. Felifax, the Tiger-Man*
Charles de Fieux. *Lamékis*
Fernand Fleuret. *Jim Click*
Louis Forest. *Someone is Stealing Children in Paris*
Arnould Galopin. *Doctor Omega; Doctor Omega and the Shadowmen* (anthology)
Judith Gautier. *Isoline and the Serpent-Flower*
H. Gayar. *The Marvelous Adventures of Serge Myrandhal on Mars*
G.L. Gick. *Harry Dickson and the Werewolf of Rutherford Grange*
Raoul Gineste. *The Second Life of Doctor Albin*
Delphine de Girardin. *Balzac's Cane*
Léon Gozlan. *The Vampire of the Val-de-Grâce*

Jules Gros. *The Fossil Man*

Edmond Haraucourt. *Daah, the First Human; Illusions of Immortality*

Nathalie Henneberg. *The Green Gods*

Eugène Hennebert. *The Enchanted City*

Jules Hoche. *The Maker of Men and His Formula*

V. Hugo, P. Foucher & P. Meurice. *The Hunchback of Notre-Dame*

Romain d'Huissier. *Hexagon: Dark Matter*

Jules Janin. *The Magnetized Corpse*

Michel Jeury. *Chronolysis*

Gustave Kahn. *The Tale of Gold and Silence*

Gérard Klein. *The Mote in Time's Eye*

Fernand Kolney. *Love in 5000 Years*

Paul Lacroix. *Danse Macabre*

Louis-Guillaume de La Follie. *The Unpretentious Philosopher*

Jean de La Hire. *The Fiery Wheel; Enter the Nyctalope; The Nyctalope on Mars; The Nyctalope vs. Lucifer; The Nyctalope Steps In; Night of the Nyctalope; Return of the Nyctalope*

Etienne-Léon de Lamothe-Langon. *The Virgin Vampire*

André Laurie. *Spiridon*

Gabriel de Lautrec. *The Vengeance of the Oval Portrait*

Alain le Drimeur. *The Future City*

Georges Le Faure & Henri de Graffigny. *The Extraordinary Adventures of a Russian Scientist Across the Solar System* (2 vols.)

Gustave Le Rouge. *The Dominion of the World* (w/Gustave Guitton) (4 vols.); *The Mysterious Doctor Cornelius* (3 vols.); *The Vampires of Mars*

Jules Lermina. *The Battle of Strasbourg; Mysteryville; Panic in Paris; The Secret of Zippelius; To-Ho and the Gold Destroyers*

André Lichtenberger. *The Centaurs; The Children of the Crab*

Maurice Limat. *Mephista*

Listonai. *The Philosophical Voyager*

Jean-Marc & Randy Lofficier. *Edgar Allan Poe on Mars; The Katrina Protocol; Pacifica 1, 2; Robonocchio; Return of the*

Nyctalope; (anthologists) *Tales of the Shadowmen 1-12; The Vampire Almanac* (2 vols.); *Shadowmen 1, 2* (non-fiction)
Ch. Lomon & P.-B. Gheuzi. *The Last Days of Atlantis*
Camille Mauclair. *The Virgin Orient*
Xavier Mauméjean. *The League of Heroes*
Joseph Méry. *The Tower of Destiny*
Hippolyte Mettais. *Paris Before the Deluge; The Year 5865*
Louise Michel. *The Human Microbes; The New World*
Tony Moilin. *Paris in the Year 2000*
José Moselli. *Illa's End*
John-Antoine Nau. *Enemy Force*
Marie Nizet. *Captain Vampire*
Charles Nodier. *Trilby and The Crumb Fairy*
C. Nodier, A. Beraud & Toussaint-Merle. *Frankenstein*
Henri de Parville. *An Inhabitant of the Planet Mars*
Gaston de Pawlowski. *Journey to the Land of the 4th Dimension*
Georges Pellerin. *The World in 2000 Years*
Ernest Pérochon. *The Frenetic People*
Pierre Pelot. *The Child Who Walked on the Sky*
Jean Petithuguenin. *An International Mission to the Moon*
J. Polidori, C. Nodier, E. Scribe. *Lord Ruthven the Vampire*
P.-A. Ponson du Terrail. *The Immortal Woman; The Vampire and the Devil's Son*
Georges Price. *The Missing Men of the* Sirius
René Pujol. *The Chimerical Quest*
Edgar Quinet. *Ahasuerus; The Enchanter Merlin*
Henri de Régnier. *A Surfeit of Mirrors*
Maurice Renard. *The Blue Peril; Doctor Lerne; The Doctored Man; A Man Among the Microbes; The Master of Light*
Jean Richepin. *The Crazy Corner; The Wing*
Albert Robida. *The Adventures of Saturnin Farandoul; Chalet in the Sky; The Clock of the Centuries; The Electric Life; The Engineer Von Satanas*
J.-H. Rosny Aîné. *Helgvor of the Blue River; The Givreuse Enigma; The Mysterious Force; The Navigators of Space; Vamireh; The World of the Variants; The Young Vampire*

Marcel Rouff. *Journey to the Inverted World*

Marie-Anne de Roumier-Robert. *The Voyage of Lord Seaton to the Seven Planets*

Léonie Rouzade. *The World Turned Upside Down*

Han Ryner. *The Human Ant; The Superhumans*

Frank Schildiner. *The Quest of Frankenstein*

Pierre de Selenes: *An Unknown World*

Angelo de Sorr. *The Vampires of London*

Brian Stableford. *The Empire of the Necromancers (1. The Shadow of Frankenstein; 2. Frankenstein and the Vampire Countess; 3. Frankenstein in London); Eurydice's Lament; The New Faust at the Tragicomique; Sherlock Holmes and The Vampires of Eternity; The Stones of Camelot; The Wayward Muse.* (anthologist) *News from the Moon; The Germans on Venus; The Supreme Progress; The World Above the World; Nemoville; Investigations of the Future; The Conqueror of Death; The Revolt of the Machines; The Man With the Blue Face; The Aerial Valley; The New Moon; The Nickel Man; On the Brink of the World's End; The Mirror of Present Events; The Plurality of Imaginary Worlds* (non-fiction)

Jacques Spitz. *The Eye of Purgatory*

Kurt Steiner. *Ortog*

Eugène Thébault. *Radio-Terror*

C.-F. Tiphaigne de La Roche. *Amilec*

Simon Tyssot de Patot. *The Strange Voyages of Jacques Massé and Pierre de Mésange*

Louis Ulbach. *Prince Bonifacio*

Théo Varlet. *The Castaways of Eros; The Golden Rock.; The Martian Epic* (w/Octave Joncquel); *Timeslip Troopers* (w/André Blandin); *The Xenobiotic Invasion*

Pierre Véron. *The Merchants of Health*

Paul Vibert. *The Mysterious Fluid*

Villiers de l'Isle-Adam. *The Scaffold; The Vampire Soul*

Gaston de Wailly. *The Murderer of the World*

Philippe Ward. *Artahe ; Manhattan Ghost* (w/Mickael Laguerre); *The Song of Montségur* (w/Sylvie Miller)

www.ingramcontent.com/pod-product-compliance
Lightning Source LLC
Chambersburg PA
CBHW060413030726
47495CB00003B/564